THE END GAMES

THE END GAMES

T. MICHAEL MARTIN

Balzer + Bray

An Imprint of HarperCollins*Publishers*

Balzer + Bray is an imprint of HarperCollins Publishers.

The End Games
Copyright © 2013 by T. Michael Martin

Library of Congress Cataloging-in-Publication Data
Martin, T. Michael.
    The end games / T. Michael Martin. — 1st ed.
        p.   cm.
    Summary: "In the rural mountains of West Virginia, seventeen-year-old Michael
Faris tries to protect his fragile younger brother from the horrors of the zombie
apocalypse"— Provided by publisher.
    ISBN 978-0-06-220180-5 (hardcover bdg.)
    [1. Survival—Fiction.   2. Zombies—Fiction.   3. Brothers—Fiction.   4. West
Virginia—Fiction.   5. Science fiction.]   I. Title.
PZ7.M36422End 2013   2012038108
[Fic]—dc23

Typography by Ray Shappell

13 14 15 16 17   LP/RRDH   10 9 8 7 6 5 4 3 2 1
❖
First Edition

For my wife, Sarah Louise Martin,
whose love is my life's very best truth

I shall tell you a great secret, my friend.
Do not wait for the last judgment,
it takes place every day.

—*Albert Camus*

Everything not saved will be lost.

—*Nintendo "Quit Screen" message*

CHAPTER ONE

Michael awoke in the dark to the screams again.

He drew up the rifle in the tarp at his side. He kicked out of the sleeping bag and ripped his gun from its waterproof wrap and raised the sights up toward the perimeter blindly. A form appeared twenty feet ahead. He tugged the trigger; it would not give. He cursed himself, clicked off the safety, resighted the shape. But the form was nothing more than a tree, a yew, arthritic and leafless. So dark: God, so dark out here. By the gunmetal moonlight, the ring of trees around their camp was all but invisible. But that was impossible. Unless—

Their fire had died.

He gasped, "Ohcrapno."

A crimson bed of cinders popped in the circle of stones. A spindle of smoke twisted.

He whispered, *"Patrick!"*

Out there in the night the scream went on. Human but not. Living but not.

Patrick didn't stir.

Michael knelt unsteadily in the snow. He felt for the Pokémon sleeping bag, torn and patched and torn again. "Patrick, get up!" The lining swished. "Bub! Let's go!"

Only when he tossed it open did he realize the bag was empty.

His heart rammed his throat.

But the lining was still warm. His brother hadn't been gone long.

Michael risked everything and shouted, "Patrick!"

Several seconds of silence, then a call reported through the darkness. *"Paaaatriiiick!"* But the echo was not his own. It was a voice without depth or dimension, choking on earth. A dead, elongated roar. The Bellow, mimicking him.

Heavy feet changed direction and dragged through the brush, maybe one hundred yards away, nearing.

Stay—frakking—calm.

Don't let Patrick be sleepwalking again. Jeezus, why did I say we could camp outside?

Concentrate. Think, like Mom.

I swear, please don't let him be out there—

Hey a-hole: Feel. Your. Blood.

Michael closed his eyes against the dark cold, and there was that moment, that ever-repeating instant, when everything inside him hissed that it wouldn't work, that he didn't have time. Then he thought of his breath, and emptied his brain.

His focus aligned on the quick warm creek within his veins, the powerful flex against his ribs, the deliberate drumming inside his ears. It felt like every fiber and thought of himself fusing into one another, until his mind and his movement merged to a single thing, seamless and bright, like a glowing radar dot.

It felt like: *yes-yes.*

His eyes leapt open, and he moved, focused, fine.

He tore open the duffel bag next to him.

"Paaaatriiiick!" said the Bellow, closer now. *"Paatriiiick!"*

Michael grabbed a safety flare from the bag and stood and

punched it on his thigh—a *whoosh*. Sparks fanned a molten dandelion.

The forest conjured orange before him, their camp and the rotten deer stand and their car ahead on the dirt road. He spun on his boot heels, wafting away flare smoke.

New-cast shadow lunged in the trees.

He saw no one.

An image jumped into his head: *Patrick, hiding behind a tree as a joke. Patrick, laughing into his elbow, until he heard the Bellow coming . . . then froze, afraid.*

"Patrick, good one! You—you got me!" Michael stepped over the sleeping bags, nearer the trees. His voice wavered as he shouted. He cleared his throat, calmed, continued, "Bub, come on out now; I'll let *you* shoot this Bellow! A hundred points!"

"*Youuuuuu got meeeee!*"

Michael whirled.

Fifty feet away, he could just make out the creature: staggering, hitching wild legs through the woods. Its limbs hung at impossible angles, a dozen times shattered. Its clothes were stripes of rot. What skin still clung to the skeleton was in some spots the color of mushrooms and in others that of wax and mostly it was as pale as the bones that jutted through it.

But a moment ago it had been coming from the other direction.

There are two of them.

"*Buuuuuuub,*" it said, "*poooooooin—*"

"Cheating . . ."

The whisper was small: so small that it could have been the voice of the flare. But Michael knew the sound too well. It was the same excitement as when he and Patrick had beaten *Halo 4* on Legendary Mode, their headphones plugged into the TV so they could stay up all night without anyone knowing; the same giddy, too-many-Sour-Patch-Kids, *One more level, c'mon puh-lease* excitement at a new part of The Game.

As the Bellow bayed once more, Michael flung himself into a nearby cluster of pines—and his knees went weak with relief.

Patrick sat on a snow-slick log, hunchbacked in a down coat and two hoodies, looking at something on a steep hill slope. His hands kneaded his hair—not in terror, in annoyance. He looked like precisely what he was: a five-year-old kid getting equal parts ticked and thrilled by what was happening.

"They're not playing right," Patrick said.

A skeletal hand shot through the needle thickets above Patrick's head. Michael automatically raised the gun, discharged a round, exploded a branch. A body fell in the shadows and slid down the hill. Michael's hands shook with adrenaline, but that did not stop his smile.

Patrick covered his ears, whined, "Hey, watch it."

Then he pointed at the twitching shadows down the steep hill by the bridge.

"THEY'RE NOT—THEY'RE—RIIIIGHT—NOT PLAAAAAY-ING!"

Michael's heart frosted.

There weren't two Bellows. There were ten, at least.

"There's so many. Fourteen, I counted 'em up," Patrick said, bewildered. "They're never in groups. You know?" And stood, suddenly furious. "Hey, cheating! You're cheaters!"

"Patrick, shut up!" Michael hissed, and seized him back from the edge of the overlook.

"But they're bein' buuuutts!"

Michael smothered Patrick's mouth, gently, beneath his fist. "Right and it's not that I don't agree, Bub, but just this sec we need to concentrate on getting *our* butts outtie here."

Because holy hell, where did all those Bellows *come from*? *Why why why are they moving in a pack?* Michael thought. *The Game Master never said they would!*

"PATRICK—UPPPP—SHUUUTTTT, PAAAAATRIIIICK!"

Images burned into Michael's head:

Bellows, in greater number than his bullets, would surround him and Patrick.

Block the bridge.

He and Bub would be trapped. Among the dead trees. And dead screams, and claws—

Stop it! If you lose it, it's Game Over.

The car, he thought. *Like now.*

"You don't get it?" Michael said. "Seriously?" He chuckled and then stopped—as if trying not to mock Patrick.

"What?" Patrick said.

"They're not cheating." Michael stood and strapped the rifle over his shoulder and took his brother's tiny mitten-hand in his own. He led him back through the pines. "It's just a surprise, that's all. Like a surprise attack."

"Surprise attack?"

Michael nodded.

They got back to the clearing.

The Bellow with the shattered arms stood fifteen feet away. *"ATTTAAAAAAACK!"*

Michael swallowed a shout and instinctively hurled the flare at the creature. The flare landed two steps in front of it and the Bellow raised its broken arms, trying in vain to block the dazzling light that tortured its never-closing pupils. The Bellow staggered backward, the illumination driving it momentarily away, like the crack of a lion tamer's whip.

At least five more Bellows than there had been a minute ago screamed in the forest beyond the creature, imitating the pain of their fellow.

A finger of terror crawled up Michael's throat.

Go move quick move quick go.

He grabbed his pillow and their duffel. He jammed a box of raisins into Patrick's hands and pocketed their small cardboard box of .22-caliber rifle rounds.

"Aw," Patrick said, "we leavin'?"

Michael rushed Patrick to the dirt road and the car. He slid his hand through the tire of the bicycle bungee-corded on the back, popped the trunk, shoved the bag and food in there. He felt his blood. Calmed.

He pulled the square ammunition box from his pocket.

Patrick said, "What about our beds?"

The bullet box was upside down: its cardboard flap came open. The little missiles fell into the snow: wet, ruined.

Michael slammed the trunk. "What, our what?" he snapped.

Patrick pointed at the sleeping bags back in the clearing. The flare had landed on top of the bags, and the bags had burst into flames. Past the bags, held temporarily at bay by the flare light but still visible, were a dozen Bellows.

Michael said, "Uh, we'll get new ones."

"NEEEWWWWWW OOOOOOOONES!"

Bellows screamed this almost as one over the hill down by the bridge. Michael jogged to the hill. Fifty: *fifty* of them. Down the mountain, in front of the bridge, the mass stumbled nearer on the dirt road that curved up toward their car.

The terror-finger grew another knuckle, nudged his Adam's apple.

No. Why? How the hell are we supposed to fight them? What are they doing?

Having a rave. Beginning a shindig. Doesn't matter. Plow through them.

That many'll crack the windshield!

Then you shoot. You shoot as many as you can.

"Get in the car, Bub," Michael said. "Go 'head and start it, then lay down in the back."

The prospect was candy to Patrick. "Okay! Really? Wait, in the trunk?"

"What?"

"Do you want me to lay down in the—"

"Just the backseat, Patrick! Go!"

Michael jammed the keys into his brother's hands and watched him go to the car.

Then Michael turned back. He picked a Bellow at random by the dark shore under the bridge and raised his scope on it, amplifying the enemy. Once it had been a man, twenty-five years old perhaps. Now its loose jawbone swayed, a pendulum clicking on a hinge; now it screamed with a power so tremendous it was as if the Bellow were not the screamer itself but the mouthpiece of some beast that blasted through its bones from within the earth. *"THE CAAAAAAR!"*

Michael's crosshairs wavered as he shot and a chunk of earth on the bank beyond the Bellow ripped away.

Idiot idiot.

The Bellows droned on.

Michael cocked the bolt again, chambering the next round. Three shots left. If he remembered right.

Breathe out before you shoot, Michael told himself. *Like Modern Warfare.*

Michael breathed out hard to steady his crosshairs, and his breath fogged the lens.

"Stupid stupid—"

"Sssstuuuuu—"

Patrick turned the ignition, and Michael heard the engine whine. *Frakking cripes, the alternator!*

The engine kicked over. Relief flooded him.

And Patrick screamed.

From twenty feet away, Michael watched a Bellow moving toward the station wagon. Blonde hair crawled over her scalp. A silver necklace glittered on her skinless clavicle. She fell on the hood, clawed toward the windshield.

"Lay down, Bub!"

Patrick's silhouette gave two thumbs-up and vanished.

The woman reared an arm back. With the power common to all Bellows, she struck at the windshield. Cracks popped across it. Patrick laughed as glass dusted down. "She's good!" he shouted.

Too good.

Michael exhaled a slow stream like a digitized sniper and he pulled the trigger. He'd been aiming for the forehead; the side of the Bellow's skull flipped away instead. The creature stopped screaming and slid from the hood and spun to the dirt with a thud. And a wild satisfaction swelled Michael's chest.

Two shots now.

"Lay—Paaaaatriiiiiiick—Paaaatriiiiiick down!"

The Bellows were moving up the hill. Sixty, seventy-five. The forest echoed, in hideous stereo, alive.

So burn it alive, Michael saw. He *saw* it, even though it had not happened yet: the satisfaction and the *yes-yes* simply loaded the image, fully formed, inside his mind.

Burn. It. Alive.

He ran to the car. Pulled out from the trunk a five-gallon nickel tank. Patrick looked through the window, said, "That's our gas." Michael sloshed rainbows in a semicircle behind the car, then went to the front, trailing liquid. Patrick said, "Michael, it's our gas."

"Yeah."

"But that's our gas, though."

"Patrick!"

"Why're you using it for?"

Just shut up, Patrick, shut your face. If you say one more word, tonight they are going to win.

He said, "Remember the Game Master talked about tricks?"

Delight spread on Patrick's face. "You're gonna trick 'em up? Yesssss!"

Michael nodded, glugged more on the downslope road, then hurled the canister.

It stopped on a rock several steps ahead of the approaching Bellows, glinting.

Michael cocked the bolt and lifted the rifle. He steadied the crosshairs. He checked the safety—*off*—and—

—*wait wait wait!*—

—and then took the rifle down and adjusted the outer aperture a quarter turn to the left, and the trigger came back with an easy tug.

He'd been right; the scope sight had been slightly off.

His shot now was flawless: the tank sang and bled some of its insides.

But didn't explode.

No.

The night went casket black. The sleeping-bag fire behind them had died, the flare, too.

Flare!

Michael rushed to the trunk and grabbed another flare. He slammed it bright on the seat of the bike, waved it once in an arc over his head to drive back the Bellows now only paces behind the car, then flung it at the tank.

Where it landed too far, the sparks hissing the wrong way.

"Michael. Michael, they're coming, they're gonna win."

Michael chambered their last chance.

He settled on the lead Bellow ahead. Maybe it would fall, make the others stumble, giving the car time to escape.

He breathed, *"Please."*

Feel your blood.

And without thinking, at the final instant, swung the bead back at the tank.

A cry of light and a flat crack. The slug punctured the tank and slung a tongue of gas forward: a liquid fuse, an airborne fuse.

The flare lit it and it detonated.

Knew it! Michael's chest shouted. *Knew it knew it knew!*

A blazing arm roared high from the gas tank, exploding the canopy above in a catastrophe of flame. Fire glimmered and traced the gas trail up the hill, raising a primal barrier between the car and the Bellows of the forest. Over the chaos, beyond the inferno, Michael could hear the Bellows' agony. His eardrums shook with it.

Patrick laughed and clapped and kicked the driver's seat in delight, and Michael jumped into the car and rammed the pedal to the floor.

An airborne moment when the car bucked off a tree root, then they were off, tearing snow and earth toward the core of the explosion. When the fire leapt onto the hood he yelled out, "Duck, Bubbo, close your eyes!" and fell down on the seat. He heard and felt the fire, a hot cloak unfurling above, then it was gone and he was moving like a pinball between the standing Bellows, feeling sick and smiling, both, as he watched them burn.

Michael cocked the wheel at the bottom of the hill, fishtailed, barreled down the length of the dogleg road parallel with the creek. He shot them onto the bridge and across it and only then slowed to under sixty.

Patrick asked, "Did we win?"

Michael looked in the crooked rearview.

"ZOMGosh, we won, didn't we?" Patrick bumped his butt up and down in his seat. "Vic-tor-ee?" he said in his computerized RoboPatrick voice. "Ach-eeved? This eeeeve?"

The night air squealing through the cracks in the windshield was blinding cold.

It felt gorgeous.

Knew. It. Would. Work.

Michael grinned and held up his crossed fingers.

"Not yet. Tomorrow, maybe.

"Game on?"

Patrick's smile didn't falter. "Ai-firm-ai-tive." Then, regular-voiced, "Ya-ya."

"Ya-ya, too."

Patrick nodded. Michael nodded.

"Seat belt, dawg," Michael reminded.

And he drove himself and his brother from the torching woodland.

CHAPTER TWO

Twenty-two days.

Michael lifted his finger from the Sharpie'd tally in his journal. *Wow. Man.* Twenty-two days since Halloween. Twenty-two days since Michael followed the Game Master's Instructions and carried Patrick through a door into the night and saw their first Bellow. Twenty-two days since that moment, since the world seemed to end, but then instantaneously resurrected to a frightening and beautiful life.

Five hundred and twenty-eight hours of The Game, Michael figured. And grinned.

Pretty good for a seventeen-year-old nerd, his five-year-old brother, and a crappy rifle.

He tossed the Sharpie into the station wagon's cup holder. Patrick murmured in the back but didn't wake up. Michael pulled out a map from the glove compartment and spread it on the passenger seat.

Outside, the predawn sky was the shade of a bruise. The station wagon sat parked on a half-paved road that was not much more than a path in the woods. A rotten-wood fence ran along the roadside, separating them from a valley. Automatically,

Michael scoped it out, taking brain snapshots of the world around him.

The valley: an ugly crater, its flat walls sheered into the rock face.

The small coal refinery: a gray factory, spired with stout smokestacks that made it look like the final castle of some ambushed kingdom.

The refinery's doors: well padlocked.

But a double-wide trailer (probably the refinery's "office") sat in its shadow, about fifty yards from the Volvo. The trailer had been knocked off its cinder blocks, probably by nothing awesome.

The erratic holes puncturing the trailer's door: shotgun.

And for just a moment, looking at this scene, Michael could almost *see* someone running in there, finding themselves cornered. Maybe the Someone had been caught by the sunset, which comes almost supernaturally fast in the mountains. Or maybe the Someone was exploring the trailer during the day, thinking they'd be safe . . . and Someone didn't bother to check the dark of the closets first. Seeing the evidence of people's Game Over was sad, of course. But it was also, at this point, pretty ridiculously predictable. That was just what happened, right? You did the things the Game Master said or you were out.

Or . . . maybe they just got surprised, Michael, he thought, his smile fading a little. *Like* you *did last night.*

Suddenly, the trailer's door slapped open, and a Bellow lurched from the shadow: an old woman with one ear, her nightgown snapping, flaps of skin coming off her face like soggy wallpaper.

Michael reached under the map for the rifle and thumbed off the safety. *No bullets left, dude*, he thought. A little thread of fear made him consider driving off.

Man, no. One little Bellow doesn't get to make *me run.*

The Bellow began staggering toward the car. Patrick snorted in the back but still didn't wake, even as the Bellow began its shapeless moan. Michael waited for an idea—an image—about what he should do. Followed his breath.

Then he checked his watch. And felt his small smile come back.

He returned to the map.

COALMOUNT, 13 MILES, read the sign on this country mountain road.

Michael found the state capital of Charleston on the map, then traced outward. This was a regional map, taken from the cabin where he and Bub had ridden out the first few Game nights. The map's Pennsylvania and Virginia were thick with cities, but most of West Virginia was simply grayed out, with patches darkened to indicate rising mountain elevations. Thick black lines symbolized the interstate; a couple of reds marked the highways; a long blue marking, the Kanawha River, shot north to south through the entire state, occasionally branching with capillaries. The state looked a little like a health textbook illustration of a diseased lung. The first few days that he and Patrick had spent on the road, traveling the switchbacks that dived and webbed through the mountains, Michael had sometimes tried to gauge the contours of the hills around him against the charted elevations on the map. He'd peered close to the paper, as if he might spot his miniature self on it, glowing like a radar dot on a video game map-screen.

Now, though, he just looked at the handful of larger towns plotted along the interstates.

The Bellow let loose another bay. Michael hummed, thought about turning on the CD player, then remembered how sick of "Ron's GOOD OL' COUNTRY Mix" he was.

And soon he confirmed what he'd already guessed:

Coalmount wasn't on this map. The map lines converged on the capital city, but he was somewhere out in the uncharted gray. With the woods and the switchback roads and the trailers. Still. He had no idea where he was—and no idea how to find an interstate road to the Charleston Safe Zone and The End.

Well, he thought, *there go my vacation plans.*

The Bellow staggered over a cinder block and found its footing again, now about thirty yards away, continuing toward him as Michael went back to his journal. He wrote:

Day 22

No one in forest. Smoke in the sky yesterday = from lightning probably :(

Camped near river last night. Kanawha? Not labeled.

In one hunting shed: Backpack/protein bars. Yum.

Last nite, way way more Bellows. 80+? Why? Never grouped together B4. One-time deal? (Plz?)

Fire EXTREMELY good on Bellows. Hate it. Theory about light/eyes = woot. (Note: let Bob know Game Master confirms! It's not their skin—it's the eyes.)

Don't know where we are. River nearby—Kanawha? Will keep heading south.

Don't want to stay outside after last night. Thought it wld be fun for Bob. Actually: just cold. And uhhh not fun.

4 Atipax left . . .

Michael lifted his Sharpie, staring at that last note. For a second, he was surprised by a stitch of an anxiety inside.

He added:

P.S. I am an awesome shot ;)

P.P.S. BUT SRSLY: AWESOME.

The Bellow reached the fence, bouncing back a little when it struck. The creature looked down, blankly puzzled.

Michael chuckled.

The Bellow raised a thin, nightgowned arm; the arm sliced downward; the wood blasted apart in a burst of shards.

C'mon over, Grandma, I've got something to tell you.

Patrick's snoring hitched again, and this time, he woke up.

Michael checked his watch, cranked down his window a bit.

Seven, six, five . . .

"Hey, newb," he said to the Bellow just paces away.

The Bellow replied: *"NEEEEEWWW—"*

Three, two . . .

"Good morning," Michael said, and the first shafts of the dawn slit bright and pink over the trees, glimmering the snow and windshield dust on their dashboard. The sunshine struck the Bellow's eyes: the creature collapsed on its knees, and its roar became a roar of pain.

Michael nodded, satisfied, slapping the dome light off as he put the car in drive.

"Michael?" Patrick said.

"Yeah?" Michael answered.

"Mornin'," yawned Patrick, stretching upright. "What we doing today?"

CHAPTER THREE

They were a couple hours into the day before the twisting, rutted road brought them to the town called Coalmount. Michael opened Patrick's door, did a butler bow, and told Patrick his butt crack was showing as he stepped out.

Then Michael climbed over the hood and glassed the new town with his binoculars from the roof of the station wagon.

"Michael?" called Patrick.

"Yeah?" Michael replied, smiling at the routine.

"Nothing," said Patrick.

The town might call itself Coalmount, yeah, but *no offense, ol' buddy, but you look sliiiightly like every other coal town ever.* Michael scoped the dozen or so buildings on the main street, all of them brick and stout. He noted, not for the first time, that the only structure that looked less than thirty years old was an office building labeled SOUTHERN WEST VIRGINIA COAL AND NATURAL GAS.

"How many *R*s are in 'Faris'?" called Patrick from behind the car.

"Why?"

"I think I spelled it wrong in the snow."

"Oh."

"With my pee," Patrick said.

"Yeah, I got that the first time," Michael laughed.

He looked back through the binocs, tracing up the length of the main drag. A statue of a coal miner stood in what, if you were feeling just ridiculously generous, you could call the town square. The miner statue carried a pickax, but its face had been either carved or blasted away.

Power poles plastered with Safe Zone flyers (he made a mental note to check if the flyers had road maps on them). Four or five pickups abandoned in chaotic arrangement in the street and sidewalks. *That's more cars than there usually are, though,* Michael thought. It occurred to him that the pickups might be a sign that people were still here, and for a second, before he could stop the thought, he pictured soldiers coming around the corner, soldiers they'd finally found.

He surveyed the crust of the snow, searching for footprints . . . but all he saw were wide, erratic imprints: evidence of the Bellows' shambling gait. He felt a moment's disappointment, but then also a relief.

There were only ten or so Bellow trails. Some tracks wound to a closed Dumpster he noted he should stay away from; most simply vanished into the dark open mouths of the buildings' broken front doors. The few scattered Bellows here had sought their daytime sanctuaries in some of Coalmount's dark crannies, but there weren't as many Bellows as there had been during the weirdness in the woods last night. Not nearly as many.

"Looks like we're gonna have to entertain ourselves today," Michael said.

"What the?"

"No people have been out since last night's snow. See?" He hopped off the car, pointing the binoculars at Coalmount.

Patrick looked through excitedly, his cheek warm and smooth against Michael's.

Bub's lips moved silently; Michael knew he was counting something even before Bub lowered the binocs and informed him, "Eight flyers."

The binocular strap looped around Michael's neck, and when Patrick saw it drawing tight, he said softly, "Sorry—whoops." Most kids would yank it as a joke.

But this kid isn't most kids, Michael thought, smiling a little. *Actually, sorta the opposite.*

"You want to Game On?" Patrick asked after he'd looked at the town. Michael nodded.

As he always did when they began the day, he hoisted Patrick onto his shoulders, letting Bub do The Yell.

"We're gonna Game On!" Patrick called to the town.

The Bellows' echo, from all their hiding places: *"GAAAAAME!"*

Patrick's own snow-muffled echo: . . . *we're gonna, gonna* . . .

"I'm a butt!" Patrick added.

The dozen or so hidden Bellows informed them that they, too, were *A BUUUUUTTT;* Patrick giggled at himself. And standing there outside the town that was shouting back Patrick's joke, Michael felt Bub's happiness like a transmission, like a tingling signal that traveled perfectly through the fingers that Patrick tapped on his head, through the ankles that twisted in Michael's hands as he laughed. And the last thread of the anxiety Michael had hardly realized he'd had slipped away. So they got in the car and drove into Coalmount, two Gamers gaming on.

Coalmount looked like it had been postapocalyptic even before Halloween.

Gray mountains, studded with dead trees, rose up and up beyond the buildings around them as Michael drove down Main

Street. The sun was a tarnished dime that only got above the peaks at noon, so the towns always seemed like an image on a screen with permanently lowered brightness. A mile or so to the east, the gentle waving of the mountain range gave way to sharp rock, severe and flat: there the coal had been mined by exploding the mountaintops. The silhouette of the range was like a heartbeat measurement that had been alive and suddenly stopped.

When you said "West Virginia" before Halloween, Michael thought, places like this came to people's minds. You thought of dusty sunlight through yellowing blinds; you thought of damp trailers; you thought of mountains that roamed and loomed and locked, like a fortress designed to keep you in. It was impossible, of course, to grow up in West Virginia and not be told roughly thirty times a week that "Coal Mining Is What Powers Your Lights." But Michael's hometown was just a "meh" suburb of the city where West Virginia University was, its own mountains tamed with Walmarts and McMansions. And in places like that, it was easy to believe that coal towns like this didn't exist.

So entering these towns was always a slightly surreal experience.

Michael parked the Volvo in front of the Southern West Virginia Coal and Natural Gas office on Main Street, which sat beside a tired-looking red church. The office and the church were the only buildings on the road whose front doors and windows were still intact; unraided.

"Pop-Tart me," Michael said, and they stepped out of the station wagon, Patrick handing Michael a foil-wrapped pastry, s'mores flavor: cornerstone of a healthy breakfast.

"So. Got the message from the Game Master," Michael said. He paused, taking a bite of the Pop-Tart, grimacing a little at the taste. They'd been old even when they'd found them in Ron's cabin, and being in the car had not done much in the way of making them less *gaaaah*.

Patrick nodded, eating his Pop-Tart with both hands. He shivered pleasantly, like he would waiting for a surprise party. There wasn't anything that Bub looked forward to more than hearing their Instructions. Nor anything that Michael looked forward to more, either—even though, with the way The Game worked, neither he nor Patrick had ever actually *seen* the Game Master.

The Game Master's Instructions were delivered in the total silence of night.

And here was how. You stop in the woods, or in a stranger's emptied house, or in the car along a frost-starred road. You wait for Patrick to go to sleep. And after he is snoring, if you are quiet (very), the Game Master materializes from out of the dark and speaks. You have to really listen: the Game Master's arrival, when it happens, is no louder than the knock of your heart. His whisper is more silent still. But ahhh man, his Instructions about how to play The Game, his directives about how to get closer to the Safe Zone and to winning: what a relief and wonder to receive.

If all of that sounded like some kind of magic—a Master fashioning the apocalypse around a Game he'd made, instructing you precisely about where you should go next in order to stay safe—well . . . it kinda *felt* magic. It was a power that would have seemed impossible to Michael before Halloween.

So add that to the "impossible stuff" list, thought Michael now.

He cleared his throat, beginning his imitation of the Game Master's voice: smooth and richly deep, an utterly grown-man's voice.

"You're getting closer to the Safe Zone. You performed well last night, Michael and Patrick. You encountered the first Bellows that seemed to move in a group. 'Why?' is a question which may be of importance. So ponder it. But not at the expense of my new Instructions.

"You will set out upon a new town. Although it is not certain,

the possibility remains that soldiers—who can escort you to the Safe Zone—may be near.

"I have left, scattered for you in this town, metallic parts for Patrick's new weapon.

"Because your stores of food and ammunition have been thinned, seek to replenish them. Before you travel from this town, you must earn one hundred points.

"Stay alert. Stay sharp.

"I will be watching. I will be waiting. And I will be, as ever, your Game Master."

Patrick did a fist-pound, said, "Booyah."

Michael and Patrick crunched down the street through the ankle-high snow with their pants cuffs duct-taped to their boots to keep out the cold. Their duffel bag was strapped across Michael's chest, the .22-caliber rifle slung over his shoulder like a fishing pole; with his other hand, he pulled the rusty Radio Flyer sled they'd found at a garbage dump last week.

In the center of town, next to the tiny fountain with the no-face statue, Michael cupped his hands around his mouth, shouting, "Hello!" to the streets. Sun glittered on the snow. Patrick switched his wool hat for Michael's huge gas station aviator shades.

As a couple Bellows' replies and his snow-muffled *Hello!* voice echoed to him—but no human calls—Michael's brain clicked over everything around him. Standard stuff. Squat mounds of snow-buried cars; soggy Safe Zone flyers (mapless, alas); charred sheriff's cruiser; gas station with an explosion-crater where the pumps should have been.

"So where ya wanna start?" Michael asked Patrick.

Patrick pointed to the snow-covered downhill street behind him.

Zoom.

They sledded down the series of hills from the square, bob-bing through the abandoned cars and trucks, Michael's arms wrapped around Patrick's waist, Bub chuckling at fake-danger every time they narrowly avoided clipping the cars.

The Coalmount grocery store was called—seriously—Food'N'Such.

The storefront's shattered windows had been boarded. Through the open door, streams of daylight filtered in, making the inside dusky.

No Bellow replied.

"All right, Sticky Fingers, let's clean out the joint," Michael said. He stepped in over the bits of glass that had been busted from the door. But he noticed Patrick hadn't followed: he was still at the threshold. Bub tried a grin, but his eyes were afraid, and he was doing that hum of his. Michael felt a tug of sympa-thy for him—and annoyance with himself.

"Right. Sorry, buddy. The Lightball."

Michael unzipped the duffel bag and pulled out the weapon he'd made last week: a ball of duct tape, almost the size of a vol-leyball, with its whole surface affixed with shards of a mirror. Bub took the Lightball from Michael (the globe had several outer layers of plastic wrap, so it couldn't cut you), looking grateful.

Then Michael took out their long, heavy-duty, red Maglite, nodding to Bub: *we're a go.* Bub rolled the Lightball into the store like a bowling ball. Michael ignited the flashlight and aimed it at the ball, the light beam striking its mirrored sur-faces, the mirrors blazing in turn and streaking star points in all directions in the dusky store, over the walls and the ceiling and the floor, traveling down the center aisle like a scanner and a light-grenade for any Bellows within.

The ball bebopped jauntily over a couple cans, then came chiming to a stop against the far wall.

"Booyah." Patrick nodded, satisfied that Food'N'Such was Bellow-free.

Then they went shopping.

The store was pretty standard, the ceiling tiles brown, low, sagging. A Little League trophy topped with a miniature brass kid collected dust on the counter. A 7UP clock, which had to be at least twenty years old, hung over the register, forever proclaiming that the time was 8:40.

"Ten points for safe cans today, too?" Patrick asked.

"You know it."

They ventured into the aisles, stepping over cans and moldy, plastic-wrapped food. There was a smell of pickles. Patrick went ahead of him—only a couple steps; even then peeking over his shoulder to make sure Michael was close—bending, inspecting labels, rolling away the cans he didn't want down the aisle.

Michael felt grateful for his brother's caution. Last week, when they'd been searching a camping supply store for ammo, Patrick had opened a gun cabinet to find a pair of clawed hands lunging at him from the dark. Michael had been right there, had shot the Bellow instantly—he never even let the creature get close, of course—but even with the points they got for shooting the Bellow, the pure wallop of the surprise had left Patrick so shaky that he didn't even use his usual *of-course-I'm-not-scared* cover-up. That was a three-Atipax night, and Patrick took the extra pills with a mix of gratitude and embarrassment that Michael found a little heartbreaking. Michael couldn't stop thinking about it, either, though for a different reason. The Bellow hiding itself from the daylight was a blonde girl, maybe nineteen. He'd tugged Bub back too quickly for him to really see anything, but she was naked from the waist up, and Michael's stomach and face had gone explosively hot: it was the first time he'd seen a girl naked. She was rotting. So would you believe there was sorta nothing at all in any way sexy about it.

Now Patrick bent and opened his Pikachu knapsack and put in two cans of Campbell's Chicken & Stars, tucking his chin as he arranged them carefully. Then he picked up another soup can at his feet, considering it with pursed lips before swapping out a Chicken & Stars for this new one.

"Hey, Bub," Michael said, loading his own duffel bag with some beef jerky, "you don't like tomato soup, remember?"

"But you do," Patrick said casually, zipping the knapsack shut.

A twist of warmth spread in Michael's chest. "Are you trying to get on my good side? Because I have to tell you: not gonna happen. Okay, low-five," Michael said, and drew it away when Patrick went to slap it. *"Pfff,"* Michael laughed.

Lunch, Day 22:

3 jerky sticks each

Soup for me :)

Two Flintstone Vitamins for Bub

(Okay, they're delicious, I ate one, also)

Between a couple buildings sat a small dumping yard, and Michael suggested that they explore it for pieces of the new weapon the Game Master told them to build for Patrick (Bub was preeetty sure it was going to be a rocket launcher). They found only some old springs and a busted recliner with no footrest, though, and Michael noticed there were some bits of glass from a shattered television; he told Bub they should probably leave. But on their way out, Patrick spotted a length of pipe sticking out from an oil-stained blanket, and the pipe, upon close inspection, was definitely the barrel for a launcher. Michael packed the pipe into their duffel bag and asked, "When we get this thing done, can

I borrow it sometimes?" Patrick said, yeah sure, yeah he could, if he gave him five bucks.

Michael pointed at the hardware store and said, "Ammo."

The windows of Mountaineer Supply were boarded, though not super well; there were foot-wide square gaps near the top of each window, which meant that the store was brighter inside than Food'N'Such. It was also less pickle-y, if more well raided. Michael noted patches in the wood paneling above the door that were a lighter shade than the paneling around them; somebody had even taken the bubble-letter words that had been hanging there. The pale patches were in the shape of these words:

GOD. COAL. BELIEVE.

The ghost words were kind of creepy, for some reason.

Michael and Patrick found an aisle with some kid-sized shovels and rakes hanging on pegs; a handwritten sign claimed that the tools *MAKE GREAT BIRTHDAY GIFTS! That just doesn't seem very likely,* Michael thought, amused. Farther up the aisle, twisted coat hangers lay scattered on the floor, some still bearing children's black sweatshirts. One looked like it actually might be Bub's fit, but when Michael checked, the neck tag said it wasn't 100 percent cotton. Which was one of the things that the idiot "doctors" who Ron thought were so awesome had been right about: the feel of synthetics drove Patrick sorta bonkers.

The glass of the store's firearms counter was shattered; not so much as a single bullet remained. They did find a couple hunter-orange sleeping bags, though, and a bathroom in the back of the store with a Bellow-repelling daylit window. Michael placed roughly half the nation's remaining reserves of toilet paper onto the chilly seat; Patrick thought that was hilarious. Well, Michael might happily do a lot in the name of The Game, but one indignity he wouldn't endure (for the third time, ugh) was getting his butt cheeks frozen to a porcelain thunder box.

They were walking down the road again when Michael stopped and said, "Wait. Wait, I'm not thinking." He looked back at Mountaineer Supply, an image flashing behind his eyes. *The boards on the windows. The holes.*

Not accidental, something in him said. Those were, like, sniper holes.

Taking Patrick by the hand, he jogged back to the store. He checked the floors around the windows that overlooked the streets and soon he discovered that he'd been right. There was a duffel bag, filled with ammunition, lying by a window behind the cash register. Boxes of bullets for every gun caliber inside. He felt good, pleased, for a second. Then he realized that the bag was camouflage, and not the leaves-and-grass kind of camo that people use for hunting.

Soldier camo.

Wait—were soldiers here? And if they had been, why would they leave this? What would happen to make them leave it?

Patrick, standing a few feet behind Michael, gasped.

Michael's hand blurred automatically for the rifle strapped on his own shoulder. But Patrick was just standing at *GREAT BIRTHDAY GIFTS*, picking up a tiny toy: a windup tin man with a pickax, like the no-face guy at the fountain.

"Michael?"

"Yeah?"

"You . . . okay?" Patrick said, sounding worried.

Michael said, "Yeah," then he wound the key of the toy for Bub. The toy man raised his arms and "mined" . . . though Michael couldn't help but think that it also looked like he was driving back invisible monsters.

"A. Roe-Bot. Like. Meee," Patrick grinned, delighted.

When Patrick turned the key, though, it snapped off in his hand.

The sadness Michael saw flash behind his eyes was swift and familiar and overpowering.

"*Whoa*, buddy, you're strong," Michael said.

Patrick looked up at Michael. "Yeah," he said. His face relaxed. "Ya-ya."

Love you, too, Michael thought. Then said: "Ya-ya, too."

loo *points already. Reloaded rifle!*

If soldiers were here, why would they leave stuff behind?

Maybe . . . some are here?

No, he thought. Anybody could have a bag like that. It probably just belonged to someone who had lived here in this town and left for the Safe Zone.

But Michael found something amazing at the bottom of the hill that made him wonder if he was wrong.

A short school bus, yellow in the road, sat longways across the span of the street, jammed perfectly snug with both ends striking buildings, sandbags stuffed underneath the belly. A barricade.

"They're protecting something on the other side," he said to Patrick, who looked up at him, excited.

The body and windows of the bus were peppered with bullet holes, though, like the aftermath of an enormous conflict, which was probably not the best indicator that the blockade had been a success. But still.

Don't get your hopes up, Michael. Don't.

Michael called out for Bellows to mimic him: "I've got butt pimples—"

"—They are narsty—" called Patrick, giggling.

But no one, and no thing, responded. They crawled through a small cove in the sandbags, Patrick going first, fake farting the whole way through. Day goes by freaking fast in winter West Virginia: it was only 3:55, but that meant they had maybe twenty good minutes for exploring the town.

The first thing Michael saw on the other side of the school bus were houses, familiar-issue: squat (also depressing and ugly); layered with dust (coal, of course); set with too many too-small windows (covered over with metal and/or wood). The cold air carried that hallmark dead-place smell: sour, rank, coiling, green. But at the end of the road was a building labeled MEETING HALL, and its lawns featured long wooden spikes, pounded into the earth at forty-five-degree angles to repel the dead.

Michael stood with his brother in the husked-out street, calling.

He got a response. But it was, alas and aw crap, the same one as always: a deadened, elongated echo from the Bellows' daytime hiding places in closets and attics and closed coal bins and woodsheds.

Except.

Wait: Does *it sound different than normal?*

Michael called out, again, "Hello!" his heart lifting a little.

An image came into Michael's mind before he could control it, before he could tell himself to calm down. He pictured soldiers coming around a corner, men with weapons, power, and looks of astonishment. *Boys!* they'd say. *Wow! Hell-oh! Wow! Lookit these boys! Lookit this kid, will ya lookit this hero!*

C'mon, let's get you out of this place, let's get you someplace warm, fellas. It's over, Michael, you did it, you won, let's get you boys to the Zone—

And Michael was already walking through the Meeting Hall's lawn of spears when he realized, in the back of his brain, that a few of them were strangely shaped.

Four or five sets of planks had been fashioned into crosses.

He realized why the responses sounded unique: the Bellows' calls, eerily, were emanating from under the ground, radiating from beneath the snow and earth under his boots. Tacked onto the crosses (the red paint, he noted, was faded) were small wooden signs:

(RANDAL VOLPE) BELOVED, GOD-BLESSED
DO NOT TOUCH!!!
(ABEL MASSEY) BELOVED, GOD-BLESSED
(GERALD BRAY) BELOVED, GOD-BLESSED
(EMMA ZARR) BELOVED, GOD-BLESSED
DON'T DISTURB, BELOVED, MOST-BLESSED

Michael shook his head, feeling a bewildered resentment. Why the crap would people keep Bellows here? The instructions from all Safe Zone flyers and endless radio announcement loops said that Bellows were to be destroyed on sight.

But seriously, even if nobody ever told you, how could people not realize: if monsters show up at your home, *you get rid of them.*

At least it doesn't sound like there's as many Bellows as last night, he told himself. *Maybe last night was just a fluke. Maybe—*

And sensed movement behind him.

As he spun, the snow grinding under his heels, several nearby crows cawed and exploded into flight. On a house where the vinyl siding had been torn off and hammered over the windows, a series of icicles stretching nearly to the ground collapsed, bringing the storm gutters they'd hung from down with them.

Nobody there, Michael thought, his heart knocking in his temples. He pictured the map, the gray zone, his miniature self lost in all that gray. *No Bellows. And no soldiers. No Mom. There's nobody here, newb. There's nobody* anywhere—

"Michael?" Patrick said. He looked at Michael, his eyes asking, *You okay?*

I—damn, Michael thought. *I thought for a second . . . I really thought . . .*

"Just tired."

"So . . . just Bellows here, then?"

"Yeah. I know where we can stay tonight, though."

Michael led them under the bus and said, "Piggyback," as they went back up the hill, Michael pulling the sled behind them.

Stupid to think . . . stupid to think that . . .

"Dinner when we get back," Michael said, crunching through sunset-shaded snow.

"Okay," Patrick replied. "I'll save some of my jerky for Mommy."

After a second, Michael nodded. "Good call."

He set Patrick down to walk when they reached the level Main Street, and that was when all the thoughts about being stupid vanished from his mind.

Starlight lay bright and crisp and strange across the snow. Patrick stopped spontaneously, his smile beautiful and alive. They could hear, from some other street, the hoof-falls of the passage of deer in snow. They could hear the crisp crackle of ice splitting in some unknown river. The night, the whole of it, felt like a private thing, as if Michael could grasp the star-rich horizon and pull it over them like a quilt and keep themselves in it forever.

"Michael?"

"Yeah?"

Patrick took his hand.

They ran to the door of the shelter for the night—the business building they'd parked beside on Main Street earlier—which he lock-picked with his multi-tool, opened, slammed, bolted, chained. By the Coleman lantern's flat green light, they ate a dinner of dusty-tasting nut bars. Michael laid out their new sleeping bags in the west of the office, tucking his brother in while the moon rose, and that moment of beauty had eased Patrick, so after only one Atipax he clicked to sleep so instantly it made Michael almost laugh, both happy and sad. *Day twenty-two,* Michael thought. They'd sledded, explored a ghost town, foraged, and Patrick was sleepin' easy in Southern West Virginia Coal and Natural Gas's office, 'cause all in all, in this weird Game world they now lived in, yeah, that was pretty much your average day.

CHAPTER FOUR

All right, Game Master, when you gonna show up?

There was this fantasy Michael had, which went like this: *go to bed before midnight.* Not fancy, nah, but when your muscles itched from a night of driving and a day of snow walking, man oh *man*, did it sound sexy. How many days without once sleeping through the night? How many hours waiting, exhausted, for their Game Instructions?

Twenty-two days, plus one day, equals I wanna sleeeeeep.

Michael sat in a folding chair with an uneven metal seat, purposely ignoring the comfortable leather chair behind the desk. He sipped the last of the Mountain Dew Code Red they'd had with them when The Game began, idly tapping the .22-caliber rifle on his lap, watching a ribbon of world through the planks of wood on the window.

A snowstorm had moved in since they'd arrived at the office. Occasional shrouded flares of lightning; thunder in the hills. The falling snow largely veiled his view. Michael wouldn't have wanted to try to spot flashlights or lanterns in the mountains tonight, anyway—not after he'd gotten his hopes up that there were people here who could lead them to the Zone. 'Cause sometimes, looking at the mountains, if you weren't careful, you could *feel* all the dark miles that lay between the place you were and the place you wanted to be. You could feel like a radar blip, marooned in the nether-zone of all those miles that weren't on the West Virginia map. You could feel like The End of The Game wouldn't ever really come.

You can feel, his brain hissed now, *like maybe the Game Master doesn't know what he's talking about—*

Man. No. Don't even think that.

A young Asian boy wearing shredded tuxedo pajamas, his cheek-skin gone, staggered past the end of the alley Michael could see down. Then the snow sealed up the view again. Bellows lurched aimlessly in the roads, like dumb undead drones without a queen, but it was still only the dozen or so Bellows he'd heard earlier. Better than last night. So there's that.

But that doesn't mean you don't have to be sharp. You still have to feel your blood. Because if you don't, you'll think too much; you'll get your hopes up. Like today, how you thought you were going to get yourself and Patrick to soldiers. And to the Safe Zone.

And to Mom.

Michael stood up, roughing his hands through his hair, blowing air out over his lips, trying to push down his frustration. Somewhere out in the snowing night came a whipcrack of lightning, not much more than a flashbulb, but it fleetingly silhouetted the shapes of two Bellows moaning past. And here was the thing Michael couldn't help but think: the Bellows were the ones remaking the world in their own images. The Game Master, not so much.

That can't be true, though, he tried to reason. Okay, yeah yeah yeah, things were frustrating now. But, true or false: the Game Master had brought them this far—safely. *True.* True or false: the Game Master had materialized in the dark of the night just before Halloween, and told Michael where to go, told him how to save Patrick. *True.* And the Game Master had told him how the Bellows were not as fast as he was, how the monsters were only mindless pawns scattered in the night. The Game Master had told Michael that he was going to gain the Safe Zone and finally find a place for Patrick to sleep that didn't have screams or need locked doors. The Game Master had given them The Game, which was a joy, and a miracle . . . and . . . and . . .

And God, but I'm just so freaking tired.

Those Bellows last night in the woods, though, Michael . . . they almost got you. They almost hurt you.

And what do you think will happen to Patrick, if it turns out Bellows really *can* hurt you two? What do you think will happen to him, *inside?*

Michael sat back down.

And his mind whispered: *three Atipax left.*

The Game Master won't come until you're quiet.

Michael stood up again, trying to lighten himself up, deciding to keep himself busy. *Well, maybe he should hurry, 'cause some of us have class in the morning, ha-ha-ha.*

Michael rooted through the business desk, finding an ancient cell phone in the top drawer. *Too bad reception ain't happening in the backwoods mountains of good ol' West "By God" Virginia.* Anyhow, he doubted that he'd be able to reach anything except the constant Safe Zone advisory recordings that you got on the landlines, no matter what number you dialed. When Michael pressed the ON button, though, he was sort of amazed to watch the screen light up and show a blinking half-bar of charge left. The 9 button had an image of a little cassette tape on it. Voice recorder. Could be useful. He turned it off to save the battery.

Newspapers in the trash can in the corner, but they were all pre-Halloween.

Headlines about the war in Iran; a guy in Pittsburgh who won the Powerball; that awful, doesn't-help-West-Virginia's-public-image story about the little boy, Cady Gibson, who had snuck into a mine and been killed when he accidentally fell and hit his head—in Coalmount, actually. MOUNTAIN STATE IN MOURNING the headline said. Photos showed the entrance to the mine, and the kid himself: a blond boy, maybe a third grader, with crookedly cut bangs that might have been cute if they hadn't made Michael realize that Cady's family probably just couldn't afford a real haircut.

Sounds kinda familiar.

In another drawer, alongside a can of nuts, was a plastic, bright-orange pistol. Michael laughed, picking up the surprisingly heavy toy from the otherwise I-am-a-serious-businessman desk. *Man, Bub would love this.*

Michael went back over to check on Patrick again, the Bellows moaning outside in the shapeless night.

But he hardly heard. Because Patrick—legs twisted, blond hair shagging his brow—looked so small, so sweet, that Michael thought, not for the first or final time, that he would shoot all the monsters in the world he had to, he would do anything to reach the Safe Zone in the capital city of Charleston, to win The Game for Patrick. And when breath came like cotton through Patrick's tiny, chapped lips and he snorted, kind of hilariously, Michael felt he *could* decorate the floors of the world with Bellow brains. He felt it in his breath and blood. Yes, he could. *Yes-yes,* he would.

'Cause you, Bub, are the best half brother I've got—

—and right then, Michael thought he heard something speak, and looked up.

Through the gaps in the boarded window on this western side of the building, the snowstorm had momentarily cleared, allowing a view of the steeple of the church next door.

It had been small and paint-chipped in the daylight. But at night the spire had become a great arrow arcing for the stars. For some reason, it gave Michael a breath of joy. *Things have worked out so far. It's like . . . sometimes it's like there's someone helping us. Besides the Game Master.* Michael smiled a little, gazing at the eerily moving building—

The moon sailed out from behind the clouds.

Michael's heart leapt to his throat, and he forced himself not to gasp.

Eyes had flashed in the shattered windows across the alleyway: eyes, in the black of the church.

People, Michael thought.

He took a shaky step away from Patrick. For a second, his blood whamming, he stood unmoving in the streams of new moonlight. Then he moved to his window, peeking out through the gap between the boards.

No. You don't know it was people, he cautioned himself. *Could just be Bellows.*

But Bellows' eyes are black! Those were *bright*!

The snow was falling, and the moon had retreated—but he thought he saw silhouettes in the church. *Big* silhouettes.

People! He almost shouted it.

But, no. Don't wake Patrick and get him excited, not if this was a false alarm. And if the Bellows heard him and realized there were humans inside . . .

But he felt a frighteningly powerful burst of longing.

Michael went to the door and loosened the chain; it tumbled quietly. Snow spurled inside. Down the alley between the office and the church, Bellows roared and staggered.

Wait a second before you go, he thought, looking back at Patrick. *Just a freaking* second. *Feel your bl—*

Except Michael had already left the threshold of the Southern West Virginia Coal office, shutting the door behind him and traveling toward the side entrance of the church.

"Hey," he whispered.

Michael lay his fingers on the church doorknob: he hadn't

been in a church in years, not since it had been one of Ron's this-will-definitely-fix-my-life ideas.

He crossed the threshold, rifle in his hand.

"Hell—" he said, and the green smell hit the back of his mouth. Ahhhh no.

The first thing he saw: the Bellow. A man, dead-eyed, wearing a blue coal-mining jumpsuit and gas mask and utility belt, secured by a rope to the raised wooden altar of the tiny house of worship. Michael stopped a couple feet outside of the Bellow's reach, then whirled.

People were clustered in the pews, watching the Bellow, as if awaiting the announcement of its deadly sermon.

Michael immediately felt his blood, but before he could stop his thoughts: *Why are these people looking at this?*

Because they weren't people.

The "people" stood utterly still, without breath, without flinch. The worshippers were mannequins. Their arms, reaching for the sky, were posed. In the eye sockets, shards of mirror glimmered and flashed: they looked like disciples eternally paused in the brilliance of an epiphany.

The imitation of life, of *safety*, was somehow hideous—like biting into a hamburger that was fine on the outside, but in the crescent of your bite, maggots squirmed.

"Stupid," he said. His own voice sounded shaky.

Fine—it's fine, he told himself. *Things are still going well. Hope is just getting some good laughs at me today, that's all.*

"Stttuuuuupiiiiiddd!" said the muffled, bound Bellow.

And out of the corner of his eye, Michael saw the Bellow lunge. For one incredible moment, the enormous altar the Bellow was tethered to tilted forward; the nails anchoring it to the ground screamed.

The Bellow's clawed fingers flew out and scraped the side of Michael's neck.

Michael recoiled at the frozen touch. He staggered back, nearly falling over a pew. He felt a sting that was mostly surprise. His hand went to his neck. The skin was tender, hot, and wet.

Freaking thing scratched me, Michael thought, in something like wonder. *I let it scratch me.*

He gulped twice, trying to regain control of himself, to push away the coppery adrenaline. He looked into the eyes of the Bellow that was attempting to lunge again from the moonlit altar—*actually, just "eye,"* he corrected himself. One eye was the normal all-black, but from the other socket, an eye hung from its stalk like a deflated water balloon.

"STUUUUUUUPIIII—"

And redness surged through Michael's head.

He raised his rifle . . . and swung the stock of it at the Bellow, cracking the creature in the side of the skull. A sound like a sweet spot–hit baseball. Its brain ruined, the Bellow collapsed.

Didn't ask you, Michael thought.

Not bothering to shut the church up behind him, he went back to the office, chained the door.

Michael felt shaky. Frakking hell, you know what "something" would help him? Getting out of this crap-hole in the morning.

He thought of waking Patrick, just to tell jokes or something.

He crouched down, reaching out to touch Patrick's shoulder. But he stopped his hand. Brain-crud coated his fingers: his whole sleeve, in fact.

Can't even hug my brother, he thought.

You know what, Game? Sometimes I am so sick of you. Sometimes I just want to qui—

But don't think about that.

Michael sat in his hard chair, feeling his blood slam in his temples.

The Game Master arrived immediately.

CHAPTER FIVE

"There's someone outside."

Michael twitched, murmuring. He turned onto his other hip, pulling the sleeping bag up to his armpits. Good Lordy, did the cold suck: his bones felt hard and thick, like the cement floor underneath him. He swam slowly out from under sleep, his closed eyelids glowing a soft red. *Day twenty-two, plus one day, equals—*

"Michael, there's someone outside."

Michael's eyes burst open.

The burn of daylight through the semi-boarded windows hid his brother's expression. Michael automatically locked his own emotions down, too.

"Huh?" Michael whispered back calmly.

It's probably not people, he told himself. *Probably Bellows who couldn't find someplace to hide when the sun came up. Bub's just confused.* Michael remembered another confusing wake-up, the one that had come only a couple days before Halloween. Patrick had shaken Michael awake, saying, *What's a "impatient picnic"?* The fist-sized bruises on Michael's arms were still spectacular that morning: even in the confusion of waking, he hid them under the cover from Patrick. Patrick continued: *Daddy came back. He said, "Patrick's goin' back to the impatient picnic this weekend. They have a openin' first of November." Mom's sad. She's cryin' in the garage. Why's she* cryin'*?* Patrick said, but from the gathering dread on his face, Michael thought a part of Patrick already knew. And the truth shimmered up to Michael, too, like something hideous breaching in a nightmare.

"Inpatient clinic," Michael thought.

Even after everything he did, Mom let Ron come back. And she's letting him take Patrick back to the psych hospital.

But, now?

Now: Michael didn't hear *any* Bellows.

If someone's out there, they can take us to the Safe Zone.

"I was making dinner," Patrick whispered.

Dinner? What the hell time is *it? Did I sleep* all day? "I didn't wake you up. You snored loud. I . . . I was trying to be a good Gamer." In his hands, Patrick held their crappy multi-tool can opener and a can of tomato soup. The top of the can was gnawed and frayed.

And when Patrick pointed out the mostly boarded window, on the far wall maybe twenty feet away, Michael had to bite the meat of his cheek to make himself not shout in joy. Because in the daylight outside that window, for the first time in three weeks, he saw a living human, not his brother, walk past.

"Oh my God." He pawed his sleeping bag off, still whispering *"A million billion points for you."*

The Campbell's soup can dropped out of Patrick's hands, striking Michael's left shin.

"Bub, be carefu—!"

But Michael stopped. Patrick could read Michael, yes, but the reading went both ways. Patrick wasn't screaming—was not giving any huge, obvious sign that things were wrong—but his mouth was twitching.

He's scared. He's trying not to be, not in front of me. But he is.

"What's up?" Michael made himself smile.

Patrick's small tongue came out and licked his chapped lips. "The people sound . . . mad."

Michael stood up.

Mad, he thought. Which meant . . . what? *Probably nothing. They're just mad because . . . because they're a search party, and they haven't found anybody in the coal towns yet. Like we haven't.* But Michael heard a squeaking door open outside—the living human apparently entering a nearby building—and as Michael looked out the window, he thought: *the person went into the church.* And he felt his stomach go cold.

The stained-glass windows of the church across the alley were mostly busted. When Michael was two paces away from his own mostly boarded window, he caught his first glimpse of the church's interior: more shapes in the pews, shapes looking at something at the front of the church. *The altar,* Michael thought. He froze.

And heard this scream:

"Do you know what God has asked me to do?"

Nearly magical lines of shock traveling up Michael's arms; Patrick's hand clamping down on his; Michael, barely aware of it, spinning to a crouch, yanking Patrick closer to him, hiding against the wall underneath the window.

The voice sounded again and Michael had to stuff his hand over Patrick's mouth.

"DO YOU KNOW—"

"Please," a female voice answered. "Rulon, I did not do this."

Patrick's eyes were big and bright with a question: *How does Michael feel about this?*

Michael just half smiled and shrugged, like: *I know, little weird, right?*

But he really thought, his pulse flying, *What the fug is going on?*

Michael attempted to peek outside. For a moment, all he could see was the wet-warped wood that planked the window. Then he craned up farther and saw across the alley to the church.

The mannequins still stood among the pews, yes, but they'd been joined by perhaps fifty people, standing and kneeling amidst them. Their faces were dust-slashed, solemn, worn. Some had slightly yellowed skin. Their winter coats were ragged and bled out dirty insulation. Most of the people were so viciously thin that they nearly vanished even within the thin tatters. Two or three were obese; they wore only T-shirts, despite the cold. One such man—kneeling in the pews, his thick combed-back hair as black as coal—openly wept.

Michael's gaze trailed up the aisle. At the altar, there stood a man in rubbish brown robes, his back to Michael. *Priest,* he thought wildly.

In front of the priest, a blonde girl, no older than twenty, pretty in a malnourished way, was on her knees.

"Rulon," she said, voice so heavy with a hill-country accent that it sounded almost unreal, "please. I swear to you, I *didn't touch it*. I protected it all day, in the basement."

"Then how did he *die*, Mattie?" said the priest. He was speaking softly now, nearly whispering, but his voice still carried. "How, when we protected him for so long? How, when we left you alone only for a single day? Did one of our mannequins come to life, is that what you believe?"

The girl—Mattie?—shook her head. "Someone . . . someone else . . ." she said.

"Yes, child. We found footprints in the grocer's. We know this, Mattie. Go on."

Grocery store. That's us, me and Bub. Michael suddenly became aware of him and his brother as two small people in the fragile shell of the coal office.

"The other person, they must've come in last night . . ."

Me, Michael thought again, and felt an almost dizzying gratitude for the last night's snowstorm, which must have filled in their other prints.

"Of course," said the priest gently. "Never thought *you* woulda killed it, child. I s'pose you must be right: the killer must have come in last night, when you brought it up to the altar, when it was late. . . ."

"Yes!" Mattie agreed relievedly. "They came in when I—"

"When you . . . ?"

"When I was asleep!" she finished enthusiastically.

Michael didn't know what was going on, not exactly, but from the girl's face he understood everything he needed to know: Mattie looked like a girl who had been caught with her hand in a cookie jar . . . and the cookie jar turned out to have jaws like a bear trap.

"From the mouth of babes." The priest—his back still to Michael—looked to the crowd in the pews. Some smiled. Some frowned. But they all nodded in agreement.

"Oh, Mattie. No, your hand would never put harm upon any Chosen. Certainly not one so special, so precious. Certainly not one that we trusted you to protect while we were gone. I know you would not betray your God like that. Or betray *me* like that, Mattie."

The girl's forehead made a wrinkle-work of emotion, and for one moment, something terrible shone in her eyes:

Hope.

"R-really?" she said.

"Of course," said the priest. "But . . . you know, Mattie, God judges the sinner the same as the one who fails to *stop* the sin. And, child?"

"Yes?"

"I do, too."

And Michael knew what was going to happen even before it had begun.

The priest reached into his robes, and from its dirty tangles a hunter's knife materialized. The blade sang cleanly across Mattie's throat, a bright silver slash trailed by a spray of red.

Michael felt a sympathetic flash of heat across his own throat.

He can't do that, Michael thought desperately.

The girl's limp body twisted to the floor.

Patrick's mouth moved under Michael's hand, as if to ask what was happening.

It's—you can't kill people, Michael thought. *That's against the Rules.* People *don't hurt* people *in The Game!*

But these people in the church didn't seem to care. While the priest stood over the body, a man came forward from the pews, his heavy boots clunking. He was the weeping man with the coal-black hair, but he was the smiling man now. The priest said to him: "We'll feed her to them tonight. But this girl does not deserve resurrection. Cut off her head first, please, Samuel." And as Samuel scooped the girl's body from the floor—like it was his everyday job—Michael saw him mouth: *hallelujah.*

CHAPTER SIX

The people were filing calmly down the aisle of the church, now, out the front door to the street.

Patrick pushed Michael's hand off his mouth, sucking air, coughing. Some distant part of Michael understood that he should shush him, but the world grayed out momentarily before his eyes.

What the hell just happened? he thought. *Why did those people do that? Who the hell are they?*

The Game Master had told them a lot of things. *You're quick, and so you're safe*, he'd said. *You're not really lost, just on your way. And if you will only do what I tell you, Michael, you will be saved, and you will save your brother.*

But: *"People* will hurt people"? "On the way to the Safe Zone, you'll encounter lunatics who have no interest in helping you"? Those were a couple that must've slipped the Game Master's mind.

"What happened? Do you wanna go to those people?" Patrick said.

"Shh a sec . . ."

"Yeahbut*whathapp*—"

Patrick, shut up! I'm trying to think; just shut up!

Michael whipped around to look at Patrick—and Patrick did more than just recoil at Michael's anger. Michael saw something in Patrick's eyes: that going-far-away look. *OhGodno.* He'd seen that look before when Patrick got too confused or scared . . . and he'd seen what happened to Patrick if nobody stopped it.

Michael snapped back into himself.

Whoever these freaking people are, don't let Patrick know that you're scared.

Michael licked his lips. "They're just some bad guys," he told Patrick. "It's a surprise."

"Huh?" said Patrick. "Another one? Like the woods?"

"Bigger one. Way, way bigger."

"Did the Game Master tell *you* about it?" Patrick asked.

No, Bub. This, he definitely did not mention. I'm starting to think the Game Master is kinda full of shit.

Michael said, "Yeah, of course he told me about it." He forced a smile. It felt real, almost, even to him.

Michael heard roars.

He twitched, nearly screaming back, then looked out the window. The alley led out onto Main Street. The people from the hideous ceremony stood there: the strange priest was speaking to them, waving his hands down one direction of the street and then another. Beyond the priest and his followers, in the hills that towered just beyond the buildings on the opposite side of the street, lay the edge of the forest. Which was bellowing.

Dusk-colored shadows were approaching from the deeps of the woods. Dozens of Bellows. Because it was almost nightfall.

Twenty-two days plus one day equals you overslept you stupid asshole!

Hurry. Hurry and get out get out get out.

47

"*Piggyback,*" Michael whispered.

"*Michael?*" Patrick whispered in his ear as he clambered onto his back.

And sense-memory overpowered Michael. . . .

It's Halloween.

Patrick rides piggyback, his hands clasped together just above Michael's heart. They stand in the hallway to the garage; on their right is the bathroom with the busted toilet. Patrick's whispered "Michael?" is warm in his ear. Michael cocks his head and puts a finger to his lips.

He presses a hand against the hinges of the door to the garage to stop its double squeak. And once the door is shut behind them, he nods for Patrick to go on.

"How do you know about The Game?" Patrick whispers.

"Like I said, buddy: the Game Master told me. He told me how we can win."

Michael goes his rehearsed eight and a half steps across the dark to a mound of old clothes in the corner. A waft of perfume from a ragged scarf. He pushes down his ache. Underneath the clothes lie Michael's backpack and a duffel bag, both filled with enough food to last through The Game they'll be playing for the next couple days.

He gives the backpack to Patrick, tells him holding it counts for five points.

"How do you win?" Patrick asks.

"You get points. But they're not as important. What's important is that you outrun the bad guys; what's important is where you get to in the end."

"Where are we going to?"

Away from here, Bub. This Game is going to take us away, *Michael thinks.*

And opens the side garage door to the jack-o'-lantern night, not knowing what is about to change, not knowing that The

Game and its bad guys will be different than he had anticipated, not knowing that when he goes outside, he will see his neighbor being eaten.

"Michael what're we gonna do?" Patrick whispered now—not in their garage in Bridgeview, West Virginia, but in a boarded office in good ol' "Almost Heaven" coal country.

"Stealth Mode," Michael made himself whisper.

One: get out of here.

Two: fast.

Three: stop thinking, and feel your blood.

One: get out. Two: fast. Three . . .

Hunched, Patrick's legs tucked under his elbows, Michael moved away from the alley window. He could not concentrate, because his thoughts were flinging through him—

—How did this happen? Why were the people so mad that the Bellow had been killed? Why?

Michael shrugged Patrick higher up, looking around the room for their possessions. *Duffel bag? Not important, leave it, no time. Rifle? Rifle? Where is the— There, behind the desk, go.*

And how are you going to "go" if your car is outside with all those people?

"But they're not *supposed* to be bad," Patrick said.

"Which is what makes it a surprise."

Something sharp caught Michael's pants. Just the side of the desk. But he'd nearly screamed.

Be quiet, Bub. Because Michael had to think—no, no he had to *not* think—he had to *not think* and get them out of here, because if he didn't—

Because: if Patrick gets too scared, if Patrick Freaks again, Atipax pills won't be enough, will they, Mikey?

They went to the front door.

As Michael looked through a half-boarded window beside

the door, the priest was finishing his talk. The snow had a strange muffling effect on the wild man's words, but every few traveled: "boot prints . . . small . . . chosen . . . find . . ." Their shadows growing darker in the bluish snow, the priest led the group out of sight, back into the church.

Michael and Patrick hadn't found any weapons in their canvass of Coalmount. Evidently, that was because they hadn't thought of the church as a possible arsenal.

The congregation reemerged with two axes, three pipes, four crowbars, and seven pistols. The priest himself cradled a rifle with a scope and banana clip.

He motioned in different directions, and the people began spreading into the streets and side streets and alleys, like a great spiderweb being spun. *Looking for us. Oh God, yeah, it's a search party, just not the kind I wanted.*

One woman was waiting in the road. A hammy woman—red coat, no gloves, a sweet, dimpled face—paced parallel to the coal office, not fifty feet from the front door. She was carrying a crowbar. She raised a hand to her brow, scouting the tree line that rose behind the buildings on the opposite side of the street. Amazingly, she seemed to have no interest at all in the side of the street where Michael was hidden.

And she had not even noticed their Volvo station wagon.

Situated between Michael and the woman—dusted with fresh inches of snow from last night's storm—was the only possible hope of escape for the people she was stalking.

God bless you, crappy West Virginia winter! "Gamer, we've got to sneak out. I bet you'll do it *awesome*, huh?"

"H-heck yeah," Patrick said weakly. And added with a struggle: "woot."

God, he tried so hard. *Ya-ya.*

Michael thought: *Breathe. Just breathe.*

Here, Michael thought, *we go.*

And *did.*

In the milli-moment when Hammy was turning and turning away, Michael, carrying his rifle and his brother both, opened the door of the office of Southern West Virginia Coal and Natural Gas, and silently stepped out.

Because he did not want the steam to rise, he locked his breath inside his mouth.

And in his temples, he felt his thudding blood.

In seconds like these—strings of seconds that seemed sewn together, tethered easily with light—everything glowed. Every thing *flowed.* His feet floated down before him, instructing themselves, finding seamlessly the empty space between the iced-over parts of snow that would crunch. *He was not thinking.* In seconds like these, he was pure *doing.*

He could smell the snow. He tasted and heard the cold. The car was sliding closer to him, and as it did, behind his eyes, he saw them driving off in it.

"Michael!" Patrick whispered uncertainly.

Michael flinched, ready to hiss at Patrick, but then everything inside him froze.

On the other side of the Volvo, Hammy was turning toward them.

Run! But Michael ignored the panic. He threw himself down, Patrick still on his back. His shoulder bucked against the side-rear bumper of the Volvo; snow from the bike attached to the back fell down on them.

He could see the woman's feet, under the car. Her fat legs were stomping in the snow.

His own legs burned and quivered underneath him.

The office was only maybe ten paces back, but it might as

well have been in another world. He'd be spotted if he tried to return.

Patrick looked panicked, and Michael understood that he had to hurry.

He crouched-crawled to the front passenger door. His hand gripped the handle, and just as he tugged it, he thought:

Locked it. I locked it before we went in the office.

The Volvo's alarm exploded the air around him. Michael's legs softened. Bright spots of shock popped in front of his eyes. He jammed his gloves into his mouth.

Patrick screamed into the glow of now-flashing hazard lights.

"Heeere!" Hammy shrieked. *"Oooooooh, they're heeeeeeere!"*

She began to run, but slid and stumbled as she made the transition from sidewalk to road, slamming onto a knee. "Waahh-*hoooo!*" she wailed. Beyond her, in all directions, shadows neared: Bellows in the woods, killers in the roads, wailing and approaching.

Patrick, his eyes white and afraid, said, "Michael?"

NOW! FEEL YOUR—

—blood, blood, hammering his heart—

And suddenly, suddenly Michael was calm!

He took Patrick's hand into his own, knowing this: he would get the keys, or it would be Game Over.

He got Patrick up, back across the sidewalk toward the office, shouldered the door, into darkness, where he tripped over a can of paint, quickly regained footing—to the desk, to their duffel bag beside it—kicking the paint can away and as the can burst open and splashed red color, Michael tore open the bag and fanned apart the Pop-Tart wrappers and there were his keys, there were his keys, winking, like they were happy to see him too.

"Michael, what are we gonna do?"

"Go to the next level."

Grabbing Patrick's hand again, squirming bones in mitten, *yes-yes*, and out the window, quite calmly Michael saw shadows that were confused and shouting. The people were twenty yards away, and jogging fast. But, ah, Gamers, that was the thing: they were *jogging*, and Michael—beginning to smile—Michael was *dashing*.

The car key went into the car lock like warmed oil.

In video games, in the cut scenes at the ends of missions, it was always this moment that snagged the good guys by the ankle. In video games, it didn't matter how perfectly you played: you couldn't go to the next level if the game didn't want you to. Bad guys could be gaining, and you do something stupid, like drop your key—but Michael's car door opened perfectly. He lifted Bub into the car, and Michael was about to enter the car, too, to put the insane pursuers in his past. So he did not expect it when there came a flash of yellow, and the Volvo's windshield finally shattered inward. And beside Michael's ear, just as he was getting ready to sit, the headrest exploded.

Stuffing flew, white and singed.

Snow wheeled into the car through the place where the windshield had been. Ducked down, stunned, his head on the driver's seat but his knees on the ground outside the open driver's door, it took Michael several seconds to fully process what had happened. His brain had been knocked, reeling, to the mat. And the *yes-yes* was gone.

"Patrick?" he made himself not scream.

Silence.

"Owwww," said a voice.

His heart iced. "What, what's wrong?"

"That was *so loud*."

"I . . . I know. What a jerk, right?" Michael said. He tried to sound calm—didn't think he was a success.

Don't Freak, please. Not now, Bub.

Michael spotted the keys. They'd fallen onto the passenger

seat. They were just out of reach—

A second shot exploded the remainder of the headrest.

A metallic *click*, in front of the car. "Come to me, boy."

Michael cautiously raised his head, peering over the dashboard. The gunman-priest stood ten feet from the hood, his long barrel aimed at Michael. He ejected his spent shell, which disappeared in the snow, steaming.

He slid the cocking mechanism of his gun forward, chambering a new round. *He's actually going to shoot us.*

"Sir, wait, WAIT!"

Wind spun snow between them. The man didn't say a thing. But his eyes were happy and glittered in his face like beetles.

"Out, boy." His whisper carried as well as a boom. *"If you know what will please your soul: out."*

Not far from the forest's edge, Bellows blew their dead calls. The last of the search party—mostly older people who couldn't run as fast—were arriving from the side streets. They began forming a loose ring around the car.

Run, you die. Stay in the car, you die.

"Out." The wild priest smiled.

"Me and my brother?" asked Michael.

"The child shall be last, thankee."

What could Michael do but nod?

He pretended to struggle to get to his feet to buy himself half a second. *"Bub,"* he whispered.

"H-huh?"

I'm going to go outside now, Michael thought, *to talk with the man with the gun. Don't Freak. Please stay here. And if you hear him shoot, don't look.*

"BRB. You just do one thing for me, okay?

"Don't eat my Flintstone Vitamins, chump, or I swear I'll punch your butt so hard . . ."

There wasn't even a giggle from the backseat. Michael stood.

And now, more than any other moment since The Game began, he had no idea what he was going to do.

He stepped away from the car and into the center of the unreal nether-zone Main Street.

The gunman-priest kept his weapon on Michael, ruddy face grinning tightly. His long robes twisted and furled, somehow ghostly. His robe and his fingers were stained red.

Michael raised his hands up. *So what I'm gonna do is . . .* That was a trick that worked, sometimes: starting a thought and letting it finish itself.

But it didn't work this time.

His stomach crawled. He was surrounded by the crowd that had happily witnessed murder in the church. He half expected the crowd to swarm him, to carry him to the altar.

The crowd watched.

Michael took a step away from the car and nodded to the gunman-priest, who did not nod back.

"Who are you, boy?"

"My name is Michael Faris, sir," Michael replied carefully, "and I'm just looking for—"

"'Michael.' Do you know who the real Michael is? 'Michael' is the archangel: God's warrior. But Michael Faris, you betray God." The priest cocked his head. "Where do you come from, Michael Faris?"

"The office. We slept there."

"Play no games," the priest said. "Before that, boy."

"We . . . came from Route 82." Michael motioned toward the edge of Coalmount with his head.

"Before that," said the priest.

"Before . . . ?"

"Beefooore!" hissed the priest. His neck popped in cords. "Before before!"

Michael did not dare look away from the priest, but he swore that he could almost feel Patrick's reaction ping across the air to him, asking why a man in The Game was so mean. Patrick, getting more and more scared . . .

From the woods: *"Beeee—fooo—heeeeeffooorrrreeee!"*

Calm again, as if comforted by the roars, the priest said: "Confess, child. In the night. You killed the Chosen."

The crowd murmured agreement. Did they sound closer than before?

Michael's groin filled with ice. "The what?"

"God's Chosen, Michael Faris."

"Well . . . I'm not exactly sure what you mean by 'God's Chosen.'"

But with blossoming dread, Michael thought he *did* know why Rulon called the Bellow he'd killed "the Chosen."

The way the Bellow was bound to the altar in the church. The way other "God-Blessed" Bellows were buried in front of the meeting hall: sealed and untouchable, as if they were being protected.

They . . . oh God. Oh effing no. Do these people worship *the Bellows?*

"You think this is your victory, don't you, child?" said the priest.

Michael blinked. "I . . . victory?"

"But you are the victor of nothing. You destroyed our First, but ohhh, more of the Chosen pass through these hills around our town and come to us every day, don't they? Your friends may have tried to force us from our homes, but we're back, now, aren't we? And you cannot keep us out of your shelter forever. This is not your victory, no, child. Tell me: Why did the others send you?"

Michael stood stone-faced, refusing to betray his emotions. But something strong and good roared in his chest. *There are others. Nearby. Others, who this a-hole hates.*

Which means, probably, they're awesome.

Others, as in the Safe Zone?

He didn't know; doubted it, actually.

But he could not help but picture the ending he'd been fighting to reach since Halloween: he pictured walking into the Safe Zone, holding Patrick's hand. And he pictured Mom, the little birthmark on her left cheek twitching, like it always did when she saw him and was about to smile; he pictured her pride in him, her happiness.

Ringed by the crowd, the madman's rifle zeroed over his heart, Michael mentally calculated how long it would take to dive back into the car, find the keys, and plow an escape through these lunatics.

Way too long.

Michael looked into the priest's eyes. And what he saw inside them—the certainty and fury—made him . . . calm.

You can't outrun him. So outplay him.

Yeah, the Game Master never told you about fighting a psycho priest, but outplay him—just do this one last thing—and maybe The Game can be over. Just like the Game Master promised.

Outplay him how?

Michael's senses searched for his pulse. . . .

He opened his heart to the fear, and the danger beat through his veins, enlivening him, amplifying all instincts, the terror fusing all his focus down to a powerfully bright, pulsing bead.

He looked into the man's eyes and took the measure of his rage, and fear. He saw who the priest was, behind that rifle, behind those eyes. Michael understood him.

Like Ron.

You outplay him like you do with Ron, how you always keep yourself—and Bub—safe whenever he's around.

You lie.

And Michael smiled—*yes-yes*—the crazy exhilaration of

knowing what to do outweighing any dread.

He took a step forward, let it become a trot, and offered the priest his hand.

The priest's finger tensed on the trigger. The crowd didn't gasp: they seemed to *become* a gasp, going taut and drawing back.

"Stop," the priest said.

"Sure thing," Michael said.

He stopped but leaned in, ignored the gasping crowd, said seriously, "You're right, though. The man in charge sent me. And if you hurt me, sir, I think he's gonna be . . . upset."

The priest's beetle eyes narrowed with suspicion. "But why would he send a child?"

Who's 'he'? Doesn't matter. Keep going.

"Hey, Coalmount, how ya doing?" Michael greeted the crowd.

One time, the governor had come to talk to his high school; as he'd walked to the auditorium stage, he shook everybody's hand. Michael imitated that now, the politician's winky-winky, grabbing limp fingers. "Everyone eating okay? Need any food? Anybody need clean undies? Besides me."

Michael felt the air shift on his neck, knew what was coming, and had to fight not to smile at things going according to his plan.

The stock of the rifle slammed down between his shoulder blades. He staggered forward, screamed for half a second in his closed mouth. He looked at Patrick, saw him between the passenger's and driver's seats; Patrick gasped. Which was good—Michael *wanted* Patrick to see that these people were breaking the Rules, even violently. *Because in a second I can show you that you're still safe, Patrick, that even with these people breaking the Rules, The Game is still under control. Just keep watching, Bub.*

But Michael suddenly thought: *Don't push Rulon too far! If it goes too far, Patrick will* know—

"Oh, you *a-hole*," said Michael to the priest.

"The foul-minded boy! The sin-thick boy!" His teeth glowed like yellow tombstones. "Do you know what I believe? I believe you are alone. Why would he send a child?"

Now a teary-voiced man in the crowd shouted, "Yes, Rulon! Yes! Get that one!"

"Wait," Michael muttered, but the priest had no intention of waiting.

Rulon began to raise his rifle. He looked to the sky.

Feel your blood. Calm down.

"Accept the sacrifice," the priest intoned, "of the one who spilled Your Chosen's bloo—"

Michael reached into his pocket and drew the old-school cell phone, powering it on, hitting the number pad, saying into the phone, "They're about to hurt me, sir!"

And the sound—*yes-yes*—issued forth from the speaker like a small cannon.

"I order you to stop!" called the Game Master.

Blink.

"Sssssttoooooppp!" wailed the Bellows from the woods.

Rulon squinted down at the silver phone in Michael's hand, as if at some unholy artifact.

Michael tapped a button. The Game Master's rich accent barked out even louder from the speakerphone. *"Again, I order you to stop!"*

"Who is that?" said Rulon.

"Ask him yourself," replied Michael.

Rulon didn't.

"These are your orders!" the phone replied, anyway.

"The man in charge," Michael said. "The master," he said louder, for Patrick's sake.

"Lies," said Rulon. But he sounded uncertain. And Michael felt a thrill of *yes-yes*, because the crowd wasn't looking to Rulon. They were looking at the phone.

"No one is our master," said Rulon calmly to the crowd. "*We* are our master. Who that man is, I don't know. When the Lord began purifying, we were left to do His good work. We were left to shepherd the first risen Chosen until His Horsemen come. We were left—"

Michael put the phone to his ear, turned off the speaker. "He doesn't believe m—"

"*Enough!*"

"*Report back to me, Michael!*" said the Game Master.

Someone in the crowd, concerned, said, "Rulon? Who *is* it?"

Rulon watched the phone.

Michael said into the phone, "I'm here, sir. This man, Rulon, still looks a little trigger happy. Are there reinforcements?"

Hit a button. Speakerphone again: "*There are soldiers nearby!*"

"Awesome to know," Michael said, and he began to back toward his station wagon.

Rage and confusion tumbled over Rulon's face. Rulon lowered the gun, raised it, then put it down permanently.

Beat you. And you can't believe I can do it. Just like Ron.

See, Bub? We are *safe.*

His fingers looped the door handle and he nodded toward the crowd, winked, gave a thumbs-up. There was no car alarm this time. Patrick peered up through the gap between the front seats, and Michael had an almost uncontrollable urge to low-five him—to *touch* him.

"Boy?" Rulon had taken a couple steps toward Michael, and for some reason looked slyly, dangerously pleased. "I have only one question. If the man in charge sent you, what is his name?"

"I—"

The voice on the phone crackled. It could have been static. But it wasn't. "*End of your recording,*" a robot voice on the phone said. "*Play your phone recording again? Press one to play, press two to delete, press three to record a new—*"

How long did it take to close the phone? Too long.

No, thought Michael. *Messed it up, I messed it up.*

His eyes locked with Rulon's, electricity leaping between them as the cell phone's voice recorder cut off—

—and Michael slammed the driver's door into Rulon's groin and dived into his car. He threw the gear into DRIVE, hoping to outrun the truth:

The voice on the phone had been Michael's own, not a phone call but a recording he'd made last night when Patrick was asleep. Because, of course, Michael *was* the Game Master. And there was no Game.

Michael had made it up.

CHAPTER SEVEN

Had Patrick heard? That was all that mattered.

Please frakking no. Oh please *no.*

"Bub?"

Michael lay low, out of gun sight, driving the Volvo blindly as the attackers' faces and arms struck the windows. Hands grabbed in through the empty windshield.

"Bub?" Michael repeated.

"Get theeeeemmm!"

"Grab the big one!"

"Move! Out of the way! I'll cut the tires, let me cut —"

And a gun crack split the dusk.

Michael's rearview mirror ripped free and flipped onto the passenger seat. He spasmed, trapping his scream in his mouth. Rulon was reloading, perhaps twenty yards in front of them, but there was something more dangerous already inside the car: the tears brimming in his brother's eyes.

Patrick was hiding in the footwell behind the passenger seat. No: no, he was *cowering* in it. He clutched his Ultraman, trying to look tough, but Michael saw the truth. The way Bub panted, thin and ragged. The way he rhythmically bit his lip, hard enough to split the skin and bring a bead of blood. The way his eyes were going blank, like a void, like a TV screen the second after the power goes out, like he was tumbling down a long dark hole in himself, a hole that had opened when the world as he understood it cracked wide open under his feet.

Patrick was trying not to Freak.

Why why why? Was he upset because of the gunshots and the crazy people, or because he had heard that the "Game Master" on the phone was only a recording of his brother's voice? Did he know that Michael had invented The Game, had lied every moment of every day and night since Halloween? Did he know that the only reason The Game existed was to keep him away from that ledge inside himself?

"Bub . . . 'sup?"

Patrick's gaze widened and snapped over Michael's shoulder. Michael looked and saw a man dashing from an alley to their right, raw lips pulled in a grin, pistol in hand. Michael gritted his teeth and heaved the wheel, speeding left, onto a road that shot off of Main Street, away from the man. They were leaving Coalmount, past the spot where Michael had checked it out with his binoculars, past the rusted sign that asked them to PLE SE COME AGA N! Gonna pass, thanks for the invite.

Michael reached the country route that had brought them to Coalmount yesterday, choosing the opposite direction from which they had arrived, hoping—oh, please—that it would take him to the Others Rulon feared.

"Michael . . . ?" Patrick said softly.

"Yo!" Michael said, his voice shaking.

"It's wrong, it's wrong."

What's wrong?! Another gunshot at their back. This one took the back right window, splashing glass.

Patrick cried, *"Breakin' the Rules is against the Rules! Other people are supposed to HELP US!"*

And Michael slid in his seat as relief made him putty. *Oh thank God, he didn't hear. He doesn't know. He's just scared.*

But that doesn't mean he's not going to Freak.

Because the only reason The Game keeps him from Freaking is that he thinks it's all safe! *He thinks the Bellows can't really* hurt *you or him, that there are Rules—that you are his safe place, that you can always* protect *him.*

And now, people *were* trying to hurt them, people were shattering the Rules, shattering the world.

And these people will make him Freak and disappear into himself—or they will just kill *him—unless you get out of here, fast, very.*

Patrick's eyes screamed what Michael now asked himself:

What are you going to do?

Click went the headlights to life automatically, as the station wagon's sensors registered nightfall. The Bellows had noticed, too: they sifted from the woods on either side of this rutted country route, screaming on the roadside like phantoms in an urban legend. Wouldn't be long before they clogged the road.

Think. Think think think.

In the rearview mirror, Rulon's maniacs were coming. They had boarded four-wheelers, motorcycles, dirt bikes. And their headlamps were gaining.

"Are they *chasing* us?" Patrick whined.

"What do you freaking think?" Michael snapped.

Patrick began chewing on his palm. Patrick's voice, shamed and quavering, said, "You're mad at me."

Oh, good effing move.

Michael swerved, avoiding a child Bellow in a ballerina tutu. "No, I'm not."

"Then why did you yell?" said Patrick.

"'Cause I'm excited."

A heavy thud, and a smashing of a headlight's glass. He'd hit a Bellow. Michael slowed for a split second, shocked. *And the motorcycles gained.*

"Michael, I want Mommy. I w-w-want her a l-l-l-little."

No, Bub, you want her a lot, and you want her now. And guess what? I do, too. And now you're going to start screaming, and I can't give you a pill to calm you down right now, so this is what is called The End—

Michael, desperate, blurted: "Let's go talk to the soldiers!"

Patrick blinked: *What the?!*

"Yeah, Bub, we'll tell on the cheaters—I saw soldiers last night, I wanted to surprise you—they're with the Game Master—*maybe we'll even get enough extra points and finish tonight.*"

And how are you going to do that? Michael thought. *How are you going to "meet the Game Master"?*

Shut up! I'll figure it out. I. Will. Eventually. Soon. Figure. That. Shit. Out.

"Are they close?" Patrick said, voice shaky.

"They're super close, next door basically, it'll just take a couple minutes, okay?"

Nothing. Quiet.

"Oka—?"

". . . Is that a good-guy sign . . . ?" Patrick whispered.

Michael turned his head just in time to see the sign zip past: a sign shaped like a badge, attached to a metal pole.

That, he thought, *is an interstate sign.*

His entire brain exploded.

Three weeks.

Three weeks.

Three weeks.

Three weeks they'd traveled on the pitted back roads, searching for an interstate entrance. Three weeks in the gray nether-zones of his useless map. Three weeks in the mountains, and they'd only seen one entrance, and that on-ramp had been clustered with empty cars, with razor wire strung across the road.

The only thing on this on-ramp was moon-bright snow.

Breathe.

He turned onto the ramp.

Uuuuuupppp, it felt like; *uuuupppppp* the incline of the ramp, the spectacular fantastic incredible on-ramp, *yes-yes*, zooming as if for a takeoff, gliding with it *now*.

Snow cometed into the car, but that was nothing, because he could look out and see the whole night in between those white streaks. He fit into the moment. The world slid into clarity around him. He struck a patch of black ice and instantly corrected the car's shimmy with a flick of the wheel.

The maniacs chasing him didn't understand: Michael was used to being chased. He'd been outmaneuvering danger a lot longer than just since October 31.

"Bub," he said, smiling, "I need your help. I need you to be a shooter. I need you to be, basically, Buzz Lightyear."

"Huh?" said Patrick.

Michael passed the flashlight and the orange toy gun he'd gotten from the office over his shoulder, just something to occupy Patrick until they got away.

"It's your weapon, buddy. If you see any Bellows, zap 'em with the light."

Patrick took his hand away from his mouth, hesitating. He gulped. "Can I be Woody instead?"

And Patrick, *yes-yes*, took the light and gun. And satisfaction and relief blossomed in Michael as Patrick stepped back, at least for a second, from the ledge inside himself that wanted to swallow him whole.

They reached the interstate's even plain. Cars and big rigs clogged the two-lane, cast ascatter like spilled toys.

Creatures within the big rigs' cargo hulls screamed.

Cargo hulls' doors roared open to the new nightfall.

Michael did not breathe and his blood soared through him, and he seamlessly slalomed the Volvo through the just-wide-enough gaps between wrecks.

But you can't outrun Rulon's maniacs here, Michael saw— not thought, but *imaged.* Gun to heart or pedal to floor: that was how it always worked. A plan, fully formed, flashbulbed in his mind, and its brilliant light seemed to transform the world around him into something like a high-definition video-game screen shot, an impromptu tutorial, with arrows and highlights and clues indicating what path to take.

Too many cars, Michael saw.

So, you stop your car.

And hide from the maniacs, in the woods past the interstate guardrail. Climb up a tree and wait it out. Then come back to the interstate in the morning and follow the road to the Safe Zone. To Game Over.

And maybe even to Mom—

"Bub, how 'bout a bike ride?"

"Huh?" Patrick began, but Michael shouted, *"Hold on to something!"* and crushed the brake.

He did not know why. The *yes-yes* was telling him to, that was all.

The car screamed over the frozen concrete, and when it finally came to a stop, Michael understood.

His headlights revealed the bottom of a flipped eighteen-wheeler, perhaps ten yards ahead. A dozen Bellows crawled over the underparts, glistening like wasps. If he hadn't braked, either the Bellows or the wreck would have ended him.

He wasn't psychic, that wasn't it. Just accustomed to the terrible. Very much so. Just ask Ron.

The remaining motorcyclists were still a half mile back, negotiating the traffic tangles. Michael hooked his .22 caliber over his shoulder and carried Patrick from the Volvo.

Michael unbungeed the mountain bike from the back of the car, Patrick still piggyback, then guided the bike through stalled cars toward the guardrail on the side of the interstate, taking out, with his rifle, two Bellows who followed from the eighteen-wheeler.

When they reached the guardrail, Michael put the car keys in his pocket, and something deep inside of him seemed to tear. He and Mom had gone to Myrtle Beach a thousand times in that car, back when it was just the two of them.

"Michael? Why're you sad?" Patrick asked, leaning over Michael's shoulder and peering at his expression with growing dread in his voice.

God, he sees everything. Control yourself.

"I'm not, *pfff*," Michael said, and turned toward the guardrail.

The falling darkness beyond the railing: a sheer downhill slope, mohawked clear of trees in the middle where power lines were strung, dense Bellow-sounding woodlands surrounding the empty lane on both sides.

It looked like a path off the edge of the known world. Like a void, waiting to swallow him.

No. No. I've done worse, Michael told himself. That ride had been when he was thirteen, and the bike had been his birthday present. In his pickup, Ron had taken Michael to the top of a mountain-bike trail in the city park. "Well go 'head," he'd said, and seemed a thousand miles tall, his smell like sweat and strong coffee, the sun glinting the gem of his championship football ring. But the trail was nasty, snarled with roots. "Your mother and I worked hard for this bike. If you think we got money layin' around, you can go on back to dreamin'," Ron said, seeing Michael's hesitation. "Do you know what *hard work* is, Michael-boy?"

"I—"

"Oh, did I know *you'd* pull this shit. You ain't sittin' on your ass with your damn video games all day while your mother and I work. A boy should *want* to ride his bike. Don't you think that's what real boys want?" Ron was a bomb. Yes, he was a bomb, and that was the first time Michael lit him. But when Michael's tears threatened—*tears a* real *boy would never have,* he thought—Ron said softly, "'Course, maybe the problem is, this boy's *really* becoming a *man*." The hairy hand Ron placed on Michael's shoulder had felt amazing, like everything that was powerful and mysterious and special about grown-ups. How easy it is to believe in kindness when you are young and your world has not yet ended. So Michael rode the trail.

He spent the rest of his birthday in the emergency room, his collarbone broken in two places.

But that was before, Michael told himself. *Back when I still thought he was safe. Before I realized I had to, like, take scary things and use them.*

This wasn't a suicide run. This was a hill made of Awesome and Getaway.

Michael lifted Patrick into the kid's seat mounted on the back of the bike. God, he felt so small.

"We're gonna hafta go purty fast," Michael said. "Sooo guess who gets to control our headlights?"

Michael demonstrated, turning the flashlight on behind the binoculars, so that a single beam entered the back of the binocs and twin pipes of bright shot out the front.

Patrick smiled a little, in awe. He put the orange toy gun into his pocket, took the light and binoculars from Michael.

The riders—Michael did not see Rulon among them—reached the Volvo, dismounting and searching the car in the light of their headlamps. Michael got shakily onto his own bike. He was toeing silently forward when Patrick screamed:

"Wait! Michael! Ultraman! *I forgotted him!*"

One of the riders shouted, "Oh Lord! There! The side of the road!"

"I got him in my pocket," Michael lied.

And he pushed off.

The mountain *whooshed.*

One instant they were on flat; the next, the world tilted up in a misty punch of snow. The drop was far steeper than it had looked, and the snowstorm thick enough to blind. But Michael focused desperately on the adrenaline-sick pulse hammering in his throat—

And he twisted around the crawling Bellow, leaning into his turn, and it felt that he was leaning onto air just firm enough to hold him gently up.

He smiled without realizing it. *Yes-yes*, this was chuckling at gravity. This was, in the depths of insanity and wrong, perfectly *right.*

Exhilaration.

Freedom.

Control.

"Left-left-left!" he said breathlessly, and Patrick shot light upon a Bellow emerging from the woods.

"Reach fer the skyyyyy!" Patrick cried in his cowboy voice.

The Bellow screamed and fell and sledded down the mountain on its back.

"Nice shootin', Tex!" Michael heard himself say, and his

brother laughed, clapping happily on his back. And Michael remembered joy.

Now came the first four-wheeler, following, flying over the guardrail.

Its headlight hung wildly among the treetops to their left, then landed down in the snow.

Michael hooked the bike into the tree line. Here the moonlight faded, so the forest was a maze of shadow. A hundred trees seemed to blast into existence just beyond his handlebars— dangerous, ah, and thank you very much for that. Michael jabbed the handlebars, surging between the trees like a missile.

The four-wheeler entered the woods, its headlight whipping side to side as it copied Michael's path.

Up ahead came what Michael had hoped for: a thick collection of trees, their trunks so tight they'd be impossible to steer through—

—except for him.

He wove straight through, so close he felt the bark brush his sleeves, and an instant later the four-wheeler tried to follow and an instant after that, the four-wheeler crashed.

"Newb!" Michael crowed.

Go.

Go.

This is mine.

I can bike every mile of moonlit snow in the world.

Chase me, 'cause me and my brother?

We. Can. Run. Forever.

CHAPTER EIGHT

Michael shot out of the trees, into the clear lane between the two sides of forest, and it began to occur to him that, despite the three motorcycle-riding crazies still coming down the snow-covered mountain for him, he was really going to make it. He was going to be safe. He would find the Others that Rulon had mentioned, and sometime—maybe soon—he was going to make it to the Safe Zone and The End. *No more secrets,* he thought. *No more lying all the time. I won't have to* do *this anymore.* He was going to find Mom, and everything since Halloween and after it—all the time away, all the battles with Bellows—would be worth it.

He was thinking those things when he gasped, because he saw something wonderful ahead that blazed through him like light.

Charleston, he thought breathlessly. *That is* Charleston.

Down the mountain, in the valley a mile below, Michael saw a golden dome, tiny from here, lit up like a Christmas tree. Spotlights beside the Capitol building traced into the sky, blotting out the starlight.

"Patrick! Bub, *it's the Safe Zone!*" Michael said.

Patrick gaped over his shoulder, going, *"Whoa-ho-ho!"* in amazement.

"We're going to win—" Michael began.

He saw the coming threat at the last, last second. A buck, a deer, hugely antlered and explosively fast, had cut in front of him. Michael yanked the handlebars, and felt his bike tipping with a slow, gummy, nightmare awareness.

The bike collided with the ground, hurling snow, its leftover speed carrying them forward. Patrick cried out; Michael felt him slip away.

Get the bike! Michael thought even as he barrel-rolled violently through the snow. *Keep going!* He sat up, his eyes stinging with snow. "It's okay, Bub!" he said. Half blinded, he was patting the ground, looking for the bike. . . .

The ground vanished beneath his hand.

Cliff.

Michael felt a screaming vertigo and paddled backward.

"Michael!" Patrick called, a few steps behind him . . . which Michael could see because of the light of the motorcycles, which had stopped maybe fifty feet back.

The Bellows were coming from the tree line, too, behind Patrick. Many of them glistened and crackled, their limbs lined with ice.

We're trapped.

The men on the motorcycles stepped off their bikes, stamping toward them through the snow.

Michael ran to Patrick, held onto Patrick, his heart thudding, and he felt his blood, and—

And, he didn't move.

He didn't run.

"Help us, Michael," Patrick said. *"Please."*

Standing between the coming killers and the edge of the

world, with no place to flee, something happened. Michael felt his own breath course down his raw throat, his blood rushing through his terror-stoked heart . . . and a feeling he couldn't name enveloped him.

It's fine, said the strange feeling.

It was deafening, inside.

But it was, too, amazingly, purely calm.

And strong: so strong that it didn't seem to come from him, as *yes-yes* did, but *through* him. It was a voice so immense and *not him* that the instructions could have originated in the stars. And the voice was telling Michael what to do.

Wait, it said. *Just wait.*

What? his mind protested. *Why?!*

"Michael, what are you doing?" Patrick said.

Wait.

"Michael—" Patrick cried, *"Michael, what is that?!"*

Michael turned, expecting to see the city. But something had taken the city away.

Awe and dread overpowered him.

Oh my God.

Over the cliff, something was rising: an orb, like the dark twin of the true moon.

"What is that?" Patrick breathed. "Is that *real*?"

"It's real, Bub. It's . . ."

The orb ignited.

"A hot-air balloon," said Michael.

And it was.

CHAPTER NINE

They stood there while the shadow eclipsed them.

Why the balloon had arrived or where it came from: mysteries.

But, a fact: the balloon was a jack-o'-lantern.

Up from the cliff's edge came twin black-hole eyes, a great triangle nose, a huge, magic, maniac, Cheshire-cat smile. The rising aircraft smelled of fire. Snow fell onto the canvas and hissed away as strings of steam. That hiss—like a cat, recoiling—was the only sound.

This is going to scare Bub! Michael thought. The panic overrode him, deleting the strange, certain feeling he'd possessed a moment before.

But Patrick surprised him: the balloon reflected in his eyes, and he gazed upward with cautious happiness, like a child playing peekaboo.

"*Whose* balloon?" he said.

Someone must have ignited it. But there wasn't anyone in the pilot's position. The basket was empty.

As startling as if the moon itself had been turned off: the balloon's flame, untouched, snuffed out with a puff.

Michael and his pursuers flinched. The balloon loomed, and the basket creaked.

A shadow rose, up from the basket's floor.

The moment stretched and twisted. It could not have been more than half a second, but the pilot seemed to rise ponderously, like a terrible jack-in-the-box unfurling in slow motion. The pilot had no visible eyes—he was total silhouette—but Michael felt him scanning them all. As the pilot reached full height, a second shape rose, in his hands. A gun shape.

Michael fell on Patrick, hugging him into the snow as the shadow opened fire.

Light flashing: thunder trying to tear the world.

The Bellows had been staring up at the pilot, like Patrick. So they had no chance. One shot each, one bullet each: skull center, every one.

It was impossible, even with an automatic, but the pilot seemed to catch all of them at once, as if some unseeable scythe had cut them with one shining swoop.

The motorcyclists who had been madly pursuing were now madly attempting an escape. There was a momentary, somehow considering pause from the pilot; he cocked his head.

As the motorcyclists reached the rim of the forest, the pilot plucked three quick gun bursts.

Three bodies fell face-first into the shadows of the tree line.

The aerial assassin pivoted one final time and aimed his weapon at Michael.

"No no no, wait, no!" Michael screamed.

He kicked back in the snow, pinned naked on a bull's-eye.

The balloon descended slowly on its own. The pilot stood preternaturally still, like a statue in a hurricane, even as the basket settled in the snow, dangerously near the cliff.

Night-vision goggles were strapped to the man's head, the lenses protruding on stalks. An oxygen unit covered his mouth.

With his breath curling from the mask's side cylinders, he looked like a knight and a dragon both.

"S-sir?" Michael said.

The gun aiming at Michael never moved.

Patrick squirmed out from under him and sat up, his eyes big and clear with awe. "Who is that?"

It could have been anybody. The man was a blank.

The pilot raised a hand.

"Name," he said. The voice rang. Hard. Cold.

And without waiting, the pilot cocked the gun's slide in preparation.

Michael shot to a stand. *"Wait—"*

"Your name!"

"What?"

"SAY THAT GODDAMN NAME OF YOURS!"

"Wha—Michael Faris!"

"Count," the voice said. This word came calmer; for the first time, Michael noticed a slight hill-country accent in it.

Count? He thinks you're a *Bellow*!

"Sorry,waitwait!Onetwothreefourfivesixseveneightnineten."

The man didn't answer.

Michael paused, swallowing dryly.

"Is that okay? Is that enough? Sir?" Michael said. "'Cause honestly, if you want me to count higher than ten, I gotta take off my shoes and use my toes."

The joke was for Patrick's sake. But Patrick didn't laugh.

"Him too." The pilot pointed his rifle at Patrick.

Michael stumbled left, shielding his brother. *"Hey!"*

"Move."

"Sir, he's fine!"

"Damn, but I *looooove* proof," the man said.

Patrick stared. "What's your name?" he asked softly.

"Count."

"He's fine. Bello—those things can't talk like he's talking!"

"Are you the Game Master?" Patrick asked.

"Patrick—"

"The *what*?" the man said.

"Are you the soldiers Michael saw?"

Pause. Pause. "Where'd you see soldiers?" the man said.

"Pretty close," Michael said; he cringed inwardly. "Sir. Please. We're fine."

The shadow considered it.

"Well. I'm Captain Horace Jopek of the United States Army 101st," he said. "And I'm wonderin' if anybody's lookin' for a ride to the Safe Zone."

A soldier. Captain Horace Jopek. Captain *Horace Jopek.*

Michael stood, feeling curiously light. *I did it,* he thought. *I freaking* did. *Oh my God, we're safe. Game, the eff, Over.*

"Jeezus, why didn't you say so?" Michael said, laughing a little.

Patrick was grinning shyly, half hiding his face against Michael's leg. "It's okay, huh, Michael? We won, huh?" Michael nodded.

"So, where you ladies come from?" said Captain Jopek.

The captain took off his goggles and mask. As Michael's adrenaline began to subside, he realized that this captain was titanic, one of the tallest men he'd ever seen. The captain seemed about forty, and somehow his face emphasized just how huge he was. The wide, stubbled chin looked as powerful as the slabs of his forearms; his nostrils were cavernous and black. And despite the cold, a kind of heat seemed to bake from his skin. A jutted brow shadowed his eyes—they were dark double zeroes—but the remaining pieces of his expression were full of the good humor of a man who has just come across a secret.

"Our bike," said Michael. Patrick helpfully pointed over the cliff, grinning.

"Just the two of ya?" the captain asked. "No soldiers with you?"

Uhh. "No," Michael replied.

"Well, ain't *that* a reg'lar West Virginia miracle," said the captain, and winked at Michael. His breath was thick with sickly sweet tobacco.

"Whelp, I guess it's time to hit the sky," the captain said. "More of them bike loonies will be back soon, believe me." He patted the rim of the basket good-naturedly. Michael became aware of the sounds of more Bellows in the woods.

God, The Game worked. I made it real. He reached for Captain Jopek's hands.

"The brat first," said the captain.

Michael hesitated a second.

In the end, it wasn't entirely his choice: Patrick slinked from behind his leg when he realized they were going to fly. The man quickly lifted Patrick up and set him on the floor of the basket. Michael felt a momentary, surprisingly brilliant pang of separation as his brother disappeared from view under the lip of the basket.

Without hesitation, Captain Jopek turned to extend his hands to Michael. *This is real. It's really over—*

But the captain's expression froze him. "What happened there?" the captain said, an odd and cold and calm smile on his face.

What happened where? Michael was going to ask—but his fingers found the same place the soldier's eyes had. His neck. Blood there. The tumble from the bike must have torn open the scratch he'd gotten last night. "Oh, crap, you know what?" Michael said, half laughing. "There was one of those monsters, in a miner's outfit—"

In a sleek blur of movement, the cold eye of the assault rifle's barrel raised on Michael. Michael recoiled, almost falling in the snow. "Jeezus!" Despite his panic, he fought to still sound respectful. "I'm not infected, sir! It's a scratch."

"Scratch," the man said.

Michael nodded.

Patrick sensed the tension, tried to chuckle, hummed.

The gun went down, the soldier's gaze came up, and for the first time Michael saw his eyes.

What happened next could have been a trick of light, a quirk of exhaustion.

The sparks of moonlight in the captain's eyes seemed to fly to the pupils and vanish. Michael realized: there was nothing to read in Jopek's eyes.

And Michael was beginning to reach for Patrick, because something wasn't right, he was *always* able to read people—but some black object was coming at him: the stock of the captain's automatic rifle, looping up and up, flying almost like his great balloon. Michael heard an explosive hollow *thwok*, and the last thing he saw were Patrick's fingers, his brother's fingers, reaching out for his.

CHAPTER TEN

The winter winds, which seemed to snarl in the alley beside their apartment before gathering strength and pouncing out, were growing colder. The night was like a thing you could reach out and snap. It didn't even matter if you were inside.

Michael shifted on his quilts on the living room floor, looking up at his mother's face. See, Michael baby, *she said, her smile floating above him, like a warm moon,* it's like a adventure thing. *She palmed the quilts flatter and fit his mittens on his fingers.* You remember *Indiana Jones? Wasn't that movie fun? That's what this is just like, baby.*

He'd heard Mom on the phone with the gas company earlier asking how could they have the heart in the middle of February, but it never occurred to him that the call and the adventure had thing one in common.

All he knew was when she smiled at him, like they had a secret, he couldn't imagine ever feeling cold again.

He whispered to her: Really?

Very really, baby, *she said.* Yes, yes.

They lay down, curled against each other, beside the crackling fireplace. He kept humming the theme from Indiana Jones,

only quitting when Mom stopped helping because she had fallen
asleep. The winds were really bellowing now: the front door
began sounding like a barrier against the boogeyman. But he
wasn't scared.

He was an adventurer.

He loved Mom's tiny, dreaming breath on his cheek.

For a while, Michael watched the snow streak past the win-
dow like a billion falling stars. He wondered if it was cold in
outer space. He didn't think so: in his mind, it was all swooshing
dark and globes of power. If he and Mom went, they could ride
comets, he thought.

And when morning came with a smooth lemony color on his
lids, he lay there, clamp-eyed. Because he didn't want to open
his eyes. Because he didn't want morning.

Nights were better. They made the world feel huge, fat with
surprise, full of doors to be opened. Morning made everything
too bright. You could see too much. You could see the water
stains on the ceiling, or the way the stuffing poked through the
stitching in the couch pillows. You could look in Mom's eyes and
see sadness in them.

He clenched his eyelids, trying to hold in the private night.
He'd been Indiana Jones, running from—

—running from a soldier—

—balloon—

Michael shuddered, and his eyes flew wide.

Light, hard white spears of it, pierced his vision. For a
moment, he was so shocked that even blinks wouldn't come.

Balloon.

Patrick.

He sat up, heart jackknifing in his ribs, and shouted as a
pain like a frozen rod pierced through his skull at the temples.

Michael sucked air, clasping his head, his brain pulsing like a black bladder.

The light was like hot, white bulbs held to his irises: the same sort of blinding, buzzy light that seems almost supernaturally bright in emergency rooms at night. *Michael—do you go by Mike or Michael?* he remembered a doctor saying. *So Michael, I'm a doctor here. Your father—stepfather, excuse me—asked me to talk to you. We understand that Patrick began screaming a couple hours ago. And this was for no reason?* (Say what Mom told you to say. Yes, he was screaming for no reason. No, Ron never touched Mom.) *Well, listen . . . you know we're here to help your brother.* He *doesn't know that. And so our thinking, pal, is we know how close you two are, and it would absolutely help us if you could hold him while we give him a shot. Just to sedate him for a few hours. We could strap him down, but we've found that it's better if— Hey. Calm down. Michael, I will say this with absolute clarity: your brother is a danger to himself. This is just who he is, and pretending he's not won't change that. He is back there shrieking and hitting himself. I believe he broke his hand. We see these things all the time with special-needs children and— Hey, Mike, you're a big boy, but if you're going to use that kind of language, keep it* down. *Now are you going to help your brother or not?*

Michael got his feet under him. And he felt something he hadn't expected, something that stopped him: something soft.

Carpet.

There was a cot behind him. He'd been lying on it.

He was . . . in*side*.

The shock seemed to short-circuit his brain. His fingertips went numb; for a moment, he felt like he might tilt over. He told himself it was another dream.

Because even if it actually existed, the room he was in was unbelievable.

It was as if he had awakened in both a courtroom and library. Small wooden desks were arranged in concentric horseshoes, row within row facing a center where there stood two podiums and something like a judge's seat. The room was cupped under a dome, ribbed and decorated by two scenes: one of men smiling in a sparkling city, the other of grimly determined miners and machines. The grand vault made him feel no larger than an ant.

But it made him feel like a giant, too: he'd been a lot smaller, last time he was here. Back then, he'd been in a line of other sixth graders, probably wearing the Quidditch shirt with gold writing Mom only let him wear on "special days." That was the day C. R. Rohrbough threw up out the window on the bus ten seconds before it could pull over to the side of the road. That was the day of the West Virginia history field trip.

He was in the Senate chambers of the state Capitol.

He would have thought, after three weeks' imagining, that anything would be an anticlimax. But this was greater and more weird than he could have predicted. It was still easy to picture governors striding over the deep-blue-and-marigold carpet, but the stately space had been transformed. It was jammed with cots, dozens of them, rumpled with thin brown blankets. Here and there among them were red plastic meal trays. Here and there were mugs.

Here were wallets, backpacks, toy trucks, an old-school iPod with no earbuds.

Here were photo albums, pizza crusts, Bibles, half-bitten doughnuts, a book Michael recognized from freshman English, *Story of a Girl*. Here was—oddly heartbreaking and heartwarming—a plastic sheriff's belt with orange-tipped guns.

The room held *lives*, in other words.

Michael whirled, looked out the windows: the glass was covered with protective mesh, which pixelated the world, and that was actually perfect, because what Michael saw outside was something out of *Modern Warfare.*

A courtyard, dotted with statues.

Government buildings—anonymous, the color of drizzle, pocked with a trillion grimy windows—hedging the plaza on two sides.

And, in the courtyard: a network system of barricades.

Layer beyond layer of chain-link fence stretched for an acre at least. The fences' tips were coiled with razor wire, which swayed back and forth in the wind, and whistled a thin, tinny tune.

Between these layers, spaced evenly, were sandbagged gun posts, outfitted with heavy artillery. Here and there were high shooting towers.

Beyond the fence, arranged in a rough arc, were Hummers. Beside the Hummers, a camouflage-colored fuel truck.

And at the very end of the courtyard, positioned before a statue of a coal miner, was a freaking tank.

Michael felt a grin spreading on his mouth. It faltered, held frozen a moment. Then it spread to a point of almost-ache. *I can't see the mountains.* The thought hovered before him, almost incomprehensible. The mountains and monsters of the gray zone were gone, blotted out by things that *people* had made. He had battled back to the sane and charted sections of the map. *To The End,* Michael thought.

I won.

I saved myself. I saved us.

He stood there, wrapped up in the sunlight and silence of the Safe Zone, and it seemed to him that the moment tasted almost holy.

And then, in a thin, cracking voice, he shouted: "HEYYYYY, YOU CRAZY MUTHAFUGGING WORLD, YOU JUST GOT *P'OWNED!*

"I BEAT YOU!" he said, then paused because this was making his headache throb like the world's worst cavity. Then went on, 'cause it was worth it. "YOOOOOU GOT OWNED, BONED, AND STALLONED! I TEABAG YOU!" He began, half realizing it, to jump up and down. "IIIII—TEEEEEABAAAG—YYYY—"

"—oh Christ—"

There was someone at the door to the Senate chambers. Michael looked over his shoulder and saw it was a girl. For one single instant, he was embarrassed by her witnessing him smack-talk Earth, but then he was flooded with a happiness so intense that he was surprised by his own small tears. *Day twenty-four,* he imagined himself writing in his journal. *Saw first new person in three weeks who IS NOT CRAZY OR DEAD.*

"So sorry!" she cried.

The girl's hands flew up to her face: the tray of food she'd been carrying flipped to the ground. She fled, slamming the enormous oak double doors behind her.

Didn't get a good look, he mind-wrote. *But I think she's kinda cute.*

Also: uh, maybe is crazy.

Michael blinked, wondering why the girl was horrified. Then he realized why, and the horror was his.

He was naked.

Ohcrapohcrap, he thought.

"*Ohcrapohcrapohcrap,*" he hissed desperately, and, several seconds too late, cupped himself.

"So *so* emphatically sorry!" said a voice through the door.

Michael stood there, his mouth working open and closed. *Bwah,* he started to say; but that was not, strictly speaking, English. A long time since he'd held a mature conversation, but he felt reasonably sure even his A-Game might not have been up to the task of smoothing out Surprise Nudity as Introduction.

"Uh," he said, "it's cool."

And cold. Understand me, girlie: in here, it is cold.

"I thought that you would have . . . There were supposed to be, like, clothes left on your cot."

There were: a blue V-neck like a nurse would wear, and a pair of camouflage pants. Michael tugged them on, wondering how and why he'd wound up, y'know, nude. But despite his bewilderment, he smiled at the door with a little awe, jittery with embarrassment but also adrenaline and a buzzy joy. He was talking to a person. A girl. A human. In the Safe Zone.

He stepped around the apple juice burbling out of a plastic bottle on the overturned tray. "H-hi?" he called through the door.

Flatly: "Yes."

"You can come in," Michael said.

"No thank you."

"I mean I'm dressed now."

"And yet," she said.

Michael smiled a little.

He waited for her to go on. But all he could hear was that rusty tune of the razor-tipped fence outside. Michael placed his hand on the cool oak of the door, leaning against it. "Hey."

No answer.

"Hey, I get it," he said. "You saw me naked. Embarrassing. Obvz. But you, I'm sorry to say, are not the first to walk in on me in the buff."

There was the tune, his breath, and then—as his heart leapt—very softly: "Uh-huh?"

"Right, so I was in marching band," Michael went on, his throat feeling stiff and unpracticed. "What it should be called is, The Club Where Sweaty Dorks Collectively Undress. Well, I don't love doing that, so I wait till everybody else is gone and even then I dress in the stalls, which works great except that sometimes I forget to lock the stall. And that is the reason that my band director, Mr. Green, who has a mullet and is *awesomely awkward*, opened the door, wanting nothing more in this world than to take a dump, and instead saw me with nothing on but a pair of socks and a marching helmet."

He pushed on in the silence. "I was literally putting the plume in when we started screaming."

The door moved between them as the girl laughed; Michael realized that she was leaning against it on the other side. Michael closed his eyes, spontaneously grinning: *laughing*, a new person *laughing*.

"That was . . . humorous," she said. "So, you should come down and eat with everyone. That is, if your brother saved you any food." Michael's heart lit with relief and excitement and a thousand other emotions that just jittered together.

"Just make sure you keep your clothes on. There's no dress code, but naked asses? They're frowned upon."

Michael laughed and was about to say something, but he heard footsteps echoing away.

The girl had gone, and the joke deflated behind her.

But still, Michael leaned back, roughing his hands through his hair in relief. *The Safe Zone,* he thought. He didn't think he'd be able to eat—his stomach felt like a home for ADD butterflies. But he looked for shoes at the cot he'd been sleeping on, and he found his old clothes, neatly piled under the cot, slit raggedly up the middle, and he felt an unexpected pang. When he went to shrug a camo jacket on, he heard a soft brushing sound, and his fingers went to his neck. He winced at the tenderness he found. He looked at his pale reflection in the windows and saw the clean, tan square taped there. The scratch had been bandaged. Which made him think of the Bellow from the church. Which made him think of the phone. Mom's number was floating in his head as he grabbed the cell from his old pants and pushed the power button down, wondering if he could actually place a call now that he was in the

Safe Zone. But he hadn't turned the phone off after using it with Rulon; it was dead.

He thought about Mom being in the same city as him . . . maybe the same *building. I. Made. It. Just like I knew I would—just like the Game Master, ha-ha, said I could. I saved Patrick and myself, and soon Mom's going to understand how I saved her, too.*

And the butterflies in his belly did backflips.

Wow. So. This level is a little nicer.

The Capitol halls evoked an almost eerie sense of dignity. It was like a brass-work, marble palace—except the palace was also interspersed with the accessories of crisis.

Bracketed lanterns and a series of chandeliers hung on the walls and ceiling, but tripod-mounted banks of fluorescents— tethered to squat, silent generators by thick cables—rested on the floors. Columns soared to ceiling arches, but countless dozens of cots jammed the floor. Daylight filtered through metallic mesh that protected the windows lacing the dome, and it cast prison-diamonds of shadow. Life-size statues of West Virginia's governors—*the Bosses*, Michael thought giddily—stood on their pedestals, their eyes darkly eternal. The governors had been mustached, ninja-masked, pirate-patched, and navel-pierced. A politician Michael vaguely recognized had a thought sprayed on the wall above his bald head: *DAMN KIDS GET OFF MY LAWN.*

The hall, though currently uninhabited, smelled over-crowded, like too much skin. It was a human smell, and shockingly, powerfully nostalgic.

Michael stood there, in borrowed socks, and a kind of awe curled over him. For three weeks, he'd fought the dead, traveling alone except for a fragile five-year-old. But he had never let despair overtake himself, for he'd been always aiming for now, for here, for this endgame moment. He had felt not hope, but certainty: *yes-yes*. And now here he stood, in the cold/sweaty/ majestic/chaotic promised land.

So the fact that the halls were so quiet simply didn't quite register with him right then.

His clothes whisperingly scratching him—that feeling other people's clothes always seem to have—Michael found his way through the halls. He came to another dome, far higher than the one before, that looked as if it were painted with gold. He imaged what it was like here: people lying together in the winter night, warmed by their generators and their own communal body heat. The soldiers patrolling through the halls. He wondered if he would see the enormous soldier from last night again, or if that strange sniper was only on rescue duty, ballooning in the mountains.

And looking at the cots, for the first time, Michael began to wonder where everyone was.

Michael took a wide stairway that curved around the rotunda beneath the golden dome and, at its bottom, he heard something that he hadn't heard in so long that his brain took a second to understand it: a group of people talking somewhere behind walls. The marble had a confusing effect on sound: there was a frustrating minute when Michael was chasing echoes.

But he found the door. A brass plaque read THE GOVERNOR'S DINING ROOM—PASS REQUIRED. He paused, feeling weirdly like he had on the morning of the very first day of high school.

He wondered if the girl had already told people about their encounter—indeed, if anyone else had seen him naked before he'd awakened. *You know what?* he thought, grinning nervously. *I don't even care.*

Michael opened the door.

CHAPTER ELEVEN

And he experienced a moment's disorientation. Like stepping down, wrongly expecting a stair.

The people at the table looked up at him, silenced. As Michael entered, an old woman with short, wavy hair put one hand to her mouth, as if delighted by the sight of him: her smile stretched past the edges of her fingers.

Michael thought for a second he had found the wrong room, and was about to mutter an exiting apology. But then he saw Patrick, drinking chocolate milk through a crazy straw from a clear plastic milk bag, sitting beside the wavy-haired old woman.

"And here he is, this new fella," laughed the old woman brightly.

Michael eloquently replied, "Hey."

Patrick looked at Michael, then the old woman, as if he wanted to get up and run to Michael but was too shy to do so in front of anyone. Instead, he threw a high five across the air with such grunting power that everyone stared at him anyway.

Michael's chest warmed, seeing his brother: his smile, his posture. Patrick was fine. Last night's emotional storm of near-Freak, however horrible, had passed. One thing Michael understood about Bub better than anyone: when the world around him made sense, Patrick could be pretty kick-ass strong.

The dining room, *Governor's* or not, was a cafeteria: all plastic chairs and wipe-down tabletops. Four people, including Patrick and the old woman, sat at the nearest oval table. One of them—a muscle-y guy staring eagerly at him—looked about Michael's age. The other person was a girl, dark-haired, whose head was down as she poked at her pancakes; Michael could just see a pale, round nose and small pink mouth. He assumed this was the girl he'd inadvertently streaked for.

And that was it. Nobody else in the cafeteria. Chairs upside down on the tables, silver legs pointing up.

"And how are you today, Michael?" said the old woman. Her softly Southern accent was lovely. So weird, hearing someone not-Patrick use his name.

She moved toward him with an old person's small, careful steps. And then she surprised him: she took his hand in both of her own.

The unexpected contact, though warm and obviously sweet, made Michael's cheeks prickle with heat for some reason. Despite how much he'd wanted to see people, he was struck by an urge to pull back.

"Well, we just want to say welcome," she said. "And to tell you what a good day you've made this. We are so thankful to see you."

"Thanks," he said, taking his hand back. "I can honestly say that it is very awesome to meet you." It occurred to him that he hadn't spoken with a sane adult in weeks. He added, "Ma'am."

"So what is your favorite breakfast, Michael? Bacon and eggs? Oatmeal? Cereal?" She went on, but Michael stopped listening around "bacon," because he saw a pile of it on Muscle

Guy's plate, shiny with grease, and his stomach went, *Baaaaa-con?* And itself answered, *BAAAAACON!*

He nodded. "Bacon works."

Food. Was. Good.

Not stale Pop-Tarts or beef jerky; not prepackaged calories served car-temperature—*f-o-o-d.* The flavors burst, so intense that for the first couple minutes, Michael's jaws ached. It was weird, being the center of attention, but not so weird that he stopped eating. Too good. I-have-questions-but-I-also-have-bacon-and-guess-which-I-love-more good.

A few times, Muscle Guy ("Henry," he said, "but I prefer Hank. So call me Hank. Question—") tried to cut in, but the woman, who introduced herself as Bobbie Louise, gently hushed him.

When Michael had sat down next to Patrick, he'd whisper-asked where Mom was, now that they'd "got to The End."

"We'll find out, Bub," Michael told him.

Patrick nodded. "Is this the big party?" he asked. And when Michael shook his head, Patrick replied, "Oh, okay." It came out sounding like, *Oh, thank crap. 'Cause that would have been lame.*

If there were other sections in the Safe Zone, Michael supposed it could be a couple hours before he found Mom. He allowed himself to draw up the image he'd had in his mind these past few weeks, the image of The End: him holding Patrick's hand as they walked across a bright Safe Zone room, spotting Mom in a crowd, her looking up at him, proud and so, so happy.

As Michael finally finished his hash browns (wonderfully greasy), Hank said, "Question," for the fifth time. "How's the situation out there?"

Michael set down his orange juice slowly. He traced his finger over the sweat on the side of his glass, struggling for an honest answer.

"Super cold," Patrick suggested to Michael quietly.

The old woman laughed. Patrick looked up at her with a surprised delight, but then almost seemed to catch himself. He looked back to Michael, doing his songless humming thing.

"And there's not many humans," Michael said. "Have you guys noticed that there have been more of those, uh, Things, sort of gathering, moving in bigger groups?"

"Have we friggin' ever," Hank nodded. His voice was clipped, though. Was the deepness of his voice changing a little every time he spoke, like he was trying to sound more manly, or something? "They were easy to deal with the first couple weeks. Scattered. Then it was almost like they started . . . coordinating, I dunno. Maybe it's just that they were looking for *people*, and they were getting better at finding us, so they all started attacking around the same time. But it's weird.

"Anyway, been out there long, man? What's your time line?" Hank pulled a tattered spiral-bound notebook from his pocket, uncapped a pen.

Michael's eyes flicked to the notebook, his stomach tightening a little. He suddenly felt wary of speaking about their time in the outside world and confusing Bub. "Since Halloween," he replied.

Hank, who had been leaning across the table, fell back in his chair. "You've been out there *the whole goddamn time*?"

Patrick, halfway through a piece of bacon, froze, eyes popping, like he had just heard someone fart. Protectiveness and a little anger blossomed hotly in Michael's stomach.

"Hey, let's keep it PG in here," Michael said amiably.

Hank snorted a laugh like Michael was making a joke. But when Michael didn't return the laugh, Hank stared, as if trying to gauge if Michael was serious about protecting Bub from cuss words in a world where there were, y'know, monsters trying to eat him.

Finally, Hank said, "Uh, whatever, dude, sure." Michael nodded, friendly . . . although he realized that Hank—good-looking in a hard kind of way; striped track pants, cigarette breath—would probably not have been his friend in the world Before. *And not just because, ha-ha, I don't technically "have friends."*

"I think what Hank is trying to say is, what were y'all *up to* the whole *daggum* time, Michael?"

The girl leaned forward on her elbows across the table, her eyebrows raised in an open, friendly expression. Her hair, short and choppy, was so darkly red that it was almost black. She wore wire-rim glasses and a bright blue hoodie over an EPCOT T-shirt.

"Looking for the Safe Zone, is all," Michael replied. He impressed himself by being able to look the girl in the eye for almost an entire second.

"It took you *three weeks*?" Hank scoffed, as if taking so long to battle lots of dead-slash-insane people was just ridiculous.

Michael's shoulders pinched back. He felt a surprising twinge that he didn't like, an ugly defensiveness.

"Yeah, well," he said, making his voice steady, "we were in my stepdad's cabin in the middle of nowhere for the first week. There were a few Things out there in the woods. Nothing me and my gun couldn't handle."

Michael paused, waiting for Hank to nod, maybe look impressed—something. But Hank kept quiet, just waiting for him to go on.

Well, who cares what he thinks? Michael told himself. He still felt a little sheepish, though, as he finished. He told Hank that they'd gotten low on food in the cabin, had heard Safe Zone announcements on their car radio. But by the time they'd backtracked on the roads they'd come to the cabin on—the only country roads Michael was familiar with, and the only interstate entrance he knew how to reach—the towns were all deserted, the interstate ramp impassable because of abandoned cars and barbed-wire blockades.

"And we had to play 'Siphon the Gas' a lot!" Patrick added.

"And you made it *without* a fortress and a bizagillion guns. It is impressed upon me that you are impressive," said the girl. "I'm Holly, by the way," she informed him.

"Patrick," Patrick said, surprising Michael with his boldness, however small.

She grinned, so wide it was actually a little big for her face. But yeah, wow: cute. Undeniably cute.

"And this cabin was . . . where?" said Hank, nodding eagerly to his notepad.

"Is it cool if I ask why you're taking notes?"

"Orders," Hank said as if it should have been obvious.

Orders from whom?

Michael told Hank it was near a popular (if isolated) ski resort in the northern part of West Virginia. "Canaan Valley. You know it?"

"I'm from Atlanta. No clue, champ."

"Sorry, slugger," Michael said. The gently ribbing joke was for Patrick, but Holly chuckled. Hank's pen paused; he looked confused.

"So, you're at the cabin," Hank said, returning to his notes, "you leave; after a while, things get worse. And you didn't see the army or any of the search parties until a couple days ago, just before you were rescued. Right?"

Patrick looked up at Michael.

Hank thinks I saw a search party. He must have talked with that captain from last night, Michael instantly understood. And giving an answer to Hank's question would only spiral to more questions about the soldiers: questions that would require more lies.

And man, I'm done with lying.

"Hey, I'm sorry. Just, do you mind a bunch if *I* ask a couple things?" Michael said. He really *was* burning with the questions that had been pulsing on the edge of his thoughts since . . . well, since he saw that first dead Bellow shambling toward him on Halloween. Except, he wanted to be careful about what he said around Bub.

"Where were you guys when you first got . . . pulled into this?" Michael asked. Hank began to speak up, but Michael, worried he might swing the subject back to the soldiers, added: "Bobbie?"

Bobbie's calm, thin smile did not falter, but he thought he saw something painful pass behind her eyes.

"Well. I don't know if it's my favorite story," she said. "But they do say a person never forgets where she was when poor President Kennedy was shot. Or when those planes hit the Towers. So I guess I'll remember it forever, whether I want to or don't.

"I was with my husband, Jack. We were playing rummy on our airplane trays. Things had gotten so bad near our home in Tennessee; the government began emergency flights to Safe Zones. One hundred and ten souls on board our flight to Charleston. Everyone on the flight was supposed to be well; the pilot snuck his wife on, and she wasn't." Quickly, Bobbie said, "And you, Henry?"

Hank sighed through his nose, as if he was bursting with other things he'd rather discuss. "In Atlanta. School. Came here when the action started. Our dad"—he indicated himself and Holly—"came up to help right after the Zeds were first on the news. Like a lot of people did. He brought us."

Michael felt a momentary—and immediately embarrassing—happiness, finding out that the guy Holly was sitting next to was her sibling.

"So there are . . . uh, Zeds, you called them, in Atlanta, too? And Tennessee?"

"There weren't at first. It seemed to start somewhere in West Virginia, actually. Now? Who knows, man. Government shut down internet and phones in the Safe Zones almost right after the Zones were set up."

"Why?"

"'Cause the only way they could keep things under control—make everyone come to the Zone—was to control what people knew about what was going on," Holly said. "'Information is power,' etc. It kept people calm. That was a good day or two, ha-ha."

There was something in her tone Michael couldn't quite read. It sure wasn't amusement, though.

"We don't even friggin' know for total-sure where the first case was," Hank said. "Some places were worse than others—it was bad here—but there was so much shit going down at first—" Hank's gaze flicked to Patrick, who had begun blushing. "Err, so much poop-poop going down."

"That's a technical term," Holly told Patrick. It drew a little laugh from Bub, and Michael felt a warmth of gratitude.

"They got theories," Hank continued. "Maybe a virus, a natural sort of deal. All they know for sure is it's some kind of brain infection. The captain thinks it's an attack from Iran, 'cause of the war. Whatever it is, thank Christ for the soldiers."

"Yes indeed," Bobbie said in soft, earnest agreement.

Then Hank picked up his pen again, sitting forward eagerly. "And then there's the people you met, right, who think it's the end-times, that the Zeds are the ones God chose to bring back to life to take to Heaven first. The Rapture, they call themselves. Friggin' rednecks actually *fought* the soldiers when the army tried to bring them to the Safe Zone."

"Wow, huh," Michael said, patting Bub on the knee, "some

98

people just don't play by the rules. So hey, I probably should get going. Is there, like, a list of where the other people here are?"

Michael felt Patrick's energy change, felt his shyness changing to a pure excitement. Michael's belly twisted, and he wanted, right then, to get out of this room and just get Mom *now*.

Then Hank laughed bitterly.

"Other people?" Holly said. A dread growing on her face.

"In the Safe Zone. We're going to go find our mom."

"If she's not *here*, she's not here," said Hank.

Michael continued grinning, trying to grasp the punch line of that weird sentence.

"We're . . . Michael, aside from Captain Jopek, sweetie, *this* is the population of this town. Us," said Bobbie. "Since a week ago, sweetie." She looked at him with pity.

"You mean . . . except for all the soldiers," Michael replied.

"There's a *soldier*. Like you said, man, Zeds are moving around in packs now. They overran the perimeters around the city a week ago," Hank said.

"I thought—no, hold up. You said 'thank God for the soldiers.'"

"All the other soldiers evacuated, along with everybody else. Everybody else who wasn't massacred, anyway. They went east, to another Safe Zone in Richmond. I meant thank God for the soldiers *you* saw."

It was as if Michael had been trotting along at a leisurely pace and then forced, at the shout of an unseen pistol, to explode into a full-out dash. Automatically, but with a little panic, he tried to find his blood—but he only felt their eyes, heavy with expectation and questions.

They think I really saw soldiers, Michael thought. *Patrick told them I did, and they don't realize that I just said that because of The Game. They think I saw Real. Frakking. Soldiers.*

Michael remembered the window in the Senate, and the courtyard outside: the *empty* courtyard, the *quiet* halls. How had he not figured it out before? How the hell had he not figured it out?

Stupid—God, so stupid. You idiot, don't you know: you're not allowed to let yourself be happy, not until you know it's The End.

And he felt Patrick's eyes, with confusion of a different kind: *Why're you nervous, Michael?*

"Yeah, no," Michael finally said. "You're right; thank crap for them."

"Thank *Something*," Bobbie laughed shakily.

"We knew somebody'd come back," Hank said nonchalantly, though Michael could tell he was enormously relieved. "The captain's been on the radio with some units that are return-ing for us, but the last couple days the transmission's been bad because of the mountains. So how far away were the soldiers? When do you think they'll get here?"

Michael paused, calculating the days. *The soldiers who were here have been gone for a week. They'll be back, but . . . but maybe the Bellows all moving together are making the trip back take longer. That's all. But the real solders will be back.*

"Ah, soon for sure," he said calmly. "Next couple days. Right, Bub? Then, party time, right?"

Relief, on everyone's face then, and in their eyes. Relief—especially in Patrick's.

Michael felt slightly guilty. He wasn't quite *lying* when he said that soldiers would be here soon, if the captain was saying the same thing. *And I can just explain myself to them later, that I was saying it for Bub. It'll be fine—*

And then those relieved gazes traveled over his shoulder.

Something tilted. The change in the room was invisible, but as real as one side of a brass scale tipping with a violent clang.

The steady clocking of combat boots. The tinny, atonal music of a ring of keys.

Michael looked over his shoulder and saw the man from the balloon.

"Well, ain't it my crew," said Captain Jopek. "How's doin's, folks?"

The captain had looked a hundred moon-blasted feet tall last night. Even up close, he'd been all eerie speed and seamless shadow: a sniper from the stars. Here and now, walking through the upturned chairs and the overhead light, the captain was a little more human, comprehensible. But man, still, he made Michael feel tiny.

Silence from the table. For some reason, it felt tense to Michael—though that was probably just because of his nervousness from a moment ago.

The captain took off the helmet he'd had cocked back on his head, took a loud sip from a Red Cross coffee mug.

"Henry, you sleep okay, or you still wakin' yourself up with your own farts?"

Hank blushed, though he didn't look displeased. "Just, ah— just when Bobbie makes chili," he said, grinning.

The captain didn't smile back, though. Instead, sipping his coffee, he watched Michael. Seemed to do it for a long time. So long that Michael got the idea that the captain was waiting for him to speak, and Michael began to stand up, to thank him for last night, when Captain Jopek suddenly said, "Looks like we got our new lady friends fed." He spoke with a slight hill-country drawl that seemed to ghost in and out; it would fade in, jab at every couple words. *Looks* like we got *our* new lady *friends* fed.

"I'm a boy," Patrick pointed out.

"That a fact? Well, *boy*, this captain's just happy he could help y'all get to his humble home."

Michael wasn't sure he *looked* that happy.

The captain set his mug down loudly, glided toward them, boot heels clocking, key ring tanging. Michael, still awkwardly hunched, wasn't sure whether to stand or to sit back again. He settled on sitting.

"Get enough to eat?" the captain asked.

"Yeah. Amazing," Michael said.

"So, Captain," said Hank. He stood up, so that it was like he was with the captain on one level, and everyone else on another. "We have some new reconnaissance. The new ladies, heh-heh, were telling us—"

"I heard that, I sure did!" The captain sat down on a tabletop across from them, crossing his arms. After a second, Hank sat back down, looking sheepish. "Pretty excitin'. Boys comin' back to town! Huh, Bobbie?" he said, yanking her into the conversation without looking to her. "Ain't that excitin'?"

"Oh. Yes, absolutely."

"Miss Bobbie, you're sweet as tea," said the captain, "but you sure oughtta sound more excited, ladylove, 'cause this is *the news*. The big one. We oughtta put this on a banner and drag it behind a plane."

Bobbie tugged at her gold wedding band, fidgeting.

"Whelp, I reckon it's time to do us another field trip. Hank, you get that gear primed."

"On it." Hank nodded. And okay, it was official: he was *absolutely* trying to make his voice deeper. "When do you want to leave, sir?"

"How about oh-now-hundred?"

Hank snorted laughter.

"I think I'm gonna chat first, though," the captain said, "with my new buddies here."

He cleared his throat.

And nodded toward the door, indicating that everyone else should exit the cafeteria. As Holly and Hank and Bobbie left, Patrick whispered to Michael, excited, *"Like a zoo field trip?"*

Michael shrugged to quiet Patrick.

Follow your breath, Michael thought. *Feel your blood.* Because the captain was probably going to ask questions about the soldiers. Which would not have been a big deal—Michael could just take the captain aside and tell him he'd white-lied. . . . But sitting there, looking up at the captain's odd, unreadable eyes, Michael couldn't help but think of last night. And the way the captain had been so quick to strike him in the head.

"So, hey," Michael said at last, "I have to say, thank you so much for last night."

"Got pretty good accommodations compared to what you're used to, I reckon. Glad I could get you some clothes, too—hope you weren't attached to the old ones; I had to check you for bites before I let you into my Capitol. We're a little low on food and meds, maybe. But of course, with them soldiers comin', sounds like that won't be a problem soon, right?"

That smile again: all teeth, no eyes. Captain Jopek uncrossed his arms, lay thick, scarred hands on the table. Relaxed, comfortable with the quiet: that's how it looked. So why did his waiting feel like a prodding finger looking for a loose board?

Imagining it. Paranoid.

"Michael, you got somethin' you want to tell me?" the captain said.

"Like what, sir?"

"Like a secret, maybe."

Michael's stomach fell a little. "Hey, Bub," he said, "I think I saw a 3DS out in the hall. Why don't you go check it out?"

Concerned, Patrick asked with his expression, *How come, though?*

"Just for a sec," Michael said. Patrick left.

"Why don't we just go on and get it out, Michael?" the captain said. Michael nodded, but sill couldn't help but hesitate. The captain spoke after the silence: "You're on drugs, aren't you, son?"

Michael blinked. "Sorry?"

The captain unbuttoned a chest pocket, on which CAPTAIN H. C. JOPEK was stitched. He pulled a rattling pill bottle out.

"This state's got a problem with pills. And this 'Atipax' is serious stuff, judgin' from all the warnings on the bottle."

Michael tried not to show his relief that the captain had not asked about the soldiers. "O-oh, no, sir," Michael said. "They're Patrick's."

"What the hell's the matter with him?"

Nothing is 'the matter with him,' Michael thought defensively. *It's everything around him.*

"He just gets overwhelmed sometimes. They help take the edge off at night."

"'Contact name: Molly Jean Faris'?" asked the captain, reading the label.

Michael flinched, hearing her name aloud. "My mom."

"And where's she?"

"We haven't seen her since Halloween. We . . . got separated."

The captain raised his gaze on Michael—and he did something that caught Michael totally off guard: the captain, this titanic Safe Zone guardian, put his hand on Michael's shoulder, and made a face of sympathy and respect. "Well, I think you done one *hell*uva job getting that little boy and yourself to my zone. Give you a medal, if I could, soldier."

Michael still could not quite read the captain, but in that moment, it didn't matter. He wanted to tell the captain, "Thank you so much for saying that," but he didn't trust his voice to not catch on the lump in his throat. He nodded wordlessly, and the captain handed him the pill bottle.

"I gotta ask, though, buddy: What you do to make those Rapture boys so mad?" said the captain, walking toward the exit, Michael following.

"I killed one of their favorite 'Zeds,'" Michael said.

"No *shit!*"

Michael grinned. He felt like a nerd who has just made the hottest girl at school laugh. "They called it their 'First.'"

"Those loonies blew their lids when we were shooting the Zeds during the mandatory evac," said the captain. "They even captured two of my soldiers, shot 'em in the head, and fed 'em to the Zeds. 'A holy sacrifice,' they said, and I ain't kidding you.

"That priest thinks he can save the whole world, protecting the Zeds, worshippin' 'em 24/7. When we started runnin' his people out of that town, he even set up mannequins in his church, so it was like *they* were 'worshipping' the Zeds, while old Rulon couldn't be around. He thinks this is the end times, and that the Zeds are the people God chose to raise from the grave so he can take them to Heaven. Rulon's got that town screaming with Zeds, locked up and 'protected' everywhere. And here's how shithouse crazy he is: if one of *his* people gets bit, Rulon takes off their heads before they can rise. Says they don't deserve to become a Zed. Says he's helping his people atone for all their sins, and if he don't keep on doing it, God will leave them and everyone else behind. I've got land mines on most roads into Charleston, but the Rapture's tried a couple times to get past 'em and into my city, to get more 'sacrifices,' I guess. Keep tryin', I say, I'll grab some popcorn."

Michael laughed. Jopek had a kind of good-ol'-boy humor that was foreign to him, and a little intimidating, but also somehow exhilarating.

"Gotta admit, though, I'd love to meet that priest in a dark alley. I've got two words for him, and they ain't *happy birthday.* Anyhow, I don't think we'll be meetin' them today, not where *we're* headed."

"Headed?"

"Downtown. Big, big city, soldier. It's been abandoned a week, and we want to be for-certain there's no-livin'-body out there."

"I—" Michael stopped walking. "I'm not so sure that's a good idea, sir. I just mean, my brother's been through a lot."

"Aw shoot, I'll get ya home by curfew. C'mon, Top Gun, we got a whole city waitin' for ya."

His hand reached out and grabbed Michael's bicep, squeezing gently, man-to-man.

"Be all you can be, right?"

CHAPTER TWELVE

The six of them, last-known Armageddon survivors in the Charleston city limits, walked down the stone steps with their shadows out in front of them.

At the foot of the grand outdoor stairs stood a statue of Abraham Lincoln, hands clasped behind his back. *Father of West Virginia, at Midnight* read the sooted pedestal. A rope encircled this pedestal, tethering the deflated jack-o'-lantern hot-air balloon to Earth.

Beside the president sat an enormous sixteen-wheeler gas tanker.

Beside the tanker waited a camo Hummer.

The sides of Michael's mouth twitched, trying a smile. It felt cool to be walking toward the Hummer. Actually: it felt sort of ridiculously badass.

The inside of the vehicle barked purpose and power.

There were no Pop-Tart wrappers, no sleeping bags filthy from a night spent on the ground. Instead of seats, there were harnesses built into the walls, like roller-coaster bars that rode your shoulders. *You must be this tall to ride the apocalypse.* A hatch in the ceiling opened to the sky and a roof-mounted machine gun. From the Bellow-maddening ambulance strobes on the hood, to the combat gurney in this rear chamber, to the "jump seat" (Hank's term, which he used as he strapped himself into it) on one of the rear double doors themselves: it was a vehicle reimagined for living-dead conflict.

As Michael lifted his tiny brother into a huge seat-harness, Patrick's eyes were big, taking it in. He put one hand out, and Michael playfully went to low-five it, "down-low-too-slow."

But Patrick didn't yank his own hand back. He held Michael's hand and pulled him closer.

Robo-Patrick whispered in his ear: *"You. Got. Us. Nice. Wheeeellllz."*

Well, what could Michael do but smile?

The trip into Charleston was like traveling across the span of a war painting: the peaceful far edges and the distance weapons, and the first battle lines and the central clash.

The Hummer departed the rear of the Capitol (opposite the barricaded plaza Michael had seen from the Senate), where layers of chain link separated them from the enormous, brown-gray Kanawha River to their left: a natural moat-barrier against attack, supplied courtesy of West "By God" Virginia.

Then the Hummer rounded the Capitol to the maze of chain link and razor wire, which stretched across Government Plaza and the long, cable-supported bridge beyond it. The Hummer paused here among the abandoned sniper posts: a series of padlocked retractable gates were set into the fencing in all directions, buffer zones like the locks of a canal that promised immunity from a breach. The captain opened the gates on their path toward downtown so his Hummer could pass through.

There was an in-the-elevator awkwardness during the repeated stops.

Patrick hummed. Holly gave a corners-of-the-mouth smile to

the floor. Bobbie politely looked out the window, then turned back when she saw a cawing crow flap with an ear hanging from its beak.

This is so freaking weird, Michael thought, *I don't even know if it's weird anymore.*

Out of the maze, the captain looked over his shoulder from the driver's seat, through the sliding plate that separated the front compartment from the rear. "Mission zero hour," he called.

Hank thumbed a button on his own heavy-duty watch, which Michael pictured him rooting feverishly through left-behind army supplies to get. "That means *set your watches,* too," he added to Holly and Michael. Michael felt another pinch at Hank's let's-please-nobody-forget-how-cool-I-am tone.

Holly lifted her sleeve; her wrist was small and milky. *"Beep-boop,"* she said, thumbing a "button" on her watch-less wrist, soft enough for Hank but not for the captain to hear. She seemed—maybe?—to flick her gaze Michael's way to see his response.

Dang, she's so cool.

Dang, don't think that.

Dang, why?

Because of on account of this being the most horrible time *to get a crush on a girl.*

Oh. Right. Daaaang.

"So," Michael called to Captain Jopek over the grumbling engine, "where to?"

The captain must not have heard, though; he slid closed the panel, cutting Michael off.

Patrick pointed double-finger guns toward the captain's now-unseeable head. "That guy," he said, "is a *grump.*"

Bobbie laughed. Patrick grinned back, delighted, like he had when she laughed in the cafeteria, and this time he did not nervously look away.

"A grump who saved your ass," Hank said to Patrick.

My God, my man, Michael thought, *will you shut up?* "Hey sorry, but remember the 'keep it PG' thing?"

Hank bristled. "Uh, sure do, big guy," he said, in a defensive, *and-what-about-it?* tone.

Just let it go, Michael told himself. But something about the condescending way Hank spoke wouldn't let him.

He shot Hank a glare. He felt his pulse speed and found himself inexplicably looking forward to the quick *yes-yes* challenge of making a comeback to whatever BS Hank was going to say.

Hank just scoffed dismissively, smirking slightly, like Michael wasn't worth the time. *"Any*way."

Hank produced a crisp detailed city map from his jacket, then spread it over the sheet-covered gurney, saying, "Let's talk objectives, people. First thing, Search. After Captain's aerial patrol last night, we can cross off Liberty and Jerry West Avenues downtown as possible hiding places for any survivors still in the city. . . ."

But Michael didn't quite hear. His face was flushing, his attempt to give a little fight frustrated.

An image shimmered into his mind: *Hank wearing a sports uniform.* Soccer, probably, and he bet Hank was very good. There was no uniform right now, of course. *But the world's full of uniforms waiting to be picked up again,* Michael thought. He suddenly remembered the first day of high school. He'd tried to sit with THE COOL KIDS, then, just sliding down his tray and sighing, like, *Gawd, another year of microwaved sewage, huh?* Theory being, they would *definitely not remember* his Middle School Wimpy Kid years. But mid-sigh, there Cool Kids sat, staring. *Oh, balls,* thought Michael, and the moment hangs; and then Bobby "B. O." Oliveto burps chocolate milk and draws laughter so Michael thinks maybe the moment could go just amazingly well until Caleb Rakestraw smiles with the same cold command he uses to bellow plays as JV QB. "Raise your hand," he says. "Raise your hand high if you want Faris to leave." Well, landslide. People at nearby tables noticed, nudged the news, and Michael stood, thinking: *No, you don't get to start over. You get to be you forever, sorry.*

Is that *what it means for things to be "normal" again?* Michael thought now.

Dude . . . no, he told himself. *Just think of everything you fought through. You're not that "you" anymore.*

Hank looked up now, saw that Michael was not enthralled by his "briefing." Hank offered that expression again: *I'm not so sure I like your face.*

Fair enough, Michael thought. *That makes us even.*

Battlelines:

As the Hummer left the bridge and entered the modest, grimy skyline (*coal dust*, Michael thought), gutters began glittering with spent bullet casings; skidmarks striped the road more and more. Hank continued talking, but Michael watched through the rear windows . . . and let Charleston's recent past echo to him.

The side streets had been armored with barbed wire and sandbags and staggered gun posts, as if the designers of the Safe Zone had sealed off all possible approaches of attack, save two or three main roads. Probably strategically smart, except for one fact: in the end, when the Bellows laid their mysterious siege to the city, the defenses sucked. The gun posts were toppled, the sandbags burst; bodies by the dozens spilled over the "protective" barbed wire, onto the sidewalks and even onto this main road itself, like ooze escaping from some cataclysmic wound. On his own long battle to Charleston, Michael had seen hundreds of walking corpses, of course. And the bodies here, which the captain now maneuvered around, were truly dead and no threat. But looking at the corpses, a cavity in Michael's chest ached. He'd imagined finding platoons of soldiers, many times. Just not inanimate: not decomposing.

The tragedy was just, like, relentless.

The green, sour dead–smell penetrated even the strong-box of the Hummer. *A mass grave,* Michael thought. *That's what the Safe Zone is. That's* all *it is.* He remembered the grave markers on the lawn of the Coalmount meeting hall, and pictured thousands of spears, pounded into crosses, spanning across Charleston.

The Hummer stopped, jerking Michael forward against his seat harness.

A sign outside their window read:

BUSTED KNUCKLE GARAGE

BEST PLACE IN TOWN TO TAKE A LEAK!!!

Hank folded his map into his pocket.

The rear double doors of the Hummer opened, letting bitter winter light flood in. The world outside was a shapeless, cruel white.

"Okay, you apes, welcome to Disneyland!" Jopek said good-naturedly. "Hope you brought your mouse hats. Now somebody get me a snow cone and I don't mean yellow."

"—*lloooowwwww*—" The calls of Bellows, hundreds of them, emanated from buildings along the road, from within alley Dumpsters, from underneath manholes.

"*Rapido, amigos,*" Hank said as the captain disappeared around the side of the Hummer.

"I love it when you speak French," Holly said dreamily.

Michael unfastened Patrick from his safety harness. As they stepped down out of the Hummer and into the street, Michael noticed that Bobbie was struggling with her own harness, her small, arthritic hands slipping on the security clips.

Before he could help her, though, Patrick climbed back inside the Hummer, undid her clasps himself, and helped lift the harness over her shoulders.

Bobbie looked him straight in the eye. "Patrick, thank you *very* much," she said. "That is *very* kind of you." She spoke with a sweet, but not condescending, tone, like she was used to dealing with kids.

"Booyah," Patrick said, and flexed his muscles.

He always says that to Mom when he opens the door for her, Michael thought. And the ache in his chest expanded.

The Busted Knuckle Garage stood in the corner parking lot of a flat downtown street. Three raised garage doors, plastered with WVU stickers, led inside. Within were cars, within were shadows, within were patches on the ground that were either oil or blood.

Michael glanced around for the captain . . . and what he saw made a little breath of happiness rise inside him. The captain was straddling the double-yellow line dead center in the war-torn street, strapping on the last of his arsenal: a bulletproof (or bite-proof) Kevlar vest; a combat knife held to his wrist by three Velcro strips; a pistol on his ankle. Compared to the chaos around him, the captain looked strangely *right.*

"*'Reach fer the skyyyyy,'*" Michael whispered to Bub in his Old West sheriff's voice. Bub giggled.

The captain's gaze snapped up to Michael. His eyes were narrowed.

"I miss somethin'?" he said.

"Just: nice equipment."

The captain nodded, looking pleased. "I'll tell you what: it's my duty, that's all. This stop won't take too long. Not too many folks dumb enough to try ridin' this out at a mechanic's."

"Not even in West Virginia?" Hank joked.

The captain ignored that. "Could still be some hidin', afraid to come out. Gotta check; standard operatin' procedure. Henry, why don't you check my oil while we're here?"

"Do you want any help looking?" Michael asked the captain.

The moment the sentence was out of his mouth, he was surprised he'd said it. *I thought you didn't* want *to "play The Game anymore."*

The captain cocked his head. "Help? Uh, nah, Private, I didn't bring y'all to come in with me: just brought you to keep you close to yer captain, nice and safe. You have yourself some lunch."

"O-oh. Right, yeah, of course."

The captain turned, strolled into the garage, and casually shouted, "This is Captain Jopek of the United States Army! If you're healthy, say the first three letters of the alphabet!"

"Ay. Bee," Patrick said softly, to himself. He paused, trying to remember. "Ay, bee, dee, gee . . ."

Watch out for holes under the cars, where the mechanics change your oil, Michael almost called out. But the captain disappeared through a door in a brick wall inside, and was gone.

"Now, how does lunch sound?" Bobbie opened the shoulder bag she'd been carrying and pulled out a large Tupperware container, which was steamed white. "I think you might like some goulash."

"Miss Bobbie," Holly said, "that looks lovely."

A picnic? *Out here?* Michael thought. *Seriously, no offense, Miss Bobbie, but this kinda isn't the place for a Martha Stewart moment.*

Patrick looked up to Michael: *Am I allowed to have some?* Michael nodded vaguely, then said, "I'm gonna see if Hank needs any help."

He went to the front of the car. Hank was pouring oil from

a plastic container into the engine. Hank said, not looking up from the engine: "Nope."

O-*kay*, Michael thought.

Bobbie and Holly sat on the rear fender of the Hummer, Patrick between them. Bobbie had her eyes closed, and seemed to be whispering. *Praying before she eats*, Michael realized. Her old-fashioned-ness and cheeriness seemed so oddly out of place.

Holly scooted over, offering him a space. But he found himself shaking his head. "Actually, thanks, I'm not hungry," he mumbled, and walked out into the street, feeling a little numb.

What's the matter with you, Michael? he thought. *You wanted to get here. And now you* are *here.*

But what am I supposed to *do* now?

Why do you have to "do" anything?

He shook his head at himself, looked across the road. Sealed-off parking lot; a Super Walmart past that. *So you want to play a game, Michael,* his mind hissed. *Okay: guess how many Friday nights Ron dropped you off at Walmart.*

Guess how many Friday nights he came home reeking like popcorn and sweat and beer—like he'd rolled in the trash under the high school football bleachers instead of sitting on them? How many Friday nights did he take you and Patrick to Walmart so he could have his parties with the buddies he only liked when he had alcohol in his blood? Michael and his brother would wander the night fluorescently, playing the demo PlayStation 3, eating Oreos, drinking Game Fuels. Michael pretended, of course—pretended it wasn't stealing, pretended this was normal and kind of awesome, actually; so the make-believe was Patrick's real life, and the happiness Patrick felt was real, and that was the only thing that could ever make Michael feel something good. And so when he was asked first by a cashier and then a manager, were they okay, he was not pretending when he said, "Hunnert percent, good buddy." And Patrick loved that—giggled inside his hoodie—but even still they had to duck suspicion, so when the manager went away, they did, too, to the bathroom handicapped stall, where after playing Hot Hands, for a couple hours, they slept. In peace.

Which never lasts.

Guess how many nights?

("A lot" doesn't count as a guess.)

No guesses?

Huh. How 'bout instead of a game, I tell you a story.

So there's this little kid, right, and he thinks his mom is awesome. The strongest, best person on Earth, in his humble opinion. And the mom and the kid are so close that they're each other's entire world; the kid doesn't even really want any friends. But they're poor, and sometimes the kid can tell his mom is lonely, and he fantasizes a lot about someone coming into their lives and lifting away that sadness in Mom that is becoming harder and harder to soothe with a joke. And then— stay with me, this is where the story gets good—then *a Someone actually does come into their lives*. Name o' Ron, this fella, and he's got muscles and this sense of humor that always feels wonderfully/scarily on the edge of becoming too dirty for a kid to hear. At first, Ron is magical. Like one time when the kid— Michael, let's call him—is in fourth grade and gets an earache, Ron blows a gentle puff of pipe smoke into his ear, and the pain evaporates. But Ron's best magic? Taking away that little bit of fear that always seemed to hang behind Mom's eyes. Then he and Mom get married. Michael takes Ron's last name, and he thinks, *This is who I am now; I'm this man's son; he's going to take care of us.* This man, who builds houses for a living, builds a home for all of them. This man pats Mom on the butt in front of Michael sometimes, and Michael, of course, groans, but every time he sees Mom smile, it's like feeling the sun on his back. Soon little cross-stitches hang on the walls of their house:

FAMILY IS THE BEGINNING, MIDDLE, AND END.

But soon . . . sometimes . . . the man comes home at night feeling mean.

And the kid learns to tread carefully, then, *yes-yes*. Learns to look into Ron's eyes and gauge the man's moods. Learns to walk into a room and instantaneously detect the emotional temperature. Learns to know how to act and speak to diffuse Ron when the kid senses Ron's countdown ticking.

Neat tricks.

But then the economy goes downhill. And Ron doesn't have anything to build anymore. So—just as another little boy, Patrick, is born—Ron begins to tear everything down.

The thing is, this little boy does not know how to stay quiet inside. He does not understand why their "big happy home" is getting filled more and more with screams. So yeah, Patrick is scared; yeah, he starts hitting himself. And so Ron puts him in this psychiatric place, sometimes for weeks, and Patrick doesn't get to go to preschool or kindergarten, doesn't really ever get the chance to realize much of what outside life is like. And nobody seems to realize that the only reason Patrick has this terrifying emotional pit inside of him is because Ron has put it there. Nobody understands that once Patrick is in a home that makes sense, he will be fine forever.

And Michael thinks: *we need someone to rescue us.*

And Ron starts hitting Mom, too.

And one time, Patrick sees Mom getting hit before Michael can get him out of the house. And for the first time, Patrick Freaks.

Punches and slaps and bites himself, yes, but that's not the worst of it. The worst is, after Patrick makes himself bruise and bleed, he vanishes. His body is there, nothing else; Patrick's eyes go glassy and he will not speak or eat or flinch, 'cause he's fallen down that emotional pit into his own secret hell. Drugs don't bring him out of it. For weeks, Patrick is just a shape in a gown, and the doctors do not know when—or if—he will come back to himself. He does come back, though; it just randomly happens in the middle of one night in the hospital, when Patrick wakes up and says he wants a cup of apple juice. Let's call this a miracle, the doctors say.

Oh, and just one other thing, they say: if Patrick has another episode like this, it's likely to be much worse. Perhaps *never-come-back, lost-forever* worse.

Right when all that is happening, guess what? The rescuers *do* come. The cops ask why Patrick got scared. Mom lies to the cops.

And Michael realizes he has to *make* Mom tell the police, somehow. So he decides to run away. He still has this *yes-yes* inside him, but it's not *quite yes-yes* that tells him to run away. Because one night, after Patrick accidentally breaks Ron's football championship trophy and Michael takes the blame, Ron hits Michael for the first time. And in the pain and terror of realizing how close Ron came to hitting his small brother, something speaks inside Michael: something that felt as if it were telling him not just how to outplay or endure all the in-the-moment dangers, but how to escape Ron's games altogether and forever. *You'll leave,* this Game Master says. *You'll run away. You'll change everything. You'll save everything, Michael. Because if no one saves Mom and Patrick, then someday—probably soon—they are going to be lost.*

This is who I am; I'm the one who can really make us safe. I can save us, by making Mom tell the truth to the cops. "Mrs. Faris," the cops will ask, "is there any reason your sons would run away? Has there been any trouble at home?"

Yes, yes.

Michael can see the image of a finish line, then: he can see The End. The cops taking Ron away, and Patrick no longer being torn apart by a world that is supposed to be safe but isn't. And Mom looking at Michael with astonishment and sadness, yes, but also with gratitude, and that smile, that smile like light. . . .

So Michael leaves on Halloween night.

And the *yes-yes* does keep him safe every moment.

But something gets in the way of Michael's great plan.

The end of the world.

EENSY DETAIL, HA HA HA HA.

Gunshots from inside the garage. The captain whooped.

"That captain," Holly said, "he's like a kid in a munitions factory, huh?"

Michael startled: Holly had walked the twenty feet or so from the Hummer to him. He felt, honestly, depressed; he didn't want to talk. Still, the automatic response, honed from living with Ron and from weeks on the road with Patrick, kicked in: Michael wiped his face of any upset emotions, made a politely interested face.

"You sure you're not hungry?" she asked. "Miss Bobbie's the best cook in town."

"Nah, I'm good."

Holly seemed to wait for him to go on. When he didn't, she said cautiously, "For sure? I mean, you're sure you're okay?"

Awesome. Cute Girl feels bad for me. Man, I must look so stupid, moping out here.

"Just tired," he said.

"*Not* that I'm prying or anything," Holly said. She laughed nervously, shook her head at herself, pulled a cloth napkin from her hoodie pocket, wiped the tomato sauce from her fingers. The confidence she'd shown in the cafeteria wasn't there. "Anyhoo, hey look," she spouted quickly, "I just wanted to say, please don't feel horrible-awful about this morning, because *I did not actually see anything.*"

Michael, despite himself, blushed, even laughed a little. Patrick looked up from his perch on the bumper with a happy, curious expression.

"Well," Michael said, "I *didn't* feel bad, except you just implied that letting someone see my bod would be something to feel horrible-awful about."

Holly grinned sheepishly, put a hand on her head. "Ahhhh, mister. I came over here absolutely convinced that I would figure out a non-awkward way to say it."

Starting a sentence, Michael thought, *and hoping it finishes itself.* He felt a surprising, glad spark of connection.

"You finally reach the Safe Zone, only to encounter Holly, the world's worst conversationalist," Holly said. "That can't be at all how you imagined."

"Yeah! Yeah, that's exactly what it is—no no, not that you're the worst."

I can kill, like, a hundred monsters, he thought, *but I cannot talk to a girl.*

"I just mean, I had all these ideas about what things I had to do to get me and Patrick to someplace that was, y'know, not awful. And now I've done them all. And if there's nothing else to do, it's like it means . . ." He paused, self-conscious.

"No no, I totally get it," she said. "You worked the whole time to get to 'the Safe Zone,' but it lacks 'the Safe,' so if *that* didn't work, then what will, right? What we've got on our hands is one highly unreliable apocalypse. A hundred years of post-Armageddon narratives! And the world ends without the courtesy of a safe place to go to."

Michael only nodded. What else was there to say?

At that same moment, as if to prove the "not-safe" point, there was an explosion.

The sound came like a cannon report, maybe a half mile away in the streets of downtown. Michael flinched, which made Holly laugh, though not at all unkindly. "Land mines," she said. "The captain's been installing them around the city. Probably that one got set off by a Zed that couldn't find someplace dark to hide.

"Anyhow, things are dreadful here, granted. But I'm now going to tell you a story that will make you feel better."

"Okay."

"So a week ago, the Zeds started pouring into the city and killing lots of people—"

"You're right. Wow. I literally cannot believe how uplifted I am right now."

"Ha-ha-ha-ha, okay, that's enough, you."

Am I, like, flirting right now?

"So the night the evacuation was going on, Hank and I were supposed to leave with our dad, but things were crazy-chaos, and we got separated from him in the crowd. Hank and I wound up on the last evac bus, and it was just about out of the city when Zeds mobbed us. The bus got overturned; people were getting pulled out through the windows. It was even less fun than it sounds.

"Hank and I locked ourselves in this tiny bathroom in the back. I will admit that I cried, and Hank . . . he really tried to be sweet, saying we'd be safe there, that we just had to wait it out. But we could hear everything. A baby screaming, and then not. Soldiers shooting, then not.

"But you know what the very worst moment was?"

Michael shook his head.

"It was when this thought popped into my head. I realized—and I don't know why—the reason the soldiers in the Zone had stopped calling the dead people 'the Infected' when everything was getting so much worse. Why they'd started calling them 'the Zeds.'"

"Why?"

"Because 'zed' is slang for the last letter of the alphabet. And the soldiers thought the world was really coming to an end, that they couldn't do anything else. And I did, too, you know? But the thing is: the captain found me and Hank, and he's taking care of us, and we're gonna be rescued soon.

"Therefore. In conclusion. This isn't The End. The world isn't over."

Michael almost said, *Hey, about the soldiers . . .* But he couldn't bring himself to spoil the moment. "So what *is* the world?" he asked instead.

Holly shrugged, smiling. Michael was again struck by how big her grin was, how open it made her face look. "Just paused, man," she said.

A couple more gunshots from inside the garage. A moment later, the captain emerged, flush faced, changing out his machine-gun clip with an almost liquid grace. "Clear and clear, by God! Pile back in, platoon. We're wastin' daylight," he called.

As they returned to the Hummer, Holly said, "May I say, for the record, how fab it is to have you guys here now? New friends rawk."

"Totally," Michael said.

Friends, Michael thought.

Daaaang.

It's hard to describe any moment on a planet rife with screaming corpses as "carefree." But that afternoon came close.

Because as Captain Jopek led them on the methodical Humvee expedition of the downtown grid, Michael felt like he wasn't just being driven through the city.

He was also being taken through a Postapocalyptic Greatest Hits Collection.

Finding Food. Check.

Collecting Medkits. Check.

Accumulating Bullets. Check.

Searching for Fellow Man. Check.

He found himself relishing the tasks, which were so awesomely familiar from almost Every Video Game Ever. It couldn't have felt more different than The Game did, and in no small part because somebody *else* was shaping the day, which—true fact—was awesome.

The captain stuck to the (landmine-free) main roads, going building by building deeper into downtown; Hank *X*'d off each successive searched street on his map (and Hank also, for no discernible reason other than it was Totally Badass, often requested to hang out on the machine gun-equipped roof of the Hummer whenever the captain went into the buildings). The captain did pick some semi-weird places to look for people, Michael thought, like a pileup of silver Red Cross trailers, which he insisted on exploring compartment by compartment, not satisfied with simply shouting into them. But mostly the afternoon passed with a pleasant rhythm of driving, finding, and talking.

Michael was relieved that he didn't feel "normal"—that he didn't feel like the person he'd been before Halloween, as he'd feared he would after his brief stare down with Hank. He'd had a fantasy, as a kid, about going to summer camp, someplace where nobody knew who he was, where he could reassemble himself and become something other than The Poor Kid or The Skinny Kid. It had only taken the rising of the dead to make this an affordable option for the Faris family, ha-ha-ha, but this afternoon trip through the "paused world" really was the closest he'd ever come to it. Michael told everyone his story of the Rapture confrontation. Holly *oooh*ed, which he pretended, all cool-guy, not to notice. Hank actually "bumped knucks" with him. ("Respect," Hank said.) It wasn't the *attention* that felt good, exactly. It was: Michael could see the pieces of him adding up in their eyes. He'd thought that up a long time ago, how people are really just puzzles, this final image that was composed of all the different moments and pieces of them that you've seen. Most people didn't seem to realize that *you* were a puzzle, too: if you were careful enough, you could choose the image other people put together. Holly and Bobbie and Hank saw the post-Halloween him, and it made that (kick-ass) him seem *real* to Michael himself, in a way that felt almost dizzyingly wonderful. And as much as he loved Bub, he had to admit that it was nice to be seen as something other than an (admittedly awesome) older brother.

The only thing that could have made it better, Michael thought, was if he could see the captain's expression beyond that sliding plate. He hoped the captain was smiling at his story, astonished and impressed by the new kid in town, and saying under his breath, *"No shit . . ."*

By the time they found the third ammo cache of the day—in a sniper post beside a McDonald's PlayPlace—the sky was burning with the pale fire of late afternoon.

"Goddamn, this light leaves fast," the captain said, his back to Michael. "Just a couple more stops."

Michael checked out the sky, too. "I don't know. Maybe we better call it a day, though?" he asked.

The captain didn't turn, but Michael saw his shoulders tense. *Is he angry?*

Bobbie seemed to notice. She put in, kind of quickly, "Yes, that sounds about right to me."

When the captain looked to them, his face seemed affable enough. *Imagined it.* "All right, Old Bones, let's get you to bed," he said. Bobbie laughed politely. "Why these walkin', talkin' dead targets only come out to party in the nighttime, though, I'll never know."

"Pssh," Hank went, like he was a 24/7 party animal.

"It's their pupils. When you die, they stop closing in response to the light," Michael offered.

Holly looked impressed.

"Respect to the scientist!" said the captain.

"Where'd you learn that?" asked Hank.

I watch entirely too much NCIS, Michael thought. "I read, tons," he replied, shrugging.

As they filed through the gate to exit the kids' playground, Michael wound up walking near the rear of the pack with Captain Jopek. Everyone loaded into the Hummer, but when Michael looked back he noticed that the captain had paused a few feet away. He was gazing at something. Michael tried to figure out what it was by snapshotting the world. *The footprints in the snow. The city in suspended animation around them.* But the captain's gaze was oddly far away—as if he were watching something beyond the scope of Michael's sight. "Well, that's the secret, ain't it?" he murmured.

"The secret?" Michael said.

"The way to enjoy this world. Figure out a way to live forever." He looked at Michael, winked. "Know what I mean?"

Uh, no. "Sure," Michael said.

But he wasn't going to let one odd moment spoil the afternoon. In the last glow of his first Safe Zone sunset, Michael leaned against the warmth and shape of the thought that there was, at last, another controller of the world. And in the rocking carriage of his Hummer seat, he found himself pleasantly dozing. For something warm was spreading out from his ribs that took him nearly the entire trip back to the Capitol, even with all its stops to open the barricade gates, to recognize.

Calm.

Ease.

Peace.

The Capitol dome was a twilit beacon upon their return. Far in the congregating dark came the sounds of moans and the Bellows' ceaseless march, but they were punctuated by the frequent *boom*s of detonating land mines.

The captain's footsteps clocked in the soaring marble halls as he took Michael and Patrick to their own room: the office of the lieutenant governor, which was gloriously boring compared to the chaos of the halls. The captain waited a moment in the doorway before leaving, the hall's fluorescence silhouetting him: gunslinger, steady, utterly adult.

Later, tucking Patrick in on his cot, Michael glanced out their window, seeing a different view than he'd had in the Senate that morning. There wasn't much moon to see by; the night was inky, and so the sharp shapes that composed the Charleston skyline were indistinguishable from the dark hulks of the mountains beyond them. And for one moment, Michael had an uneasy notion. The West Virginia that he'd traveled through with Patrick for all those weeks, the West Virginia that was an unmapped nether-zone ruled by insanity and impossibility, the West Virginia that he'd survived only by his exertion to control his thoughts and give shape to his days: that West Virginia was consuming the city.

Well . . . I'll just stay up for a little while, Michael told himself. *To watch the barriers, just to make sure we're okay.*

But by the time he'd brought a bottled water from the next room for Patrick to take his Atipax with, Bub was already deep asleep, without pills to help calm him for the night. And within a minute—for the first time in twenty-four days—Michael was asleep, without waiting up for the Instructions, too.

CHAPTER THIRTEEN

The first thing that Michael was aware of, even before he learned that Captain Jopek was in the room, was that he felt good. He woke up on a cot with sunshine on his chest, not freezing, not suffering a whacked-in-the-skull headache, and his anxiety didn't self-activate.

Still okay, he thought. *Still alive.*

And that relative calm was the only reason he didn't cry out when he looked over, expecting Patrick, and instead saw Captain Jopek sitting in the lieutenant governor's chair.

"Soldier," the captain said, "welcome back to the land of the livin'."

Michael tried to not look weirded out by the fact that, uh, the captain had been watching him sleep. "Hey, 'morning," he replied, not wanting to *feel* weirded out, either. But out of habit, Michael's gaze clicked down to the desktop the captain sat behind. The body of a huge green-black rifle sat centered among a spread of metallic parts, apparently in mid-process of being cleaned and reassembled. Some reflex in Michael tried to judge by the progress of the gun's assembly how long the captain had been here. But besides the fact that you hit the X button to reload them in first-person shooters, Michael knew *nada* about such heavy-duty weaponry.

"Anybody ever tell you," the captain said, "you sleep like the dead?"

Michael laughed a little; the captain looked slyly pleased. Michael pushed his blanket aside and sat up. Then the captain did something amazing: still looking at Michael, he went back to reassembling the rifle, intricate fingers seeking out parts and *snick*ing them back into their homes.

"Me, I'm not much of a sleeper. Sleep always feels like wasted time," the captain said. "How is it that a feller like yourself can get such damn good shut-eye, d'you think?"

"How do you mean?"

"Well, is sleeping so good just the gift of the young? Is it good genes? Just a blessin' from above?" the captain said musingly. "Or do you think it might be"—*snick-snick*—"that you can sleep"—*snick*—"because you don't have nothin' weighin' on your conscience?"

Springs, taut-coiled, entering gun guts, *snick*; bullets, five small morning flashes of gold, eaten in the clip, *clack-click*.

Michael suddenly thought, *He knows I was lying about the soldiers.*

"It could just be that I'm a weakling," Michael said, trying not to sound nervous.

The captain didn't laugh at Michael's self-deprecation. He only stared, his eyes oddly unreadable, his expression a blank, and Michael was reminded of that unease he'd felt during his conversation with the captain in the cafeteria, that vague sensation that the captain was somehow dissecting him.

Finally, Michael said, "That's awesome," indicating the captain's assembling skills.

An enormous grin split the captain's blank face. "Thanks for noticin'!" He seemed to consider Michael for a second. His fingers paused.

"So, uh," Michael said, "is Patrick around?"

"Bobbie's got him. . . . Can I ask you somethin', soldier?" the captain said.

"Sure."

"You ever feel like you were born for some special greatness? Like even if the world didn't see it—*wouldn't* see it—every day of your life, a marvel was coming your way? Like you were something they could never imagine?"

Michael tried to consider the question honestly. But he was distracted, because he noticed something strange: the captain's accent, which had faded in and out yesterday, wasn't there at all—hadn't been, actually, since Michael woke up a minute ago.

At Michael's hesitation, the captain waved a hand almost angrily, his enthusiasm apparently dampened. And when he spoke, the accent was back. "You want to know why I'm here, I guess." He slapped the clip into the bottom of his now-assembled rifle, stood, and looped the strap over his shoulder. "Well, I want to tell you a secret. Walk with me, I never could stand sittin' still."

Michael followed him into the marble hallway with its disordered scattered cots and vandalized governor statues. Still feeling anxious, he allowed the captain to lead him around the ring of the Capitol's central rotunda. Above them, the great golden dome glowed with daylight.

"I tried to get on the horn this mornin' with the rescue unit again," the captain said. "The signal ain't great. Actually, to tell you the truth, I'd rather yackity-yack on a tin-can telephone. The mountains're pretty, but they sure don't love radio signals. Wish I knew how to boost the signal, but I'm a good ol'boy, what do I know?"

Michael could hear the voices of the others somewhere.

He wished he were with Patrick.

"Did they say how far away they were?" Michael asked.

"Neg. But I'm guessing two days. They were askin' about how many we got here, and I told 'em about you and your brother. Since they're from the Richmond Safe Zone, I asked 'em about your mother."

Michael stopped in his tracks, the sun suddenly painfully bright. His heart hammered.

"They couldn't answer before the signal went out," the captain went on. "So I did a little research on my own. I found a list that the government was making before the Charleston Zone went down last week."

Captain Jopek reached into his camouflage jacket and pulled out a folded white paper, columned with names. And written at the top were these words:

CONFIRMED DEAD (FEMALE), WV SAFE ZONE

Michael felt his insides go liquid. *Oh God,* he thought. *No. No, please—*

But then, after allowing Michael to gaze at this terrifying header for a full second or two, the captain chuckled, "Whoops, heh-heh. Other side, soldier." He flipped it over, handed Michael the paper.

CONFIRMED CHECK-INS (FEMALE), CHARLESTON SAFE ZONE, 11/1–11/5.

This list was far longer, but Michael spotted the highlighted name immediately.

MOLLY JEAN FARIS. CONFIRMED CHECK-IN: 11/4.

Tears pushed on Michael's eyes. He didn't smile: he just felt lightheaded. *Mom made it,* he thought. *God, she really did.*

"Thank you," he breathed.

"Yessir," Jopek said nonchalantly, and clapped a hand on Michael's shoulder.

Michael had not actually been thanking Jopek, though: he'd

been thanking . . . he wasn't quite sure what. "Thank you for showing me this, Captain," he said.

What about Ron? Is he on a list, too?

But Michael realized . . . he didn't want to know.

"You're welcome. I just want you to remember one thing, okay, Michael?"

Suddenly, the enormous hand on Michael's shoulder squeezed, with enough force to power over the border from "buddy-buddy" to painful. The captain's other hand shot up, ripped the list from Michael's grasp, left Michael holding just two torn triangles of paper. "The reason you can sleep?" said Captain Jopek. "It's me, Michael.

"So next time we go out in the city, you don't goddamn ever tell me when it's time to go home, how 'bout that, shithead?"

And before Michael could respond, the captain stuffed the paper back into his jacket, and walked away.

Michael felt his cheeks flare and prickle. The captain's echoing footsteps dwindled down the hall, but Michael stood still, feeling dazed . . . and oddly ashamed.

Why the hell did the captain have to do that? he thought, anxiety creeping up his throat.

He stared at the jagged paper in his hands. *Maybe he was right, though,* Michael tried to tell himself. *I mean, maybe I shouldn't have said we should go home. He's the soldier; he knows what he's doing.*

But Michael still felt hot-faced, and a little angry.

He began to follow the dim sounds of voices through the halls. He was almost to the Governor's Dining Room (aka a random cafeteria) when Patrick came out of a bathroom and waved.

"Michael, hey! Don't go in there, it stinks now. Hi!"

Michael grinned as Bub approached, comforted by Patrick's excitement to see him. He slipped the torn paper into his pants pocket—and despite his happiness, he felt a sudden gloomy pang in his chest. He'd never been more aware of the gulf that lay between himself and Bub. Michael had just received news that 100 percent validated The Game, that justified all the danger he'd guided them through since Halloween. But Bub was still unaware of the tightrope that they'd run together. And until he had solid earth under his feet in the Actually Safe Zone in Richmond—until they reunited with Mom, and began to remake their lives—Michael couldn't tell him, *Bub, I was scared Mom didn't make it to the Safe Zone. I was scared that running away didn't actually save anything, 'cause nothing worked out in the end. The "yes-yes" and "the Game Master"? I was pretty much terrified that they were full of shit.*

Michael settled for saying, "Awesome shirt, duder."

Patrick wore a new hoodie: blue and gold, with a deer silhouetted by a sunrise. The shirt was a little long, but otherwise a good fit. "Bobbie gave it! It's soft. I drawed this for you." He handed Michael a piece of paper covered with red and silver scribbles. "It's Ultraman."

Michael replied, "Obviously." As they headed toward the dining room, he could smell something sweet and buttery. Sweet baby Jeezus, *cinnamon rolls.*

And he'd begun pushing open the cafeteria door when he heard the sound inside—a sound so familiar and so foreign, and it stopped him. *Is someone* crying? Michael thought.

He cracked the door, peeking through. Hank and Bobbie sat alone at a red cafeteria table; the cafeteria was only half lit, the sections beyond them dark, but there was light enough to see by. Hank leaned forward with his elbows on the table, one hand in his hair, his other holding Bobbie's hand. And standing at the door, secretly looking in, Michael realized something that left him a little awed:

Hank was crying.

"It's hard, I know it's just so hard," Bobbie was saying softly. "But Richmond, it's just waiting for us. You have to focus on that, Henry. And you said yourself how smart your father is, you know it? And this captain of ours, he's a good ma—"

Bobbie paused, as if reconsidering.

"He's so good at what he does," she finished.

"Y-yeah. You're right," Hank said, his voice warped and throaty. His face looked so weird to Michael, like a little kid's. "But . . . what if the other soldiers get here before the captain can do it?"

"Do what, sweetie?" asked Bobbie.

"What if the captain can't find—"

"Why's Hank crying?" Patrick whispered.

Michael flinched away from the door just as Hank's head sprang up. Patrick's brow knitted, confused and troubled by what was happening. "I bet he just has a stomachache," Michael whispered to him.

A chair scraped in the caf. "Gonna go fill the generators," Hank said to Bobbie. A moment later, a door (not the one beside Michael) opened somewhere, and the sound of Hank's footsteps faded away. *He must not have seen me,* Michael thought. Though, he wondered. . . .

Patrick opened the door to the Governor's Dining Room. Bobbie was clearing plates from her table, her head down, speaking softly. Michael glanced around, expecting to see Holly (and honestly, really looking forward to it).

There was nobody else in the room, though.

As the door swung shut, Bobbie flinched and looked up, startled. She looked much older than yesterday, somehow.

"Good morning to a handsome sleepyhead," Bobbie said, trying for lightness, not quite making it. She collected spoons into a bowl half filled with oatmeal. "I did make you breakfast, Michael, but I am so sorry, a puppy named Patrick ate it."

The bowl of oatmeal suddenly slipped in Bobbie's hands.

It crashed onto the tray, spoons clattering.

Patrick, who had been walking toward a table covered with blank papers and Crayolas, stopped, his shoulders pinching back. Michael could feel Bub's tension ping through the air, his emotional radar lighting up. Michael considered making an excuse for both of them to leave.

But, no. I don't want to just leave her by herself, not if she's upset.

"Miss Bobbie, I can get those," he said casually as he walked to her. He picked up the tray. "Would you show me where the dishes go?"

Bobbie shook her head absently. "Just back in the kitchen," she began, but then she understood the meaning behind Michael's question. Gratitude made her worry lines relax. "I will, certainly. Patrick, would you do another sketch of that robot for me?"

Patrick had sat down at the table and picked up a red crayon. He looked relieved at Bobbie's new tone, if still confused.

"Heckz. Yez."

The door to the cafeteria's kitchen was past an empty salad bar. The kitchen was darker than the dining room: light filtered through the porthole, swinging as the door shut behind Michael and Bobbie, glimmering across the stainless steel of the sinks and counters.

"That was very kind of you," said Bobbie. She pulled a red handkerchief from her pocket. She raised it to her face, then seemed to realize she wasn't actually crying. She wiped spots of oatmeal off her hands instead.

"Miss Bobbie, can I ask: What's got you so upset?"

"It's just something the captain said," Bobbie replied.

Remembering how small the captain had made him feel, and now experiencing a little anger about how Jopek had upset Bobbie, Michael asked, "What did he say?"

"Oh, Henry asked last night, after we got back, if he could help the captain with his patrols in the fences outside the

Capitol. Henry is always so eager around him. But the captain just said, 'You ain't got no job other than sittin' on yer butt 'til I tell you otherwise, Henry.' Maybe it's good that the captain is taking care of everything, I suppose. Maybe he was only trying to be friendly. But something about the way he said it felt . . . not friendly. I don't know why, but sometimes, when I look at the captain, it's as if there's a secret in everything he says."

Like when I said we should get back to the Capitol at sunset, and the captain pretended it didn't make him angry. But Michael pushed that thought down: he'd only imagined the captain's anger.

"I'm probably just thinking too much. It's all this waiting; it's so difficult." Her voice trailed off; she shook her head, frowning in wonder. "I can't imagine how it must have been for *you*, out there. The cold. The lonesomeness. The not-knowing. I don't know how you did that."

"Aw, it wasn't that bad," Michael said, downplaying the difficulty out of habit.

"You sell yourself short, honey," Bobbie said, looking him earnestly in the eye. "You do."

Michael paused, tempted to again shrug off the compliment from this sweet old woman. He'd never known his own grandparents, but he'd always thought that old people's smiles and their "Hey, good-lookin'" and "I think y'all might be the best marching band in the state" were too sweet—*unearned* was maybe the best way to put it.

But there was something far different from that too-sweetness in Bobbie's eyes now:

This is painful, Michael. It's safe for you to admit that to me.

"It was . . . tough," he said.

"That's one way to put it," Bobbie chuckled, momentarily brightening. "Michael, may I ask a strange question?"

He nodded, wanting even more, after her kindness,

to make Bobbie feel better.

"When you were out there, when you were just trying to get through each day," she said, "did you ever pray?"

He started to say, *No*, or, to be polite, *My family's not really religious*. But then he remembered seeing the Coalmount church, before he'd found the mirror-eyed mannequins. How the steeple had pointed for the sky. And he remembered the feeling he'd had on the cliff just before the balloon arose from nothing: that sense of awe, both good and terrible, as if a plan were being invisibly synced together for him and Patrick, like unseen clockwork behind a curtain. Those cliff-and-church feelings had not been *yes-yes*, exactly. *Yes-yes* was an inner quiet, both weapon and joy, that supplied an understanding of how Michael must handle himself in any present moment. The church-and-cliff feelings had felt *different*, somehow.

But now, Michael shook his head at that, inside. It was like a movie: real in the moments, but afterward you sort of laughed at yourself.

"I only ask because sometimes I wonder if this world *is* all . . . well, the end-times," Bobbie said, and Michael got the feeling that letting her talk was the best thing he could do to help her feel better. "Because the plane that brought me to the Safe Zone? It was a crash, Michael. The pilots were attacked, and we fell out of the sky, a hundred souls on board. I should have been killed. And my husband—did I tell you Jack is his name?—only broke his legs. The government began to evacuate Charleston just a few hours after the crash, when those creatures began overwhelming the city. The injured were on the first buses, and you could hear the soldiers fighting downtown, trying to clear a way through for the buses, but Jack was so calm, so brave, when they were loading him onto that first bus."

"So you'll be seeing him soon, then," Michael said, trying to cheer her as her voice trailed off. "Also, I think you're doing pretty good in the bravery department."

"Thank you, Michael," she replied. "But I just mean, such incredible things have happened in this world. I've always prayed: it's like talking to yourself, then it changes. And I used to think that God answered all prayers—that if you honestly gave yourself to His grace, and if you treated people with kindness, you'd be safe and carried through whatever was to come. I still pray. But with all the terrible things around us, now I'm finding . . ."

"What are you finding?"

"I'm finding that I don't want God to speak back to me," Bobbie said. "I do not think that I'm prepared for what He has coming."

Michael didn't believe in what Bobbie was saying, but he couldn't help it: chills crept up his spine.

"I know those people in the mountains believe this is The End, too," Bobbie said, so softly it was almost as if she were speaking to herself. "But I think I understand them. I grew up in a coal town; I *know* what it's like to have all your hope tied up with the mining company. Then they had a little boy *die* in their mine." Michael remembered the newspaper he'd found in the coal company trash can, the article about the accident that killed Cady Gibson, the young boy with the ragged, crooked haircut. "And then the dead rose. And I believe that the people in that town needed hope, and the only thing they could do was try to believe that these awful things *meant* something, even if the meaning is something terrible. Their priest took their pain for his own purposes. And I believe that makes him a dark man."

The idea gave Michael pause. It struck him that, if Bobbie were right, then the Rapture's situation felt uncomfortably like Patrick's and his own: after all, Michael was using The Game to shape meaning out of their pain. *But no, it's totally different,* Michael thought. *When The Game is over, Patrick's going to be fine.* The Rapture's only goal seemed to be destruction.

"But Miss Bobbie, there's no reason to believe that

anything bad is coming."

She looked back to Michael, seeming to snap out of the small reverie. "Oh. No, of course. I'm so sorry to go on like this," Bobbie said.

Michael nodded, and then Bobbie, still looking distant and shaken, headed for the door. He felt a need to interject again, to repay her for her being kind to Patrick—to feel useful again after the moment with Jopek, which had made him feel so small.

"Miss Bobbie?" She turned to him. "You know, you're not going to have to be 'waiting around' too much longer with the soldiers on their way."

Bobbie nodded, but didn't look reassured.

"And you don't even have to just 'wait around' at all. I don't pray, but you know what did make me feel better when I was out in the mountains? Keeping busy. That's the big thing. And carrying a gun didn't hurt, either."

Bobbie smiled, said jokingly, "Maybe I'll try that sometime, honey."

"Heck yeah. Maybe those soldiers will recruit you; I just hope your husband will recognize you in camo."

And, finally, looking like her bright self again, Bobbie laughed.

A reminder that soldiers were coming back soon; the obvious truth of the awesomeness of Bobbie's survival mirrored back to her: these things added up, slightly refocused the world, to give her a picture of happiness. And not *just* her.

I'm good at this, aren't I, making people feel better? Michael thought as he headed out of the kitchen.

But you never saw any soldiers, Michael, something in him whispered.

He felt a small pang of guilt. *Well . . . even if* I *didn't see them, soldiers really* are *coming. And if this little not-even-half lie makes Bobbie feel better, isn't it worth it?*

Yes, he responded, with warmth in his ribs. *Yes, yes.*

CHAPTER FOURTEEN

The rest of the day passed quickly. Michael ate a couple cinnamon rolls for breakfast, which gave him this mostly pleasant mix of sleepiness and sugar-jitters, and afterward, he asked Bub, "So what do you wanna do today?"

Patrick seemed almost confused by the question. After Michael reassured him—*yep, anything*—Patrick took him to the cots in the marble halls, where they played with a couple of Nintendo 3DSes. Michael was delighted to play a game with a *screen*; he told Patrick about the time that he'd beaten the original *Super Mario Bros.* in eight minutes. "I gotta try it again one day," he said. "With my eyes open this time."

Patrick didn't find that funny, though. And when Michael tried to show him the secret warps on the *Mario 2* cartridge, Bub replied, seeming oddly restless and grumpy, "Michael, I *know* 'em all already."

He asked if they could go explore.

And Michael said sure, partially hoping to bump into Holly. Patrick led them through most of the Capitol, but they didn't run into her. The "exploration" of the building was dampened also by another fact: Nearly all of the Capitol's corridors and chambers were identical, and the novelty of the whole *mayhem-meets-marble* decorating scheme had already kinda worn off. Michael traveled through these Safe Zone halls with his brother, the mesh-filtered winter light streaming around them, but he had a vaguely depressed "stuck" feeling, as if he were repeating the same screen over and over on a scratched game disc. Patrick began doing things that he usually only did when he was uncomfortable or bored: he counted the cots, up into the hundreds, as well as all the left and right turns of the halls. Even when Michael and Bub discovered a two-lane bowling alley in the east wing of the Capitol, they wound up quitting after only one round: resetting the pins themselves turned out to be brain numbing . . . and when Michael told Patrick that he couldn't remember how to keep score, Patrick seemed—uncharacteristically—almost angry.

He remembered how Bub's doctors had once mentioned that "children like Patrick" could get upset if their diet was not monitored. *Maybe Bub just had too much sugar this morning?*

So after a tuna-fish-sandwich, sugar-free lunch—after an unsuccessful attempt to get Bub to take a nap—Michael suggested they play a game of *Sorry!* in the Governor's Dining Room. Bobbie, who had found the board game, played as well. Even though it was one of his favorites, though, Patrick was uneasy, fidgeting and saying, midway through, "Can't we do somethin' *else*? Michael, can't we?"

And Michael began to realize what was the matter with Patrick today.

That realization made Michael's stomach drop a little, for it implied a dimension to Patrick's anxiety he'd not previously considered. Michael always knew, of course, that Bub needed to *understand* the world around him in order to feel safe.

Now, though, the world around Patrick finally *was* safe . . . but because hanging out aimlessly at the Capitol wasn't what The Game said they should do, *Bub could not understand that he did not have to feel his horrible anxiety anymore.* It struck Michael that the respites Patrick had received from that anxiety—the way he'd been so happy around Bobbie, for example—were only temporary. *Patrick can't really get better, can't really feel comfortable—can't really* change—*until I get him to the real Safe Zone.*

Michael's watch read 2:30 and the sun outside the windows of the Governor's Dining Room had begun its sure descent toward the skyline. *Okay,* he thought. *So, just give Bub a "Game task" to do.*

And so, at the tail end of that afternoon, just as Patrick was putting away the board game pieces and Michael was still trying to come up with a new task, Captain Jopek elbowed open the door to the cafeteria and announced: "Headin' downtown for a quick trip, troops. Load up at the Hummer in three minutes." The captain saw Michael check his watch, said:

"Got a problem with that idea, Faris?"

Michael shook his head, both because he felt that unaccountable Jopek-seems-strange shame and also because, for the first time that afternoon, Patrick seemed excited.

So Michael dressed his brother in his coat and wool hat and mittens. He loaded Bub into a rear-compartment harness in the Hummer, Hank and Holly and Bobbie following him. He comforted himself with the knowledge that it was 2:47; sunset was almost an hour away. He caught Holly's eye, nodded, both nervous and happy when she took the harness right across from him, with only the white emergency gurney to separate them.

The captain revved the engine, beginning their "mission."

And very soon after that, everything began to go wrong.

CHAPTER FIFTEEN

Aren't there, like, land mines here?

Michael shifted in the harness, looking uneasily out the Hummer's rear portal window. The captain had taken them across the Capitol bridge, into the downtown grid, but instead of simply continuing yesterday's systematic search of the main, mine-less streets, Jopek had unlocked several thick layers of fencing, and taken them into an alley so narrow that the sides of the Hummer nearly scraped.

Michael looked to Holly, wanting to know what she thought of this, but the captain had opened the sliding plate between the front and rear Hummer compartments: the unfiltered sound of the engine was so loud that nobody in the back could hold a conversation.

Calm down, man, Michael thought, feeling a little panicky. *The captain knows what he's doing.*

They got to their destination safely. The side streets didn't contain as many mines as Michael had thought, perhaps because the recent influx of Bellows into the city had detonated them already.

But still.

The Hummer stopped. Captain Jopek hurled open the rear double doors.

The pale fire of late afternoon burned on the captain's grinning, eager face. "'Mon out," he said, strapping on his Kevlar vest, his wrist knives, ankle pistol. "This little mission shouldn't take too long."

They'd parked next to an enormous fake-corn maze, set up in a shopping square across from an old movie theater as a Halloween decoration, Michael supposed. Scarecrows hung inside the maze, ragged and off-kilter on crosses; jack-o'-lanterns rested on bales of hay, their puckered mouths stuffed with snow. Much of the corn was flattened; all of it was browned. Michael felt, again, that sense of vague depression: seeing the maze was like walking past a water park closed for winter.

"Rock 'n' roll," Hank said as he disembarked. *Observe the badass* is what it sounded like.

Michael helped Bobbie out of her harness, then waited with Patrick as she and everyone else piled out of the Hummer.

"What're we gonna *do*?" Patrick whispered as Michael set him down on the street, heading toward the maze behind the rest of the group.

"Just wait while the captain looks for people," Michael replied. *I guess.* "Hundred points for each one."

"Points for people?" Patrick said, and stopped walking. "There's *never* people in buildings, though."

And just like that, the momentary relief that Bub had gotten from Jopek's "mission" announcement was gone: his small face crinkled down with disappointment and frustration; his mittened hands clenched and unclenched. Michael could feel, like something electrical, the tingling signals of Patrick's anxiety through the air between them.

Michael's heart hurt a little. He saw the scene around them through Bub's eyes.

The snow, all slushy and gray.

No gentle hills to sled.

No Lightball-able places to explore.

And most of all: no real reason to believe that The End was one step closer than it had been before.

Michael remembered the other night, in Coalmount, when he and Patrick had been taken aback by the brilliant starpointed sky, how it had seemed that they almost owned the world. Now the captain was standing beside this dreary abandoned maze, talking to "his troops," undoubtedly telling them to wait outside "while yer captain does a little explorin'."

Uh, Michael, are you seriously *feeling nostalgic for the good old days when you and your brother were trying not to get eaten?*

Well. Actually: yeah.

"Maybe can we look for more pieces for my weapon tomorrow?" Patrick murmured, almost to himself, walking toward the maze, his shoulders slouched. He pulled his tiny orange toy gun from his coat pocket, then put it away again forlornly. "I can't even make it shoot, the trigger's too hard to pull."

"Bub, hold up." Patrick looked back. "Why don't we go look for the pieces *now*? Secret style."

'Cause who's it gonna hurt, if I do what I want for a couple minutes?

"Nuh-*uh*, really?" Patrick replied, his face coming alive. Michael nodded, and Patrick offered him a double fist-bump. And it was as Michael led back around the opposite side of the Hummer, going away from the captain and the maze and everyone else, heading toward an Ace Hardware storefront, that in the back of his mind he realized something was off.

Footsteps, coming toward him, fast across spattering snow.

Michael turned.

And when he looked, the captain's face was there, filling his vision.

"*Hi! What'cha doin?*" Captain Jopek said.

Michael startled, trying to search the captain's eyes, finding instead only that perpetual blankness. But he told himself: *I'm just taking my brother for a walk, captain, and I'm allowed to do that.*

The captain's checking to make sure you're safe, that's all.

"Taking Patrick for a quick walk," Michael replied, trying to sound confident.

The captain's brow darkened. He nodded, like a man in contemplation.

"Taking Patrick for a walk," Jopek repeated. "Takin' P," he said, grinned blazingly, "for a . . ."

The captain paused.

And growled:

"*WAAALK*?!"

The sound rumbled and cracked the winter air between them. In that moment, the captain exploded toward Michael, stopping inches short of Michael's nose.

"What the," Patrick breathed.

Michael opened his mouth to say something, but the captain shook his head with such authority that he silenced himself. Michael became aware of Hank smirking in the background, though Bobbie and Holly were nowhere in sight. Michael suddenly felt like a kid who had struck out at Little League tryouts.

"Maybe you're too dumbass to recollect this, but I told you to start listenin' to my orders, Mikey," the captain whispered, close, so close, his hot breath like a small invasion.

Jopek's just trying to . . . to . . . He hoped the sentence would finish itself. But, no.

Jopek put his right hand, shaped like a pistol, to Michael's

145

temple. The crescent of his nail pressed inward. Before Michael knew what was happening, tears pushed on his eyes. He took an awkward step backward, but his butt struck the wheel bay of the Hummer.

"I—I didn't think it was a big deal."

The captain smiled ugly humor. "Aw, I think you *proved* you didn't think."

Hank guffawed. Michael did not understand the malice: He'd thought he and Hank had formed some degree of rapport yesterday.

The captain cocked his thumb back, like the hammer of a gun . . . and, finally, with a light push, drew it away from Michael's skull.

"You just gotta be careful, boyo," he whispered, and clapped Michael happily on the shoulder, without at all changing those dark eyes. "You just want to make sure you follow my rules."

Hank chuckled. The keys on the captain's hip sang like a ring of knives as he left.

The captain is like Ron, Michael.

Jopek is just like Ron.

Welcome home.

Patrick's expression was an honest blank, as if someone had taken an enormous pink eraser and wiped away everything that made sense to him. "Michael?" he said uncertainly, and reached out to take his hand.

"*Bub,*" Michael hissed, snapping his hand away. "Not now."

What the hell is the matter with you? he thought. *What is* wrong *with you?* Why, when he'd looked down the barrel of Rulon's rifle, should Captain Jopek's gun hand seem so horrible?

"'Kay but, why you fighting with—"

"I said not *now*. What part of that is confusing?"

Patrick's face crumpled. The expression should have broken

Michael's heart. And he realized, resentfully, that Patrick seemed to think it should, too.

Michael did what he knew would hurt most: He rolled his eyes and shook his head, like he was trying to hide annoyance at a little kid who wants to play but is too small to do it right.

Patrick made a face of raw pain and walked away, around the Hummer, toward the maze.

Okay, so the captain's being an asshole, Michael told himself. *So what? So freaking what?*

By the corn, everyone else stood in a circle that looked sealed to him.

"Just had to fetch Mikey, is all," the captain was saying lightly to Holly and Bobbie. "And I tell you what: y'all come in with me this time." He looked at Michael; a subtle sneer. "Yeah, I think the man in charge is gonna keep a real close eye on you from now on."

"Captain? Pardon me, Captain?"

"Bobbie."

"Since it's still daylight, I'd like to do the lookin' out," Bobbie said. "If Henry doesn't mind letting me use his gun, of course." She elbowed Hank's arm, looking nervous but also a little giddy. Like there was nothing wrong in all the world.

The captain tipped his helmet to her. "Bobbie Lou, I think you just got Henry's job."

Hank didn't look super pleased.

Bobbie looked at Michael, offering him her smile: that bright revelation of wrinkles and white teeth and eyes. She winked, and silently mouthed, "Maybe they'll recruit me"—but Michael still felt so sick with shame that he looked away.

He followed everyone else around the maze. Holly kept trying to catch his eye, asking with her expression: *you okay?* Michael felt a swell of embarrassment, again cast his gaze elsewhere, saw Bobbie on the Hummer out of the corner of his eye.

Hay tugged and danced across the ground between them. Bobbie's silhouette stood crisp against the orange sky. She lay a hand on the roof-mounted machine gun, as if it were a possibly warm stovetop. Her small shape looked so fragile, as if a wind could lift her into the sky, and for no reason Michael could name, that idea made a moment of fear chill his chest. He had a frighteningly childlike urge to call out to her. Then she was raising her hand to her forehead, saluting them, pretending to be a soldier.

Michael turned without a salute back.

The captain led them into the shadow of the movie theater's marquee: MAGIC LANTERN THEATER—HORROR-A-THON—GET UR TIX EARLY—SHOWS SELL OUT. As he kicked in the door, the smell of stale popcorn rippled out. Hank screamed when a body pitched out of the shadows, but it was just a cutout of Vin Diesel.

Michael looked into the dark. *No, I am* not *that old "Michael" anymore. I explored places, just like we're doing now, for twenty-three fugging days, before I met Jopek*, Michael tried to reassure himself as he stepped into the theater.

An old movie theater lobby: dips of velvet rope, moldy pretzels and lumpy nacho sauce, fake coffins propped against the walls.

Captain Jopek's face, floating in the dark, turned toward them.

"Stay sharp, ladies." His breath was a ghost.

"This is Captain Horace Jopek of the United States Army! I am here on a search-and-rescue! If you're alive, call out the first three letters of the alphabet!"

Now everyone felt for one another as they moved in past the last of the light, holding the shoulders of the person before them like a blind-man's chain: Captain, Holly, Hank, then Patrick and Michael.

Captain Jopek, his gun light lancing like a glisten-sharp sword, looked like the point man of a covert team in *Battlefield*

3. "All right now, check your corners," Jopek said, "staircase over there, Jopek, check it, clear, bet your ass it's clear."

His body moved with the precision of a machine. Every step was solid and certain of purpose and stealthy—but Michael did not feel any admiration for Jopek's power right then. It seemed arrogant to him, and ugly.

Heading through a theater-room door, which was splattered with dried blood.

People were in their seats, Michael saw, *when different villains shambled in. One scream. Popcorn arcs in the cut of movie light and the audience boils up with panic. Stampede for the too-small door. Panic when people begin to be bitten; panic, and in the half-light, it is not possible to tell who is good and who is not.*

Cold wind uncoiled through the theater door, whickering dead leaves up the aisle. Patrick slipped a little; Michael did not look at him but gave his shoulders a reassuring squeeze.

"What's under there?" Patrick whispered. "What's under the leaves?"

Something weird, under the crackling leaf-carpet—soft, but with a gooey weight.

"Ho', shit," said the captain, as if seeing something up ahead. "Ho' *goddamn."*

"Captain," said Hank. "What's the situation?"

The captain swung the gun light up and speared the silver screen.

A shape seemed to shift beyond the movie screen.

"Captain," Holly murmured to herself. "Should we be here?"

The captain was striding toward the screen now: fast and sure, until he skidded again, on something slick, the gun light a quick slice across the movie screen. And it was at that moment that fear began to rise in Michael like poison

149

water rushing up a well, because there were other shadows behind the silver screen; they were growing, now they were more defined, like something drawing closer in a nightmare from the other side of the veil. Patrick grabbed Michael's hip and said, *"Look."* Down the aisle, the captain regained his footing and his weapon rose, and while Holly gasped in revelation and Hank began to holler, Patrick said, *"Look! Michael, LOOK!"* And, now, Michael did. In the reflected silvery half-light, it was hard to tell what Patrick held pinched between his thumb and index fingers.

But Michael looked closer.

And the thing dangling from Patrick's fingers looked directly back at him.

It was an eye, a human eye, torn with the ropey rosy stalk still attached.

The movie screen. It bulged. Teeth and hands burst seams through it. And there in the vivid gun light were Bellows, two dozen Bellows, coming forth like three-dimensional demons breaking free from the scariest movie ever made.

Hank hollered. Holly cried out, stumbled back on a seat.

The captain only laughed and opened fire, filling the room with his perfect, video-game-hero's fire, the gun bursts flash-bulbing his perfect hero's face.

Michael watched Holly, saw the relief on her face, the same that he himself had felt when the captain mowed Bellows from his balloon—

—but this is different! The captain isn't just "saving us" right now! Michael thought. *The captain isn't noticing something!*

Eyes. The eyes!

The Bellows coming from the movie screen: they had no eyes.

"Uh-oh!" Patrick shouted at something behind them, his voice half-fright, half-fun as he pulled out his toy gun.

Michael spun, seeing the several shadows lurching through

the theater door. The captain paused to reload.

Michael listened to the monsters' footsteps: like glass, like crunching broken glass.

They came in through the front door, he understood. *Even though it's daylight, they came in through the front door, and stepped on the glass the captain broke!*

"*Captain!*" shouted Michael. "*We have to get out* now*!*"

"For twenty points," he added under his breath. Michael picked up Patrick and sprinted down the aisle toward the captain.

"Captain, we have to leave!"

"*Stand down*," the captain barked, still smiling, his eyes glittering. He was firing on the screen again. "Captain's got this; can't be that many back there. Ha!—sons-a-bitches can't even *see!*"

"*Captain*," Hank shouted, "*behind us—*"

The captain whirled and popped four perfect shots to destroy the brains of the Bellows in the theater doorway. He spat tobacco, spun back, resumed his firing on the theater screen . . .

. . . and were there more Bellows there now, even though he'd been massacring them? . . .

Yes-yes.

Michael reached the captain, forcefully grabbed his shoulder. The captain tore his shoulder away, and his glare blazed into Michael.

"Listen!" Michael shouted. "They're all coming from outside! If we don't go, they'll trap us in here!"

"Outside?" The captain laughed. "It's still daylight."

"I know it is, but . . ." Michael began—and the thought finished itself: "*—they tore their eyes out so they could go outside in the day!*"

The captain glowered. "Get back, and that's a goddamn order."

You have to get us out, Michael! he thought. At that moment he remembered: *The captain's got another gun strapped to his ankle.*

Michael knelt so quickly that even the captain could not react in time. Michael found the Velcro and unstrapped Jopek's combat-issue pistol in one seamless, *yes-yes* move.

Michael felt a joy at the captain's anger.

"The *hell?*" said Captain Jopek, gaping at Michael, as if astonished that this skinny kid stealing his gun could exist at all.

And that was the only reason Michael had time to turn and run up the aisle, saying to Holly and Hank, "This way," firing his own three perfect shots at the new Bellows streaming in through the theater door.

What am I doing what am I doing.

Answer: Grabbing the controller, FTW!

Michael charged into the hall and Patrick held on piggyback and Michael felt Patrick's excitement and his own blood and spotted his reflection in the glass poster cases and thought, *Hot diggity—badass.*

"Faris!" Hank barked, running behind him, voice strained with confusion. "Wait for the captain!"

Two Bellows moaned in the lobby—a fireman, a thin woman in a polka-dot dress. Shot down with his huge handgun. "He'll catch up," Michael told Hank, because he *did* hear the captain firefighting his way out of the theater, and at the last moment before Michael led Hank and Holly into the blazing sunset, the captain dashed around a corner into the lobby and shouted:

"Don't you go out there! There's still m—"

But the rest of the captain's shout was drowned out.

Because Michael had been right.

Outside Bellows roared and echoed death-calls, clots in the bright bloody light, moaning from the sides of the shopping square corn maze, coming closer. Despite the joyous adrenaline of the moment, the previously impossible sight made a clean run of terror through Michael. The walking dead. The dead, in *daylight.*

"C'mon!" Michael said, leading everyone from the infested theater.

"Goddammit!" the captain shouted. *"Ho' up!"*

The stalks of the corn maze ahead surged and whipped. *"Daaaamn—GOOODDD—"* the maze roared. Bellows reached out from the corn sightlessly, their eye sockets cored to oval pits of gristle. Michael gave the maze a wide berth.

He had just begun running past it when the captain opened fire in his direction.

The maze exploded. The land mine, on the other side of the maze's fence only ten feet to Michael's right, blew high as the captain's bullet struck it, raising a man-tall spiral of concrete and fire. Hot air displaced into Michael; he cried out and stumbled to the ground. Debris peppered down; more camouflaged mines detonated. *Whampf!—WHAMPF!* Corn and walking corpses leapt.

Michael's ears rang. He blinked down at Patrick, who had fallen on a hay bale beside him. "Too *loud!*" Patrick said.

Now the captain was long-strong striding, gun nocked, past him.

"What was *that*?" Michael spat.

The captain said, his eyes glittering both bitterly and happily, "Didn't think you'd seen the Zeds in the maze. Just protectin' you, Mikey."

The captain led Hank and Holly around the maze, first clearing the route ahead with three grenades, lob-shot from the undercarriage of his gun. Michael picked up Patrick and rubbed his back, dashing through the avenue the grenades had cleared.

At last, they came around the end of the maze . . . and Michael realized one of the screams did not belong to the Bellows.

"Bobbie."

The creatures had surrounded the Hummer. Bobbie was on

top of the vehicle, at the gun. It should have been fine; *should have*. But the gun was clicking drily. It was a thing he would hear in dreams for the rest of his life: despite the Bellows and the distance, that heartbreaking and toylike *click!*

"Here! HERE! Captain, I am here!" Bobbie called. *"The roof-hatch won't OPEN!"*

"God, no," Holly moaned miserably.

Michael raised the handgun, but his finger froze on the trigger. His hands were still quivering: what if the bullet flew wild?

Patrick, in his arms, moaned, "What's happenin'? What happens if they get Bobbie?"

And yet here now came the most awesome thing Michael had ever seen.

It was a great enormous sweeping majesty, a sight that should have been projected widescreen, HD, two hundred feet tall and twice that wide to tower in glorious slow-motion. The captain's gun flying up to his shoulder as he sprinted. His eyes were single glowing firing pins. His face was a tuned searchlight. Like some tremendous flame exploding through the glass and rafters of a structure that can no longer contain it, Jopek was *force*. He was *unleashed*.

The Bellows fell like a sacrificial ring around the vehicle, with the Hummer never even dented by a single imperfect bullet.

Dumb gratitude overpowered Michael. The captain plucked the pistol out of Michael's hands.

Do what you want, Jopek, he thought. *Whatever it is; just get us back.* The Bellows were beginning to clog the street and the way back home would be rough, but who cared; now everyone was rushing to Bobbie, and she was shaking but beginning to smile. Holly and Hank piled into the back of the Hummer; Michael put Patrick in there, too, and the captain was getting in the front. Michael said that he'd help Bobbie down from the roof, went to the passenger side, which was the area most cleared of corpses.

"Come on! Hurry hurry quick, we've got you!"

Bobbie put a shaky hand on her chest and sat, scooting her legs over the edge. Her coat ballooned at her waist. And she slid off.

It was Bobbie who first spotted the monster's arms shooting out from beneath the Hummer.

She was beginning to fall toward Michael's awaiting arms when her face went shock pale in the last of the dusk. She tried to turn back, to grab out, to regain the roof.

She landed between Michael and the Hummer, one ankle bowing in.

The Bellow's rottening hands grasped Bobbie's jean-clad calves.

Not happening.

The monster's face emerged from the darkness beneath the Hummer. In life it had been a girl, no more than eight years old. The Bellow opened its mouth and an insect slithered out, went up its eaten nostril.

Yellow teeth met Bobbie's pants just below the ankle: *riiiiiipp!*

NOT HAPPENI—

Bobbie's head tossed back; her spine rattled. Michael grabbed her, kicking the Bellow's head until its neck snapped and its head lolled.

He didn't look at Bobbie's face. He looked straight at her leg. No blood. *It's fine. She didn't get bit.* The denim had stopped the teeth. *A miracle.*

Then, blood.

A thin single streak of red leaked out of the hole in her jeans and began to fill her sock.

Bobbie locked her horror-white eyes with Michael's.

And as she began to scream, he clapped his hand over her mouth.

Though panicked, he felt his breath, his quaking chest.

No one was watching.

"*Don't,*" he whispered to her. "*Don't—don't tell anyone.*"

What are you doing, *Michael?!*

Bobbie's eyes shouted: *But—*

I can't let her die, Michael thought. *I should have seen that Bellow—she is* not *just going to die!*

"*Listen to me,*" he said. "*We'll—we'll figure something out.*"

Bobbie's gaze trailed down to her ankle. Total terror, that's what was in her eyes. But was there also a faintest hope?

Lie to her, Michael. Lie, hurry, she's going to die, this is a lady who's actually going to die so lie, LIE.

His stomach hurt, and yeah he felt sick, but he said the thing that activated the only chance he had:

"I have an idea. T-trust me."

Was it enough?

Michael watched her nod.

She didn't scream when he lifted his palm from her dry lips. But her mouth still moved.

As Bobbie offered her desperate face to the dying bright heart of the sky, Michael realized: she was praying.

CHAPTER SIXTEEN

"Soldier! Drive the 'Vee!"

Startled, Michael looked up. The captain's silhouette stood on the roof.

"Move us!" The captain slapped a clip into the mounted weapon, tugging back the slide. Dozens of blinded Bellows, after all, were gathering, their shadows scrawling out in the square, remaking the world in their images.

Michael numb-nodded, got in the car.

How long does it take to become a Bellow? He'd never actually seen it happen. And Bobbie's bite was small, barely bleeding, which had to help, right? Would the change take an hour? A day? He thought back to the first infected people he'd seen on Halloween. *Just* move, *Michael!* He sat down.

"How did they know to tear out their eyes?" Hank was asking Holly, like she would Google it.

Where was Michael going to drive them? *Just get Bobbie to the Capitol, then figure out what to do. 'Cause if you tell the captain, right now, that she got bit, he's so freaking "tough" that he'll just leave her.*

And what exactly do you think you *can do to help her?!*

I don't know—I'll figure it out!—I know I can. Maybe the soldiers will have a cure. Maybe we can just amputate her leg. Horrible but it might work, if Bobbie didn't lose too much bloo—

Feel—

"*Faris, take us home, goddamn it!*" boomed the voice above him.

Michael cranked down the window, answered, "I don't know the way!"

And from the back:

"Bridge, left, left, right, left"—a sniffle—*Shit!*—"right, right, movies," said Patrick.

"It'll be reversed going back, though," Michael said.

"So *do* it!" Hank squealed.

And Patrick began to reply with the correct reversed directions, but Michael spoke over him: "Bub, sit up here, Bobbie can fix her harness by herself this time, stop trying to help her!"

All at once:

"Go—"

"Faris, drive—"

"*MOVE—US—OUT—*"

Have to go, oh fug, bad bad bad, Patrick be careful!

Michael ignited the engine, wheeled a wide arc, turned the correct direction. To the sounds of screams, arms of Bellows swished in through his open window, through the open doors in the rear.

The mounted weapon above their heads, manned by Captain Jopek, roared doom.

Bellows in the headlights were spun from their shoes. Spent copper shells cascaded across the windshield.

"Go right?" Michael called to the back of the car—not because he had forgotten the directions, but because he did not know if the screams included one of pain from Patrick.

"Left, retard!" Hank cried, slamming the double doors closed.

"Right," Patrick sniffled.

Michael told him, *"Ten points!"* thought again, *How long does it take to change into a Bellow?*, swerved to the right and everyone screamed, like riders of a roller coaster that has begun to tilt homicidally from the tracks.

The new road was filled with twice as many Bellows.

Didn't matter. The captain unleashed fury like chains of fire, shot out land mines that raised roaring towers. The monsters flew, flipped into gutters, splashed through dusk-filled storefront glass and into cars, whose alarms went *REEEE!* And the only Bellows Michael had to avoid lay already dead on the ground.

Michael felt a powerful, frightening love for the captain. He looked in the rearview; Bobbie was nodding off, Patrick clinging to her, trying to shake her awake.

"Up here, Patrick!" Not loud enough, Patrick didn't hear.

Suddenly, Hank stood and pointed out the windshield. *"Plaaaaane!"* he screamed.

The sight through the windshield was so huge, so surreal, that at first its danger didn't register.

An airplane.

It was a jetliner, enormous, and it had used the street as a landing strip. Its nose had ruptured the concrete. Only one wing was visible, for half the plane was *inside* a gray building. It was the plane that had brought Bobbie to Charleston. One hundred souls, fallen from the sky; welcome to your final destination.

The visible wing was coming like a brilliant guillotine.

Michael swung the wheel wildly, knowing even as he did that it was too late.

The great steel of the wing came whistling, and struck. The

car bucked wildly on its shocks. Friction drew sparks in a fat line down the edge of the car, the shriek hideous and bright.

The captain's voice, from above, growled, *"Switch."* Combat boots materialized in Michael's window, pushing him to the passenger seat as the captain monkeyed from the roof into the driver's seat. He took the wheel and looked at Michael.

"Goddamn near threw me, you dumb asshole," said the captain.

Michael nodded. *Just take us home. Just make everything work.* Why had he not told the captain about Bobbie? Just then, he couldn't remember.

"Sorry," he breathed to the passengers in the back as they flew past the gate that separated the explosive side streets from the mine-free main roads, careened by the Busted Knuckle Garage, BEST PLACE IN TOWN TO TAKE A LEAK! And Michael did feel terrible, he felt ashamed, but he was also looking back because of Bobbie. *How much longer before she changed?*

Bobbie moaned, then slouched, unconscious, against the chest-bar of her seat harness.

And for the first time since the insane drive from the Magic Lantern began, someone noticed that Bobbie looked unwell.

Holly, sitting across from her, said, "Miss Bobbie, what's the matter?"

Beyond her, through the portholes on the rear doors, Michael could see mobs of Bellows; dozens more were out front, too. Many were eyeless, but by now the last slice of sun had slipped beneath the horizon. Even the Bellows who had not learned to destroy their sight were emerging from the city's hidden darknesses, from doorways and manholes and Dumpsters. *What're we gonna do if the captain isn't up top shooting? Omigod, what're we gonna—*

"Throw 'er out the back!" shouted Captain Jopek.

They're going to throw Bobbie out!

Hank, slimed with sweat, stood from his seat and threw open the double doors.

But he did not reach for Bobbie; he did not seem even to have noticed her new unconsciousness. Instead, Hank reached for the gurney in the back. He grabbed the sheet off the gurney, pulling it upward like a matador; the wind sucked it out the open rear door.

The gurney was loaded with grenades, which were stuck to the mattress pad and the bars with duct tape.

"When?" Hank called.

"Wait till we get 'round the corner to cut it! We got a ten-second delay on those frags. I want to clear those assholes on the bridge. I wanna watch them try to swim." Jopek's face was smiling, his voice was so, so calm. Like it was all a game.

They swung around the corner, the last one.

Hank loosed the chocks from the gurney's wheels, then yanked upward on the silver line that had been strung among the grenades: all the grenade pins flicked up at once, like bright popcorn. He thrust the gurney out the rear, where its wheels met the road, squealing smoke. A rope-tether, tied on one end to the gurney and on the other to a pole on the inner wall of the Hummer, unspurled rapidly then tugged, taut.

"Henry, my good man: cut it!"

Hank's face was hard and determined, but his eyes were also shiny with joy.

He nodded and reached for his pocket. And that was when, with slow dreamy terror, his smile transformed to a frown.

"Dropped it," he breathed to himself, disbelieving. "Captain, I dropped my knife in the theater—*THE GRENADES'RE TOO CLOSE THEY'RE GONNA BLOW US U—*"

"Aw, hush," the captain said.

Did the captain ever flinch? No. He took the handgun from Michael's lap—the same one Michael had stolen from his ankle—and turned in his seat and, only half-looking, single-shot the thick nylon rope that tethered the deadly gurney to the back of their speeding car. The severed rope zipped through the back and out to the screaming street, and a moment later the crowd of Bellows swallowed the homemade mass-extermination device whole. The explosion was huge, scorching, a great radius of blast that burst Bellows away from earth and their own limbs. The sun had set now, but for that moment the captain resurrected the day, and *his* light still had the power to hurt all the Bellows, blind or not, as much as he pleased. Holly put her hand to her chest like she was trying to push down her pounding heart. Hank reached out for Holly's hand, which she took. So everyone was looking out the back, at the captain's fire, when Bobbie opened her eyes and raised her face to Patrick, and turned into a Bellow.

CHAPTER SEVENTEEN

Michael knew that he should move. He should dive into the backseat and grab his brother.

But he couldn't. He couldn't help thinking of Halloween.

The expression on Patrick's face had been the same, then . . .

. . . *as Michael opens the door on the side of the garage, telling Patrick about The Game. Now there is the night with its smell of leaves and its feeling like freedom, and of course Patrick is afraid of the dark; but, of course, he pretends not to be. "This is so* cool, *huh?" he only whispers, and clasps his hands tighter on Michael's chest.*

And then, shattering the dark: the scream.

A man's, from the blue house across the street: "I don't know you, darlin', but you best get outta this house, pronto! You— HEY! You come at me again, I swear I'll shoot! Get back! Get baaAAACC—" A burst of sound and light from the neighbor's living room window: a woman's body crashes out through the glass, landing on the jack-o'-lantern in the concrete driveway with a sound that makes Michael's throat crawl.

Michael freezes. His brain shouts, fleetingly, that this is a Halloween prank—but then all thought comes to an end when a light turns on in his house, and he realizes Ron is coming, Mom is coming, and she is going to ask him what he is doing out here. . . .

Michael looks back, to maybe reassure Patrick. But though Patrick's frightened hands are unclasping and clasping on Michael's chest, his mouth is also fidgeting to not smile. He thinks this is The Game, Michael realizes. He thinks that lady was a bad guy. And he's trying to look brave.

Because becoming brave means something—maybe everything—to him.

And just before the front door of Michael's house opens and the night falls apart, Patrick's eyes hold a hope: a hope that maybe this time, he, Patrick, can finally be strong, even when things are scary. That hope that if he is just brave enough, he can outrun the pit inside him.

That hope that is so beautiful, and dangerous.

As the Hummer roared across the bridge to the Capitol, Bobbie's eyes widened . . . but not just to whites. Her eyes were a rapidly pooling black. It was as if the old woman's pupils had been pierced by a pin, and the darkness was leaking out.

Holly turned away from the fire behind them and noticed Bobbie again, this time recoiled instinctively and without sound.

"What the?" Patrick whispered.

"WHAAAAAATTTT!" Bobbie screamed.

Her hands curled into claws, her jaws a nest of fangs. She meant to kill; there was no doubt.

She lunged.

And with no more than a half inch between her claws and Patrick's face, her seat harness caught her, with a *click!*

Michael dove for her. His ribs struck the hard top of his seat and sang. For a terror-syrupy moment, he was caught atop the seat, wriggling.

"PATRICK, GET AWAY!" he cried, and finally thudded into the rear of the Humvee. Hank and Holly watched in shaken awe.

The monster wearing Bobbie's skin lunged again, this time throwing the harness off with impossible strength, and Patrick was just staring in confusion.

"What the hell's goin' on back there?" Jopek shouted, heaving the steering wheel back and forth as he dodged the few remaining Bellows ahead.

Michael snagged Bobbie by the arm of her coat, redirecting her momentum, slamming her to the floor. Something inside her snapped, hard and loud. Tears leapt to Michael's eyes, his stomach going hot and loose.

The wind was shrieking with each swerve of the car; the rear doors flapped and zoomed, back and forth.

"What—what—what—" Hank kept repeating.

Without warning, Patrick burst into tears, collapsed onto the floor.

"She got bit, oh Christ, she got bit somewhere!" Holly cried.

Everything was screaming. Everyone knew.

Bobbie squirmed beneath him like a weasel in a sack. But her eyes: they hadn't turned all-black like Bellows' eyes yet. Thin white strands still remained in her eye sockets, and the dark and light in her eyeballs were churning, as if warring for domination of Bobbie's body.

Bobbie, in her own voice for one millisecond, said, "Michael?"

She's not all-dead yet—oh God, maybe we can still figure something out. We're almost to the Capitol, just hold her down, just for a few more seconds—

Michael called out, "Hank, help me, hold her—*Hank!*"

But in that moment, roaring again, Bobbie's hands flew up and shoved Michael toward the sucking door. He grabbed out blindly, and somehow snagged underparts of a seat, stopping on his back; he could feel the vibration of the tires beneath him.

Bobbie stood again, seeming to flood the compartment, huge in her hunger. An image rose, unbidden, in Michael's mind: *let her come, grab her again, throw her out the door.*

Because you can't save her, Michael's mind hissed, and the hopeless thought flooded him with a new variety of terror. Bobbie had been kind, utterly good, but she was going to die, this was her ending. And there was no controlling that.

And as despair struck him in the endless milli-moment, Michael pivoted out of Bobbie's path, caught Bobbie by the left shoulder of her coat, and spun her, flung her perfectly into the jump seat mounted on the door.

"Michael—" said Holly, her voice quaking and teary, "do you need help?"

Michael ignored her, slamming the roller-coaster safety-bars down on Bobbie's shoulders, incapacitating her at least for the moment.

"Bobbie. *Bobbie.*"

He smelled her breath: stale and old.

In the dueling blacks and whites of her eyes was a slowly dawning recognition.

"Are you there?" he heard himself say, from far away.

There was a sniffle behind Michael. From the floor, his chin trembling, Patrick asked Bobbie, "How come you're being *mean*?"

Bobbie blinked.

Her eyes went normal-white again.

She touched her face.

And burst into tears.

And then the captain was stopping the car at the statue of Abraham Lincoln, opening the rear door.

He didn't holler or rage. He only gently motioned everyone to step out to the fenced-in rear promenade of the Capitol, like a slightly tired crossing guard. "Bobbie, girl, you come on out now. And I mean nice and slow."

Michael felt himself step down out of the car. "Captain, can't we wait?" Michael said. "Do you have to do this?"

The captain just nodded.

Michael felt the pain and terror from Bobbie and Hank and Holly, circling in the air over their heads. He felt Patrick's confusion. He was even vaguely aware of everyone, himself included, following the captain's orders to go into the Capitol. At the top of the great stone steps, Hank opened the double doors. Patrick, still sniffling, whimpered, "Michael . . . what's he gonna do? Michael, w-what happens if a Bellow bites you?"

Holly took Patrick's small hand with her big one. Michael looked at her with an almost painful gratitude. She was silent, though, and didn't look back as she guided Patrick inside the Capitol.

Michael didn't follow. From the top of the stairs, he looked back down to the captain and Bobbie, beside the camouflage Hummer. Michael noted numbly that the buffer-zone gates in the barrier fences were all open, even though the captain had never stopped, tonight, to unlock them.

Bobbie was clutching her stomach.

Suddenly, she bent over from the waist, dry retching.

The dark sky with its scud of stars seemed low, suffocatingly low.

"When'd you get bit, girl?" asked the captain.

Bobbie retched once more. As she leaned back up, her gaze flicked to Michael. She looked back at Captain Jopek.

"On top of the car," she rasped, her voice hoarse and weak. "While you were inside."

Why is she lying?

She doesn't want Jopek to be mad. She's protecting me.

But you *couldn't protect her. . . .*

"Why do you ask?" Bobbie said to the captain. And the same

expression came across Bobbie's face that had come across Patrick's earlier: hope. Was it always so hard to look at?

"Captain," she went on, "do you think I might be all right? Do you think the soldiers can reach us and help, somehow—"

The captain didn't answer. It was unclear what he *was* doing, pacing calmly away from her, boots clocking. Then he seized two handfuls of the chain-link fence.

He tugged, and the section of fence ran along its tracks, shutting in front of Bobbie's face, locking her out. Far beyond her, from the other side of the downtown bridge, figures in the dark steadily approached and steadily moaned.

"Ain't nothin' nobody can do," said the captain. He cocked his pistol. "Shit. Damn, Bobbie Lou, what a mess. I swear to God: I'll make it quick."

Tears glided down her face. "Wait," she said softly.

"Can't talk me out of this, girl."

"I *know.*" And for that moment her voice was strong again, her anger beautiful with its vitality and life.

Bobbie raised her eyes, away from Jopek: her gaze pointing to the low stars. She was speaking to something she could not see. Was praying going to make this better? Michael wondered desperately. Was it—?

The gunshot flashed and illuminated Bobbie. She had no time to scream. Captain Jopek of the United States 101st turned in the starlight, watching Michael with eyes like guilty verdicts, the gunshot still echoing through the night, through Michael's screaming heart.

CHAPTER EIGHTEEN

Michael undocked.

That was how it felt: one moment, he was an inhabitant of his body. And then he was floating into the Capitol.

End. Dead. Thanks for playing.

Screams, in the black of Capitol rotunda. Hank, screaming. His white shirt glowing like a spirit. Hank kicking out and striking the pirate-patched head of a bronzed governor, sending it ponging between cot legs, away into the dark.

Somebody turned out the lights.

The hall's only illumination was coughing out of the tripod fluorescent light-banks. They were knocked over, thrown on the floor. . . .

"What the HELL!" Hank was shouting.

Grief, Michael thought. *The world is full of dead people, and that is the first grief I've heard.*

"What the HELL IS THIS?! DAMN IT! GOD! DAMN IT! GOD!"

Everything looked oddly unhooked. A wind through the door could knock this building into the sky.

"Hey!"

Michael turned.

His brother was running to him, dashing as fast as a little boy who is rounding third and heading for home. *But this isn't home. No, this isn't home* at all. A wave of homesickness, sharper than any he had ever felt, threatened to overwhelm him.

Patrick collided, hooping Michael's waist like steel, hugging him with fierce need. And for some reason, the homesickness felt so much worse.

Across the hall, Holly sat on a cot, her back locked straight, her eyes big and dully hard, like unpolished glass.

Patrick said something into his right thigh, the skin tickling there. Michael looked down, which seemed to take a very very long time.

"Is Bobbie gonna play, still?" Patrick said.

Michael watched his brother from the far theater of his own skull. He knew that he should flick out a lie, a comfort. But all that came to his mind were funeral scenes from games like *Gears of War.*

She was a good grunt, a damn good one! Raise your guns to her, men! She'll be missed!

"Where is she?" asked Patrick.

Michael said, "She's out."

And now the hugeness of her death seemed to send a dizzying kind of vertigo to his heart. She was dead. Away away. Call in a thousand doctors; collect a million med kits; none of it would help. *Jeezus, it is not fair that she died.* That was a stupid thought, what everybody thought when anybody died. But that didn't make it untrue.

If I'd just seen the Bellow . . . If I'd just been quicker . . . Bobbie would have been fine, Michael thought. *And maybe she wouldn't have stayed out there by herself at all if it wasn't for me trying to make her feel better.*

"But how *come*?" Patrick said.

Michael lifted his head, began taking in other things around him. Their shapes and meanings vague at first, like pixels seen too up close. He looked at the walls. And understood that Hank's screams were not totally grief.

During the captain's "mission" into the city, his Capitol had been invaded.

Crucifixes glimmered on the walls. Letters flickered in the twitching light, like runes.

GUIDE OUR HAND, ALL MIGHTY WRATH. Shadow. GOD O WE BEG FOR THE SON. Shadow. THE SON O GOD GIVE US THE SON. WE SACRIFICE

WE SACRIFICE ALL

WE SACRIFICE OURSELVES TO YOU

Michael swooned with distant horror, because he realized that the markings slashed across the walls were red—and the red did not look like it was paint.

The Rapture are sacrificing each other *now,* he thought. *Not just other people who try to hurt the Bellows.*

'Cause, you know what Rulon is doing now, Michael? He's changing the rules. You know how he's making his followers believe that they can be saved?

Just look at the walls.

He's making them feel their blood.

"What's 'out'? Why? Bellows aren't s'posed to h-h-hurt people," Patrick was saying. He was not even trying to hide his rising anxiety. "Was Bobbie hurt real bad?" He grabbed his right ear and twisted on it once, hard.

"Bub, don't—" Michael said.

Patrick lowered his hand, but his chin still trembled. "I l-l-like Bobbie, she said Mommy was going to see me soon. Where's Mommy?"

"They were here, Captain!" Hank said, striding past Michael. The captain had entered from the night, through the double doors. "The Rapture. Bastards came and broke right in!"

"What gave it away, Detective?" the captain said softly.

Hank blinked. "The walls—the—over here, see?"

The captain looked at Patrick, trying to smile sadly about Hank's stupidity or something.

"There was a letter nailed on the door," Hank said. He handed Jopek a closed envelope, which was addressed like this:

TO THE DEVIL IN CHARGE

Jopek took it, half interested. Nodded. "Class-A move with that knife in the car, by the way."

Hank frowned, blushing and wounded.

Suddenly, Jopek whirled, drawing his weapon, and firing into the darkness of the hall at his back.

"I see you, sumbitch!" he shouted, and his machine gun belched a ten-second, sweeping burst. The gun flashed the empty halls, the rotunda, the dome above.

As randomly as he'd begun, Jopek stopped. "Checking," he muttered. "I think they're gone. But, shit, they broke into my base, didn't they? Got past all the land mines and into my city, didn't they? Even stole the weapons in the fence maze, I saw. Bet they stole my caches in the Capitol, too. But yeah, I sure reckon they're gone now. I reckon they don't wanna screw with ol' Jopek—GODDAMN YOU—"

This time, the captain's bullets were not random: Jopek hollered like a fury of thunder, accompanied by lightning from his own hands, shooting out the chain that held the chandelier within the dome. The chandelier plummeted past the balcony by which they stood, shattering in the well of the lower level.

"Sore loser," Michael whispered huskily to Patrick. But suddenly this rotunda felt very small.

Holly stood from her cot, moving closer to where the rest of them stood, in front of their panting protector.

"You think they took all our other guns?" she said.

"What'd I say?" the captain replied petulantly.

"So . . ." Hank said, a question in his voice.

So is it safe here? So when do we leave? But Michael said nothing. He didn't want any attention on himself right now. Or any questions about Bobbie.

"So . . . do we need to do anything with Bobbie?" Holly asked when Hank didn't go on.

The captain shook his head. "She's in the Kanawha, now."

The image of Bobbie's body, floating in the Kanawha River among six-pack rings and coal-dirty water, sent grippy rolls of nausea through Michael. He felt Patrick's arms tighten on his waist, questioning. He felt it, but ignored it, trying to think of what to say, what to do.

"So we should go," Patrick said.

The captain looked at Patrick. Michael looked at Patrick.

"The bad guys are coming. And Bellows're . . . bein' jerks. We should *go*, duh."

"No, boy, ain't nowhere we're goin'. Ain't nowhere but bed."

"Sleep?" said Hank, a little incredulous, even angry. It was the first time Michael had heard him speak to Jopek with anything other than absolute respect. *"Here?"*

"Hankzilla, cool down," Holly said. She touched his shoulder, and there was real *care* on her face as she calmed her brother. "The captain's right. We are all shaky right now. And we aren't sure what's going on yet, with anything."

"We know the frickin' maniacs are stealing our shit!" Hank said. "And we know *They*'re starting to tear out their damn eyes and move around in the day now!"

"But we don't know *why*," Holly said. "We're safer here than anywhere; we can put new locks on the gates for tonight, and—Look, I am burnt. I am tired, and I want to lie down. And I want to cry. The morning is when we can figure things out." She looked to the captain. "Right?" she said, then added, "Sir?"

The captain held her gaze.

"Absolutely," he said simply.

They stood there, their remade halls rising into new darkness around them and ringing with sounds of the Bellows approaching in the night, and it was a moment Michael would remember for a long time: when he looked back on that night among the wicked graffiti, the night before so much changed, it was the moment that seemed to sum it up.

Because Hank said, "You're right."

Patrick said, forlorn but cooperating, "I'm hungry."

No objections. No fights.

"So y'all best get on to bed. Me, I got some securin' of the perimeter to do."

No one is asking why the Rapture are attacking now.

Or why Jopek made us go out.

"I just got one question," said Jopek. "You helped Bobbie down, yeah, Mike?"

Michael's pulse butterflied in his throat. Slowly, he nodded.

"Did you know she was bit?" the captain said.

They watched him. And what Michael realized was, there would be no good in telling them the truth. The words would leave him and become theirs, and everyone would put together the wrong puzzle. They would only see a reckless, skinny kid who'd grabbed the captain's gun. A kid who'd put them all in danger by trying to save Bobbie, and to what end?

Michael shook his head. "No clue."

"None? Genius," Hank scoffed. Hank was going to apologize for questioning the captain by being mean to Michael.

But to Michael's shock, Jopek only said, "Take the man at

his word, Henry." He rubbed the back of his neck, his forehead crinkled in what looked like pain. "Shit, we got a lot ahead of us now, but I'll guaran*tee* somethin' we ain't gonna do: rip our platoon apart, not trust each other. Now y'all get to sleep. Things'll look brighter tomorrow, guarantee you that.

"Anyhow. Like Michael said. The soldiers will be here soon."

CHAPTER NINETEEN

Soldiers will be here soon. The words, clanging and swooping inside his head. *Like Michael said.*

Patrick lay down on a cot in the Senate chambers later that night, the tips of his hair sharp with water out under the edge of his WVU wool cap. Their previous bedroom, the lieutenant governor's office, had been ransacked by the Rapture. Black night dipped in through the windows: this side of the Capitol was a face turned from the moon, and the objects cast across the floor—an iPod, two toy guns—were only weird buoys floating disembodied in the dark. Hank's vague form, far away on a cot, shifted. Wind like a far train in the halls.

Michael pulled Patrick's blanket to his armpits, to let him tuck it under himself the way he liked. But Patrick didn't.

How long do you think until that unit gets here? everyone had asked. *What road were you on when you saw them? Are you sure you don't know?* Not in so many words, not in words at all. But building up to words, which Patrick would hear and be confused and frightened by: Michael could hear it in the way their breath kept pausing as if on unformed sentences. And suddenly, barely, Michael got an idea: "I'm going to give Patrick a shower." They had, after all, not had a real one in weeks. They had, after all, earned it, getting to this, ha-ha, Safe Zone. Hank had still been asking questions as Michael carried Patrick away.

Who was it that said people need hope?

It was Bobbie.

When Patrick stripped in the showers attached to the Capitol's weight room, the rodlike appearance of his ribs sent a black surge of helplessness through Michael that nearly made him shake. Patrick's hands were going up to his ears, and Michael knew that he was going to begin scratching at them, yanking at them, and Michael looked in his eyes and saw a flash of what Patrick saw—him, bewildered and depressed and scared—and understood what he *wanted* to see instead. So Michael "slipped" on the shower's clean tiles until Patrick smiled. His smile was no more real than Michael's.

While they were showering, Captain Jopek sneaked into Michael's frightened mind. In his imagination, Jopek placed the cold eye of his pistol to the back of his head. *"If you care 'bout Bobbie Lou so much,"* he whispered, *"I'll be glad to send you to her."* Michael knew it was not real, but he turned again and again, almost expecting to see the captain pixelate into existence from the shower mist, like some grim phantom coming to issue judgment and death.

Michael sat down next to Patrick's cot. He noticed dust on the blanket and brushed it clean. Brushed it, brushed it.

"Michael?" his brother said.

"Well, better hit the hay," Michael replied too quickly. He stopped brushing the blanket, couldn't figure out where to put his hands instead. His thighs.

Stop looking at me, Patrick. Stop trying to figure out how I feel. You won't like it.

"Are you gonna talk to the Game Master tonight?" Patrick

said hesitatingly. A bitter, frightening laugh tried to rise in Michael's throat. "Will you ask him why's he lettin' the Bellows change? And the cheaters keep cheating? And what we're gonna do tomorrow?"

"Sure."

And it won't matter.

"Time to sleep, though. Do you want a pill?" Michael said.

Patrick hesitated, obviously divided.

You didn't need one last night, when you thought I got us safe, Michael thought.

After a moment's pause, Patrick nodded.

Michael got the Atipax bottle from their bag, angling it so that Patrick couldn't see how few were left. Two more pills after this one.

Patrick stuck out his tongue and carefully put the pill on it. A little water dribbled down his chin as he drank from the Red Cross plastic water bottle. Red crosses. Madness written on the walls.

"Thank you," Patrick said, wiping his mouth.

"I'm sorry," Michael blurted. Couldn't help it. *I'm sorry I don't know what to do. I'm sorry that I didn't realize that the Safe Zone didn't mean The End. Sorry we're in this room, breathing the same air as these people. Sorry you want to be like me. 'Cause, what exactly do you think you'll be if you* are *like me?*

"Sorry . . . I snapped at you when we were going to the movie theater," Michael finished.

"No, you did a good job, Gamer!" Patrick said. His face was a mask of enthusiasm. And right then, Michael realized something. Lying on an abandoned cot in the dark heart of the Capitol and all of its false promises, Patrick was not pretending to be brave or to feel okay.

Patrick's trying to make me *feel better.* Michael's face prickled, a burn of shame. *Michael is my protector,* Patrick had always thought. *Michael is my own Safe Zone.* But that image of Michael was breaking apart.

Who are you, Michael? he seemed to be secretly asking. *Who are you, and what's going to happen to me?*

Patrick turned onto his side, facing the window. *Turning away because he knows I'm upset. Sleep tight, don't let the Bellows bite, Bub. But they will in your dreams. Because you think I can't protect you. Because—*

"Do you know what a jack-o'-lantern is?" Michael said.

Patrick rolled back to Michael after a reluctant pause. "Pumpkin," he said, his brow knitting, rubbing his nose on his sleeve.

"R-right," Michael said, nodding in what he hoped was a thoughtful fashion. "But do you know where they come from, I mean?"

Patrick answered, "Walmart?"

"Ha, no. They're actually this tradition from Ireland. People used to believe that on Halloween night, ghosts came back to earth." *You're gonna scare him, idiot.* "They believed this 'cause they were newbs," he added.

"See, the Irish people thought that ghosts would go from house to house on Halloween, so—"

"Ghosts eat candy?"

Michael barked laughter. A sleep-mutter and a creak of springs sounded from Hank's cot across the room. It felt wonderfully warm, wonderfully whole, to laugh like that.

Patrick's face brightened a little.

"No, Bubbo, ghosts don't trick-or-treat. They can't hold the bags, for one thing. Ectoplasm all over the candy. Buzzzz killll."

Patrick's smile, touching his sleepy eyes, felt even better than Michael's own laughter had. Actual fact: it wasn't even a close call.

"So yeah, we got Ireland, dead folks, Halloween—"

"Heh. It's funny," Patrick said. "Monster stuff coming on Halloween. Like in The Game."

Michael blinked. *Jeezus cripes,* he thought. *Yeah. Wow.*

He felt that feeling of things *syncing.* He thought of the church, of the hot-air balloon rising out of the night. He understood that Bobbie would perhaps have said that the feeling inside of him was the voice of something supernatural: a whisper emanating from some secret, tremendous Power that commanded everything that had happened in this world and everything yet to arrive. Michael had never believed in that sort of "God" before Halloween—and he certainly didn't believe in it now, after Bobbie died so hideously, so unfairly. But he didn't quite know *what* the feeling was. He knew that it was a little scary, a little out-of-control. But (perhaps because the feeling overpowered the pain) Michael didn't push the feeling away.

He rode it. Like a dark wave.

"Yeah," Michael whispered, *"the ghosts did come back on Halloween. They came to possess living people. They used living bodies, like people-suits. But do you think the Irish wanted to be taken over?"*

Patrick shook his head, happily engaged.

"Right on, duder. So they found a way to trick the ghosts into taking over something else," Michael said. "Because the ghosts were looking for a warm body . . ."

The words hung there, Patrick looking confused.

"Warm body with a face . . ."

"A jack-o'-lantern!" Patrick exploded, like a kid yelling BARNYARD BINGO!

"Hey!" Hank hissed from his cot across the room.

"Hey-hey!" Patrick replied. To which Hank had no retort.

"Yep: jack-o'-lanterns. Like guards, to keep things safe. And Bub, guess what we got right here?"

Michael pointed out the window; they could just see it, the crest of orange-bright canvas on which snow fell. The jack-o'-lantern hot-air balloon.

Patrick finally slept.

Bub had just begun snoring when a hand grabbed Michael by the shoulder.

He flinched, the springs squeaking beneath him. But the person who grabbed him wasn't who he'd been afraid it would be.

"*Good evening,*" Holly whispered. He could smell her citrusy gum, but he couldn't see her expression: his own shadow obscured her face. "There's something I need your help with," she said, and cocked her head toward the door, silently leaving the Senate chambers before he could answer.

He thought: *No, I shouldn't go. I shouldn't talk to anyone. I'll have to just lie more, anyway.*

But Michael couldn't help it: he *wanted* to follow Holly.

The windows in the hallway looked out on the courtyard of Government Plaza. Michael saw that, for the first time since he'd reached the Safe Zone, Bellows had breached the defense systems on the bridge between the Capitol and downtown. Two dozen or so monsters—who must have gotten in through the fence's "buffer zones" before Jopek could relock the gates—roamed freely in the fence maze.

Holly stood by the last window at the very end of the hall, looking outside, the moon so strong that she cast a shadow. Michael hesitated momentarily again, thinking it would be better to go back, but then walked on.

"*Hey,*" he whispered as he reached her.

Before Holly turned to him, she started a polite grin. The grin never made it to her eyes—although Michael got the sense that she was trying very hard to *make* it do so. "Hiya," she said, not quite meeting his gaze.

There was a long silence.

Michael said, "Sorry, um . . . you *did* want me to help you with something, right?"

"No. Yeah, I mean. Kind of." Holly gave up her not-smile and shook her head in aggravation—*at me?* "Sorry I'm weird. Shit." She didn't say it with her usual self-deprecating jokiness, though: she was being mean to herself. "I saw that you were awake, and I was thinking I could change that dressing on your neck for you," she said. And before Michael could respond, she opened a door across the hall into a small fancy-ish sort of break room.

Disappointment settled heavily in Michael's chest. *Well, what the hell did you expect her to want with you?* He'd just been thinking of their possibly flirty conversation yesterday, how good it felt to experience a distraction from the horrors of the "paused" world.

"Over here, if you please," Holly said, pointing to an over-stuffed chair.

Michael stopped in the doorway. "You know, don't worry about it."

"No worries, won't take two minutes." She pulled a stool next to the chair, opening a first aid kit.

I don't want to do something that's "good for me" right now, Holly. I don't want to "take care of myself." I want to just be with you.

"Holly, I can do it myself, really—"

"I know you can," she said, her voice shaky. "But I really would like to be able to do something useful right now."

For the first time since leaving the Senate chambers, Holly's gaze met his full on. What he saw there was sadness, confusion, fear about everything that had happened today.

He offered tentatively, "I guess I'm just a little nervous it'll hurt."

"Huh?"

"Yeah, you might not be able to guess this, Holly," Michael sighed, "but I am a man haunted by a tragic bikini-waxing incident."

He watched her frown relax, warmed by the joke. "Oh no, I totally got that vibe from you. It felt like bad manners to bring it up, though."

That slightly too-big smile momentarily spread over her face. That smile pierced Michael, somehow; there was something about it that was so open, so unguarded, that it let out a little of the heaviness in his chest.

He sat down in the chair. A window in front of him overlooked a dark alley; he watched Holly's reflection in the black glass as she scooted closer to remove the square of tan tape holding the cotton to his neck. Just before she did, Michael thought, *This is the first time a girl ever really touched me. Yeah, okay, maybe this getting-scratched thing isn't so bad after all, ha-ha.*

Except that Holly made what looked like a disturbed face. "How's the war wound lookin'?" he asked, trying to sound light, though suddenly distinctly insecure about his neck's physique.

"A little inflamed . . . ," Holly murmured. "But it's fine, I'm sure. I know you figured this out already, but scratches aren't really a danger. The virus doesn't transmit through anything except bites.

"*Okay, mister, prepare to be zapped,*" she whispered, and pulled, fast and hard, on the adhesive. Michael grunted. "You are welcome," Holly said. She rooted through the first aid kit in her lap.

"So. You're pretty good with the science-y stuff."

"You're pretty good with the flattery-y stuff," Holly chuckled. "But I'm not so good. Mostly, I just repeat what my daddy taught me."

Michael saw Holly's reflection smile. In the dark glass, the expression was difficult to read, but something about it became strangely distant.

"He's a doctor?" he said after a pause.

"Pharmacist," Holly replied. "But, like, a fancy kind. This'll be cold; that's your warning."

She gently circled a cool, sterile-smelling cotton ball over his neck. "But, yeah, the virus—do you mind if I geek out a second and tell you about it?"

Michael shook his head, happy to hear the eagerness, even excitement, in her voice.

"Rad! Oh Nerd Joy, you are one of the things I miss most about the world Before."

I don't miss anything from Before, Michael thought.

"So yeah, the dead-people virus: It's a *new* virus, obviously; you don't see the dead rising every flu season. Like Hank was saying yesterday, a lot of people think the virus is man-made— maybe in Iran, because of the war."

How can people do that to each other? But after everything he'd seen at home, maybe cruelty shouldn't surprise him. "God . . . ," Michael said.

Holly suddenly took a deep, nearly angry breath. "If God is around," she said shortly, "maybe He should be trying harder." She breathed hard again. "Like, Christ, with this shit with Bobbie . . ." She stopped herself, then said, "Hold this," and taped a new cotton square to his neck.

Her voice sounded far away, as if already mentally deciding what to put where in the first aid kit. *Bring out the awkward: "Well, thanks" and "So, yeah."*

"So yeah," Holly said, "we should probably get back to bed now. I don't think the captain really wants us walking around. You and I should totally hang out tomorrow, though. Did that bandaging ordeal hurt as much as you thought it would?"

Michael held in a sigh. He didn't want the respite from the

crappy world to be over. "Nah," he said.

"Tell the truth," said Holly.

"You'll be hearing from my attorney."

"Heh. But . . . thanks for this, Michael," she said. Seriously, no jokiness at all. "It was really sweet of you."

Michael made a "no big deal" gesture, and bent over to move the stool out of his way to hide his blush.

They went out the door and headed back to the Senate, and Holly was saying, to fill the quiet: "Yeah. So. The virus. The government was working on a cure. The CDC, the Centers for Disease Control, basically the FBI of the germ world, they even had this lab in town. They had to keep moving the lab to different places, though; people kept trying to overrun it and get the cure for their infected families. The CDC scientists were supposedly on the verge of getting a working formula that would reverse the virus's effects on the brain. I don't know how soon after getting bitten you'd have to take the cure for it to work; the scientists were hopeful, though. But then Charleston got overrun. I don't know if the CDC even was able to get the 'cure' out of the city during the crazy evacs." Holly sighed. "Anyway—it's hard to make a cure, because viruses evolve and go through mutations."

"Like how a cold changes all the time?" Michael said.

"Exactly, because a virus's job is to survive. So it keeps changing, but on a deeper level—that's my dad's fave phrase: 'on a deeper level'—it's not changing at all. It's becoming what it already is. The environment becomes hostile; maybe antibodies are introduced, new proteins or something. So the virus does what viruses do: it adjusts. But it's not reacting, because what it mutates into was already a part of it. Coded, like a secret, all along."

They were walking past windows: light and shadow.

"But what's it heading toward?" Michael asked. "Like, does it have a 'goal'?"

Holly nodded. "I guess, sort of, it's heading 'home.' Viruses do that literally, sometimes: there are some that actually make infected animals migrate to the place on Earth where the virus originated. Which gives me the jibblies. But even if it doesn't do *that*, the goal of every virus is to 'go home' to itself: to make the ultimate, purest form of itself. It's why the Zeds' behavior is changing, why they seem to be growing . . . not smarter, but savvier. Like you said, they tore out their eyes, they're just using sound now—which, *holla*, dork points for figuring that out. But yeah, as with every virus, this one is evolving to its most powerful-slash-purest form."

Michael asked if that form had a name.

Holly said, "The endgame."

Michael stopped, a few feet from the Senate. That odd, soaring feeling again—like things syncing together. *Like . . . clockwork.*

"What's up?" Holly asked. "You okay?"

And now was as good a time as any to admit how much he liked her. In the long, empty, snow-lit hall, it would have been easy to imagine that they were the last two people left on Earth, that he could just say good night and see Holly tomorrow, and continue his limited-time crush at the world's most bizarre sleepaway camp. And maybe that was cheesy pop-song stuff, but to Michael nothing felt false about it. It was right then that Michael understood, in his bones and heart and breath, that this moment was what he'd wanted: to be just a normal teenager, to not have to worry about anything other than the mystery of a cute girl's feelings for him, to just let an adult instruct and protect him.

And Michael could not stand it.

Now that he had reached this endgame, he realized he could not stand feeling regular, smiling breathlessly at his own minor-league daring. Going back to his Senate bed would be safe and not-scary, because he would be following Jopek's orders instead of this "what-does-she-think-of-me" feeling. Yeah, it would be not-scary, but here was a true fact about Michael Faris: right then, he *missed* danger. He missed the type of recklessness that somehow also made him feel safe, the kind he dashed into blindly, trusting only that he would feel his heart and breathe his breath and smile his way out of it.

When he replied, "I'm fine. I don't think I'm tired yet. Do you want to maybe hang out right now?" he felt sort of terrified, because one: she was beautiful, and two: he wasn't, and three: Jopek, who'd seemed unhinged earlier, might catch them.

But mostly, at last, a little *yes-yes—that* was what Michael felt.

"Absolutely," Holly said. Genuinely happy. Almost like, despite Jopek's rules, she had been wanting him to ask.

Which was, of course, The Best Thing Ever.

So after they ran through the marble halls that sang with moonlight and rang with calls of Bellows, after they reached the rotunda with the ruined chandelier, after they jokingly high-fived the rows of governor statues—after all that, Holly opened an oak door padded with leather, identical to the one at the other end of the hall, and whispered, *"Welcome to the Capitol Sanctuary."* Pews and a pipe organ, and no cots or postcrisis clutter. "They used it for state funerals and stuff. I think they sealed it after things got awful-awful. The captain actually had to move a coffin out of here and down into somewhere in the Capitol's basement—that kid who died in a coal mine, remember? Cady Gibson. But it's just beautiful in here, you know? Anyway, what do you wanna do?"

In a movie, the hidden meaning of the question would be something like: *baby, let's smooch.* But he didn't think it was now. Anyway, he didn't really *have* anything in mind.

Michael shrugged, his heart pounding from running and from nerves.

Holly thought a second, then she wove through the pews, to a podium at the front of the sanctuary, flicking the microphone it held with a fingernail.

"So. Everyone," she said in a game-show-host voice, "welcome to *The Holly Hour*! Tonight's guest is a very special friend of mine: Holly. Holly, how have you been?

"Not so bad. Just hanging out with dead people.

"And how is that?

"I find them beautiful.

"Is that so?

"Especially their skin.

"Because it's beautiful?

"Because it's a-peeling."

Michael chuckled, did a rimshot.

Holly faked an awkward pause at her joke, pulling an "eesh!" face to a "camera."

"Now, our next guest here in West Virginia is a guy who hails *all the way* from West Virginia. Please welcome Michael . . ." She gave him an expectant look.

"Oh," he said. "Michael Faris." Holly's *"Come on down!"* applause echoed in the chamber as Michael walked to the front of the Sanctuary and sat in a fancy priest's chair, a few feet from the left side of the podium.

"So Michael." Very "Oprah" solemn. "Tell us about yourself. How old were you the first time you got pregnant?"

And for the next couple minutes, sitting there after curfew in this secret sanctuary, Michael joked with this cute-hot girl. Which felt kind of enjoyably risky in itself: he kept checking the sanctuary door out of the corner of his eye, making sure that Jopek wasn't coming in. And he really did want to impress

Holly, to keep the conversation light, so that she would see the purposely-and-perfectly-selected Michael.

Then Holly said, "Now, let's get back to something we started discussing before the commercial break: what *are* the things you miss about the world Before?"

"Um, how 'bout you first?" Michael said, keeping his tone casual.

"I miss knowing what I'm gonna do every day. I mean, I don't miss *class*, necessarily, but I miss knowing I have class, and then I have lunch and more class, and then I have Quiz Bowl or Mathletes or Readers' Regime—Michael! Don't laugh! A-hole!"

"I'm n-n-n—" Michael chuckled.

But she was laughing, herself, and her smile was somehow even more open than usual. It was a little like a live wire. "I miss who I got to be in class," she said, playing with loose wood paneling on the podium. "Because now . . . okay and maybe this'll sound cocky, but whatever—it's like I'm still *smart*, but who cares? Not that I want all y'all to worship at The Altar of Muh Brain, but I liked being that girl. It's like with Hank, though: that kid makes me in*saaane* sometimes, but I also feel sort of profoundly dreadful for him, 'cause I don't think he really knows how to *be* in this world. He was so cool in school, and—not that this is the world's great tragedy, granted—he's kinda trying to figure out how to feel okay without coaches telling him what to do, you know? That's partly why we were so relieved when Jopek found us. We had this soldier who was going to protect us, and then we'll get to the Richmond Safe Zone, and . . . and if the CDC did make a cure, everything will get back to the way it was before."

A thought hit Michael, and it hurt. *You wouldn't have liked me in the world Before, Holly. I don't even think we would have ever talked to each other. My only friends were 1) people on Xbox LIVE, 2) my mom, and 3) my little brother. And my*

*main hobby was trying to rescue them from their awful lives.
I didn't do such a hot job of winning that game, either, so yeah,
you could say I'm still a loser.*

She pulled the piece of wood paneling off of the podium and
flicked it at Michael. "All right, mister, your turn."

Just keep it light. Michael began: "I miss being in school, too,
definitely. . . ."

But the sentence didn't finish itself.

Something odd was happening inside him: he thought,
with surprise, *I—I don't want to lie anymore. I didn't come
for that.* He'd believed, a moment ago, that he'd sneaked to
the sanctuary to *yes-yes* his way out of things, to feel nervous
but in control, too, with the "danger" being the dance of what
pieces of himself he let her see. But he didn't want to look
in Holly's eyes and just see his puzzle reflected back to him.
Tell her.

"No. I—I don't miss Before. At all," Michael said.

Stop, Michael. It's going well, don't eff it u—

"I ran away," Michael said. "On Halloween."

"What a cliff-hanger! More in a minute after a word from our
sponsors—"

"I mean it though." *God, what am I doing?*

Holly blinked at him. "Whoa, wait—really? Like, from home?"

Michael nodded, and she responded, "Okay . . . ," sounding
cautious but not unkind. And that settled it.

The more he went on, the realer it became. Holly listened,
not interrupting as he told her the CliffsNotes version of Ron:
Ron was the one always pushing Patrick into the psych hospital; Ron was the first person Michael had ever hated, a feeling
that was enormously mutual, and so big between them that
it had to come out somewhere, and one time it came out of
Ron's fists.

"Sorry if this sounds weird," Holly said gently, "but why doesn't your mom just leave?"

"Because that's just what she is, you know? It's like, when The Game started, Patrick and I called the Zeds 'Bellows,' because 'bellow' is what they do. And Mom is someone who can't leave someone who loves her; she's someone who needs to be rescued. And I just realized, if I was quick enough, I could rescue her. . . . But . . ."

Michael had no idea why he was telling Holly this; it just felt important that he do so.

When he paused, Holly asked, "When what 'game' started?"

"I lie to Patrick, about everything. To protect him from this thing one of his idiot doctors called 'Freaking.' Bub just disappears into himself. I tell him everything is a Game; that this whole *world* is all a Game."

"Wow. So that's why he feels so safe with you. I can see why the kid loves you so much."

But Michael suddenly felt sadness and an incredible loneliness. He wasn't so sure Holly was right about Patrick. In a way, Patrick didn't really *know* him.

He guessed Patrick worshipped him.

And there was a difference—huge, he sensed—between worship and love.

"Anyway, on Halloween," he went on, "Bellows crashed the party, and Mom comes outside and . . ."

". . . and?"

Michael gulped.

And shut up, Michael, he thought. He'd felt almost sure that there was a point he had to make, something vital in the retelling, something that he was missing . . . but he just felt exposed, now.

Holly tried to meet his eyes, and he felt his blood.

He said, "Ron came out; Mom wouldn't get in the car. That's it."

"Michael . . . that is so *hard*, man. But you know that it's not, like, your fault, right?"

"Right," Michael said noncommittally.

"No, listen, you are not even slightly allowed to feel bad about that," she said earnestly, leaning forward, her eyes intense. "Getting to Charleston, protecting your brother? I'd say you're sort of amazing. And things are going to work out, the soldiers will be here any day, and then . . ."

Michael nodded, his chest hurting.

Holly noticed how upset he was, and said, "You know what? I'd like to share something with you."

Now she moved out from behind the podium, through the pews, through bars of moony snow-light, her skin like smooth milk, and he followed her, until they reached a patch of darkness, and her hand floated through space and found his hand, and his heart was alive in his throat.

A ladder was set against the wall, stretching up toward a recessed balcony. "You first," she said, and when Holly followed him, he took *her* hand, helping her from the ladder. He noted, *First Initiation of Hand-holding.*

"It's quiet up here. Why, I don't know. The Zeds' screams don't seem to reach—I guess because they're all out in front of the Capitol. And it's kind of generally wonderful up here, don't you think so?"

The balcony *was* generally wonderful. There were seats for an audience facing out over the bowl of the Sanctuary, but behind these seats was a wall of glass, which looked out on the Kanawha River. It was the river that ran from one tip of Michael's West Virginia map to the other, the connective tissue through coal towns and McMansions, gathering pieces of the poor West Virginia and carrying them to where less-poor West

Virginia could pick them up. The river was polluted, of course, and Bobbie was there now, but you couldn't tell. The Kanawha only shone like a black ribbon, its surface spangled with the reflections of star points, as if the heavens momentarily had come to earth.

It would be easy to pretend the world was a world without the Bellows. And as Holly sat beside him, Indian-style, a warmth spreading in his skin when their knees touched, Michael understood that this was the gift she was giving him: a little piece of a world that made you think the whole thing was different.

The world can *be different,* Michael thought. *I don't have to let myself and people I care about get cornered. I don't have to pretend that someone else is going to save me. I can leave, and this time, I can take* all *of us.*

"I think we need to leave Captain Jopek," Michael said. "Soon."

Holly looked over, confused. "What? Why?"

"Because he's dangerous, Holly. He never should have taken us into the city so late. It was pointless. And I swear, I think Jopek made us go into the Magic Lantern because he was pissed at me for questioning him."

"That . . . doesn't sound right, Michael," she said.

Yes, it does. "Even if it isn't, though, Jopek is letting us get cornered. The daylight doesn't stop Bellows anymore, who knows how long it will be before they get through the barriers outside? There are more Bellows here all the time. Jopek is being stupid. I *never* let Bub and me get cornered when we were out there by ourselves. We can take the Hummer and get out of Charleston, and the . . . other unit, the one I saw," Michael said, feeling a twinge of guilt and regret for having to lie, but pushing it down. *It'll be worth it in the end,* he thought. *I'll get us to the Safe Zone, and we'll all be safe.* "They've gotta be close. But even if we can't find them, the other Safe Zone is just across the border to Virginia."

Holly looked not at all convinced.

"Holly, you've *never* thought that there's anything weird about Jopek?"

"Well. I don't know, maybe he's too bossy sometimes. But that's probably just the army, y'know?"

"No, I don't think so at all," Michael said. "I don't know what it is, but when I look into his eyes . . . it's like I'm looking over the edge of a pit. Even Bobbie said, 'It's like there's a secret in everything he says.'"

Michael saw Holly flinch a little—because of the mention of Bobbie, he supposed.

After a moment, she said, in a light tone of voice that Michael didn't quite buy, "I guess I've thought the captain can seem a little weird sometimes. Let's make a deal, Michael: if you get me a week's supply of food, a gun, and a charger for my iPod Touch, I am in on this road trip."

Michael nodded, wanting to push for a more serious *Yes*, but Holly looked out the window, and he saw her face become that same, strange—hurt?—faraway thing that it had been after she'd mentioned her father.

"Do you think," she asked, in a soft voice, "that things happen for a reason?"

"Huh?"

"Do you think that they work out 'like they're supposed to'? Bobbie thought so. Even though the world is so messed up, she told me she really felt like things would be okay, if you held on to hope, that Something was in control. When I couldn't sleep, she'd, like, pray for me. She said praying could . . . not control things, but help them. Sometimes I felt like her praying did help me sleep, so I gave prayer the old daughter-of-an-agnostic-scientist try. But I never heard any voice or whatever. This sounds crazy, Michael, but I just wish, so bad, that I could know if Bobbie still believed things happen like they're supposed to, after she got bit. I wish she could tell me that she did, that even though the worst possible thing happened to her, she still felt like there was a reason to hope. I . . . I think she would. I don't know about God or anything, but I definitely believe in hope. Because even if awful-awful stuff happens, sometimes out of nowhere, there's okay stuff, too. Good stuff. Kind-of-great stuff."

Holly looked at him. The river chopped. Michael's heart thudded.

"Like . . . what?" he said.

And although the truth burned from her eyes to his, Holly only shrugged.

Michael took his second shower of the day. This one cold. Very. As arctic as he could fuh-reaking stand.

And against the pelting freeze of it, his mind spun, clocking like a magnetized needle on a pool of oil seeking out its North.

The first *yes-yes* truth came to him at 11:47 p.m.: *some part of Holly still wanted to believe in Captain Jopek.*

Why?

For some reason, Michael suddenly thought of Jopek's eyes flashing in the darkness of the Magic Lantern, so much like those mannequins in the pews and aisles of the Coalmount church.

First escape plan, 12:03 a.m., thought up en route to the Capitol Senate: *Since Holly might not want to leave Charleston, we can just hide somewhere in the city.* Yeah, Michael and Holly and Patrick (and Hank, if Michael could convince him) could find a building and barricade themselves, and wait for the soldiers to return from Richmond and rescue them.

There's a whole city out there, Michael told himself.

But his blood sped in his excitement and he sensed, immediately, the lie in that.

The Capitol was moated by gates and locks and the Kanawha River; all other roads apart from the main ones were tacked with mines; there was not a whole city for him.

There was this building.

There were these blood-splashed, echoing halls.

How the hell did I not realize that?

That thought felt frightening. *Good.* Michael focused on the fear.

And stood at the starlit windows of the hall and gazed across the empty city. He imagined the city and the mountains around him as a vast electronic pixilated videoscape, its surface teeming with countless characters . . . before being cleared with an apocalyptic swipe of a virus's god-hand.

Reset.

Michael thought of the wasteland gamescape, where two sprite figures—he and Patrick—encountered a man, a huge-rendered soldier: a man whose mere existence seemed to promise to keep them safe. He was, after all, a guardian, in the old world. He was a protector, a good guy, by all the old rules. He was, after all, supposed to be The End.

And suddenly, Michael understood:

The eerie magnetic hold that Captain Jopek of the First Division of the Crapocalypse had over the others came not from their stupidity, not their fear, but their empty idea of the future. It came from not realizing that they were clinging to an endgame—"A soldier will save us"—from a world that no longer existed.

Michael had once believed there were two West Virginias, one composed of coal towns, the other of cities.

But the truth was that *no* West Virginias existed anymore. The state from Before was simply gone, and in its place there was only a blank slate, a void.

That was a truth that Michael had known, somehow, since the Halloween moment when he saw his first Bellow, and took the reigns of the apocalypse: this was a new world. And what was a world, in video games or in life? It was an arena on which you placed an avatar: an image of yourself.

But everyone's still trusting their old pictures.

No, Jopek was not the saving soldier who would be found at The End.

Jopek was the accidental idiotic survivor of a war that he was convinced was his destiny.

And who are you, Michael?

I'm the one who can save us. I'm a Gamer. And the Master.

So what are you going to do?

I'm going to remake the world.

And after that? I'm going to beat that world.

Day 25:

First date ever. (I think.) Went well. (I think.)

Also:

I know why Jopek's eyes look empty.

He's lying to himself.

He believes that he knows best. That he's The Man

In Charge, even though the world changed around him.

"You ever feel like you were born for some special

greatness?"

Like the mirror-eyed mannequins in the Coalmount church, the captain looked so much like what he pretended to be that it was hard to tell the difference. Until you looked very, very closely.

And then it was the clearest, most *yes-yes* thing in the world.

So I am going to lie, Michael thought, and grinned to the

jack-o'-lantern in the secret dark of the Senate chambers. *I will lie to save Patrick and Holly and Hank, and leave.*

Tomorrow.

Tomorrow, Captain, you get your next mission. You're going to become part of The Game.

CHAPTER TWENTY

"What's a Betrayer?" Patrick asked.

Michael gripped the metal bars on the end of the gurney and ran down the hall. Patrick, sitting cross-legged on the gurney, whooped for joy and wrapped his hands around the sidebars.

"It's what the Game Master said we have to find today," Michael explained.

"Yeah, but—waaaaahh my *butt tingles*!" Patrick shouted as they rumbled over a patch of busted marble.

"The Betrayer is the reason The Game's been all weird, Bub," Michael said. "It's a person who's not playing by the Rules. He's someone who looks good, but isn't. The Game Master wants us to figure out who it is, so he can't mess up The Game anymore. And guess what, duder? After we find the Betrayer, we're road tripping to the real Safe Zone."

"The Game Master said so? He said we can *really* go to The End this time?" There was hope on Patrick's face, but Michael's heart ached at the skepticism and worry that were also there.

"He promised. And we'll do whatever it takes."

"Michael?"

"Yeah?"

"Ya-ya."

"Ya-ya."

So that was the first thing Michael did that day.

"Hank. My *man*," he said, an hour later. Hank stood at a urinal in the bathroom.

"Faris," said Hank coldly, "do you notice the piss I am taking?"

Michael nodded, raised his palms up: *my bad!*

He leaned against a stall, sucked the strings of his hoodie, waited until the pee-sounds stopped. Then said, "Man, the captain can shoot, but his handwriting sucks, right?"

Hank went for the sink. Their eyes met in the mirror. "Huh?"

"So the note he left *you* wasn't messy, too?" Michael said.

The implications of the question settled on Hank's face. He looked like a fangirl who has asked for her favorite singer's autograph and received a "maybe later, babe." Michael actually felt a twist of guilt, remembering what Holly had said about Hank last night, but he couldn't help but feel a *yes-yes* satisfaction that his lie was having the perfect effect.

"What did it . . . what did yours say?" said Hank.

"To talk to him, later, where he sleeps."

"I don't think that crazy asshole *ever* sleeps," Hank replied, trying to sound like he wasn't upset about Jopek's "snub." "I heard, uh, Michelangelo never did, either," he added.

"And the note didn't even say where that *was*, which is super nice," Michael said.

Hank raised his eyes, quickly, and Michael was suddenly afraid he'd overplayed his hand.

Hank squinted for a long moment, then dropped his stare moodily. "Governor's office, Faris, if that's what you're here to ask me." He left the bathroom, his broad shoulders hunched so low that Michael felt sorry for him. Aaaaalmost.

* * *

Michael had been in some semi-exciting situations since Halloween.

But as he jogged past a headless governor and climbed the rotunda stairs, he decided that the best had been Halloween night, before the first Bellow appeared across the street from his house. In those seconds, there was only this: his brother, his plan, and his total control.

That was the first time he had ever felt that way.

Except. Right. Fuggin'. Now.

The marble stairway, which curved wide and stately around the rotunda, overlooked Government Plaza. A snowstorm was swishing against the windows. Fun weather to drive in, if you could get the right car.

He became aware, as he neared the governor's office at the end of the empty hallway, of his heartbeat. Heavy and somehow thick, yes, but perfectly calm and even.

Michael mentally replayed what he was going to say if Jopek was there, then knocked twice on the double doors, lightly. Ron's voice echoed in his head: *You always want to knock on my door, Mikey. Because then I can come out. 'Cause this is Ron's den, and believe me when I say:* You *can't come* in.

"But hey, Ron, if I did that, how would I have stolen the money to pay for, uh, running away?" Michael whispered.

He waited there a few seconds more, feeling that anticipation like waiting for a game to load the next, last level. Then he opened the door.

Stormy half-light poured through the great plate of glass on the opposite wall.

Whatever Michael had expected a governor's office to look like, this wasn't it.

It wasn't oval; it was about as big as his principal's office; there *was* an American flag, and a West Virginian, but they lay tipped, crisscrossed, on the floor. Maps spilled off a humble desk and across the carpet. He recognized a map of Charleston: like Hank's, almost all the streets had been X'd out in red.

There were no cots or couches in here, not even a rumple of blankets on the floor. *I guess he* doesn't *sleep,* Michael thought, half-joking. But the thought made him uneasy.

Michael went to the governor's desk and got his first surprise of the day. He had expected—he wasn't sure what. A struggle, anyway, before finding the extra keys.

CAPT. H. C. JOPEK, he saw, stitched in fraying black thread on one end flap. The shoulder strap snaked lazily over the top, which yawned wide, like an open mouth.

The captain's canvas bag.

No, I don't pray, he thought. *But sometimes? My prayers come true, anyway.*

Michael opened the flap, and heard, unmistakably, a muffled key-jangle somewhere inside the bag.

He palmed aside a *Playboy*, and all at once, he became aware that he had left the door to the office open. He suddenly imagined Captain Jopek hiding behind the door, crouched there like a dark troll beneath the bridge of a castle, and now Michael's palms broke sweat and he plunged his hands deeper into the bag but he only found one old walkie-talkie, three maps, no keys. *Don't freak out,* he thought, but the keys weren't in any of the side compartments, either, and Michael thought, *Oh God, I just imagined the jangle.* He swallowed. Noticed a tiny, zipped pocket on the front of the bag. And when he opened it and slid his hand inside, he finally did hear the sound of the keys, yes, but another sound, too, not the keys and definitely not imaginary.

"Reckoned I'd find ya here."

The light through the window seemed to go cold on his clothes. *Don't spin,* Michael thought. *Don't scream.*

"Hi!" he said, turning. There was a method to moments

when you've been caught. You didn't want your smile to look too guilty and give away the extent of trickery. But then again, looking *not* guilty, when you're obviously off-limits, rang alarm bells, too.

"Got a secret, Mike," Jopek said. The captain's bright, excited face shone like a searchlight. And for a horrifying second, Michael thought Jopek was questioning whether *he* had a secret.

"Don't you got an itch for what it is?" the captain said.

Why isn't he asking why I'm here? Michael thought, but said, "Absolutely. What's up, sir?"

"I was on the walkie this morning, tryin' to raise up the units, out there in radio land." Jopek grinned at his wit. He walked closer, halved the distance between them. "And do you know what, fella? There I am with my coffee like always, and this mornin I *did* get a call. From some mountain folks who had tales to tell."

Jopek's smile crackled, so wide it looked as if his flesh could split.

"Mikey, c'mon, you know what I'm gonna say, ha-ha! I got in touch with the soldiers you saw, boy!"

A round rim of his bike tire, flying over the edge of the world, had seemed to suck free of gravity. The same feeling as now: cliff-fall vertigo.

Made it come true, Michael thought wildly, his vision puckering dizzily at the edges. *I made it real.* He kept his smile, but he could not stop the blood from boiling to his cheeks.

"Yep, they're 'bout thirty miles out, oughtta be here by tonight," Jopek nodded. "Told 'em take their time: me and my troops will make sure the roads they need to get into town don't have any mines on 'em."

Was the captain joking? Lying?

And then, arcing like a flare: *No! Telling the truth! Real unit, coming!*

"I know we had our differences, buddy. Yesterday, I was pissed at you, I won't lie. But I'd sure be glad to have you come out to town with me today. I mean, just think," Jopek said sincerely, "your mama's gonna be so happy to see you."

And somehow, Jopek's attempted emotional manipulation gave Michael a gift of focus; a power-up, he thought. Calm washed over him again.

Here are two warriors, playing a game, and both are lying. I don't know *why* you're lying, Captain, but I know that you are. And actually, know what? I think I do know why. You know that *I'm* lying about the soldiers, don't you? Maybe you've always known. You want to make me feel safe, want to make me feel like help is coming, so I'll trust you . . . and then you'll make an excuse. "Oh, the soldiers changed their minds, sorry." "Oh, let's keep camp here, like I was sayin'. Those monsters and those Rapture ain't nothin' that ol' Jopek can't handle."

"Sir? I couldn't find—" someone said.

Jopek swiveled toward the door. Holly had been entering hurriedly when she stopped short. Her eyebrows flicked up, surprised to see Michael.

"Well, here he is. And good timin'. This storm's really kickin' things up. If we're gonna get goin' . . ."

Jopek shrugged: *then we better.*

Captain Jopek was leaving the room, already drawing his key ring from his belt. Finally, Holly looked at Michael, and though it was dangerous, *because* it was dangerous, before Jopek even sailed out the doorway, Michael reached into his own pocket, grabbed the keys he'd stuffed there, and held them up for Holly to see.

CHAPTER TWENTY-ONE

But she didn't smile.

She wouldn't even look at him. Not when they corralled Patrick at the rotunda, not when Jopek asked Hank to stay behind and be watchman in case the Rapture returned, not when Hank looked outright depressed that Jopek was taking Michael along instead of him.

Not even when they went outside to the rear Capitol steps, and everything got so weird.

"What the!" Patrick said—*shouted*, actually. He had to, it was so loud out here.

Past the Abraham Lincoln statue and the deflated balloon tethered to it, two hundred eyeless Bellows roared in the falling snow and pushed en masse against the security fences that ran on both sides of the Hummer. Last night, Jopek had relocked the fence systems on the bridge after the Rapture's invasion; Michael had seen only a couple dozen Bellows on Government Plaza afterward. But somehow the monsters had found a way across the downtown bridge, and they penetrated every layer of the security barriers, except for one final double layer of chain link. He saw, with whooshing relief, that the Hummer's escape path through the fence system was still intact. But the final layer of fencing was bulging dangerously with the force of the Bellows, and Michael could hear more Bellows on Government Plaza around the corner of the Capitol—"more" as in "freaking hundreds."

"Them tricky bastards started comin' in from the river last night!" Jopek said. He looked almost excited, like this was a fun, new challenge.

Michael looked at the enormous Kanawha River, past the Hummer and the fence. The river had seemed like peace itself last night. Now Bellows were churning past in the current, sinking and then surfacing downstream, screaming white jets of water into the air. And by luck or something worse, some Bellows *were* ending up on the shore, *were* shuffling toward the fences, as if trying to gain the Capitol.

Michael pictured the fences popping like over-tight wire. *We have to get out of here. Like* now.

Jopek, whistling, strolled down the marble steps toward the Hummer, walking needlessly close to the rotting hands shooting through the fences. A Bellow with a LeBron James–caliber reach swiped at him, smearing green goo on the captain's right shoulder. "Open wide, honey," he said, and—without looking—unstrapped his ankle pistol and shot off the Bellow's jaw.

Michael called to Jopek, "Captain, why can't the soldiers clear the roads themselves?"

Jopek put the pistol in his belt, cocked a hand behind his ear, grinned, "What's that? Couldn't hear ya."

"Is it really safe, Michael?" Patrick said over the din. "It's really how to win?"

"'Course it is, Bub!" Jopek shouted, apparently hearing just fine now. "C'mon, now, buddy—let's get *The Game* started!"

The blood pulled out of Michael's face. He felt his windpipe close to the size of a pinhole.

How the hell does Jopek *know about The Game?*

Hearing the captain speak the term Michael had created to protect Patrick—created to protect Patrick from monsters, and from people just like Jopek—felt like a violation.

"Okay!" Patrick called brightly, relief in his brother's voice. Relief, Michael thought, because *someone else* told him that he was safe.

As Patrick practically skipped to the Hummer, Michael glanced to Holly. She had bluish circles under her eyes—as if she'd stayed up late last night, talking to someone after she and Michael had parted.

"Holly," he whispered, *"did you tell Jopek about—"*

She walked away, down the steps, got into the rear of the Hummer.

Michael, seeing no choice now that Patrick was excited, followed. But when he boarded the Hummer, he saw Patrick crawling through the sliding slot, to the front seat.

"Hey, Bubbo, what're you—"

Jopek loaded into the driver's seat and looked back at Michael. "Thought it might be neat for him to ride up front. I'll make him buckle up—standard Game procedure, right, ha-ha?"

Patrick grinned at Michael.

Jopek snapped the sliding plate closed before Michael could say anything.

Outside, the sunlight pulled free through the storm for one split second. Bellows moaned, as if in approval.

What. The hell. Is going on?

"Holly, why did you tell Jopek about The Game?" Michael whispered as he strapped himself into the harness across from her. He felt as if Holly had somehow handed Jopek a

weapon. Maybe that was just paranoia. But that was only part of the reason that he felt so stung. *Holly, I trusted you,* he thought.

"Just to be careful," Holly replied. "I didn't want Jopek to say anything that would make Patrick realize this isn't a game."

"Taking care of Patrick is *my* job, Holly."

"But why would you even risk someone saying anything that could confuse Patrick, since we all live together in the Capitol?"

"We're going to *leave* the Capitol."

Holly turned away from him, looking out the window of the rear door, stripes of shadow and light flowing over her face as the Hummer moved forward. She murmured, "Yeah . . ."

Oh man, Michael thought, afraid suddenly. *You didn't change your mind about leaving, did you?*

As Jopek drove them across the bridge, Michael's chest tightened once again: Bellows on the ledges were throwing themselves over the guardrail, down into the Kanawha River chopping far below.

"What's going on?" Michael whispered.

Holly didn't look.

The city mutated, Michael. Everything did.

"Holly, we should not *be in this city anymore."*

The panel to the front slid open; the captain called, "Comfortable back there, lovebirds?"

Patrick chuckled.

The panel sliced shut.

Michael began to bite the nail of his thumb, stopped it at his lips, put his hands to his thighs, realized his hands were blotting sweat.

He had outsmarted a thousand living dead with a station wagon and rusting gun, but he hadn't felt this choking-terror feeling for weeks.

Captain Jopek took the main roads into the downtown grid.

Perhaps as a result of the Rapture's infiltration of the city's defenses last night, Bellows now roamed freely even on these previously secured streets. Jopek sped every few seconds, rammed into the Bellows, laughed. But bizarrely, as the Hummer progressed farther into the city, the number of Bellows in the streets actually decreased, until there were practically none at all. *What are the Bellows doing? Are they all going to the Capitol? Or the river? Why?*

It doesn't matter. I'm still going to get us out of here.

You don't know what's going on. You didn't think of any of this.

Through muscling will, Michael pretended he wasn't here in the Hummer. He was an avatar in a video game, waiting for the next screen to load. *Because that's what's true: this is like a game, and you're in control of it. You are. Do you freaking hear me? This is just a game and you are the Game Mas—*

The car stopped.

The sliding panel between the rear and front compartments was still closed, save a thin slit. Michael peered through. Jopek was speaking to Patrick, gesturing with his hands. His head looked so enormous next to Patrick's.

Michael leaned closer, trying to hear what they were saying over the loud engine—hoping, in fact, that Patrick might look back and smile, and Michael could draw just a bit of confidence and strength from his little brother's image of him.

Patrick suddenly tossed back his head and burst out laughing at something Jopek said.

Jopek affectionately ruffled Patrick's hair.

Patrick low-fived Jopek, looking as happy as Michael had seen him since Halloween.

A thread of jealousy and low panic stitched through Michael. But he dismissed it. Patrick wouldn't *really* change, not without getting to the Safe Zone ending that Michael and The Game had promised. Patrick wasn't capable of that. Definitely not,

Michael tried to tell himself. Definitely not.

A moment later, the rear door swung open and light crashed in.

They were in the parking lot of a shattered shopping center: Kohl's, a Christian bookstore, RadioShack, Little Caesars, lots of FOR RENT signs. Mountains loomed in one direction, the skyline in the other: the captain had brought them to the final edge of downtown. A few Bellows staggered about under the swinging stoplight at the exit of the lot, a hundred yards away. But the Bellows were separated from Jopek's Humvee by an obstacle course of Hummers and tanks positioned throughout the parking lot. The number of military vehicles in this seemingly inconsequential parking lot seemed bizarre, but Holly didn't seem to react at all. Jokes came to mind about why the vehicles were here—a sale on "tank tops"—but Michael said nothing.

"I thought we were going to make sure the roads are clear," Michael said.

"Just got one last place left to search, big boy," said Jopek. Affectionate and buddy-buddy, but Michael sensed a sharp edge under the smooth voice.

Past a pair of overturned, silver-trailered army trucks sat the only non-raided building in the lot: an enormous and shockingly well-preserved Walgreens pharmacy. Jopek led Michael, Patrick, and Holly to it, stepping over a few sandbags and several truly dead corpses clustered beside the trucks.

He put a couple bullets in the Walgreens's door lock; a kick took care of the rest. "This here's the last place on my list to look for any survivors before the soldiers get into town," Jopek said as everyone followed him in. "And maybe someone could pick up some A-t-i-p-a-x, how's that sound? Faris, you shop for us."

Jopek thrust a cart to Michael. It rattled quickly. Michael tried to catch the handlebar one-handed, but it hit so hard that the cart lurched sideways, hitting his foot. "C'mon, Faris, be a team player."

Jopek turned away to the heart of the store, cocked his hands on his hips. "Attention, Walgreens customers!" he crowed.

"*Cuuuuuuussst . . . eeerrrrr . . .*" The Bellows' echo. It came from the rear of the store, flattened by layers of doors and walls. The idea of being in a building with Bellows, after yesterday, seemed insane.

"Ready a-go?" Patrick said happily. "The captain and I are going to explore, okay, Michael?" A genuine request for permission. That made Michael feel better.

Jopek said, "Patrick's gonna come 'round with me. Boy in this world should learn to fight. *Has* to. Otherwise—well, s-h-i-t."

"Yeah, to be honest, I'd rather he not go *looking* for Zeds."

"Hey, you let him wander 'round coal towns with ya, huh? Let him crawl under a bus, he was tellin' me."

"Always in eyesight," Michael said, cringing at the childish defensiveness in his voice.

"'Course, he *must* have been safe 'cause you got them magic, protectin' eyes. Ha-ha, just teasin'!"

Michael felt a kind of low rage, suddenly wanting to throttle the captain. But he pushed down his objections. If Michael wanted to get out of here he had to speak to Holly about what was going on . . . maybe even about how to get away from the captain. And Patrick *would* be with a man with an assault rifle, which meant he would not be totally unsafe. "Right," he returned the smile. "Go for it. Hey, just don't do anything I wouldn't do."

"Doing what you wouldn't do," Jopek called over his shoulder, walking down an aisle, "is the whole point, kinda."

They all—Holly included—went.

Michael stood.

Scared. Nervous. Embarrassed. Confused.

And, then: royally fugging pissed.

He swiveled on his heels and marched, gaining speed, the cart's wheels squeaking to a higher and higher pitch. He propelled himself down not the medical aisle, but the food ones; he held out an arm to the shelves and let it knock in protein bars, mints, crackers, a plastic barrel of pretzels, baked chips. The glass doors of the drink cases at the end of the aisle were webbed with cracks that had let out the cold, but who cared, Pibb Xtra and Red Bull don't go bad. He stuffed the child seat with the cylinders of pure, sweet, awesome sugar explosions that Patrick loved best.

Who does Jopek think he is? He think he can just jab me around and never be jabbed back? Who does he think he freaking is?

Michael, turning from the drink cases, touched the Hummer keys in his pocket like a talisman, and shouted, "Whoa, I bet you could live for a *week* on all this food!"

And that's enough, right, Holly? Okay, maybe you had second thoughts, but once I show you all this—that I do what I say, that I can do what I want—that'll be enough, right? You'll let me save you, right?

"Liiiiivvveee . . ." called the Bellows in the parking lot. They had begun winding closer through the field of Hummers outside.

Doesn't matter. Move.

He rattled back down the snack aisle, by the book racks, celebrity magazines flapping in his wake.

At the checkout counter, Michael grabbed Reese's Peanut Butter Cups with jack-o'-lantern wrapping, some Peppermint "Batties," and a display's worth of 5-Hour Energy. He grabbed a pair of new aviator sunglasses for Patrick off a spinner rack, put them in his pocket.

The cart was now packed half a foot high.

Andbutso, now what? He drummed his palms on the

handlebar, his eyes going closed, trying to find his pulse. *So get it out into the car.*

He thrust the cart toward the front exit. It powered its own way and stopped between the anti-theft sensors. *Now . . . now get Patrick and go out to the car—*

Except one thing—

—kinda a biggie—

How are you gonna get Patrick out without Jopek being suspicious?

He couldn't. He knew he couldn't.

A triple-burst of gunshot leapt from the rear of the pharmacy, silencing a Bellow. A double burst followed, a single shot, another triple. How long before there were no more Bellows back there to occupy the captain?

Outside, a scud of phantom-colored cloud loomed over the sun, casting a pallor over the aisles like early twilight.

3:27. Jopek was going to come out front and announce their departure. 3:28.

"Holly?" Michael said. No reply.

Feel your blood.

He did.

And it told him the logical, pure truth: there was nothing he could do.

Standing there, his heart a fierce coil in his throat, a sudden bloom of despair nearly overtook Michael. Why had he thought he could take control of this? *Why* had he thought he could escape a captain in the army? *Good one, Mike. Tell us the one again about the tank tops.* It was just like what Holly said about the virus, his life had returned to where it had come from: his and Patrick's lives, commanded by a man who did not play by any sane rules.

No! Michael thought. *I am going to get us out of here!* But that voice rang hollow.

"Holly?" he tried again.

Not even a Bellow responded.

Do you pray? No, I don't. But maybe I should, because those maniacs in the woods do, and even they can control their lives more than I can. So, yeah: God, if you're not too busy figuring out where to put all the people who showed up recently, HELP M—

And he became aware that he was being watched.

The lot outside was grim with shrouded sunlight. He turned and turned. There were no monsters near the storefront yet; but goose bumps nonetheless lit across his arms and neck. A few deer were cantering peacefully just outside. They were arranged, the three of them, in a triangle. And they seemed, instantly, a family. The spotted fawn sniffed the cement with a kid's curiosity; the mother doe's eyes warily flicked over the bodies on the ground. The buck led them. It had power, you could see that; its muscled shoulders and thighs looked thick and fast and beautiful. The sharp spread of its antlers gestured, somehow kingly, with each stride.

I saw you two nights ago, Michael thought. *Or something like you. At the cliff. Right before I almost fell off, I did.*

That sensation: like clockwork behind a curtain. Filling Michael now. Like *yes-yes*, but not. Stronger than *yes-yes*. Beyond it.

Michael realized that the sight of the deer was making him hold his breath.

He tried to let it out softly, but dust hitched his throat. He coughed.

The doe's and the fawn's heads sprang up. They eyed Walgreens. He felt certain that they couldn't see him because of glare on the glass, but he froze, for some reason. The clouds, however, did not: they gusted, spilling sun, so the fringe of the deers' coats looked momentarily lit on fire, like cave paintings of majestic creatures of a higher world. Their own sudden shadows frightened them; the doe and fawn fled across the parking lot, weaving like spirits through the disinterested Bellows now emerging from the field of tanks.

The buck remained. There seemed to be a field of *power* emanating from it, almost humming. Its moist snout blew two strong plumes of breath. Its coal eyes held the glass.

Michael told himself, *It's just looking at itself. It can't see in.*

But no. No, he felt that the animal was staring at *him*.

Chills, not entirely pleasant, powered across Michael's skin. He stood in stunned silence, mentally and physically frozen. *I didn't see the cliff coming, and there wasn't anyplace left to run . . . but I still survived.*

Was it possible . . . something *was* helping him? Was that real, or was it him *hoping* it?

He felt a quickness of warmth fill him: small at first, a candle in a cave; but it grew. In truth, it began to torch. There was no reason that he should feel good. None. There was no clear path for escaping Jopek right now.

And yet . . .

And yet, Michael suddenly knew: *I'm going to get us out of here. Somehow, I am.*

He jumped when Holly yelled, "Captain! Not here!"

She was in the rear of the store, behind the pharmacy counter, just past the glass condom cases he always pretended not to notice when he went to a pharmacy with Mom.

Michael took one last glance back at the buck.

It was gone. Must have left to find the others.

How do you know you can get out of this, Michael thought, shaken a little out of that nearly eerie silence.

Because . . . he answered, smiling, *because that's what I always do.*

And then he was dashing down the aisle to the pharmacy, not even caring that the keys were tambourining in his pocket.

He slapped his hands on the white pharmacy counter. *"Hey,"* he greeted in a whisper.

Holly had been looking at a door with a square of darkened glass that led to the storerooms. "Oh. Hey," she said, trying to sound friendly, then turned away again. *"Capta—"*

"Heyshutupwaitwait," Michael hissed, scrabbling over the counter. He came down on a collection of empty pill bottles, half-skated on them. He reached Holly and without thinking, put his hand over her mouth.

"Can I *help* you?" she said, muffled and angry. She shook her head out of the muzzle, leaving Michael's hand slimy.

"Sorry, but please don't yell for the captain."

There was a scuffy sound beyond the door—the sound of steps moving over spilled boxes and coming closer. Sounds of Patrick talking to Jopek. *Hurry.*

"We're getting out of here," Michael continued. "Grab some Atipax and we are gone."

"What?"

"I'm going to tell Jopek I got an alert from the soldiers, on the radio in the Hummer."

"That's . . . not gonna work, Michael."

"The food is ready, though. And I've got the keys."

"He'll just get on the radio and check—"

"I'll drive away before he can—"

"He'll take the keys—"

"He doesn't know I *have* keys—"

"He will if you say you used the radio *in the car!*"

"So I'll say something different, I'll figure it out," he said, stringing the moments together, *riding* the words as they sledded from his mouth, not sure what to say until he was hearing the words, too. And God, it felt right, *yes-yes.*

"Michael," she said emphatically, *"I'm not leaving."*

"Why?"

Another firecracker string of gun bursts, this time closer, this time accompanied by a strobe, visible through the dark glass. He heard Jopek laughing.

Jopek called through the closed door: "Searched all the rooms, Holly! It ain't here!"

"What 'ain't here'?" Michael said to Holly . . . and in that moment, something flashed inside his head: Hank crying and saying, *What if the captain can't find it?*

"What are you looking for, when you go on these 'missions,' Holly?" he said. "What is it you and Hank want the captain to find?"

All the defensiveness, evasiveness, and forced friendliness that she'd used that morning evaporated from Holly's face. Right then, she was just the self that she had shared last night. The kind-but-frightened self. "I . . . don't know what you mean."

What does she want more than anything? "Is it your dad? Is he still somewhere in Charleston?"

"What? No, he's not in the city," Holly said, and Michael knew by the surprise in her voice that she was telling the truth.

"Whatever it is, I can find it for you, too. I can help you better than Jopek, he's an idiot—"

Holly snapped at him, "Stop! You're not perfect, either, Michael! You got scratched!"

He physically drew back, his face stinging with surprise and hurt and shame. Suddenly, all the good things from their time together deflated inside him.

He could see that she instantly regretted her outburst, but it didn't make him feel any better.

"I'm not trying to hurt you," she said. "Honestly, I didn't think you'd go through with this 'leaving' thing. I like you, Michael: you're funny and you're kind, and one day, I swear to

God, you and I *will* go on a road trip together. But . . . you aren't a soldier, and nothing you say to me right now will turn you into one."

There was a kick at the stockroom door and it flung open and the sight that was revealed made Michael feel, for a moment, sick, because Patrick peered through the night-vision scope that Jopek had unclipped from his gun, and Patrick held it with only one hand. Because his other hand was holding Jopek's.

A thready blue mitten in Jopek's fingerless, blood-spattered glove.

Jopek's happiness was so ugly.

"Roll 'em out, doggies," Jopek said, and Patrick laughed, "Arf!"

Michael spluttered, trying for time, "I gotta use the bathroom."

And Jopek said, "Funny guy," and Patrick delightedly nodded: *he* is! The two of them left the counter, went down the makeup aisle. Holly followed, avoiding Michael's eyes, arms folded over her stomach. Disappointment rose in Michael, and yes, anger, too, but there was something else, worse, something he could immediately name.

He felt . . . betrayed.

Cloud cover had resumed outside. The day was the color of gravestone.

The silhouettes of Patrick, Jopek, and Holly had stalled at the glass, gazes angled upward.

Michael jogged toward them. "What's going o—?" he began.

"They're. All. Hiding," hissed Jopek to Michael. His eyes were wide. And for the first time since he had met him, Michael thought he was seeing Jopek's true feeling: fear.

Jopek said: *"Rapture."*

A mound of shadow, on the roof of the Little Caesars facing them across the parking lot, shifted. And it sprang.

The assassin rose perfectly between LITTLE's faded-orange T's.

The obese man wore only camouflage pants and a plain black T-shirt. He had swept-back, coal-black hair. And in that infinite moment as he raised his weapon and prepared to unleash war, Michael recognized the assassin. He was the Weeping Man from Rulon's church: the worshipper who had decapitated all the corpses his priest said did not deserve to rise from the dead.

The Weeping Man now held a grim cross, a metallic crucifix, hallelujah hallelujah.

No: a crossbow.

Michael curved his arm around Patrick's chest and fell upon him like a fire tarp, both of them still tumbling as the first arrow burst through the wall of glass like a sword through water, and Michael felt—*oh God!*—the sting.

And there was blood on the floor, blood on the floor, whose . . . ?

CHAPTER TWENTY-TWO

Something had cut him below the left knee. The arrow's triangle head was pinned to the polished tile floor. Beads of red on its tip. The thin, black shaft above it nodding lazily.

Heyo, lost some health points, he thought with a brain that seemed roughly seven miles away from his skull.

From far away: "—back!—fall!—"

And then, pain.

Shot! he thought. *I'm shot!*

I let myself get shot!

The world snapped back in sudden, close high-def. The blood. Holly hiding a couple feet away, behind the spinner rack of sunglasses.

"Michael," Patrick said, half underneath him, and Michael registered something in his voice he did not like. "W-w-w-why is—?"

Why is we under attack, why is there a man with a weapon above the midget who says *Pizza pizza!?* Why is there more shadow-people standing up on that roof now and even more coming through the parking lot, and Michael, why is you lying there like a frog pinned to a bull's-eye?

Another arrow screamed toward them with a building whistle, flying through the hollow air where the glass had been. The projectile struck the checkout counter and ricocheted up, smashing an endcap of cookie jars.

Jopek was crouched at the counter, his back against the candy bar racks. Now he roared up like a freight elevator, firing a sweep of bullets that splashed out several windows, then aiming, truer, single-shot, at the assassin.

The C in CAESARS popped, a shattering bulb.

A second shot, and Weeping Man went twitchy. He pawed his neck, shaking his head, tipped forward off the roof, and he all at once was shaking his head in denial of his free fall. Hallelujah, hallelujah.

A thud.

"Faaaaall baaaaack!" Jopek shouted. It was a good thing he was shouting. There were, after all, a half-dozen men screaming on the Caesars roof. There were shadows on four-wheelers and motorcycles speeding across the twilit parking lot. And there were Bellows that had finally navigated through the maze of tanks and Hummers and were now only fifty paces away from the Walgreens storefront.

"FAAAAALL!" the monsters called.

Yes, fall back. Oh, awesome idea. Oh, put on your boogie shoes, Michael. "Scoot, Bub," Michael said, desperately pawing backward into an aisle, afraid of standing . . . and finding he was unable to stand. In this same moment, Holly was crawling toward him, using bins of discount DVDs and water bottles as barriers. She reached Michael and, her face very close to his, looped an arm around him to help him stand.

She said, "Upsy baby."

Patrick said, "Michael got *hurt?*" Genuinely surprised.

Oh Jeezus. Oh shit. "Nah," Michael gulped nickel-plated adrenaline, "takes more than that to—"

"Oooooh *NOOOOO!*" Patrick squealed, for he saw Michael's blood.

Just a little blood on the floor, but Patrick's eyes popped. The color shocked out of his flesh. His hands flew to his cheeks, pulling and pinching. It was the look of a boy who has watched Superman enter the ring and get his head knocked off his shoulders. It was the face Michael had seen in his own nightmares: his little brother's horror as the last shreds of his world disappeared from under him, leaving only the abyss.

Michael, this isn't how you promised it would work*!*

Patrick burst into tears. *Oh God no no no no no!* "I'm fine, buddy," Michael said.

"It's the *cheaters*, isn't it? It's them!" Patrick tried to punch himself in the leg; Michael grabbed his wrist, feeling sick.

"FALL BACK, I GODDAMN SAID!" Jopek hollered—but all the same he also *laughed* as bullets stitched across the counter and sent wood-chip shrapnel flying around his face. His expression burned with insane good humor, his eyes alive like black fire ignited by the chaos. "Got a wound, Mike? Suck it up before I give ya one to grow on!"

The barrel of his gun bladed to Michael's face.

Michael, shot with terror, managed to scramble to a stand.

Jopek's gunslinger furnace-face laughed and laughed and winked.

"Got this 'un covered, so you know." He cocked a casual thumb over his shoulder, indicating the battle.

He loaded a new clip, spat out tobacco.

And then Jopek trampolined, leaping up, landing two-heeled on the platform of the checkout counter. He blew out the last of the window glass with a machine blast from his gun. And standing there while war swept closer across the parking lot, the captain hollered with huge, wordless joy. Captain Jopek looked, for all the world, like the king of this apocalyptic land. Not just a Gamer, but the Master.

"Do you need help?" Holly asked Michael. She was looking at him—and at his furious expression—with a kind of horrified awe, as if she had seen him take off a mask, show a hidden face.

No. No, he didn't need help. He could get going just fine now.

With his sobbing brother's hand in his own, his leg barking every step, Michael stamped a fast course up the aisle. *Eff you,* he thought, not just at his leg. *Eff you very effing much.* Ignoring Holly's questions as she followed him into the shadowy stockroom of the pharmacy, he stepped over a Bellow with blue trousers that the captain had killed. Set in the far wall was a red exit door and Michael rammed his shoulder against the closed door with anger rocketing in his blood, acidic and hideous and good.

And Patrick said the thing Michael had, for the last few weeks, most feared: "M-M-Michael, I want to quit!"

Sounds of building battle, the captain firing, roaring at invading men. Not too long before the Rapture got inside. Poor Captain.

"Michael," Holly said uncertainly. *Whamp!*—He slammed his shoulder against the door. "I don't think we should go outside—" *Whamp!*

Screeching rust, the door flew into the snow-blinding alley. Fearing another volley of arrows, Michael yanked the door closed; a moment later, cracked it again. He heard men running past the end of the alley:

"Where is the boy? Rulon swore the captain would bring the boy."

"Rulon swore we'd be saved after the sacrifice last night. Rulon can lie. . . ."

"Don't say that. God, please don't say that. . . ."

"The boy"? Rulon thought Jopek was bringing "the boy"?

Me?

Oh my God, Michael realized. *Jopek knew the Rapture were going to come here!*

But—if he and the Rapture were *supposed* to meet here for Michael, then why were the Rapture attacking?

Maybe because they're insane, Michael. Because they're freaking insane.

The neighboring roof on the other side of the alley was clear. There was no one in the alley. *Go now,* Michael thought. *Game time, final round, you bet it is.*

"Michael, ohhh, I'm quitting, I want to time out. . . ." His brother's eyes were going glassy and he shivered, like a freezing puppy in a towel. *He's going to throw up. He's going to start screaming. And then the fun really begins.*

"I know you do," Michael reassured calmly. He stroked Patrick's hair, and had an image of a ticking bomb inside the soft case of his brother's skull. "But there's no reason to cry, dude. We just got tricked. *He* knew this was going to happen."

"Wh-what?" said Patrick. "Who knew?"

Michael listened to his heart thuds. "The Betrayer knew," he said.

Patrick's eyes went wide.

Just his eyes going wide, that was all . . . *but they weren't glassy.* They were interested. Michael, for the moment, had stopped the bomb.

"The *what*?" said Holly.

Several motorbikes sped past the mouth of the alley, perhaps fifty feet away. Rapture people. Firing with the army's guns, entering Walgreens through the front doors, boot steps on the shattered windows, shouts of confusion, coordination—

—and then Michael's play at redirecting Patrick's anxiety and remaking his world didn't matter.

Patrick struck himself on the ear with a tiny, terribly mean fist. It sounded like it hurt a lot. He whimpered and scrunched his face and began to sob, powerful and hoarse. Patrick was through trying to hide it: he was five years old, and exhausted, and Freaking.

Michael felt fury at everything.

This isn't supposed to happen.

Use the rage, thought Michael. *Just use it!*

Something inside him told him to look back at the corpses the captain had killed in the stockroom. On the edge of the light, Michael saw the one with dark-blue trousers. He went back and felt for the cop's waist. Found something metallic and cold. A silver revolver, six-chamber, pebble grip, blue in the twilight.

"Oh please, let's go," Patrick said urgently. His brow was feverishly popped with sweat. "Pleeeease."

"Holly, hold my brother for me."

"What? Where are you going?" she replied fearfully.

"To get the Hummer."

The shopping center was being raided, yes, but the raiders hadn't set up a perimeter, hadn't even blocked the exit at the traffic lights. *Haven't you assholes ever played* Halo? If he could just sneak through the lines of tanks, he could bring the Hummer back here and drive away. He began to jog. "And then you'll get all the time-outs you want, Bub, I promise—"

"Don't lie to him anymore, Michael."

Michael stopped, turned back to her, feeling a hideous wonder that the girl he'd ever come closest to having a date with was now a second away from imploding his brother.

"We cannot leave. Michael, they will k-i-l-l the captain." She looked at Patrick, then back to Michael and hissed, "*They will kill him in real li—*"

"Holly, shut the hell UP!"

He might have given away their position to the Rapture.

"Look at Patrick," he spat, leaning to her. "I don't understand it, I don't, but stay here if you want. I just want you to know something: Jopek will keep doing pointless 'missions.' Jopek knew someone was coming. He's doing it for a couple reasons, maybe, take your freaking pick. One: he's an idiot and a bad soldier, which is probably true. Two: he hates me, which is ridiculously true.

"Either of those is enough to make me want to haul a-s-s, but there's also the biggie:

"I think Jopek is insane."

For a second, he thought he'd convinced her. He truly did.

"But—" she began.

"Then I'm sorry, I can't help you," said Michael. He picked up the quivering collection of nerves that was his brother. *I didn't even get Atipax in there. Stupid, so stupid.*

And Michael was almost to the end of the alley when a thought, a simple thought, stopped his boots in their snowy tracks: *Mom wouldn't get in the car.*

I . . . I can't do this, he thought. *I can't leave her. Oh God, I just* can't.

What Michael did next did not come from *yes-yes:* it came from the desperate roar of his mind that was telling him, *hurry, leave, now.* Something inside seemed to slap back, *No!,* but the gun rose in slow motion.

Holly went stone faced, the desperate venom in her eyes snuffing out: a jack-o'-lantern, smothered by a gust.

"Come on," he said.

"You're *kidnapping* me?"

"Holly, it's—it's for your own good, okay?" Out loud, that sounded so grossly *Father Knows Best.* He began to say, *Trust me,* but stopped. That was what he'd said to Bobbie.

"I'll get you someplace safe, Holly. I can do it, I swear."

But he never got to the Hummer and escaped, not right then.

Because there were explosions.

And though Michael didn't know it yet, what he would find out soon was that Jopek had just killed the Bellows in the store and the attacking members of the Rapture with several (perfectly thrown) hand grenades. Panic told Michael to run, but he stood there, with Patrick coldly mute against him—which was so much worse than screaming.

Michael walked around to the front of Walgreens, where smoke coiled out the shattered windows. He heard someone cough inside.

"You know not to say anything about the gun, right?" he said to Holly as he jammed the pistol into his pocket.

"Or you'll bust a cap?" she replied, hurt.

The door swung open, glass tinkling from it. Captain Jopek came out grinning a boy-on-Christmas-morning smile.

"Well, thank God for little favors, there ya are! What a hoot, huh? You see that? Huh? Hoo! Was that a rodeo, or *was* it?"

Make yourself look upset, some part of Michael instructed. *How?* A thought came easily: Patrick, lying speechless and far-eyed in his hospital bed. "Th—that was scary as crap," Michael said.

And, as Holly looked at him like he had lasers flying from his nose, Michael improvised. He told Jopek how scared they had been, and how this attack made no sense, did it, Patrick? Michael told him how relieved they all were to see Jopek's living face, how lucky they were to have such a good soldier as Jopek drove them to the Capitol. *But I'm the one who's really taking us somewhere,* Michael thought from the passenger seat, holding his brother, inches from a grown soldier who could fight off an ambush but couldn't see who was really sitting right beside him. *Yes-yes*, a new plan accumulated in the bottom back of Michael's brain. *Load 'em up, Captain,* he had to fight not to say, and he touched the gun hidden in his pocket. *Load 'em on up: we're headin' for a new game.*

CHAPTER TWENTY-THREE

Abraham Lincoln watched them.

There was something eerie about the way the marble president stood, unchanging, even as snow slashed his face.

The storm had built: the sky above the golden dome boiled with storm heads. Michael lifted his face toward the clouds, willing his eyes wide open to the cold, bringing fresh tears as Jopek threw open the double doors to the Capitol and exclaimed, sounding both angry and happy, *"Gaawwwd DAMN!"*

Michael brought up the rear of the group, and he set his brother down as they entered the Capitol. Patrick stood in the marble entryway, sniffling. He hooked an arm around Michael's leg, but loosely. The ride had calmed him a little; Michael knew that his own agreement that things *didn't* make sense, that they *did* need a break, had helped, too. But Michael also wondered how much his own new certainty—his total *yes-yes*—had made a direct, comforting transmission from his own heart to his brother's. This weird Charleston nightmare was going to end soon, Michael knew; Michael felt that as absolutely as he felt his tears and his blood and the gun in his pocket. Yes, he was almost sure that Patrick could sense that. *Oh, I ya-ya, Bub. Just a few minutes, and I'll get you out of the Capitol, and we can finally, really win.*

Hank was in the rotunda, which was lit by the tripod light-banks and by the very last of the twilight that showed through the windows. Hank whirled at the sound of Jopek's shout, pulling a bottle from his lips, a little liquid spilling down his front.

Hank blurted, "Captain, I think I saw enemy movement."

"Holy shit, Eagle Eye, you want a medal?" Jopek threw his head back, laughing.

Hank blushed. Beside Michael, Holly breathed out hard, like she was trying to force out inner tension. Hank took this for silent laughter and shot her a look of burning sibling contempt.

"Ambush out there, Henry. Damn near Charleston's own little Alamo."

Jopek marched to Hank and swiped the squat brown bottle from his hands. "Thankee," he said, and sucked several noisy gulps. Hank's empty hands hesitated, then went to the pockets of his striped track pants, from which he drew a lighter and cigarette from a pack. He fumbled with the wheel of the lighter; it spun out of his hands.

Drunk, Michael realized. *Hank is drunk.* Was that going to hurt his plan?

"Rapture, Henry," Jopek said, wiping his mouth on his wrist. "Looks like they got the main road into the city pretty well locked up. I will get on my knees this night, I tell you. I will get down and thank the Lord that I found out when I did, folks. Yes I will."

"What do you mean?" said Hank.

Jopek stood there in the dusk, his chest huge inside his shirt, his pointer finger emphasizing each word like a teacher giving a lesson. And it was fascinating, the way Hank took the bottle that Jopek gave back to him: grateful and respectful, and a bit afraid. It was fascinating, the way Hank watched Jopek speak:

I'm the good guy. Here are your Instructions on What Is Next in Jopek Land. And it was fascinating, because Michael knew exactly what Jopek was going to say.

"We're safe for now, thanks to your captain," Jopek said. "But folks, we're a platoon, so I'll be honest: that's the last piece of good news I got. You-all can believe that the Rapture bein' near the only road into town is powerful bad for the unit coming into town." He put his hands to his hips, shaking his head regretfully.

Holly sniggered bitterly at this, so softly that only Michael heard it.

Hank nodded, comforted with the routine.

Jopek locked eyes with Michael.

"Until we know what we're dealing with, I'm sad to say it's my duty to advise all units that enterin' Charleston is currently too dangerous—"

"The Rapture told you to meet them there," said Michael.

He felt Holly stiffen beside him; he sensed Hank's mild confusion. But he didn't feel Freaking from his brother: he only heard Patrick's humming, a light anxiety being lessened by a development in The Game.

"What, now?" replied Jopek. He had the mildly annoyed expression of a teacher who has been interrupted.

"You knew exactly what was going to happen."

Now Jopek dropped his hands from his hips, his head cocking. He half smiled.

Hank laughed at Michael, but its dismissiveness sounded a little uncertain.

"They were saying the captain was supposed to bring the boy. And you know what's funny is, you didn't seem too upset that they were shooting at us."

Should he go on? Should he say the last of it? *Yes-yes.*

"'Cause Jopek, you're the Betra—"

231

But Jopek interrupted: "And you know what's funny is, how you're pig shit retarded."

"Wait. Uh, sorry. Captain, so you *did* know they were going to be there?" Hank asked cautiously.

"Henry. Hell yes, I did. And I don't think I like your tone."

"I didn't mean anything by it," Hank protested, surprised and confused.

Jopek turned to Michael.

"That priest, Rulon, he left me a letter last night, Mikey. He said he wanted to negotiate some kinda agreement, said we could have our weapons back, and yeah, he mentioned I should bring 'the boy.'"

"Bull," Michael said, nearly laughing at the audacity of Jopek's lie. "If Rulon wanted to trade me for weapons, or if he wanted to trade"—he silently indicated Patrick with his eyes—"then why would his people start by *shooting* at us?"

"Their community is not a shinin' goddamn example of sanity, genius. His *letter* didn't even make sense, just rambling shit about coal and 'the Son.' I think Father Asshole up in Almost Heaven, West Virginia, is going a little extra batty lately since Jesus hasn't invited him to dinner yet. I think he's gettin' desperate and 'sacrificing' more of his followers. Judging from the tiny number of folks he sent to Walgreens, it don't seem like he's got all that many followers left alive, neither. So I think Rulon's runnin' low on options about how he can 'atone.' My guess? Since you killed 'their First Chosen,' Rulon wants to sacrifice *you*, Mikey. He thinks that offing you would make everything just dandy again."

Now slowly Jopek marched toward Michael. "But you might'a noticed something, big boy: even though the Rapture broke the bargain and attacked us out there—*you're still alive and safe*. So I guess that ol' Captain Jopek knew what he was doing."

"Yeah, except you know what I think, though?" Michael

replied. "I don't think you just wanted to get the weapons back; I think you wanted to *get back at Rulon* for stealing them. I think you 'wanted to have two words with Rulon, and they weren't *happy birthday*.'" Michael imitated Jopek's voice: "'Broke into my city, didn't they? I better show them I was born for some special greatness.'"

At Michael's mocking, Jopek's eyes went wide. He stopped a few feet ahead of Michael. "Mike. Mike. Oh, Mike." His voice quavered with controlled fury. "I shoulda thrown your ass over the cliff."

"Hey . . ." It was a weak protest. But it came from *Hank*.

"Hank, why don't you shut your mouth up, candy-pants?" Jopek said.

"Don't be a bunghole," sniffed Patrick, and pulled his hood over his head and shrank it shut with the strings, cupping his hands over his ears to hide the sounds.

Michael braced himself, feeling the pebbled grip of the gun in his pocket.

"Is Michael *wrong*, though?" Holly asked.

Jopek's nostrils flared. "You know, I'm *damn sure* I don't like that tone, girl."

"Well, Captain, I don't like that you drove me to a bunch of people who want to shoot me," Michael said. Jopek tried to protest, but Michael almost-shouted over him: "Is it just me, or does that break one of a platoon's basic *rules*?" He emphasized the last word for Patrick.

The words rang.

Jopek stood in the center of them now—the center of his platoon—and in the burning silence he sensed what was occurring: the image these people held of him, which always stood on solid ground, was teetering at a cliff's edge. Captain Jopek circled on his boot heels, scanning their faces, finding a dangerous uncertainty that he could never have predicted.

And Jopek smiled. He seemed true, in the same way that he had seemed true as he fought the Rapture. More than ever before, Michael understood that, like himself, Jopek was most awake when in danger. Jopek was coming alive now, and he was about to do something to take control of the night.

So am I, Michael thought.

Guys, he imagined himself saying, as he had on the car ride to the Capitol, as he had every night Before when things were bad and Mom pretended they weren't, when home was pain but freedom and life were just one opened door away. *Guys, I think we need to leave now.*

But Holly took the play out of his hands.

"Captain, Michael wants to go."

What are you doing? Michael screamed silently.

"And sir," Holly said, "I think that it's absolutely under-standable that he feels that way. He's had a terrible day, we all have, and I think it's possible, sir, that you did put us in danger needlessly. With things getting worse with the Rapture and the Bellows, doesn't it make sense for us to leave—all of us?" Her jaw was strongly set; she was trying to appear calm and reasonable. But there was something desperate in her voice, as if this moment was her final chance to salvage the hope she had placed in the captain.

"We," said Jopek, "are goin' nowhere. And you-all know *that* is rule one. Rule one."

A hundred feet tall, all muscle—that's how Jopek seemed as he slung his machine rifle over his shoulder and turned. He marched away, and each of the steps sounded like doors slam-ming and sealing.

"Why the hell not, Jopek?"

Hank's voice was soft, so soft. For this a-hole Cool Kid,

Michael suddenly felt something like love.

Jopek stopped, but didn't turn.

"Why not?" Hank repeated, louder. "Why can't we leave?"

Thumpuh: Michael's heart, a fist in his throat. Jopek looked at Hank, his face incredulous and hateful, like a jack-o'-lantern with a butane torch inside.

"We're doin' what I say, and I say—"

"I—I think you're wrong on this, Captain," Hank said.

Jopek asked, "You think I'm wrong?" He sounded politely interested.

"Yes, I—"

But somehow Jopek had cleared the distance between him and Hank before any of them realized he was moving and his fist pistoned out and he slugged Hank, cracking across his jaw. Holly gasped. Patrick's blind-hooded head looked up, momentarily startled, then hummed and looked back down.

Hank managed to catch himself before his face struck the marble, but it was close.

"You wanna compare guns, Hank?" asked Jopek softly, leaning over him. "Boy, you ungrateful shit. Who's been savin' you this whole time?"

"*Michael* saved us in the Magic Lantern," spat Holly miserably.

"Little girl, don't be smart."

"Somebody has to."

"You'll want to watch that mouth."

Can a whole body quake with a heartbeat?

After a moment, Holly replied, "No, Captain."

Hank touched his blood, looked at the captain, sneered.

What happened next was as palpable as a burst of electricity traveling across the rotunda: *the final control in this room shifted to Michael.* They looked to him for his response. In that dizzying moment, he knew what it must be like to be

Jopek: the trust . . . and the power.

"Screw y'all, somebody's gotta patrol," said Jopek, and this time his departing steps were loud and angrily undisciplined, but even with that noise and even with the moans of the Bellows, Jopek stopped at the unmistakable sound: the click of a revolver, being cocked. . . .

CHAPTER TWENTY-FOUR

Jopek turned, and blinked, "Lower that, little fella."

"I don't feel like it," Michael replied calmly.

Jopek's gaze dissected him. "Where you get that?"

"We're leaving," Michael said.

Outside the door at Michael's back, the throat of the storm roared snow and fury.

"You're playin a losin' hand here, mister. Oh yes, you are."

"Slide your rifle to me," Michael said. "Unstrap it from your shoulder *slow*. If I think you're going to try anything, I'll shoot first." Jopek searched his face. "Stop it, you know I'm telling the truth—"

Suddenly, Jopek's gaze darted above Michael's shoulder. *"YEAH, THAT'S IT, YOU GOT HIM, HANK, TAKE HIM OUT!"* he roared.

Michael flinched, braving for the impact.

But when he checked out of the corner of his eye, the only part of Hank that was moving was his head, nodding: *keep going, Michael.*

"Rifle," Michael said. "And the pistol on your ankle."

"Well, goddamn you," Jopek said casually, unstrapped the weapons from his shoulder and ankle, and placed them on the floor. He kicked both, rattling, toward Michael.

Everything inside Michael's chest seemed to fill with light and wind.

Holly's gaze met his and locked: *I am freaking scared. Okay? I'm going along but I am goddamn petrified.*

Michael felt a dull ache of longing to let her know she was safe. *This is the real me, Holly: the real me is the one who can save you. I swear.*

"It's okay," Michael told her.

"Naw it ain't, though," Jopek said.

Michael looked at Hank—whose jaw was already beginning to swell—and asked him, "We good to go?"

Hank nodded.

Michael sensed Jopek step closer; without looking, as smoothly as if he were lighting a Bic, Michael's thumb double-cocked the hammer.

Hank and Holly moved toward Michael and Patrick, in front of the doorway.

I am safe, he felt. *Little brother and me, safe.*

Control.

Joy.

Victory.

Promise.

The keys.

Holding the pistol steady, Michael fished the keys from his pocket and tossed them to Hank. He handed both the ankle pistol and the cop's pistol to Hank as well, switching Jopek's assault rifle to his right hand, keeping a bead on Jopek.

"Get the Hummer," Michael said. "Gas it up with the tanker out there and then pull the Hummer up."

"To where?" Hank said.

"Honest Abe," Michael replied, then nodded toward the door to direct Holly to go with Hank.

Jopek watched, and the reality slowly settled on his face: *This is actually happening. A seventeen-year-old is actually beating me.* For only the second time, Michael thought he understood Jopek. He looked emotionally destroyed. It was the face of a man who is watching his worst enemy sail away on a rescue boat from the island without him.

"Faris?" Hank called from the door. "Aren't you coming?"

"One sec."

Michael nudged Patrick with his knee. Patrick grunted, but he took his hands from his ears and pushed the hood back from his face. His hair was wild.

He looked up at Michael, expectant.

This is it, Patrick. This is finally it.

"Captain, we're going to go out to the Hummer now," Michael said. "We're going to leave. We're going to look for the soldiers, and we're going to Richmond. We'll have the machine gun up top. We'll have food. And you can't come."

"You'll die, my friend," Jopek said. "That's a guarantee."

"Want to know how I know you're wrong?" Michael smiled. And he said the last line of his speech, the final piece of the puzzle that would make the world understandable for Patrick, that would reassemble and fortify The Game for him, all the way to the Richmond Safe Zone:

"Because you're the Betrayer, Jopek."

Except, he didn't. He'd gotten to *you're* when he had to stop, because something terrible and impossible had occurred. Jopek's moonlit face went dark: a shadow fell across it, a shadow that blocked the moonlight through the Capitol hall's high windows. And it was at that moment that Michael heard the shriek from high above him, from the sky, like a keening lunatic commandment from some deranged god.

Suddenly the windows behind Jopek's head cracked.

Run, Michael thought. *Just run now.* He went for Patrick, picking him up.

Above, one of the hall's chandeliers was pitching, glittering wildly, the glass eerie music, clawing drags of light on the walls. There was something on the chandelier. Something like a clot of blackness, a moving thing, and hanging upside down.

There was a dead boy above them.

A dead boy, that was all. A living corpse. Something he had seen a thousand times. But Michael's fingertips suddenly went numb with terror. His stomach flooded with ice. The *yes-yes* shattered in a single, flying instant.

The boy hung above them, knees hooked on the chandelier, like a kid on playground monkey bars.

No. That's not real, Michael thought. *No, no, no, my God that can't be real!*

Because he recognized, with one glance, the boy's crooked, poor-kid haircut.

Cady Gibson, one month dead, still in his funeral suit, peered down at them, teeth peeled back into a smile like an arc of fiery bone.

Can't be right. Doesn't work like that. He just died in a coal-mine accident! How did he come back? HOW DID HE COME—

"*Is that the Betrayer?*" Patrick whispered.

The boy, inverted, swung from the light, spearing through the dark. He struck the wall with four quick limbs . . . and he did not fall. He clung to the wall; perched, the all-dark lamps of his eyes on them.

Doesn't work like that!

Sections of his blond scalp hung loose in flaps. His brow was thin enough to see the skull. In his left temple was a ragged hole, perhaps the head wound that had taken his life when he fell in the mine. And the reason that he seemed to smile was because his lips had rotted off. *Hi! Wanna play? I'm new here!*

KILL IT! Michael thought. His gun was rising, rising. *You have to kill it NOW!*

Cady opened his mouth and out exploded Hell.

Two summers ago, Ron had lit a bottle rocket in an empty beer bottle that tipped over, and the firecracker screamed a hot bright slash past Michael's head, close enough to scar his ear. That scorching cry was the only thing Michael could compare to what now came from this kid's gray, quaking jaws.

The lenses of his machine-rifle scope shattered from the shriek. Michael recoiled, and at the same instant, involuntarily yanked the trigger: fire burst from the end of the barrel.

The creature dodged on the wall, flitting gravity-less from bullets like a snake inside a nightmare. His shrieking was a trapped siren.

The creature leapt over Michael, and landed on someone two times his own size. *"Off!"* Hank screamed in a hysterical mixture of revulsion and horror. *"Off Jesus get off shit shit get it off get it off!"* He spun wildly and jerked in a dance of terror.

The creature twisted upon him like flame.

Patrick grabbed Michael's waist. *"What the?!"*

Holly cried out, lunged to help: stopped, then screamed her brother's name as if her heart might break.

The creature's jaws snapped. Hank began to weep.

Michael placed his finger on his trigger again, knowing it was too late, knowing that Hank was bitten, that Ron and Jopek had been right about him: he *was* too weak. But then a miracle happened.

As Cady arched his jaws for the bite, Hank, spinning, spinning, snarled Cady's legs.

He hurled Cady at the wall. The creature flew, flailing like a beast kicked off a cliff.

Hank crowed, apparently as much in surprise as in triumph, and upon his face there was a savage joy.

Cady met the wall, but instead of the impact shattering him, he bent his legs to catch the momentum. Elegant. Cady launched back like a swimmer making a turn at the end of a pool: he launched back at Hank, jaws first.

Insanely, in that same moment, Jopek was running at Michael like a fullback, head down.

"Hey-back-get-back!" Michael shouted and raised the rifle and Jopek kept coming anyway, and Michael fired over his head. And Jopek stopped.

"Michael, shoot it!" Holly screamed. "*Shoot it, MICHAEL, PLEASE SHOOT—*"

The creature landed on Hank and roiled and hissed on him like spilled acid. "*NAAAAAAA—*" Hank screamed. He stumbled backward at the creature's impact, and his head struck the wall with a *crack!* loud enough to make Michael feel sympathetic pain.

The monster went blurry with speed and it was hard to tell where Hank ended and where the monster began—

—*feel your* blood—

—and a thousand movie scenes of hostage standoffs flashed in Michael's brain—

—*feel it*—

—each of them ending with the cop reluctantly lowering his gun.

Oh eff that, thought Michael.

The rifle slammed into Michael's shoulder like a rapid fist.

His firepower was enormous, his aim flawless. Ropey blackness slung out of Cady as the bullets shredded his little-boy's suit. The fusillade threw Cady off of Hank, and for one incredible instant, the boy-monster corkscrewed in the air. Cady struck the wall, and with a shriek—like a steel rod being fed through a buzz saw—he threw back his head, impossibly far. Unlike any other Bellow, Cady seemed to be experiencing *pain*, and there was nearly human shock and rage in his voice, as if he was furious that his plan had been interrupted.

I guess that makes us even, you asshole!

Michael kept firing, torturing the monster-boy.

Hank had kept his head together just amazingly well: he'd ducked down to the ground to avoid the bullets the moment Cady was off of him, hadn't even flinched when some of Cady's viscera splashed on him. "Hank! C'mon!" Michael shouted behind the rifle.

Hank stayed perfectly still.

"Hank, over here, *now!*" Holly cried, moving toward Michael and Patrick. Michael had the monster seized in the bullets now, but what about when the clip ran dry? And Jopek was only maybe ten feet from Michael, and maybe he'd attack, too, and—

— and Hank didn't move.

Blood trickled from the back of his skull and spread into the lanes between the marble tiles.

"No. Oh, Christ, no," Holly breathed.

The gun stopped quiet in Michael's hands.

Hank had been dead since his head had struck the wall.

Cady Gibson stared, smiled, smiled, and he looked like a boy who had wandered across an executioners' firing line and thought it sort of tickled. Michael's eyes locked with his—*its*— dark sockets, and chills flew through him like black wings. Because, beyond the nine-year-old eyes, he saw some poisonous truth flash:

This Thing was newborn . . . and it was very, very old.

Cady Gibson shrieked one final blast, and this time the windows blew out, like glass curtains. The monster leapt out the window and vanished into the white void of the storm. And as the boy's shrieking faded off across the night that had promised Michael freedom and future, Michael could not help but think that the sound seemed to become laughter—yes, laughter, at him. . . .

CHAPTER TWENTY-FIVE

Patrick, Michael thought. *You have to tell Patrick it's okay. That you're not scared of what just happened. You . . . you have to breathe, Michael. Breathe. Rule one, breathe.*

Now, look down, champ. Look down, and see Patrick disappear into himself. Look down, and see your brother Freaking. Because you were too late. Because you forgot the Atipax. Because Game freaking OVER—

Michael looked down.

His brother was watching him. But Patrick was not terrified. The cry of the impossible monster still rang, but Patrick was not the panting and quivering kid he had been in the pharmacy. Bub was, sort of, smiling. As if he was just slightly bewildered that a boy had somehow clung to the wall and gotten one of the Gamers.

How the hell is Patrick okay? Michael wondered distantly.

Patrick said, "You just shot the Betrayer, right?" And that was the moment Michael saw the numbed desperation in Patrick's strange expression. "Hank got hurt but we're okay because *we* play right, right?"

He knows that Hank got hurt. Maybe even dead—if Bub

even totally understands what that means. But The Game still makes sense to him. For now, it still does, because he thinks Hank just didn't follow the Instructions. Even with Patrick's limited understanding of the world and his need to believe in The Game, Michael didn't think that this deception would last long. And even though Michael knew that he'd *had* to build The Game's illusions for Patrick's safety, he still suddenly felt the dreadful power of his own deception. *He feels better when someone is "logically" dead than when someone is just "cheating."*

Oh God, Patrick, what the hell kind of world have I made for you?

Patrick repeated, this time a little shriller with need: *"You got the Betrayer, right?"*

Which was when Michael remembered that Jopek was still nearby. He whirled toward Jopek, raising the rifle to his shoulder. The world puckered at the edges of his vision; a bitter yellow heat spiked up his throat. *Oh, I think I'm in shock,* he realized with dim interest. *I think I'm going to puke.*

Somewhere behind him, Holly sucked a gasp, like she'd forgotten to breathe, too.

Jopek wasn't running at him like he had feared. He was kneeling at Hank's body—*Hank's corpse,* whispered Michael's mind, and his stomach rolled. Jopek's expression was a battle surgeon's look, a face of compartmentalized concern that was, somehow, everything in the world grown-up and strong. It said, *Trust me;* you said, *Always.*

With his face angled toward the fallen Hank, Jopek raised his blistering eyes. *Shoulda listened, Mikey,* they said, hideously triumphant. *Oh yes, you shoulda let ol' Jopek stay in charge.*

Not *going to puke!* thought Michael fiercely. Not *in front of you.*

"*No-no-no-no-no,*" Holly whispered. She stood alone before

the open threshold of the snowing night. He pictured two pixelated characters, Holly and Hank, walking toward the bright
block letters that read THE END. They had made it this far
together by virtue of their grudging love. But as they make their
ending move, there comes the shriek of an invisible ax to tear
one of them away.

Holly shook her head: slowly at first, then speeding. Her
dark hair swam and slapped across her face. *No, no,* the motion
seemed to say. *Doesn't work this way.*

"Hey-it's-okay!" called Patrick brightly, his crescendoing
distress causing uncharacteristic emotional tone-deafness.
"Hank just played wrong, pff. We played right, huh! Michael
said there was gonna be a Betray—"

"Holly, I am so sorry," Michael interrupted. He moved slowly
toward her, gun still raised. He wanted to touch her, to hold her;
most of all, he wanted to shield her eyes from the sight of her
brother, the blood pooling under her brother's head and mix-
ing with the black Cady-core that had splattered on and around
him. But he had to keep the bead on Jopek. "I am so sorry that
Hank . . . that he—"

Holly sucked her lips into her mouth. *She's going to freak,*
Michael saw. *And maybe she'll be too upset to leave.* He felt a
flash of guilt for analyzing her grief.

Holly asked as if to herself, "Is he *gone*?"

"Yeah—God, I'm sorry."

"Got shot, that's my thinkin'," muttered Jopek. He stood from
the body, brushing his hands, shaking his head as if in mourning.

"I thought maybe he was going to get bit, but . . . I didn't
think he hit his head that hard. . . I—I didn't think he—"

Patrick tugged Michael's waist. *"We* always *play right, huh?"*
he whispered, with a building urgency, his voice beginning to
quiver. "That's why we're awesome, huh? Low-five, huh?"

"Is he going to come back?" Holly said to herself.

Michael didn't think so—Hank had died only of his head wound—but he still pictured himself having to shoot Hank in the head in front of Holly to keep Hank from possibly rising again. His throat clenched sickeningly and he had to fight back a moan of dread and despair. That was too much. He looked at Jopek and silently told him, *You killed him. You. We should have been gone.*

Then he said, "Holly, we've got to go." Holly looked past him, far-eyed. "Patrick? Okay?" Nothing from either of them, and Michael thought: *I'm going to have to touch Hank. I'm going to have to go through his pockets for the keys.* "You guys go outside, I'll be there, we have to go before that Bellow"—he stopped; calling it a Bellow somehow didn't feel right—"before that . . . kid comes back."

"How *did* that kid come back?" Holly asked suddenly, watching Hank. Tears spilled from her eyes, unblinked.

"The ceiling?" offered Patrick.

"How did it come back?" Holly repeated to herself. "He wasn't bit. When things were getting bad, the CDC checked every goddamn coroner's report, my dad was helping, and they dug up *any* body that had been bitten. I remember my dad told me the CDC checked Cady's body too, to make sure his head wound wasn't a bite from a Zed. *I'm saying Cady wasn't bit*, this isn't possible, this can't be real!"

She jammed a shaky hand through her hair. "Changing," she said. "The virus is changing." She sucked a single sob, a low, humorless laugh sliding from her.

Michael didn't like the off-kilter edge her voice had. "Well, that just means even more that we should go, right?" he said quickly, double-checking Jopek as he did. "Since it's changing?"

Holly nodded fervently. For one single second, she looked like a girl who has not been sledgehammered across the mouth with grief. "I guess I'm just kinda like, 'how?'" she said, her voice cracking. "You know? How did it happen? I guess . . . it's just . . . I just . . , *how goddamn it did it* happen!" she cried. "HOW DID MY BROTHER DIE, HOW DID THIS *HAPPEN*, THAT KID NEVER GOT BIT! THEY CHECKED CADY AND THERE WEREN'T ANY BITES, THEY CHECKED AND ALL THAT KID HAD ON HIM WERE A COUPLE GODDAMN *SCRATCHES*!"

And, as if by command, Holly's voice cut quiet.

And Michael did not understand why.

He did not understand why Holly's hands plummeted. He did not understand why her eyes flicked to Patrick with sudden and heartbreaking pity. He didn't understand why Jopek's lips twitched, as if to contain a smile.

And then—

—*my neck scratch*—

—Michael *did* understand.

"Oh my garsh, what a shame," Jopek said softly.

"*Stay,*" said Michael. The gun slipped in Michael's grip. His fingers were suddenly jellied with sweat.

"Naw, I ain't your puppy dog." Jopek grinned. "Not no more." And took a stride closer.

"*Stop,*" Michael said, finding the trigger.

Patrick slid closer, asking, "What's a-matter?"

"Holly—Holly, tell Jopek."

"What?" she replied. Her voice was soft and quivering.

"Tell him, tell him the truth, tell him my scratch looked *fine.*" But his stomach iced. "*A little inflamed,*" he remembered her saying.

Jopek took another stride closer. Michael double-checked the safety.

"Captain, wait," Holly said, obviously torn. "He's—he's probably fine. . . ."

"*Probably?*" Michael sputtered. "Scratches can't do anything to people!"

Michael was very very very aware of his pulse beating in his neck.

"But like the lady said, Mikey: the virus is changin'."

"B-bull! If anything was going to happen to me, it already would have."

"Took Cady a month to come back," Jopek said. "It could be the same for you. 'Course, with the virus changin' it could happen right now, couldn't it, Holly? Yes indeedy."

"What could happen right now?" said Patrick, confused.

"Holly," Michael said.

But there was silence, except for Jopek's clocking, snake-patient approach.

Jopek saw the weakness on his face, and lunged. Michael made his own move without thought: he aimed the gun above Jopek's head, a warning shot. He pulled on the trigger.

Holly screamed. Jopek's eyes widened and he tensed to flee.

Click, the gun went.

Michael, dreamlike, blinked at his weapon. His hand floated out to the gun's slide. He pulled on the slide to feed new bullets from the magazine. And fired again.

Click. Empty.

Patrick realized something was wrong, and shouted, surprised, "OOOOOHHH!"

Michael said, "Please don't—"

But Jopek lunged again, saying absurdly, "Ha!" and Michael hurled the empty weapon at him and was down the hall, was racing down the marble stairs that circled the rotunda, when the captain grabbed a pistol from Hank's corpse.

"NO!" Michael heard Holly cry out. *"HE'S NOT CHANGING, CAPTAIN, DON'T SHOOT H—"*

Marble chips exploded to Michael's right as he reached the bottom stair.

He flinched, screamed, and in between the first shot and

the second he had time to pivot toward a tour information booth, had time to think, *Where am I?* The second shot rang, and something like a high-speed needle tugged the shoulder of his coat and he shouted again and spun reflexively. *Don't lose control of yourself, don't, don't!* He saw a pair of shadowed governor statues ahead and ran toward them. He had smiled at them two days ago and thought this zone was the safe End; now Michael thought, *Where the hell am I going to?!* just as a third bullet hit a mark not two inches wide of his ankle. *TURRRRN!* his mind screamed, *TURRRN!,* and his whole skull felt soaked with terror and his vision pinholed and shimmered, and he tried to feel his blood and instead tripped on his own frantic feet and splayed face-first and struck his jaw on ice-cold marble. *So this is what it feels like to lose control.* Michael scrambled desperately up and into a hallway to the left of the statues just as Jopek's fourth shot struck the statue's hand like some unthinkable stigmata. Michael cast one last look back up at the ring of the rotunda above, over the railing of which Captain Jopek smiled like a portrait painted on a ceiling of a cathedral, like a man having the time of his life. Michael wasn't dead, only because Captain Jopek didn't want him dead. Not yet.

Michael dashed blind into the dark hall.

Where am I going to turn into a Bellow?

This isn't happening, he thought. *I was too careful! I played too well for this to happen! Seriously, it's wrong, Holly was wrong, I don't even know if I'm infected!*

But an image came to Michael's mind: the Bellow that had scratched him, the Bellow in the miner's suit.

One crumpled eyeball hanging from the monster's socket when it attacked him. As if the Bellow had already undergone the mutation that instructed the Bellows to tear out their eyes; yes, as if the virus within that miner-Bellow was already changing into something more dangerous.

Michael's mind, shrieking like a disaster siren: *Infeeeeeect!* *Infeeeeeect!*

He thought: *ruined everything, oh I hate myself, I hate myself, so freaking* stupid—

He thought: *Patrick!*

"*Mike! Hey, c'mon back, Mike!*" Captain Jopek's voice chased through the echoing black. He sounded friendly enough: he was even laughing. "*Where you runnin'? Where's there* to *run, fella?*"

Jopek won.

I'm infected, and I'm running away from Patrick. I'm infected and there is no safe place.

Shut up! Just freaking run! Just run and you will figure it out, the future you will figure it out!

But the future Me is probably a Bellow—

Feel—feel—feel your bl—

Tears scorched his throat and eyes, and Michael wanted to scream but heard himself just saying, "*Please, please, please, please,*" thought, *Do you pray? No, I run,* and the blood ramming inside was not his blood, it was not the blood he'd gotten from Mom and it was not the blood he shared with Patrick, it was not the blood that saved anyone any pain: *it was the blood that was going to kill him*—

Michael saw a door, slammed it open.

Michael skidded, stopped no more than inches from the hands and faces shooting through the chain link: the Bellows were thirty-deep against a single final double layer of fence. *I'm outside.* From the sound, there were thousands surrounding the Capitol, thousands and thousands that had surged through all the buffer zones of the bridge or entered through the Kanawha River, as if the resurrection of Cady Gibson had ignited some riotous undead beacon.

And the instant of danger, amazingly, made Michael realize: *I'm behind the Capitol.*

He could see the Hummer (useless to him without the keys still on Hank's dead body) stationed in the clear lane between the fences.

But another transport was back here, too.

The balloon!

The jack-o'-lantern face lolled, grinning, perhaps one hundred yards away, aglow softly, inflated, its butane burner readied by Hank for Jopek's night patrol. Michael could just see the top of it past the camouflage gas tanker beside him, but yes, it was there. Ready to fly.

Where? Oz?! he thought wildly.

Virginia!

What!

Other people—cure, cure—

What about Patrick?

I'm saving him—

By leaving him?

Yes! Only way!

Was that true?

He told himself to shut up.

And ran.

In the thin and deadly lane between the fences and the steps of the Capitol, electric over crumbled concrete, the green smell of death overpowering, every step aware of an image: Jopek coming out the grand double doors like an insane senator exacting revenge on his would-be assassin.

Michael gripped the wicker and he leapt into the basket. He tugged the silver lever on the burner. The flame ignited to life, carnival-colored.

Slowly, slowly, the balloon began to rise.

Hurry! Please *freaking hurry!*

The fire filled the pumpkin face, roared.

The double doors to the Capitol opened, and when Michael spun, he did so already feeling a phantom bullet in his back.

"Patrick?" he gasped.

Patrick stood waving at the top of the grand steps to the West Virginia State Capitol, smiling. *And there was no one else with him.*

How did he get out here by himself?

Doesn't matter, just get him, you—you probably have time to get to Richmond—you can still save him—

Extra life. The thought was a sunburst. *Another chance!*

"B-B-Bub!" Michael swallowed, tried to control his voice. Patrick was moving down the stairs already, with the careful-footed caution of exactly what he was: a five-year-old who is afraid of slipping on ice. *"Hurry!"*

"Trick!" Patrick said, delighted, leaving the bottom stair. "It was all a trick, huh?"

"Yeah," Michael said. *"Trick"?* What was Patrick talking about? *Doesn't matter!* Michael suddenly thought of that night they'd spent in the woods. Eighty Bellows versus one gun. Easy Mode. "It *was* a trick. Pretty cool, the way I—*Patrick*—" he interrupted himself, "—*ya-ya, I ya-ya.*"

Patrick smiled, held his arms up in the air.

The basket was hovering a couple feet off the ground.

"Crap, sorry!" Michael said. He considered simply jumping out of the basket himself, grabbing Patrick and climbing back in, but the image of the unoccupied aircraft hovering away across the Kanawha River stopped him. Though everything within his brain cried not to—though there was no time to do it—Michael dropped his hand from the burner.

The flame sputtered, *fwoop*, to a small blue ring.

There was a moment of stillness while the two brothers watched each other, unmoving, as the snow fell around them. And despite everything, Michael thought that moment tasted holy.

"It was all a trick!" Patrick repeated, whispering with bright, coconspirator's joy. *"It was* such an awwwwwesome one, *Michael!"*

Michael leaned over to grab his brother, and Patrick bounded into his arms, hugging him fiercely. And wild joy was what Michael felt. And that moment would haunt him forever, because it was, in so many ways, the final moment—the endgame—of everything he'd imagined his life would be. *"Freeze, sucka!"* Patrick giggled. And as Michael set him back down, Michael thought: *What the?*

There was something, huge and dark, in Patrick's pale fingers.

The fire had sucked the oxygen from the air.

His brother was aiming a pistol, the policeman's pistol Michael had gotten in the Walgreens, at his stomach. Its barrel looked large enough to shoot the moon.

A distant thought: *doesn't work like this.*

"Bub," Michael said. "What are you doing?"

"Tricked you," replied Patrick. "You're the *Betrayer*, I *know* it," said Patrick. He swung his head, saying it singsong. *"Jo*pek, the *Game* Master told me."

Terror.

"Pffft." Michael licked his lips. "What're you talking about, newb, Jopek isn't the Game Ma—"

"He *told* me you'd say that!" Patrick laughed.

Michael held Patrick's stare, and then lunged toward the burner.

"STOP!" Patrick shouted.

"—STOOOOOOOOOOOPPPPPP—"

Jopek and Patrick. In the Hummer. Talking.

"Patrick . . . Bub, listen to me, that gun can really hurt people. I need you to put it down."

"The Game Master said it can't hurt people real bad," Patrick said, confused.

"Jopek's lying."

"You said the Game Master is always right."

Oh God, no.

Footsteps echoed to Michael's ears, from the Capitol steps.

Tell Patrick the truth! There is no Game!

And while Patrick stared behind his gun, Michael stayed silent.

Jopek had known. Because Holly had told him about The Game and the reason it existed, Jopek had known Michael would never tell Patrick the truth—that he *could* never.

And now Jopek, saying, "'Scuse us, fella," captured him in a headlock, and pulled Michael from the basket.

"Let me go!" Michael said, twisting uselessly.

"Ahhhh, I don't feel like it."

From some black well inside Michael: *Bite! BITE him!*

And horror filled him. What did that mean?

The fences on all sides of them surged and bowed with Bellows. A musical twang of ripping razor wire. The roar of a thousand dead throats. One of the two remaining layers of chain link had given way. Bellows swelled across the overturned fence, a tsunami of flesh.

"Look at this Betrayer!" Jopek called, laughing, dragging Michael up the marble steps into the Capitol as Patrick climbed out of the basket. "I think these ol' Bellows know the Betrayer's here, don't you, Bub? I think the Bellows want some *action*! What do you think we should do with Michael? Throw him to the Bellows, maybe? They're kinda his new brothers, wouldn't ya say?"

Michael looked at Patrick, and he remembered telling Patrick that they had to stop the Betrayer, "No matter what it takes."

N-no. Patrick won't hurt me. He doesn't know if things are safe, but he won't take a chance.

And that seemed like it was true, judging from the indecision on Patrick's face.

They reached the rotunda. "Captain, what is wrong with you, *stop choking him like that!*" Holly shouted.

"Awww, he's okay," said Jopek.

"Ho—Holly—*help!*" Michael's croak seemed to blend with the chorus of the dead outside.

"Michael, listen to me," Holly said urgently, "you're going to be okay. I told the captain, we're going to keep you safe, right here."

"No! Please! Have to get to—to Virginia!"

"The soldiers will be here anytime now. They'll take us, soon. You'll be fine." She added, "I think."

Now! Tell them! If you do not tell them, there won't ever be another now!

"I lied, Holly! There are no other soldiers coming for us, we have to leave!"

"No. No. Michael. Please, don't make it worse for yourself," Holly said, her eyes pain and pity.

"Holly, please, oh God, *I made it up!* I always make *everything* up!"

"See, bud?" said Jopek. "Now he admits it, don't he?"

"Michael," said Holly, and began to cry. "Michael, stop lying."

"*BUB! THERE—IS—NO—GA—*"

But he was already at the door of the Senate.

It was open, looked like the mouth of a cave.

Going to run, Michael saw. *Jopek's going to throw me in, but I'll be smooth, I'll land and Jopek will be surprised and I'll grab his gun.*

The best Michael did when Jopek launched him, however, was not break any bones.

He stumbled, knocking against congress seats as he fell.

And in the moment before Jopek locked him in alone, Michael looked at his brother, in the lit doorway. His brother, who always sensed when something was the matter, even when Michael wished he didn't.

His brother, next to the pistol tucked unguarded in Jopek's belt.

Patrick looked deep into Michael, and the understanding came almost immediately, with a look of surprise and pity for his frightened big brother.

"Michael?" said Patrick.

"Y-yeah?"

"It's just a Game, it's just a Game," Patrick replied, like it was a prayer. "Just a Game, just a Game . . ."

The door swung shut.

Losing!

Lost!

I am lost!

Michael slammed his shoulder into the door, but it was, of course, strong wood. He tried to focus on anything. He punched himself in the thigh, hard. His mind ran: *Get Patrick. Get away. Get a plan!*

Outside, Jopek was laughing.

Michael paced frantically, feeling that if he paced into a wall he would begin walking straight up it . . . like that Thing . . .

Patrick laughed nervously back outside the door. Then his laughter sounded like it was going farther away.

Michael whispered, *"Bub . . ."*

Michael screamed: "BUB? HOLLY?"

No reply from the halls of the Capitol.

The cold column of panic in his chest uncoiled and spread to his limbs and tongue and eyes. His jaws wrenched open and over them a sound tore forth. Michael slid to the ground and jammed clawed hands into his face, and yes, and yes, he bellowed.

He ran to the window overlooking the rear of the Capitol, the Hummer, the Kanawha River.

Jopek was running toward the Hummer. Michael had not seen Patrick and Holly get into the vehicle, but he thought, *Oh God no, they're leaving me.*

And that was when something that once had been unthinkable occurred: A seam opened in part of the last of the Capitol defenses, and suddenly Bellows were pouring through, coming for the Hummer, twenty feet away from the Hummer, fifteen . . .

Jopek jumped into the car and slammed the door. In his mind's eye, Michael saw the Hummer, smashing through the few series of gates and fences that created the exit path for the Hummer, heading out, bye-bye, Mike, thanks for the memories.

A thought occurred to him: *Pray. Michael, pray.*

Michael placed his hand on the cold, moon-bright window.

What if Bobbie had been right about there being Something that could help you? What if . . . what if he had misunderstood why the deer made him feel safe and good? What if it wasn't some deep *yes-yes* aspect of himself that controlled things, but some other Power?

What if he *did* pray?

Please, he thought. *Please . . . God. Please—Universe, what- ever—if you're there, you'll help me! Please help, please let me not be infected, please save me, please* make Jopek stop!—

—and Captain Jopek, at that very instant, got out of his Hummer.

The captain threw open the roof hatch and climbed out onto the vehicle's roof: the gunslinger, stark and great against the stars.

"Oh-my-God," breathed Michael. A dizzying hope raced through him.

Only for a moment.

Captain Horace Jopek of the United States 101st slammed a clip into the SAW atop the Hummer and tugged back the machine-gun's slide. The snout barked, hurling deadly fireflies into the gas tanker staged between the Hummer and Michael's window. Flame, gory-bright, pyred up and out of the tanker. Bellows tossed and Bellows flew.

Please God.

The window roared in. Solid heat found Michael.

He lifted, watching his own feet rise over his eyes, like a kid zooming on a swing.

Please no. It was the last thought he remembered. And if anyone did answer his plea, he didn't know it. Michael soared, and when his head struck the corner of a senator's desk, the world went funny, upside down, back-asswards, game over good buddy, try again with your eyes open, newb: everything tumbling up and up into his own starless void; everything falling lost and gone, like the worldscape of a game board that has been overturned by a very mad man.

CHAPTER TWENTY-SIX

Rock-a-bye . . . Rock-a-bye . . . *Mom hummed.* Rock-a-bye . . .

Her bracelet, the one with the fake acorns, tapped on Michael's ear as she placed the damp washcloth on the back of his neck.

"Any better? Do you want more saltines, baby?"

Michael tried to answer, but felt too weak. Oh, pizza line. Why oh why oh why had he gotten in the pizza line? Bad call, newb. That stuff was famous for making stomachs stand straight, salute, and go kamikaze. Seventh grade sucked enough *without puking lava, thanks for asking.*

Mom had called in sick to work to take care of him, and she had her hair in a ponytail and was wearing an N*SYNC T-shirt and jeans. She smelled good, too: like soap and hot water, not like too much makeup. And her boyfriend wasn't here.

"No more saltines, baby?" Michael shook his head. "That's good. Because I ate 'em all. That was a joke. Do you think you'll laugh later?" She snorted: he felt her breath, cool and good, on his neck.

"Upboy . . . ," *someone called.* "Get up. . . ."

Michael's heart fell a little. He tried to open his eyes . . . and he found he couldn't. Sweet mother of crap, I am siiiiick.

"Upboy!" *called Ron's voice.*

Michael opened his eyes.

A shocking, thin blue in the sky. The sun ate up his vision like a white bomb. He blinked and looked away, the stalks of his eyes aching.

Michael tried to sit up, and saw he already was. Fell asleep sitting up? Huh. Hadn't done that in a long time. Not since the night before Halloween, when he'd stayed up so late putting the finishing touches on his wonderful and 100 percent foolproof escape.

His arms were stretched above his head. *Reeeeach fer the skyyyy,* he thought dimly. And when he tried to lower his arms, he couldn't. There were glittering loops on his wrists. Metal.

He was handcuffed to a wicker pole that stretched above his head.

Jopek, across from him, blew smoke in his face.

"God!" Michael shouted. He tried to dance back. The wall behind his back was solid, but *shifted* at his push; the floor swayed.

Jopek said nonchalantly, "I get that a lot." Behind him, clouds dipped and nodded.

He sat on a short stool across from Michael, his hand draped over his crossed legs, his flak jacket casually open, his presence impossible. This couldn't be real. Michael had been scratched, and the captain had left him behind. Michael's bad blood was now just showing him a nightmare, that's all, because he was in the Capit—

Not the Capitol.

Balloon, Michael thought. *I'm in the balloon.*

"So, soldier—"

"What's going on? Where's Patrick?"

"—hope you're rested up 'cause—"

"What happened?" blurted Michael. "Am I still infected?"

He recognized the desperate hope in his voice; it was the same that Bobbie'd had in the moments before her death. That feeling made him sick, but he could not stop it.

"I know I said it before, but shoooo," Jopek replied as if to just make conversation, "you sure sleep like the dead."

"So Mike, did I pick the right size? Hope it ain't uncomfortable—just gotta make sure you don't bite or scratch nobody."

Size?

Jopek indicated the space suit Michael was wearing.

In his shock, Michael had not even noticed. He had seen such things in newspaper photographs before: a camouflage, full-body biowear suit. His breath bounced off the plastic faceplate and hissed back on his cheeks. The sleeves were clammy and tight, an alien skin pasted on his own. When Michael jerked in surprise, Jopek threw back his head and laughed.

"Boyyyyyy, you're funny, but you're sure not sayin' much today. You learn that stealthiness from the soldiers you saw? *You like tryin' to sneak up and kill people?*"

A single cloud shaded the sun, then fled.

Michael gulped, dizzy with confusion and fear. Where was Patrick? Where was *here*? The view over the top of the basket's walls was only empty sky, the balloon so elevated he could see neither buildings nor coal company–blighted mountaintops. He sniffed, desperately searching for any clue . . . and what he smelled made him nearly gag. Even inside the suit, the scent of the Bellows—amplified, at least quadruple the worst he'd ever smelled—was overpoweringly, sickly rich.

"Where . . . where are we?" Michael said.

Jopek took a final drag and flicked his cigarette out of the basket.

He's gonna do that to me.

Michael held Jopek's gaze. He held it as carefully as he would hold a bell jar filled with poison gas that could cause a nightmare death at the slightest mistake.

"Why am I here?"

The edges of Jopek's grin hardened. "'Cause you and me got business, Mikey."

He drew out from within his jacket a handgun, tugged back the slide then let it bite forward, chambering a round from the banana clip. "Would you like to talk? I'd love to talk."

Michael had precisely zero idea what he should say: He wasn't sure about anything with Jopek just now. He had believed, before, that he understood the captain: that Jopek was nothing more than an army-issue Ron who only wanted to be worshipped and in control, and God help anyone that got in his way. Yet by that logic, Jopek should have abandoned the skinny kid who had aimed a gun at him last night. *But I'm still here, strapped in the freaking sky with this psychopath.* Michael did not even try to feel his blood; *yes-yes* and the Game Master had failed him last night; they had been shredded by the cry and claws of an impossibly resurrected boy who carried a virus that now quite probably lived inside Michael. No, Michael couldn't decipher the captain, not any more than the field mouse can fathom the lion.

But he had no choice: he nodded.

Jopek returned it.

And the air between them electrified.

"What I want to talk about," Jopek said, "is a game. I reckon that may sound fa*mil*iar."

"Where's Patrick?"

"We'll maybe get to that, but answer me first: Are you good at games, you bet?"

"I'm okay," replied Michael.

"Don't lie, now."

"I'm . . . very good."

"We'll see, won't we? Now, as to why *are* ya here? Last night, I could've put a bullet in ya. I could have left your ass behind. But I dragged you outta Hell, 'cause you and me still had business."

"What bus—"

"So here's the rules," interrupted Jopek. "The captain asks questions. The kid answers. If you lie, it's a strike. White lies, half lies, fibs—strike, strike. Three strikes and we find out what that space suit looks like with brains on the front plate and oh, Ramboy, you are in *troub*le, you know that?"

Jopek's eyes glittered.

"Question number *uno*: What's your favorite color?"

Michael tried to calm his thunder-some heart. "Purple."

"Gay, a little bit. Two plus two?"

Michael answered.

"Where are ya right now?"

"I don't know," said Michael.

"No idea? That scare ya?"

"Yeah, but I'll live."

"That's your opinion, I guess," said Jopek. "So where's 'Bub' Faris?"

Without even thinking, Michael heard himself reply, "Safe."

Jopek put a dumbstruck hand against his own cheek. "And how," he said, "would you know *that*?"

Michael breathed deeply—still scared, still bewildered. But for just a second, he felt his brain stretching, searching, and holy crap, did that feel good right now. "Because I think you want something from me."

"What the hell could *you* help me with, you reckon?"

"'Business.' But that's the only reason I'm still alive. And I wouldn't do anything for you if Patrick was hurt."

Jopek's mouth slanted into something like disgust. "'Cause you're *such good brudders.*

"Here's a easy one: you never saw no soldiers. Did you?"

Michael hesitated. Then shook his head.

"And you don't know nothin' but nothin' about other units."

Had Jopek come back because he wanted Michael's "information" on where other soldiers were?

"*I* ask the questions," Jopek said, seeing the thought on Michael's face.

"No." Michael shook his head. "I never saw any soldiers. It was just me and Bub."

Jopek asked, "Then how did you do it?"

"Do what?"

"Coulda swore I said I ask the questions! Coulda *swore it*!" Jopek said, giving a vicious, bitter laugh. "How did you *live* in this world, all the way to Safe Zone?" Jopek asked.

Why is he asking this? "I don't know."

"Well. Hey. Strike one."

Michael's eyes flicked to the gun, any *yes-yes* feeling he'd had falling away. "I just . . . *did*," he said. "I kept us pretty safe. If somebody was just watching us, they might have gotten worried. But just because they wouldn't have known."

"Known what?"

"What I could do."

"Which is?"

Michael hesitated again. He saw himself through Jopek's eyes right then: trapped; outplayed; the loser.

"I thought—think—I could just breathe and like, understand things. Almost feel what was coming."

"Is that how you knew the answer about where your screwed-up brother is?"

It felt like pushing on a bruise. But Michael nodded.

"And why do you play The Game?" said the captain.

"To help pass the ti—"

"Strike two!"

266

—Jopek's hand, huge and meaty on the pistol—

"—to protect him! To protect him."

"What from? Boo-boos? Diarrhea?"

"No—look, you know everything, you know all this, why do you want me to say it?" Michael blurted.

"And what do you think would happen at The End of The Game?" asked Jopek, ignoring Michael's question . . . and smiling.

What the hell? Had Jopek returned because he wanted to understand *The Game*?

"We win," Michael said falteringly. "There's a party."

"Search party?"

It was as if Jopek was forcing him to read his journal aloud. "An . . . Ultraman party."

"Except it didn't work that way, huh?"

"No."

"Why?" Jopek said. He looked eager.

I can't lie.

Michael said: "Because of you."

"Now here we go!" crowed Jopek suddenly. "Speak it. *Say* that shit, Michael!"

He leaned forward: his stool was about to tip, supported by only thin blades of wood.

He's pissed.

A whisper of thought, coming from the back of Michael's brain: . . . *keep making him pissed . . . .*

What? NO!

"SPEAK IT—"

"We all would've been safer without you, Jopek."

What are you doing? Look at him! He's not just pissed, he's freaking deadly right now!

Good!

What? Why?!

Because you're right about Jopek: he's just like Ron. Jopek isn't a genius; he just got lucky last night. Piss him off, like you did with Ron, and Jopek will get sloppy, yes-yes.

Michael did not totally trust *yes-yes*, but he could not help but think, *Maybe this is The End—Beat Jopek, beat the final Boss, and I can save everyone.*

Jopek's composure shattered. "You think you're so smart?"

Michael made himself smile. "You don't want me to answer that."

"When did you start thinking that?" Jopek growled. *"When did you start thinking you were better than me?"*

Oh my God, is this why he kept me alive?

To try to show me—and himself—that he's "special"? That he didn't *just get lucky last night?*

Yes!

The things that shot across the basket next weren't Jopek's bullets.

They were Michael's words, tumbling, tumbling:

"The first second I saw you, seriously, I thought, 'Look at that Shortbus Kid, I bet he asks me to tie his shoes.'"

Jopek was booming to a stand and his eyes were fiery with anger and joy, side-by-side like complementary poisons. Jopek tried to pull back the hammer of the pistol with a clumsy-with-emotion hand. He tried again. Got it the fourth try.

"Strike thr—"

"It's not a strike; it's just true. Are you too stupid to get that?"

Jopek slammed Michael sidelong into the wicker wall of the basket, and the moment was so *yes-yes* that Michael had to fight to keep himself from shouting victoriously.

Jopek panted.

"Heyo, the truth stings," said Michael.

The basket swung and swung in the sky.

Jopek aimed the gun at Michael's heart . . . and opened his fist.

The gun dropped between the *V* of Michael's feet, bouncing once before settling.

Jopek lunged at him: he keyed open the handcuffs, then hurled the cuffs over the side of the basket in a glittering arc.

"Who do you think you are? Think you're better, let's *see* it, let's play! Move, gunslinger! Sling! *Sling!*"

Michael gaped. At the gun between them. The gun in the pool of shadow between them.

"N-no," he faked.

Yes, he thought. *Yes!*

THIS IS IT! This was what Jopek was! Jopek was stupid, Jopek was jealous, and *this* was the final standoff the Game Master had promised Michael!

Jopek's breath rose to the high canvas. "Go for it. Draw. Sling it! Let's us see who's faster, see who's better!"

"No," said Michael.

"Sling!"

"I was kidding before," Michael lied.

"*I* wasn't."

"Captain!"

"—*Caaaaaaappppptttaaaaaaaiiiiiiiinnnnn*—" called Bellows a world below.

"*Suh . . . ling . . .*" Jopek whispered. His voice was hoarse, and for a hovering, trembling moment, Michael felt pity for him. Almost. "Sling," Jopek said, collapsing into the stool, thudding his head against the first aid kit that hung on the wall.

"Jopek—Captain—Horace, I'm not going to shoot you," Michael said in what sounded like desperation. "Let's just talk this out like two grown-up dudes."

And that was when Michael made his move for the gun.

The world clicked into *yes-yes* as he kicked the gun toward himself, straight into his space-suited hand.

Jopek shot up from the stool, shouting.

Michael knew, absolutely, that Jopek was going to strike him. He braced for it. He had taken everything a world of corpses had: he could take anything Jopek could offer and still get him to lower the basket and let him go free.

Jopek's fist leapt—

—but not at Michael—

—because it went for the first aid kit. He grabbed it and the kit clammed open, so for a second the red cross blazed before the sun like a sign, and out of the case spat—*no, no, doesn't work that way*—a large, black pistol that Jopek had hidden and now snatched from the air. The gun in Michael's hand began loudly clicking. *Empty,* he thought, *fool me twice oh my God NO,* and the basket exploded beside his head. Michael's screams were trapped in his space suit and he could only hear the missiles revving past his skull while Jopek laughed and shot at his head, *Which is how you kill people who were too slow and became Bellows, like me—*

—*I was wrong—*

—*Jopek isn't like Ron—*

Jopek's eyes were blastingly bright with intelligence.

With cunning.

With bad genius.

Smart! He is smart*! His secret is that he is* smart*!*

"Hey," said Captain Jopek. "You missed me."

No accent, Michael thought.

"Who are you?" Michael said.

The captain's face flamed: new mask, same fire.

"Don't you know yet, Mikey? I'm whover I damn well want to be."

Michael paled. "Are you . . . even a soldier?"

"What I am," Jopek replied, "is better than you. I want you to remember that.

"I want you to know that I put a kill switch on that Hummer, so even if you'd gotten out of the Capitol last night, you never would've gotten away.

"I want you to know that there are no other survivors in Richmond, you goddamn dumbass, 'cause *every Safe Zone except mine got overthrown last week.*

"I want you to know that this world is my world, and the only reason you breathe in it is because I let you.

"Every day of my life I have known that this new world was coming down the pike. You breathe and you think you can feel the future, Michael? No: *I AM the future.*"

Michael tried to back away but the balloon only bucked. "You're—you're lying," he said, his stomach falling. "There are other people."

Jopek reached into his jacket, pulled out a stapled collection of crumpled white papers. Michael recognized it instantly: the list that Jopek had shown Michael that had Mom's name on it; the registry of all those who had checked into the Charleston Safe Zone.

Now Jopek pushed the CONFIRMED DECEASED list at Michael's face.

Michael's chest swooned. "No please no," he moaned, and tried to look away.

Jopek grabbed Michael's chin through the space suit, forced his face back.

Highlighted in yellow: Michael David Faris, killed 11/24 (KIA; Infected; Security Patrol)

"Wh-what?" said Michael.

"Yeah! Huh!" laughed Jopek. "It's almost like somebody faked the list!"

"Why the hell did you lie? About everything, about who you are?"

Jopek cocked his head, as if vaguely amused.

"The same reason as you," he replied. "Because I want to."

That's not true, hissed Michael's mind. *None of this is. Oh God, it can't be. Mom. Mom can't be dead—*

"All right, buddy, let's get down to business."

Jopek seized Michael and thrust him up, forcing his face over the edge of the basket, and the stench of the Bellows sailed up at him like ripe disease geysering from a well.

CHAPTER TWENTY-SEVEN

A thing can hide right in front of your face, Michael had learned, if you're searching for something else. So at first, Michael almost didn't trust what he was seeing.

They were in downtown Charleston.

The unbroken sky had been an illusion: Michael had mistaken the smooth, blue front of a *Rush! Fitness* for the open air. He and Jopek had not been high up in the balloon, either, no more than fifty feet in the air. Which seemed impossible when you considered how far away those thousands of Bellows had sounded.

Except it was not impossible. Because *there weren't* thousands of Bellows roaming the Charleston roads below. The road was covered in Bellows, yes . . .

But all the Bellows were dead.

Actually dead.

Sprawled blindly and choking the road, like the aftermath of a massacre.

"What the hell happened to them?" Michael finally managed to say.

"Head wounds. All of 'em," replied Jopek. He reached up and

turned off the hot-air balloon's burner. They began descending toward the Hummer, which the balloon was tied to.

"You killed all of them?" Michael said. But as they got closer to the ground, he understood immediately that these monsters, which had overtaken the Capitol last night, had not been destroyed by a gun. The Bellows' head wounds weren't bullet holes, all circular and neat: the holes in their skulls were ragged crescents, cleaved into their foreheads or above their ears, a ruptured chaos of black blood and bone.

They were bite marks.

"My guess? That little boy—that new Thing—got hungry in the night," said Jopek as the balloon touched down and settled atop the Hummer: he got out, tucked the pistols in his belt, secured the balloon with something like heavy-duty bungee cords, and turned off the balloon burner so it would begin to deflate. A moment later, Jopek climbed down off the side of the Hummer, and Michael followed him. "By the way, Michael," he said, unlocking a gun case in the front seat and pulling out his AK, "you say a word about the other Safe Zone, and I'm afraid I'll have to kill you. And I'll make it hurt."

And he was Jopek again—or at least the person Michael had thought of as Jopek: redneck voice and cocky smile.

Michael nodded. He felt dazed by the Bellows' massacre. But he still did not understand something basic about his situation: "If I'm infected, why did you bring me?"

But right then, Holly and Patrick got out the double doors in the back of the Hummer. Michael hadn't expected to ever see them again. It seemed miraculous and absurd, the way they casually unloaded, as if their car had just pulled into a rest stop.

"Hey, Bub," Michael said, voice uneasy. "Like my new outfit?"

Patrick whispered to Jopek, *"Still the Betrayer?"* Jopek nodded, ruffling Patrick's hair. It was the same thing Jopek had done yesterday in the Hummer outside Walgreens, and back then, Patrick had look pleased. But Patrick flinched tensely this time. There was something haunted in his face: that dread-filled and desperate searching for something to believe. Patrick looked like a windup toy whose key has been turned too many times, as if the gears that had supplied the power to carry him through this nightmarish world were drawing tighter, tighter, tighter. And if just a couple more things went wrong for Patrick, Michael knew his brother was going to break.

"'Morning," said Holly. Her arms were folded across the belly of her blue hoodie. The skin under her eyes was puffy and red; she wouldn't quite look at him. Her voice sounded small: he didn't know if it was just the faceplate, but Holly had never sounded so far away.

"H-hey," Michael replied.

Not: *I'm infected, help me, help me.*

Not: *Holly, why the hell did you have to tell Jopek about The Game?*

Not: *Why didn't you just leave with me yesterday?*

"Damn, Cady had one hell of a midnight snack," Jopek said to himself, high-stepping over the corpses. The Bellows nearly carpeted the road, at some points stacked two or three on top of each other: Michael saw a bloated old woman on top of a priest.

He wished he could ask Holly for an explanation of why this had happened. If what she'd said before about viruses was true—if they only changed in ways that helped them survive—the idea of Cady slaughtering carriers of the same disease . . . it didn't make sense.

Michael didn't like it. Oh man, he didn't like it *at all*.

But what exactly do you know, his mind hissed at him, *about things working out the way you thought they would?*

"No sign of Cady this mornin', but there's a few reg'lar Bellows left roamin' around," said Jopek. "And I bet that those Rapture folks are just a mite pissed at us after our little shootout with them yesterday. The Bellows riotin' and all that last night might've kept them off for a little bit, but I doubt for too much longer. Let's get going."

"Get going where?" asked Michael.

"You ain't figured it out?" Jopek said. "The only place left to search in the city."

You still want to "search"?

Jopek pointed up the road.

The ruins of the passenger jet lay shattered and enormous and grim with snow. It was the same jetliner that had attempted to escort one hundred souls, including Bobbie, to salvation, but been betrayed by its own pilot and fallen from the heavens. The jet lay on the ruptured landing strip of the road, its nose disappearing into a building labeled FIRST BANK OF CHARLESTON, its fuselage and wings pointing at the building like an arrow.

Jopek said, "The last place that ol' secret lab could be."

"In the *plane*?" Patrick murmured.

"Inside the bank, Bub," said Jopek, and Michael cringed at the use of Patrick's nickname. "We're gonna go make a withdraw."

"Wait—what? What do you mean 'lab'?" Michael said, looking up at the face of what had survived of the front of the bank above the point where the crashed plane's nose had burrowed in, like a dog's snout in a hole. It was an old building, with three stories of faded, flat-red brick—the kind of building that seemed to say, *And this is where we put our* especially *boring adults.*

But then two ideas crashed together in Michael's head: his suspicion about why Jopek seemed so intent on his "rescue missions" in the obviously empty city . . . and Holly saying that the Centers for Disease Control were working on a cure, with a hidden lab located in Charleston itself.

Brain-stunned, Michael said, "There's a cure."

"Could be," said Jopek.

"You want it."

"Sure do! Hey, sounds like a real nice way to end The Game, don't it? Mean ol' world. How else can you *really* be safe, huh, Patrick?"

"So . . . why don't *you* get it?" Michael said.

I mean, you're brave. You're smart. You're . . . you're better than me.

Then Michael said, realizing: "You don't have that many bullets left. And you don't know how dangerous it might be."

"What do I look like," said Jopek, throwing his head back, barking laughter, "some kind of idiot who thinks they see the future?"

Cure.

Dimly, Michael understood that he should have been blowing kisses, tap-dancing, singing "Yankee Doodle Dandy." But the shock wouldn't let him.

I didn't see this coming, he thought. *Idiot. Stupid. Why didn't I see this coming?*

"And we can go to The End after we get it. Really, right? It can make the Bellows go away, right?" Patrick asked Jopek anxiously.

Michael tried to calm himself. *If a cure is in there,* he told himself, *I get to CONTINUE.* For the first time, that felt so stupid, imagining his life through the lens of a game.

"Wait. I get to *use* the cure, right?"

Jopek signaled for everyone to follow him. Just like old times.

"Have to think about it, you being the Betrayer," Jopek replied, nodding reasonably. "But y'all know, I'm a generous man."

"Will it even . . . work on me, though?"

He realized that the question was really for Holly.

Holly's mouth set, like a doctor about to give bad news. Her gaze flicked to Jopek, and she said, "Yeah. Of course it will."

Michael understood, from her uneven tone, that she did not know if that was true. He wondered fleetingly whether Holly was trying to deceive Jopek (by making him think that Michael was safer than he really was), or deceive himself (by encouraging Michael with the false hope of a cure). Then he realized that it didn't affect the facts of the cure, anyway. *And also,* he thought, *I'm pretty damn tired of trying to figure out Holly's lies.*

CHAPTER TWENTY-EIGHT

Michael walked into the jetliner with the point of Jopek's AK-47 pressed into his back, Patrick and Holly somewhere behind.

He had always wanted to go on a plane—there had been class trips; he couldn't afford them—but he didn't want to be on this one, because it reminded him of those pictures of the *Titanic* at the bottom of the ocean. It was a dead place. Oxygen masks in the darkness dangled like nerves; snow hissed through the crimson-stained seats on a breeze that stank of smoke and flesh. It was easy to imagine Cady pouncing from the floor . . . or the ceiling.

"*So it's scary.* Be *scared.* Use *it,*" Michael tried to pep-talk himself. His breath fogged the front of his space-suit faceplate. He tried to wipe the fog away; couldn't; it was on the inside. Claustrophobia enwrapped his chest.

"Say somethin'?" asked Jopek.

Michael shook his head. He hadn't tried to *yes-yes* himself outside the jet; he did not know if it would help. But now, as he walked through this dark, Michael understood that he was either going to grasp *yes-yes* or fall totally into despair. He was either going to believe that there was some truth to the Game Master's promises that such a thing as salvation existed. *This is the last chance I've got to save Patrick.*

Yeah, keep tellin' yourself that story, Mikey. But if any of that yes-yes crap worked, you'd be out of here by now.

Michael pinched his leg through his space suit, hard, forcing himself into the moment.

The captain's gun light found the door to the airplane cockpit. He prodded Michael with the barrel of the assault rifle. Michael opened the door. Wire and copper tubing sprang from the ceiling of the cockpit like Medusa hair. The nose of the plane had been chewed off in the crash.

The pilot seats were situated not in front of instruments, but in front of nothing. Where the controls should have been, there was a new world.

The enormous lobby of a great bank.

High ceiling.

Marble floors.

Framed posters showing smiling people.

Brick walls soaring with stained-glass windows, through which daylight streamed.

As his eyes adjusted, something else became clear: the bank had been divided into two sections by the airplane's unplanned touchdown. The collision had brought down a section of wall, maybe fifty feet from the airplane, so that the ceiling of the higher floors had collapsed inward.

Rubble rose, floor to ceiling. The ruins were stacked so tall and tight that they had effectively sealed off the rest of the bank from the entrance area.

"So you see why this was last on the list," said Jopek, his voice hushed. "But there's a tunnel to the other side, sorta."

Emphasis on "sorta," Michael thought. He saw the entrance: a small mouth in the rubble at floor level, dark and jagged with debris. Just big enough for him, the tunnel shot way through the ruins to absolute blackness.

Just big enough for him, Michael thought. By *"chance."*

But he suddenly had a dreadful feeling. It was that *clockwork-syncing* feeling again, yes, that sense of the world aligning for him. But this time, it felt like a dark clockwork, a wicked clockwork, conspiring against him. It was irrational but Michael thought: *Cady's in there.*

No. No, there was a whole city of other places for Cady to be.

Michael felt his breath and tried to look back at Patrick, but Jopek pushed the gun into Michael's cheek and forced his gaze front again.

"Time's a-wastin'," the captain said.

Michael nodded, and said, "Yeah. Okay. Here I g—" But then he realized that Jopek had not been speaking to *him*, because Patrick replied, "Yes, sir," took a little flashlight from Jopek, crouched down at the tunnel, and said, "Clear." Jopek stared blankly at him, then replied, "Oh. Five points." Then Patrick brushed his nose with his sleeve, and began to crawl into the tunnel.

CHAPTER TWENTY-NINE

"What are you *doing*!" Michael cried. He lunged for Patrick.

Jopek's hand seized Michael's shoulder. "You watch yourself, boy. Don't you get called for interference, now. Bub, you let us know what you find."

"Bub, do not go in there!"

Patrick gazed down the tunnel another moment, then turned around. He had never looked smaller: his mouth so tiny and pink, his nose so slender. He got those features from Mom, but right now Michael saw something on Patrick's face that he had never seen on their mother's: a stubborn determination.

He's trying to be brave. He wants The End. And he's not going to stop until he gets it.

"You said *you* would go in with *Michael*, Captain!" Holly shouted.

And that broke the pause: Patrick wriggled forward, the snow-stamped bottoms of his sneakers slipping away.

"Why did you do that, Jopek?" Michael said. "Why the hell did you do that?"

"He volunteered," Jopek replied in a "who me?" voice. "He's used to getting through tight places, he said. Kinda got the impression he didn't trust you to do it."

The feeling drained from Michael's face.

"You didn't say Patrick would go by himself," Holly breathed.

She was so smart. She had once seemed so good. So how could she still be surprised?

Michael spun from Jopek's grip. He got two steps toward the tunnel before Jopek shoved him and knocked him sprawling, rubble-pebbles poking through the chest of his suit. *"Pay-trick!"* Michael called desperately in his Game Master voice. *"Ten points for comin' back right now! Ten p—"*

Jopek, towering over him, a boot on each side of his chest, cocked the AK. "You play nice, Mikey. Now, your brother's safe in there. There ain't no monsters in there, just calm down—you hear anything talkin' back to us?"

"What did you even freaking bring me for?" Michael spat.

Jopek bent, offering Michael a hand up. Three drops of sweat glided down his brow and fell on the barrier over Michael's mouth.

"'Cause I need a backup in case the retard gets killed."

Michael roared, his fist flying to hit Jopek's belly. Jopek slapped away, no problem, grinning like a man at a carnival game.

Patrick's voice, flattened through the tunnel: *"Maaaade* it!" he said. "You're right! There's something in h—"

Then, a shriek.

The shriek of Cady Gibson.

CHAPTER THIRTY

Michael waited to hear a cry of pain. He waited for the snap of his brother's bones. And he waited to hear Patrick shouting that it was Michael's fault.

There was a second shriek, sounding like it had the night before: a knife tearing into this world from another.

Rocks clattered in the tunnel.

Patrick screamed.

Running footsteps. And an enormous, metallic shutting-slamming sound.

Then Patrick's scream stopped. Echoed. Stopped echoing. And Michael suddenly was on his feet and running.

A boot flew out and sent him spilling. He flipped onto his back, ready to punch through Jopek. But it was Holly who had tripped him. *What are you doing, Holly?*

Michael got to his feet. "No, wait wait, that Thing is in there!" Holly said, grabbing him, rough-handed.

"*Patrick* is in there!"

Tears of relief shimmered in Holly's eyes. "I think he hid, though. Didn't you hear that slamming sound? *I think Patrick got into the vault.*"

Michael knelt, peering in the tunnel. He could see flickering, fluorescent light. No child-sized lumps of clothing. No tossed-off shoe. No blood. And no movement. As if the Thing—*the Shriek*—had left . . . or hidden.

Jopek pushed Michael aside and threw a lit flare down the throat of the tunnel. "Patrick! It's the Game Master, bud! C'mon back!"

Silence.

"Yeah. The vault. Sounds like it," Jopek agreed. He sighed in relief, almost moaned, and Michael knew it was not a relief that Patrick was alive. It was relief that his mission had not just been screwed up.

Patrick was in the vault. Locked away. *He found a Safe Zone,* Michael thought, and felt a clutch of love.

Michael tried crawling toward the tunnel again, but Jopek grabbed him.

"Let go!"

"You're going nowhere till we're sure that Thing's gone."

"Because you need a backup?" Michael spat.

"Yeah," Jopek said simply.

"How long, exactly, do you plan on waiting, sir?" Holly spat with mock respect.

Jopek glared. "A while."

There were choices.

Patrick. Patrick.

"Then I'm going outside," Michael said.

Jopek scoffed, "Bulls—"

"I'm going to start a fire in the road. To keep Bellows away. You said there are some Bellows left; we've made enough freaking noise to bring all of them here. Look, do you really want to waste your ammo on them before we have to? Do you really think I'm going to try to run away and leave my brother?"

Jopek actually had to consider the last question.

"Have a ton of fun," Jopek said.

Holly tried to ask if she could come, too, but Michael was already heading for the fuselage, his mind stretching, trying for a plan, desperately, oh God, don't let this be The End—

He was ducking through the fracture in the fuselage when Jopek barked: "Faris!"

He turned, prepared to see Jopek raising the gun.

An unlit flare batoned through the air.

Michael caught it against his chest, and let his heartbeat devour the airplane.

The Game ends with stopping a Betrayer, right? I knew that, Michael thought. *Jopek and the Rapture are each other's Betrayers. Let's see what happens if they try to stop each other.*

I don't like what you're planning, Michael. The Rapture tried to kill you, too, remember?

Yeah—but I'm thinking they want Jopek even more than me, after he killed all those people yesterday.

They're still the bad guys!

But that doesn't mean I can't make them change teams for a while.

"Michael?" Holly called from behind him as he marched out into the street.

She emerged from the plane, her face all confusion, scrunched against the wind.

Michael grabbed at the back of his space suit, found a zipper, unhooded himself. He got a cinder block that had smashed into a candy store window, a swirly lollipop stuck on the bottom. "What are you . . . ?" said Holly. Tears glittered in her eyes.

You want to cry now?

Michael hurled the block over a chain-link fence into a

nearby alley, where it tipped end over end, drunkenly strolling toward the cluster of mines.

Boom. One land mine lit, exploded, sending up a mini-rocket of fire and sound.

"The Bellows are coming. Down the road. Be careful. Michael? Hey?" Holly's hand touched his shoulder, lightly.

"I don't care," Michael said, spinning on her. "I don't *care* what you have to say, Holly. I don't need your help—I don't *want* it!"

She cringed.

Michael threw a stray boot and he got two mines in the chain-linked-off alley; double kaboom; the explosive fire leapt up and the sound ran past him, traveling across the city. It was his signal to the other people in town. But where were the ears to hear it?

Michael checked the horizons.

Look at me, he thought. *Calling in backup.* Please *look at me, Rulon!*

"I know I . . . don't deserve you talking to me right now. I know that," Holly said, wiping her tears clumsily.

Look! he begged. *LOOK AT M—*

"I was wrong to trust him, Michael. I should have left with you last night. I was just so goddamn wrong—"

"Yeah, I was pretty wrong, too. I thought you cared about Patrick and me," Michael spat.

Holly shook her head. "I—I do! I care a lot. I was trying to help you guys. I just thought that Jopek . . . I thought we all had a better chance with him. I screwed up, but I didn't see any other way, okay?

"Do you remember when I told you that my dad was a pharmacist?" Holly said.

Michael walked toward the four or five Bellows that were staggering toward him and Holly from fifty yards away.

"What are you doing?" said Holly.

"Holly, just shut up. You've messed up enough—"

"My dad made *the cure, Michael!"* she said.

Michael blinked. *"What?"*

"I'm trying to tell you that he was the leader of the CDC team, and he made it! And—and—the day everything got overrun, we got separated and so many of the buses out of town got swamped. Hank and I didn't know what happened to our dad—we didn't know if he got out safe, or if he was bit. I don't even know if the CDC had had time to get the cure out of the city.

"Hank and I were alone. Jopek said he'd help us find the lab. He said we had to keep it a secret because *he* was the leader. I know that was stupid, but I just wanted to get it so, so bad. I *needed* to hang on to that. I needed—"

"Jopek's training, yeah, I remember."

"No. Yeah," she said. "But . . . I needed *hope*, Michael."

Michael didn't question whether the disgust he felt was real then; for that word, *hope*, was hideous on his heart. Mom lived behind a hope of her life changing; Bobbie hoped to run her fingers over her husband's smile one more time; the Rapture worshipped their undead hopes and let them devour them. But hope was a weak wish, Michael knew now: a dream from which you wouldn't let the real things wake you.

People say they have hope for the future, but no they don't. Because hope wasn't about the future, not truly. Hope was: *make me feel better now.* Hope was: *tell me, this second, that I'll be all right.* Hope was: *tell me I don't have to be different, but things will be.* Hope made you feel better by letting you feel a false future.

Michael forced himself to think of Patrick. He looked away, back down the street, at the nearing Bellows—now almost a dozen of them.

God, where was the Rapture?

"When the captain asked me today how to take the antidote

to make it work," Holly said, "I said I'd only tell him if he gave you a dose first. I'll tell you how to make it work, right now, but please—promise me something."

Michael whispered to the dead.

They heard it. They echoed the message: the next Bellow picking it up, casting it to the next and next, carrying it away like a series of undead tin-can telephones strung across the city.

Heeeere! The soooooooldier heeeeeeere! Baaaannnk!

—Shooooot sooooooldier!—

"Promise what?" he said.

"That you were lying last night. About there being no other soldiers that can take us to Richmond. Right?"

She touched him again, looking at him like she had in the middle of the night, watching the Kanawha River, that bare and desperate confession of want for Before.

He did not say: *I never saw soldiers.*

He did not say: *Jopek told me we're alone.*

If she needs hope to get her through this, fine. The hope's false, but without it? She won't trust me to get through this, and we won't get any *future.*

He said: "Y-yeah. There are soldiers."

Holly's brow knitted, and she nodded, and tears of relief shimmered to her eyes, and Michael remembered then, from the pure unhidden gratitude on her face, how much he liked her. And as she looked at him with trust, he pretty much hated his life.

Am I doing the right thing? Michael thought. *Am I?*

"Thanks," Holly breathed shakily. "You're a good guy."

I lie for the same reason as you, said Jopek's voice in his head. *Because I want to.*

And now Jopek was coming out of the plane. Michael put the hood of his space suit back on.

"You have to inject it at the site of the wound," Holly whispered

289

to Michael urgently, and spun around to face Jopek.

"You said you'd be right back," Jopek growled from the airplane door.

Blocking the view from Jopek with her body, Holly grabbed Michael's hand and gave it two squeezes.

Michael thought, with a painful ache in his heart: *Facebook update—Michael is IN A RELATIONSHIP WITH A GIRL HE CAN'T STOP LYING TO.*

"I lied," Holly replied.

CHAPTER THIRTY-ONE

They both did, easily enough.

Jopek asked what the hell was taking so long and they told him what he needed to be told. By now the Bellows' imitations of Michael's message had blended into each other, and there was only a sound of fire in the alley where the mines had blown.

Through the airplane and out the cockpit, Jopek kept the gun on Michael.

Back in the lobby of the First Bank of Charleston, with the gun still aimed at Michael's belly, Jopek approached the tunnel and spied down it. Holly stood halfway between the two of them, as if still on neither team, her eyes nervously cast down. The last of the day streamed in through the high, stained-glass windows.

When are the Rapture people going to come?

Michael stared at the sun-struck colors in a window to his right. Words began to form inside him. *Please, just let us get out of here. Let me out of this.* He realized that he was praying . . . and as he did, the glass darkened. A shadow had passed over the window—a movement so momentary it might have been imaginary. Until it stealthily moved again.

Michael's mouth became cotton.

The sniper setting up, he saw in his mind.

The human form in the window shrunk, lying down. *Hold B to enter Prone Position,* he thought wildly.

Michael was going to kill a man.

The idea slit him, and thoughts he could not stop rushed through. It wasn't him pulling the trigger, but Michael was going to cause Jopek's life to leak from him. He had to, he knew that. But the idea still made him sick.

The shadow on the glass grew a line: the dark limb of a barrel. The shadow snuck across the floor of the bank, laying itself behind Jopek's feet.

I'll get the cure. I'll keep everyone safe.

Not everyone, his mind said. You. *You never keep everyone safe. You can't even keep* one person *safe.*

Michael swore he heard the click of a safety snicking off.

Patrick's not safe yet. But he will be. In the end.

Holly moved in front of Jopek just as Michael was closing his eyes against the coming fire. Her dark expression told her motive instantly: she was furious. She was going to demand Jopek help Patrick, or else.

Won't work, Holly! You do not KNOW HIM!

Michael found he was holding his breath.

Michael dived for her, catching Holly at the waist, and they flew through space.

A second thud followed their own: a brick, tossed from outside, splashing through the window.

The brick landed in a crash of color.

Jopek spun. Alarmed, not yet comprehending. He looked at them. At the splayed rainbow. His stare then trailed up into the new shaft of sun. It was blazing him, transforming his face and, for one single second in that light, he looked almost like an angel.

The first shot came with a rocket of sound, a solid crack that made Holly kick out her feet on the floor beside Michael in a dance of terror. Shock registered on Jopek's features as the floor tiles at his feet blew up in a storm of particles.

Jopek had been blinking blindly in a spotlight . . . *and the shot hadn't come close.*

Jopek leapt out of the dusk light. In one single movement, he rolled into a crouched shooting stance, aiming for the high gunman through the shattered pane.

A second shot rang. And what followed was a sound Michael had never heard before:

Jopek's pain.

The captain's face contorted with naked surprise. His rifle fell, discharging. The bullet had taken him in the left leg, midway up the shin. The spot became a sudden rose.

DID IT! Triumph, frightening and powerful, roared in Michael.

Jopek tried to pull his sidearm pistol from his belt, but the silhouette fired again and Jopek was grabbing a curve of blood that traced down his screaming face.

Captain Horace Jopek collapsed.

Enemy Team down, Michael thought madly. *I did it, he's down, Enemy freaking* down*!*

Michael's blood towered up his throat and seemed to drive him onto his feet and he thought, *BRB, Holly,* even as she screamed, *"Wait, Michael, wait!"* Jopek's pistol had skidded across the floor and Michael grabbed it and put it in his spacesuit pocket, and he ran and dived into the tunnel. Darkness ate up his vision through his panting-fogged faceplate, rocks sliced through the knees and palms of his suit; now gun sounds from the sniper spiraled after him and he flinched and something shifted in the stone layers overhead: a chattering of rock crashing down. Michael squeezed forward, scrambling insanely and, a second later, shot out the other end of the tunnel.

The bank was a pharaoh's tomb.

Bills and coins in every direction, dust and debris covering all. Brass-rimmed nameplates still sat on rows of parallel desks, winking dully. On one desk, a water-bird paperweight dipped down and up, down and up. Electricity came and went in pulses, desk lamps and ceiling lights crackled on and off; computers kept booting momentarily before the power shorted, the Apple start-up *gong!* echoing like some eerie electronic doom-song. Flickering light, lots of shadows. Oh, too many.

Holly's voice from the other end of the tunnel: "Michael!"

"Come *on*, Holly! The tunnel's safe!"

"I—but—" she said.

Why wasn't she just *coming*?

She's just afraid, he forced himself to think. *She'll come. No time to wait. Move!*

"Bub!" he called across the shadowy lobby.

Only his echo. Where did they even *keep* vaults? Basement? Some kind of manager's office? Behind the counter—

Yes!

"*One-two-three!*" Michael called as a precaution, but he realized he didn't know if the Shriek would echo as a Bellow would. A banner over the counter read BEFORE YOU CHANGE YOUR DREAMS, GET A SECOND OPINION! and Michael dashed, hurtled over the counter. He landed awkwardly on his side, tried to pull out the pistol in his pocket; it got caught in the space-suit fabric. He grappled desperately for another weapon, came up with two things, a plastic capsule used to zip cash through pneumatic tubes to drive-thru customers, and a pen on a chain; he chose the pen, wielded it knifelike, whipped around, and saw nothing.

Except the vault.

Tens and twenties and hundreds eddied over the dozen

pneumatic bullets that lay between him and the vault at the end of the tellers' lane. The vault door was no heist-movie prop: no great steel circle, like a stone rolled in front of a cave. But it *was* steel, and larger than Michael, with a spoked wheel dead center like a spiked eye.

He said, "Hey!" padding to his feet. "Hey-hey-hey! Hey, Bubbo-Gum!"

A large dent on the vault door—an impact crater—twisted his reflection. There were thin scratches marring the door, too. *Shriek scratches! It tried to get at Patrick in there! Bub's really here!*

Without thinking, Michael threw himself into the door with everything he had.

It didn't even buck.

He fell back from it, shoulder throbbing.

His panting fogged the faceplate.

Michael wiped at the faceplate madly, realized wiping the outside would do nothing, felt for the suit-back, and tore the hood off messily, the zipper screaming.

He threw himself against the door again—

—*and it wouldn't open again.* It was like a door in a video game that was not designed to be opened.

"Bub!"

There was no reply, save a dry clicking behind him. Michael tensed. But it was only a mini rock slide on the debris.

Calm it. Calm calm calm.

But in his brain he saw: *Patrick, clawing the door, wheezing 'cause there wasn't air in there, fingertips bleeding.* How long had Patrick been in there? Michael guessed, *Eight minutes and forty-three seconds.* Excellent skill, very helpful.

He threw an inarticulate yell of rage, but it was more than a yell, was more like a protest. He had done everything: he had rescued Patrick through a series of Hells, had talked Holly to his side, he'd killed a dark genius with a sniper he'd conjured from nowhere. He had mutated their future.

And now, now Patrick was in there, with no air to breathe—

How, said a small voice, *did he get in there?*

It was as if someone—or Something—had dropped the thought into his head.

Patrick couldn't have opened the vault. The door was too heavy.

The Shriek hit the door and shut it, he imaged.

PULL IT open! You have to *PULL!*

The vault door swung open lightly in Michael's hands.

Not only oxygen had been sucked from the vault: time had, too. As the door swung open, a terror, beneath the neat rows of safe-deposit boxes, was revealed eternally. It was far worse than Cady Gibson. It was Patrick. His face was blue, pinched. He wasn't breathing.

This wasn't real. It wasn't true. His brother wasn't sitting here, dead.

Because Patrick was pretending. His candle was not snuffed, Michael insisted.

I know it's not real, he thought. *I* know. *I know it's not, I know I* know—

Michael cried, *"Please, Bub—!"*

—a gasp—

Patrick's eyes blew open, his breath flying out.

Michael, quite quickly, slid against the door, to the ground, began to laugh and cry. . . .

It was like Patrick was shooting up and out of a pool after a breath-holding contest. He bent forward, his hands on the floor, coughing. "It got hardta . . . hardta . . . breathe . . . . I held it *in*," he said. Hacking still, he flexed his biceps over his shoulders, his orange toy gun in one hand. *Look at me, World's Awesomest Holder of Breath and Kicker of Undead Badonkadonk.*

Even though Patrick wasn't looking, Michael gave a thumbs-up. He wiped his eyes, his fingers coming away shaking, but he couldn't help but chuckle.

"Guess what, Game Master?" Patrick said. "Guess what, I found—*Hey.*" He raised his eyes and saw Michael. If it was possible to cough indignantly, that was what Patrick did. "No. Out."

"Huh?"

"You're not s'posed to be here."

I just saved his life, he thought, *and he's acting like I pooped on his b-day cake.*

"Get *out,*" Patrick repeated, getting to his feet.

But Michael had just seen something.

There was something else in the vault with them.

There was a clear plastic tunnel stickered with BIOHAZARD. The tunnel led to a zip-up plastic door. Past the door, a metallic halo secured in the ceiling draped a pyramid of heavy plastic biomedical sterile tarps. Banks of ultraviolet lights, flickering, gave them the look of arctic ghosts.

Within the tarps was a laboratory. Steel tables and charts and tubes and a gyroscopic machine sporadically spinning beakers. A moment of joy, then a sense of unreality washed through Michael.

It's too small.

That was it. This lab was *too small.* Was it . . . like, a decoy? How could the hope of every possible future fit in here? It couldn't contain the importance.

It wasn't big enough to be the . . . the, like, Last Level.

Don't you know *yet, Michael? It doesn't look like the Last Level because this isn't a game.*

"No you doooon't," said Patrick, singsong. Michael stopped; he hadn't realized it, but he'd been walking toward the transluscent tent. "You can't *geeeet* it in *theeeere*." Patrick was teasing, as giddy and scared as if he were about to launch a tickle-attack. *Why?*

He put his orange gun in his pocket.

And from another pocket, like a magic trick, he pulled a vial, sticky with lint. The cure.

It was no thicker or longer than a number-two pencil. The reddish liquid within glimmered.

Michael's blood seemed to try to leap through his skin, but he conjured calmness on his face.

"The Game Master said only *I* had to get it, not *yooouuu*." Patrick was delighted, because he thought The Game was almost over. He just had to get that vial back to the Game Master.

So get it from him. Charm him. You've done that crap a million times.

Michael smiled. "Duuuuude."

"What?"

"C'mon."

"Nerp."

Michael shrugged, acted like, *Hey, let's make a deal,* scooped up a bill from the floor. "How's 'bout for a hundred bucks?"

Patrick reached in his own stuffed pocket. "I already got, like, a million." Which was true.

"*Cha-ching!* Can I borrow some?" Michael took a cautious step toward Patrick. "I'm hoping to get butt implants."

"No."

"Well, *that's* really inconvenient, because I already changed my name to Booty-Meister Mike."

The joke seemed to slap the playfulness from Patrick's face. Suddenly, his brother wasn't laughing. Wasn't holding anything on his face except a mask of anger and determination.

Despite the madness of the moment, it stung. When you got right down to it, it kind of broke Michael's heart.

"O-*kay*," Michael said. "How about just a little . . ." He peeked over his shoulder, pretending to be making sure they were alone. He looked back, winked. "Just a little sip? I'm just thirsty."

"You're tryin' to trick me!"

"Patrick!" *Guilt-trip.* "C'mon, Bub. I do solids for you."

"*Pfff*, like what?"

Michael, very briefly, wanted to slap Patrick. *Like save your life*, he thought, *like run away for you.*

"I . . . gave you the last s'mores Pop-Tart," he finished lamely.

Patrick gave a dismissive, "So?"

And somehow that was too much. The heat burst in Michael, bitter and fine.

"Don't be an asshole, Patrick."

Patrick didn't recoil or gasp. His face squinched down, becoming like a hard stone. His lips pursed white. It was the first time he or Michael had ever—*ever*—been mean to each other. To Michael, the anger felt like good poison. *Just because you're screwed up doesn't mean you aren't a brat.*

Then, as if Patrick couldn't hold the hardness anymore, his face became his own again. "Michael, I'll *tell*."

And with that sentence—said as a pitiful beg—Michael realized that he had no chance of getting the cure from Patrick peacefully. What Michael saw now was the same thing he had seen in Holly's eyes when she asked if Michael had been lying, in Mom's eyes sometimes: Patrick trying to hold on, for dear life, to a lie.

He won't let go of The Game. Not even for me. He can't. It's the only thing that makes sense anymore. Michael felt a crush of sympathy for his brother . . . and hate toward himself.

"Just . . . *please*, Bub," he tried, without hope.

"I'm. not. 'Bub,'" Patrick said emphatically. "I'm a *Gamer*. *You're* a Betrayer."

"Your brother, too."

"Not right now," Patrick said.

Pull the gun out of your pocket and point it at him, Michael thought, *so he thinks it's The Game. It's what the Betrayer would do. Just point the gun at him and take it!* But he felt instantly sick with himself.

You can just run. You can tackle him and get it. But he would break the vial; it was so small, and—

And now an image floated up in him, like a gift.

More vials. There was more cure. *Had* to be.

Patrick sensed Michael's thought and threw up his hands, panicked. "Wait wait, you sure you don't waaant it? Here!" He put the vial of cure between his feet. When Michael ignored it, Patrick nudged it a little closer to him with his foot.

Michael wheeled for the tunnel to the lab.

Patrick whispered, *"Wait . . ."*

Michael reached the tunnel, lifted the flap.

"Michael! Wait, *Michael! It's back here, outside the vault!"*

Michael had to hand it to his brother: he actually sounded afraid. "'Kay-yeah-no, nice try. Mine's in *there*."

"No. Not 'the cure,'" Patrick replied.

He showed his teeth, like a monster.

He said, "The 'It' . . ."

At first it was just peripheral eeriness.

Outside the vault, on the ceiling of the bank proper, visible through the frame of the vault door, a new shadow hung, like a great bat. With a whispery *click* sound, the shadow moved.

Eyes shone, like black lamps.

Michael's heart seemed to have shut off.

The Shriek moved toward the vault. Something gleamed: its finger bones. The skeleton of its fingers flashed clean white, the skin and sinew there ripped away like tips worn from old gloves, so its fingers were not just bones, but sharp exquisite axes that could pass your throat and make it smile red.

Michael's first shot, fired while whirling, missed by yards, two more he squeezed coming closer, not much.

The Shriek cried out and skittered out of sight.

Michael held frozen, the echo of the gunshots cracking around him like caged earthquakes. Then he burst out of his shock and went to the door. *It was too fast last night, it will be now too*, he thought, panicked. But he also thought: *if I can kill it, if I can shoot it in the head, it will die.*

Every bad guy has a weak spot in every game.

It's the last really dangerous one in Charleston. Kill it, and all this is over.

How do you know that's true?!

Because . . . it has to be.

"Bub," he whispered, *"you stay here while I go out and—"*

Except Patrick was at his side as he stepped out of the vault, flattened himself against the wall, like a SWAT member.

"Stop tryin' to trick me! He's on your team!" Patrick hissed.

"What?"

Far too loudly: *"You're the Betrayer!* The Game Master told me you're even supposed to *have* guns!"

"Bub, shh—"

"You have to play right! *MICHAEL, PLEASE!*"

"Sit. Down!" Michael whispered.

"Pfft, you sit down!" Patrick came back.

Oh my God, omigod.

A call of claws, clicking the ceiling. Shadows coiled all across the ceiling like snakes in a basket. Then the Shriek cried out.

The sound was followed by a second cry, nearer, and suddenly Michael knew where the creature was, on the dark ceiling above the bank's rows of desks, so Michael breathed out like a *Modern Warfare* sniper, aimed, and tugged the trigger.

The shot struck absolutely nothing.

One reason: Michael heard another *click-click-click* movement now, far from where he'd aimed. The Shriek was using the echo in the Bank of Charleston for misdirection.

The second reason: Patrick had laced his finger into the triggerhold, attempting to take the firearm, and this sorta compromised his aim.

Patrick tugged the gun down with a grunt.

Another round accidentally discharged between their four feet.

"Play *right*!" Patrick pulled the gun toward himself, like he was fighting over a TV remote. He spied down the barrel.

Michael said, "I'm not the Betrayer, let's switch teams, I want to be on your team!"

"A-la-la-la-la-can't-hear-you!"

Stone dust rained from the ceiling, this time the cry of the Shriek issuing from directly above. The rippling air pressure came down on Michael's head like a cold cap. *It's trying to paralyze its prey, shock us, like it shocked us last night, right before it jumped.*

The corpse landed on all fours in the aisle leading to the counter and wove among the desks, like a feral wolf.

Michael shoved Patrick and gained the gun.

Patrick stumbled back, over a rumpled orange carpet, and landed on a black metal box, grabbing his butt in pain. Michael was wheeling his aim back to the Shriek when the box began to roar. The creature echoed the cry. But this box's roar was mechanical: this box was an air pump.

The carpet jerked, which would have been odd except it was not a carpet; it actually was a tarp, a great orange inflatable man with pennants for limbs, and in the adrenaline-soaked brightness of his mind, Michael knew that it had been used as a Halloween decoration, and the employees had brought it in for the night, not knowing the tarp-man would never dance for customers again. Now the tarp-man furled high.

And slapped the gun from Michael's hand.

The pistol zipped across the marble, skidding underneath a wooden desk between him and the Shriek.

The Shriek stopped, head cocking, as if amused.

The orange, faceless giant jigged.

"Stay," Michael whispered, *"down."*

"Pfff, whateve—"

Michael ran. He ran for the gun.

The Shriek dropped behind one of the desks like a magician into a trapdoor, then rematerialized behind the desk closest to Michael. Michael grabbed a leather roller chair, and thrust it at the Thing.

The creature bounded over the chair, seemed to hang midair before coming down in a cougar's crouch.

The creature scrabbled toward him. Michael reached behind himself blindly, found on the desk an energy bar, *not helpful,* then something better: an orb-crystal paperweight. He hurled it. A thud and a snap: the ball slammed into its target's neck, both a bludgeon and a blade because it shattered on impact. Blood hit a floor fan and flew up: black mist.

The creature went still. Surprised or angry?

Its cry answered that.

"Oh, you are effing pissed," Michael whimpered.

Michael reared his hand back like he had another weapon,

and the Shriek responded by going for the nearest wall, which, with its bone-grips, it scaled in a vertical sprint.

For glowing moments, Michael thought it was over, the Shriek was retreating to some secret place in the ceiling. Then the pattern of the monster's movements on the ceiling became clear. It wasn't searching for an exit: it was circling overhead, as vultures do.

Michael rotated on his heels with a craned neck, not daring to let it out of sight. Speed and shadow hid the creature: it would slip out of one shadow and seem to teleport to the next instantaneously. But its all-black lamp eyes were always on Michael, even when its body faced the opposite direction: its head twisted and contorted to unnatural angles, its neck breaking again and again.

Its circle was tightening.

The click of its claws was a race of scorpions across the tops of tombstones.

"You guys are butt-monkeys," Patrick said.

At Patrick's voice, the Shriek came at last into a jag of light.

The Shriek was wearing torn, striped track pants.

"Hank?" Michael gasped.

It wasn't Cady Gibson. It was *Hank*.

If you hadn't known Hank had been mauled—if you'd just been looking for Hank, and seen this Thing—you wouldn't have known they were the same.

Hank's face was riveted, as if he had been dragged across a field of razors. Cady must have bitten Hank after Hank's death, for Michael saw a bite point above his ear. He could see the black brain.

Hank.

Dead.

Changed.

Alive.

Mutated.

The ramifications went like chain explosions in Michael's mind. *The Bellows outside.* All those *Bellows outside.*

Cady bit Hank, and Hank came back.

Cady bit the ones outside. And they're all *going to come back—*

"*Haaaaaaaaaaaaannnnk!*" The word, coming from Hank's throat, was like hearing your own ghost call a warning from beyond the grave.

"Patrick?" Michael said. All things considered, he thought he sounded good: his voice trembled only horribly. "Get ready."

"I'm—not—" Patrick replied, singsong, "—*listening*—to—the—buuuuutt-monkey—"

"Hey, Hank," Michael said softly, sliding his feet over the floor. He was inching diagonally toward the counter. If he moved any quicker, it wouldn't work; the Shriek would spring.

Michael felt the tarp-man's fingers whisk his scalp. Hank's spirals tightened. . . .

The gate that led behind the counter swung open at Michael's hips, like doors of an Old West saloon. A pneumatic tube tangled between his feet. For one electrifying moment, he thought he would fall.

He moved toward his brother. Patrick, beside him, still had his hands cupped on his head, grooving back and forth to his tune, now a club mix: "*Listening—not—listening—not—not—not* listening—"

Hank's stalking circle ceased.

The Shriek hung upside down, watching.

It hung over Patrick, luminous like a guillotine blade.

Black blood dripped from Hank's forehead. It struck the crown of Patrick's head. Patrick's face raised up slowly, still vaguely singing, now to Hank.

And Hank: he smiled.

"HEY, COME EAT IT, YOU NEEWWWWWBB!" Michael roared.

The Shriek burst from the ceiling with the fused strength of four coiled limbs. The frozen wind of its hypersonic monster-cry slammed into Michael like a blast of cold bullets. The computer monitor beside Michael shattered and exploded.

Midair, the Shriek's jaw unhinged like a python's. The back of its throat was brilliantly white. Suddenly, Patrick's song died. And now he was screaming and so was Michael, and the Shriek flying more quickly than seemed possible—

—and so was Michael—

—dodging himself to the ground and to the left, tackling Patrick alongside him—

And the Shriek bayed while whipping through the empty air and it crashed into the mouth of the vault—a drumroll of bones—slinging against the far wall, and safe-deposit boxes sprang open, like surprises.

Michael rushed his shoulder into the vault door.

But the door did not swing with crazy ease. Slow, nightmare slow: it began to inch. A ruined arm shot through the opening, Michael thrust harder—the dead arm snapped—the Shriek cried out, withdrew the limb. Michael closed the door, swung the pirate-wheel locked, and slid to the ground.

Patrick, freshly tackled, looked at the vault. At him. At the vault. At him.

"Hey," breathed Patrick. "You *triiiicked* him."

And gave a tiny gobsmacked, admiring smile to the "Betrayer"—to his brother.

Just a smile, that was all, but it was better than his satisfaction at outsmarting Hank the Shriek; better than his almost-insane gladness that he had not, in fact, been eaten. Yes, it was something so much finer.

So Michael hardly heard the sound at first, barely audible

through the steel door. Then he paid attention to it; and everything within him tumbled.

It was the shattering of the vials of the cure being destroyed by the Shriek.

CHAPTER THIRTY-TWO

Everything you do will be worth it in the end: You can control it.

One belief. One point on a compass. One guiding Instruction.

The belief had been Michael's comfort, and his weapon, for a very long time. He'd walked with it inside himself through mountains that roared and hungered around him. He'd lain with it on nights Before, when he had to wrap a pillow around his head to erase the sounds of slamming doors or crashing dishes or tears. When Michael knew so many secret pains that he could share with no one, the thought, the belief, had talked to *him*. Comforting him unconditionally. Like a best friend. Or like a mother.

You can control it, Michael thought.

As he sat in the bank, the thought seemed far away. Weak. His ears were filled with roaring wind, like a television with the AV wires cut.

Glass breaking. *Vials.*

Day 27. Dear Diary, Today I was a foot away from the cure.

I almost made everything okay. I almost changed

everything for—

—for myself—

—for Patrick. But then I kind of messed up. LOL, actually,

when you get right down to it, I pretty much effed the world.

No, said the thought. *It will be okay.*

Really?

Yes.

What about the shattering?

Michael screamed and roared and kicked at the money-cast floor, as if afraid the world would open a pit underneath him and swallow him whole. The oxygen vacuumed out of his lungs. His tongue was cracked sandpaper. *I'm Freaking,* Michael thought.

"WHAT THE?!" Patrick shouted.

Michael's head turned slowly, as if on a screaming rusted hinge.

He looked past Patrick. The vault door. His blurry reflection. His own black mouth and screaming face, pale and blank as the moon. Michael saw himself and his throat tore with his scream and oh my God stop, Michael, seriously stop please, stop Freaking.

Gone, he thought. *I lost. It's gone it's GONE.*

Patrick scrabbled away from his brother. His mouth was quivering, his hands went to his hair.

"Michael, you okay?" he said. "Hey, are you—?"

Michael stopped screaming, not because he'd regained control, he'd just run out of breath.

Tell Bub everything is okay, even though you just accidentally locked the monster in with the only things that can save you and Bub, his mind said—*Instructed.*

Patrick blinked at Michael, then yanked, hard, on a hunk of his own hair.

Tears leapt to Michael's eyes. He shot to a stand, his stomach going hot and loose with shame and terror. Patrick ripped at his hair again. He whined in his throat, his face smashing down in pain.

Yes, tell him everything will be okay, Michael. You're so good at promising, aren't you, asshole? But how are you going to lie your way out of this?

Michael lifted a hand that seemed to weigh seven tons. He made a thumbs-up.

Inside the vault, he could hear Shriek-Hank really going to town.

"Don't do that, Bub," Michael said. It was all he could manage.

"Why's you screaming?" Patrick looked him up and down, as if trying to decide if he recognized a stranger. "Why's . . . ? Did you get a splinter?"

Michael clapped a hand on his mouth. Hysterical laughter had nearly ejected. Then he understood Patrick's question, and felt like doing anything but laughing.

Asking if I got a splinter because he's never seen me like that. He thought I was . . . his Safe Zone. He didn't know I could lose it like that.

Oh, his mind hissed, *but there's a lot Patrick doesn't know about you.*

Suddenly, Patrick looked away, turning toward the tunnel across the dark of the lobby. "Hey, Game Master!" he called.

"Bub, wait." Michael's voice came out as a croak.

"But . . . you're hurt?" Patrick began. He uncertainly stepped away as Michael came closer. He gulped, and now his voice was a little plea: "Michael, you're *hurt*, right?"

Everything is still okay, right?!

"I—"

"Michael!"

Holly.

Small and muffled from beyond the mountain of rubble. She'd never made it through the tunnel.

Patrick stood there between his big brother and the tunnel, and he shifted foot-to-foot, in a heartbreaking dance of gathering dread.

"Michael got hur—I mean, *the Betrayer* got hurt, Holly!" he called desperately to the tunnel. "Time out, Game Master!" Whispering: *"And we can still quit real soon. Right? Michael?"*

And when Michael didn't reply, Patrick pivoted and cried toward the tunnel, "Can we *time OU—*?" and Holly replied shakily, "Patrick, hey," and Patrick went, "Where's the Game Master?" and Holly asked, "Jopek?" and Patrick said, "The *Game* Master!" and Holly answered, "R-right," and paused.

"The Game Master's out, Patrick," Holly finally called.

Patrick asked, *"Timed* out?"

Silence.

"Out out," Holly replied.

Patrick's face grew slack. Ghostly. He looked at Michael, his eyes going wide . . . and also, far away.

"Oh no, Michael," he moaned softly. "Ooooh, what did you *do?"*

Michael tried to take another step toward Patrick, but he was so sick with adrenaline and fear that the step wound up being more of a lunge, like a kid's pantomime of a monster.

Patrick ducked back through the saloon doors to the front side of the counter, color draining from his face.

"Michael, there's something freaky going on out here!" Holly called.

Oh God. "Are the Rapture here? The Bellows?" Michael asked.

"No, it's . . . I don't know *what* it is!"

Patrick paled even more; Michael remembered the Bellows in the city streets with dark bites in their skulls: bites delivered by the new kid, by the changed one, Cady Gibson. How long until the other Bellows came to life, like Hank? How long until all the bitten creatures sat up in the streets, their hollow eye-pits blinking, their skeleton fingers uncurling? How long until their thousands of shrieks raved in the night like sirens on a raid from Hell?

Better question: How long until you *change?*

"It's not safe out there!" Michael shouted, panicked, his voice cracking.

"Michael, listen—" she called. "Jopek's—he's—*something weird is—*"

"Now!"

"But—Christ!" she said, frustrated and afraid. "Fine!"

The mountain of rubble clattered as Holly entered the make-shift tunnel.

And what will you do after she gets in here, Gamer?

What are you going to do? Use them magic protectin' words to make some more cure, Mikey?

"Bub. Listen to me. When Holly gets in, we're going to have to . . . to . . ."

"We were supposed to work together. You said we could just play. You can . . . you can . . ." Patrick paused.

He's starting a sentence and hoping I finish it. And with a wave of self-hatred, Michael realized that that was the way it had always been. Patrick would start to feel something and look to Michael to make sure it was okay. That was his world: trusting Michael, playing The Game. *'Cause even if he didn't know I was the Game Master,* Michael thought, *he still thought I was in charge.* Michael had forged that world for him.

And now the apocalypse had come.

* * *

Michael looked toward the sound of the shattering behind the vault door again, and his reflection looked back. He could not tell what he looked like, but he did know the truth.

I . . . I can't lie anymore.

It won't work. There's no secret passage and no code; there are no alternate endings.

I can't *control this,* Michael thought. *Why did I do this? Why did I think I could do this? Who the hell did I think I was?*

"Bub, I'm sorry," Michael said. "God, I—"

"NO!" Patrick wailed, bringing his knuckles into the soft flesh of his cheeks. "DOOOOON'T TELL ME STUFF! IT WON'T WOOOOOORRRRRKKK!"

"Bub, please—"

Patrick's face screwed into a vicious mask of anger and desperation. "*You* said The Game would be fun! The Game Master said I just hadta get the elixir to win—I thought I could *WIN IT IF I WAS BRAVE*—but I'm *nooooot BRAVE, Michael, Daddy's right, I'm NOOOOOT and I CAN'T BE—*"

"Bub, it's not your faul—"

"*NO! BETRAYER, YOU CAN JUST* HAVE IT!"

Patrick reared back one tiny fist. For a single second, Michael thought his brother was going to hurl the hand into the marble counter beside him, to strike it hard enough to shatter his small bones as he had done in the psychiatric hospital. And this time there was no Atipax to help him.

But something was glittering in Patrick's closed hand.

Michael understood what the small silvery object was only as it shot up and out. The vial of cure arced and twirled, catching the semi-strobing light like a comet. It was the last dose, the single vial that Patrick had brought from the vault and kept safe through the battle with Hank. Michael cried out and raised his hands to catch it.

The vial struck him on the chest, the zipper giving a cheery *tink!* as it bounced off.

The vial struck the stone floor, hard.

But it didn't break.

Instead, it rolled, back and forth. Settling. Unharmed.

Whisper of thought: . . . *miracle* . . .

"Just take it," Patrick said. He was sobbing now. "You stupid Betrayer, I don't care. I don't even *wanna* win. I can't, I *can't*."

Tears found Michael's eyes. He saved me. *He* saved *me.*

"Bub," Michael breathed, "thank y—"

Patrick said, "I hate you."

CHAPTER THIRTY-THREE

And that was when Patrick sat down on the ground and began to Freak.

As if from another world, Michael heard Holly running breathlessly toward them.

She reached the end of the aisle between the desks. Her hoodie was spattered with blood at the cuffs; a bruise had blossomed underneath her left eye. She stopped with an almost comical swiftness, her sneakers squeaking as she spotted what Michael had in his hands.

Her eyes glistened. *"Oh my Lordy,"* she whispered. "The lab's really here."

Michael tried to figure out what to say about the miracle in his hand.

But Patrick began to scream.

Michael watched Holly's face transform as Patrick's sound—so loud; how can such pain fit into such a small body?—echoed through the lobby.

"I just want it over!" Patrick screamed. *"Why can't it, why why why why?!"*

Patrick punched himself again, both hands beating his

thighs; a sound like the slapping of raw meat.

Michael moaned, "Patrick—"

"P-Patrick, you stop," Holly said, hurrying past Michael. She leaned down and grabbed Patrick's flailing wrists.

"Don't touch! No! Don't try a' make me feel better!"

"It's going to be fine—"

"That's what *he* always says!" Patrick spat viciously, and in the strength of his agony, wormed his arms free. His little fists roared back downward with incredible speed to strike his legs, over, over.

Holly pushed him to the ground. She looked astonished, horrified. She had known about Freaking, Michael thought. But this wasn't what she'd imagined.

"I *hay-hay-haaate* it! I'm *not* good enough to get to The End— I'm—I'm—I just need my *mommy!*—"

"We're going to her," said Holly hurriedly. "Aren't we, Michael?"

Michael thought: *I can't lie.*

"Help me with him," she implored him, and he nodded distantly, kneeling, careful to keep the vial away from Patrick's erratic movements, hating himself for even thinking about that. Patrick—accidentally?—kicked Michael in the stomach. Michael pinned Patrick down. His brother looked like he was being crucified.

"Dude, take the GD vaccine," she said to Michael, picking Patrick up and pinning him against her chest, ignoring his fists and cries. "Inject it and get the rest of it and leave with us."

From the vault, more shattering. Shrieking.

"What's that noise?" Holly asked.

Michael began, "I don't have—" *anymore of the cure* he planned to say, but Holly interrupted him:

"You need a syringe, right. There's one in the Hummer— Patrick. Please. We're going home now, honey, okay?" Carrying

Patrick—dragging him—Holly started back toward the tunnel.

Take the vaccine, Michael thought, floating after her. Yes. That's what he could do. He could just say, *"Yeah—'the rest of the cure.' Which I've totally got."*

He could tell himself: *the Centers for Disease Control still has the formula.*

He could tell himself: *there is more of the cure in Richmond.*

He could tell himself: *even if this is the last of the cure, I have to take it, because I'm the only one Bub has left.*

He could pretend that the futures "the Game Master" promised him were real, instead of a series of evaporating illusions that led to a corner he could not lie his way out of.

He could take the cure.

But what then?

"His legs," Holly said. "A little help, Michael." She attempted lightness, to keep cool for Patrick, but there were tears of frustration in her eyes. "We have to hurry, we have to *leave*."

"Michael . . . ?" said Holly.

Leave, he thought.

But he couldn't answer. . . .

Because it is Halloween, and he stands frozen in the very center of a world tilting.

His plan was to silently get into the Volvo station wagon and go; to drive to Ron's cabin a couple hours away. But an almost mystical shock stops him.

His neighbor's scream pierces the quick of the night: "Get back! Get baaAAAA—!" *His brother's heart beats through the shirt on Michael's back.*

Mom's bedroom light clicks on. A second light follows. . . .

Patrick's bedroom, *Michael thinks dimly.* Mom wants to make sure he's okay. *And he can almost picture her flinging* open Patrick's door but keeping calmness on her face. She's good that way. One thing about Mom: she makes you feel good now. She can make you feel so good this second, you don't even realize that soon now will mutate. She can make you keep continuing, and you don't realize that all your life is running out.

A police car screams down the street, a red-blue missile through the dark.

A jack-o'-lantern disintegrates under its tire as it stops in the driveway next door. A husky cop—Wally Hawkin, the cop at school who always jokingly steals Michael's Tater Tots—gets out, running for the MacKenzies' front door, leaping a tricycle as he pulls out his pistol—and Michael has the odd feeling, not for the first time or the last, that he has somehow stepped into a night of make-believe. Wally looks like Leon in Resident Evil 6.

"Michael?"

Mom stands in their front doorway. She clutches her sky-blue robe closed at the neck with one hand.

"It's happening here, too," says Ron behind her.

"What?" says Mom.

"The TV stuff, the stuff from earlier toni—"

Screams.

The door of the house across the road has been kicked open by Wally, and Michael's skinny, sweet-faced neighbor, Harry MacKenzie, materializes on the threshold. His shirt says: WORK IS FOR PEOPLE WHO CAN'T DRINK.

Harry moans and throws himself at the cop.

Michael does not understand, but instinctively says, "Ten points for closing your eyes," so that Patrick will not be able to see whatever is about to happen.

Wally puts a bullet, heart-center into Harry. Harry keeps moving. Ron goes, "Oh shit!" and Mom gasps, and Patrick tightens on his neck and he says, "What's happenin'?" Harry curls his hands around the policeman's throat, and Michael thinks, I have to go, but he is frozen by the impossible sight of blood erupting from Wally's mouth, which will never taste a Tater Tot again.

"Get yourselves in here," says Ron. His voice is oddly flat. "I don't mean yesterday. I ain't playin'."

Mom dashes barefoot for them. "Michael," she hisses, "what are you doing out here?"

And stops, seeing the backpack, seeing the keys in Michael's hand.

Many times, Michael has seen Mom look hurt. He has seen her angry. Those are not things he sees now.

Honest revelation is what is on Mom's face.

You were going to leave me.

For that moment, this is the world:

He and Mom.

Silence on the moonlit dew-cold grass.

He and Mom on their front lawn.

Which is just sixty feet square, pebbled and rooty, and its grass wilts brown every July. But as they stand together in this shocked quiet, their yard seems to hum like ordinary earth transformed by a magic circle. He remembers the day he and Mom moved in, the downpour that day, Mom so eager for their own home that she carried boxes through the rain. He remembers the birthday when he awoke to a Slip 'N Slide set up right here, where they now stand. He remembers Mom taking his photo on the first day of school, every year, with a disposable camera, while he held up fingers to show what grade he was in.

These memories twist through him in seconds.

Then a pistol shouts somewhere, as if signaling the start of a competition.

"I'm sorry," Mom says. She comes closer. "I'm sorry, so sorry, about everything. I know it's been . . . wrong. I know that; I do. But Michael. Michael David." Tears in her voice. "You cannot do this."

He remembers the first night Ron came home drunk, his pickup leaving tire marks on the yard.

Suddenly, Ron is at her side, his bald spot gleaming sickly in the houselight.

"I'm not stayin' here while these happy assholes are shooting," says Ron. "Get in the car."

He is already wearing his jacket, the letterman with COACH stitched on the breast. He's ready to go. And just like that, Ron has ruined everything.

Except Ron reaches into his pocket and finds it empty. No keys. And Mom meets Michael's eyes with gathering fear.

"Where in the blue Hell's my goddamn keys?"

"I left them inside," Michael says. "The Snoopy tray. I went to Dairy Queen."

"Why you little sack of . . ." But another gunshot snaps Ron out of it, and he goes for the house.

Mom does not go for the house.

She doesn't move.

"Michael. Give your mother the keys. Before he gets back, baby."

She is using her Mom Voice.

"I'll lie for you. You'll be safe."

But that mask does not fit her anymore.

He does not think of Patrick.

He does not think of Mom.

He thinks of himself.

It's not like an adventure. Adventures, you control. Mom, you lied to me.

A cloak of smooth, cold fury unfurls from his heart. Go, the Game Master says. And Michael drifts away from Mom, to the car, loading his brother into the backseat as Patrick struggles with everything he's got to maintain his smile.

Mom stutters, paralyzed by shock. And the moment she

hesitates is the moment Michael locks the doors.

Mom's palms strike the glass. She shakes her head, screams. Patrick says something, who knows what.

"It's going to be okay. I know what I'm doing," Michael shouts now.

"Say 'See you later,' Bub," says Michael.

And drives.

He clears the driveway and careens by Wally, who lies in a pool of black moonlit fluid. He speeds past Harry MacKenzie, who stumbles like an otherworldly pilgrim.

And when Michael sees Ron's dashing form dwindling in the rearview mirror, he feels a joy so intense it's almost blinding.

Michael has found a door, he believes: a door to the next world, to another life. Yes, he is seizing this mysterious catastrophe and barreling toward The End.

It's over. I'm changing everything. I'm saving us.

I'm saving *me.*

He does not understand that tonight the earth has been damned beyond his comprehension or control. He will not consider that he may have just murdered Mom. He doesn't allow himself to think that, no, because he feels his blood now, feels good now, and the only thought he will allow is:

IT WILL BE WORTH IT,

IT WILL WORK OUT,

IN THE END.

So each yard he travels is like a wakening from a long nightmare, a wakening to control, a wakening at last to who he really is.

LOL, that's a good joke, Mikey!

It is waking in the dark to the screams again.

CHAPTER THIRTY-FOUR

"Michael?"

Mom.

"Michael," Holly said loudly over Patrick's crying, walking backward toward the tunnel, "it's road time. What is *wrong* with you?" Michael shook his head. Patrick sobbed harder; Holly's face clouded with urgency. "Dude, please. Jopek is dea—"

She paused, looking unsure whether she could do Patrick any more harm.

"He's out-out. I think. But there's something weird going on outside—*are you even listening to me?*"

"I never saved anyone. . . ." Michael said to himself.

"What?"

And I can take the cure, and I'll still be alive. But everything that's wrong inside and outside Bub will still be there, and all of this will just keep repeating, like it did with Mom. It will just keep echoing, like a Bellow.

This *was* The End, Michael suddenly knew.

This night in which Patrick's only recourse was to betray Michael, just as Michael had betrayed Mom, was what The

Game's lies and false promises had led them to. This was the absolute end of the line, with no place left to run.

Everything not saved will be lost.

Save your brother.

Remake his world.

Michael felt tears burn his throat. But he nodded and thrust the vial of cure toward Holly. "Take it."

Holly gritted her teeth. "Okay, no offense, but you are *pissing me off right now.*"

Michael opened her hand and jammed the cure into it. "Go. Leave. If you find the Safe Zone, tell them I'm here. If the scientists can copy that vial, send them back with more for me. But go."

Holly blinked at him. Michael began walking away from her, not trusting himself to stay. "Patrick, one second," she said, and set him down on the ground. Patrick hit his head, sobbed.

"Michael, what the *hell* are you doing?" When he wouldn't take the vial with his hand, she jammed it into the pocket of his space suit.

"Holly, no!" he said. "You'll need it. Please just let me save Patrick! This is the only way to make everything right."

"You're not thinking. You can use this dose, and we'll bring the rest to Richmond with us."

"There is no more, Holly."

Holly's brow knitted: *What?*

"I lied. There are no soldiers coming for us. I didn't see any, and Jopek said that Richmond is overrun, too. I . . . I guess I don't know if that's true, but getting the cure to the scientists is the only chance you've got. I'm *not* going to hurt anyone anymore. Not like when I left my mom. Go. Move."

He went to put his hands on her shoulders, to turn her back toward the tunnel. But Holly slapped him away. Like Patrick, she seemed as if she was trying to decide if she recognized a stranger.

"You *promised* that there were other soldiers. Now you're saying that the Safe Zone where my dad went might be gone? You're saying that was a *lie?*"

She really sees me. Finally.

And in that moment, horror flooded him.

But he didn't answer Holly's question. He'd just seen something behind her.

The tunnel.

Something coming out of the tunnel.

The passage to the outer lobby had been cored with the very last fire of dusk, but now that dusk light was flickering. *Something's blocking it,* he thought.

"Who . . . ?" breathed Holly. Patrick looked at the tunnel, too. And seeing what was there, stopped sobbing.

A man emerged from the tunnel.

Not a bellowing man. Not a shrieking man.

A living man.

A soldier.

Something flickered on and off in Michael's mind like a busted sign: REAL. NOT REAL. REAL. NOT REAL.

Real breath curled out from the gas mask that disguised his face, and Michael thought wildly: *it's Jopek!* Jopek had beaten death. Jopek was gonna live forever. But no—this man was way too short.

Patrick had been sitting perhaps fifteen paces away, halfway between Michael and the tunnel and the man who had come from it. Patrick sat up from the floor now. He turned to Michael, his face raw and streaked . . . but filling with a little amazement.

"Did we *win*?" asked Patrick.

The camouflaged man raised a gloved hand and beckoned Patrick with one finger.

Other soldiers crawled out of the tunnel behind the first. Michael heard Holly laugh a little in relief, perhaps in joy.

But in that moment, as Patrick stood and looked cautiously to the soldier, a memory arose in Michael: a memory of a circus Mom had taken him to when he was four. He remembered the big-top acrobats that seemed to dangle from the very dome of the sky; he remembered the rich and wondrous kid-smells of cotton candy and salt and animal dung. But mostly, as he watched these men emerge one-by-camouflaged-one from the debris passage, Michael remembered a car speared inside a spotlight's ring: a tiny car floating out in the dark that opened its door and vomited forth an endless parade of men with false, blood-bright grins. Michael had screamed, but the crowd's roar had consumed his own, and Mom, not realizing his terror, had asked, "Isn't this just *fun*, baby?"

No, it wasn't fun. And it was not right. Those clowns weren't *really* happy people.

They're just wearing *the suits!* Michael thought now.

"Don't move, Patrick!" Michael shouted as he finally broke his paralysis and ran toward Patrick. *"Don't go near that guy!"*

Holly said, "What—what—"

"Won!" Patrick crowed, voice croaking with a kind of terrible, desperate joy. "Michael, it's soldiers! We won The Game! Mom! *Mommy!*"

Patrick ran away from Michael, toward the soldier.

The soldier peeled off his mask.

Rulon.

The leader of the Coalmount Rapture stood there, as obvious as anyone, but it took Patrick a few seconds to really *see*.

He cried out, a high, ringing note.

Patrick tried to pedal back, but Rulon was quicker: his hand shot out and seized Patrick's shoulder.

Patrick bit the man's fingers.

Rulon drew back his free arm and struck Patrick, hard, across the face.

Patrick's head rocked backward. But he didn't even scream.

No, no, no.

Holly cried, *"PATRICK!"*

"Don't you touch *him!"* Michael screamed, and he was still running even as Rulon raised his rifle.

Michael experienced what happened next only as a blast of light and sickly pain flowing through the core of his arm up to his elbow. The world vanished, shimmered out in a reddish fog.

Michael shook his head, trying to clear it. He was on his ass, about ten feet out from Rulon. Blood pulsed through the hole in his space-suit glove. *Shot,* Michael thought. Rulon raised his gun again, and Michael could not move, and the only thing he could think was: *not in front of Patrick.*

Holly stepped in front of him, her arms spread like a shield.

"My name is Holly Bodeen. My father is Dr. Gordon K. Bodeen with the Centers for Disease Control. He's embedded with a special military unit tasked with retrieving the CDC's cure from Charleston. According to his latest radio transmission, which we received three minutes ago, he and his unit are less than two miles away."

Rulon smiled pumpkin teeth. "Child. Don't you know the liars' punishment?"

"Rulon," someone said calmly, "stop." A "soldier" stepped forward from those dozen or so ranged behind Rulon—the only Rapture people, Michael supposed, who had survived the lunatic sacrifices Rulon had conducted.

When Michael realized who the soldier was, he felt a wave of wonder: It was the heavy woman with the sweet, dimpled face who'd spotted him while he tried to escape the Coalmount office of Southern West Virginia Coal and Natural Gas. "Hammy," he'd called her. She looked so strange, squeezed in the military uniform.

But she also looked *worried.*

"Oughtn't we let the older boy go?" she said carefully. "Rulon, shouldn't we just take the young boy and leave the others?"

Rulon kept his poisonously glittering eyes, and his gun, trained on Holly. "Perhaps more than one sacrifice would be finer. . . ." he said dreamily.

"But didn't you say earlier that we only need the 'most innocent blood'?" she said. "Isn't that what you said . . . Father?" she added.

The silence carried on; Rulon seemed to have not heard. Then a skinny man carrying a red ax began to speak, too. "She's righ, Fa . . ." He stopped, then cast his eyes to the floor, sheepish and confused.

Rulon's losing control of them, Michael thought. And it was not hard to see why. The priest had become even more skeletal; his flesh was drawn severely against his cheekbones, his hair was streaked with blood. Rulon looked like he hadn't slept for days, and his dark eyes seemed almost to roar in his skull, like twin tornadoes.

"Their sins . . . ," Rulon said, and Michael saw tears of frustration—of building rage—in his eyes, which were now fixed on a point somewhere far overhead. "All I wanted was the boy. All I wanted was the chance to atone for my failure. I knew God would not have taken so much from me without reason. I knew God could not have raised the dead for no reason. All I wanted was the son. Oh, why do you hide him from me?"

Who the hell is he talking to?

"My letter *told* your captain that all you had to do was bring me the boy," Rulon said, and now his gaze bore straight into Michael. His breath hitched. A sob rolled up out of him.

Jopek did *bring me.*

"Oh God, I have done so much to atone. What else must I do? All I want is my son."

Hammy said worriedly: "*Your* son?"

The gaunt features of Rulon's face contorted, changed into a mask of agony and helpless fury; and even as this mountain priest cried out in a wordless reckoning of rage and of love and venom, the understanding hit Michael like a cold bolt.

"All I want is *MY SON*!" Rulon bellowed. "All I want is MY BOY, MY CADY! All I have ever wanted was to bring my Cady back! But they would not give me his body when the Chosen began to rise, and YOU hid him from me, Michael Faris, you and YOUR CAPTAIN WOULD NOT GIVE ME MY BOY!"

Devastation and confusion fell across the faces of the Rapture. Michael saw the idea they'd had of Rulon evaporate. Their priest had told them that everything he did, every person he ordered them to sacrifice, he had done in order to protect them, to win them all their entry to Heaven.

Was that belief insane? Yes. It was.

But their priest had been a purposeful deceiver. Rulon had been attempting to atone for the accidental death of his son, the little boy who died in the Coalmount mines only days before the dead began to rise. Rulon must have taken that resurrection as a sign, a hope that his son, too, could return. . . . And so Rulon had tried to retrieve his son's body from its casket in the Capitol; but the Capitol had been already become the Safe Zone. And so Rulon tried to summon the assistance and powers of God with worship and with blood; but that would not work, no, so perhaps just a little more blood would, yes, a little more . . .

And now Rulon was going to sacrifice Patrick, to try to trade one other innocent dead child for his own son.

"Bub, *RUN*!" Michael said, pushing past Holly, who only then lowered her shielding arms.

Rulon fired over Michael's head, close enough for him to hear the song of the bullet. Holly screamed, pulling Michael back.

"Speak one more word," Rulon said through gritted, bared teeth. "I beg you that."

Rulon picked up Patrick . . . and Patrick's head lolled back like a broken doll's. Vomit threatened Michael's throat, sudden and violent.

"'Michael,'" murmured Rulon softly to him in the still, dead First Bank of Charleston. "'God's warrior.'"

The priest shook his head: a nearly wistful gesture. His forehead was kneaded as if he might weep. And yet, as he looked at Michael's little brother, he smiled, too.

He looked like . . . hope.

"Michael Faris," Rulon said, "you are no one's warrior."

And that was the end.

The Rapture retreated through the tunnel and, after a second, Michael ignored Holly's screams and crawled into the shaft, heedless of his wounded hand's anguish, out to the outer lobby, where he saw the Rapture vanishing into the cockpit of the jet. Rulon fired; Michael was forced to scrabble back, like a frightened dog. But in the last moment before he retreated, the only thing he saw, really saw, was Patrick: slumped over Rulon's shoulder, his eyes glassed, his mouth slack and speechless. He was not screaming. He was not crying. He'd been dragged over the final ledge inside himself. He was gone, with nothing and no one to pull him back out this time. He'd Freaked. Welcome to the endtimes, Michael. Welcome to The End.

CHAPTER THIRTY-FIVE

No. No. Please please please, no.

Michael rushed from the tunnel, his hand a burning pulse, out across the never-ending lobby and into the street, where he saw the Hummer. He had one shining moment, before he spotted the deflated jack-o'-lantern balloon on its roof and realized that it was Jopek's Hummer, not Rulon's.

Michael'd had to wait in the tunnel in the bank, to *cower*, making sure the Rapture's silence wasn't a trick. He'd dashed out the moment he heard the motorcycles and Hummers revving.

But the Rapture—and Patrick—were gone. The only moving thing out here in the street was the snow falling from the black sky.

Run, run, as fast as you can, a voice growled in his head. *You can't catch him, he's the God-fearin' man.*

Michael dashed farther out in the street, straddling the yellow double line.

Skyscrapers choked out the rising moon, and snow muted the little remaining light. The air carried the thin stink of motor exhaust.

He whirled, throwing his gaze to the west, past the colossal tail of the jetliner. Patches of purple in the darkness: cars, lampposts, buildings. The world totally motionless except for the storm, as if the world had transformed into some nightmarish snow-globe in which Michael was suffocatingly sealed.

He screamed out, "Bub!"

No reply. And he did not see any taillights.

You can't catch him, he's the game-endin' man!

Isn't this just *fun*, baby?

No taillights in either direction. He nearly screamed; he closed his eyes; he tried to hear the telltale buzz of engines.

But heard only his heart, exploding in his ears.

An image loaded unbidden to his mind: Rulon's knife arcing up over his head, Rulon's knife screaming down, and his brother screaming back. . . .

Holly emerged from the plane.

She marched to the Hummer, not looking at Michael. He stood there, knowing why she was mad but powerless to say anything. Holly popped a compartment above the passenger seat. A moment later she came to him with two flashlights, planting one, unlit, against his chest, still not sparing him a glance.

She strode to the center of the street, her light beam racing back and forth. The light caught the falling snow in a bubble around her, like a storm of meteors, and Michael was again struck with utter loneliness: she looked like a girl firing a distress signal while the world ended at her feet. Michael started telling her the Rapture had left already—then he realized what she was doing. He turned on his flashlight, copying her search for vehicle tracks.

All he saw were footprints: so many.

"Here. This way," Holly said brusquely after a moment. "Let's go."

"W-wait—"

She jabbed her light beam at wide tire imprints in the snow that receded into the west. "The *tracks* go *this* way, Michael. *That's* the way out of Charleston, to the mountains where their *town* is." She had the tone of a teacher explaining something simple to the least favorite student in the class.

"Some already filled in, though," Michael replied. "What if that's the way they came *from*? I mean, the new tracks could've been covered by the snow, or the wind, or . . ."

Holly shook her head in frustration and shot her light into his face, blinding him. Michael flinched, raising a hand to block the light as she stamped toward him.

"Okay—fine! Absolutely!" Holly said, her voice quivering. "Where do *you* think we should go, captain? It must be convincing, since I know you wouldn't say anything that wasn't true. So please: hi, I'm Holly, please inform the damsel what you're *thinking*."

Michael began to defend himself, but there was no time. And there was no defending himself. Yes, she saw him plainly now.

"Fine," he said softly. "We'll go to Coalmount. That's probably smart."

"Oh, excellent. I'm oh-so-glad you trust me." Holly moved toward the Hummer again.

"Holly, I'm—"

Who are you?

"—I'm sorry. Look, you don't have to go. This is my fault."

She spun on him, then. Her glasses flashed fiercely; Holly hurled her flashlight at the ground. The bulb exploded in a burst of bright that illuminated the tears tracing down her cheeks. She thrust a finger at him. "Stop. Right now. Stop talking like you think I don't care."

Not defensive.

Furious, misunderstood.

Michael nodded.

And his injured hand beat like a bomb and countdown both.

"Then we should hurry," Michael said. He went to shut the open rear doors of the Hummer. *Maybe Rulon* won't *think of me following him to Coalmount. I mean, he is insane.*

Yeah, but you have a history of underestimating evil, you goddamn idiot.

He grabbed the handle of the left rear door, and when Holly shouted, *"Wait wait wait, there's somebody in—"* Michael jerked away, and accidentally yanked the door with him.

Jopek, coming out of the darkness at him—

Jopek, lunging into the bright tube of his light beam—

Jopek—his *corpse*—was strapped into the jump seat, his eyes closed, his head lolling bonelessly against his shoulder. Jopek's face was slack; he might have been sleeping (if he ever *did* sleep) except for the cake of dark blood on his forehead. *That's where they shot him. Dead.* Michael tried to feel . . . he wasn't sure what: relief, or something. But the sight, the reality, of the corpse made his stomach roll over as if in a cold grease. It wasn't tidy; the body didn't fade away like in a game. *Killer. Killer.*

But why was Jopek's body out here, when he'd been shot in the lobby of the bank?

"Eff," breathed Holly shakily at his side. "So this is where he went."

"What? When?"

"Jopek got up after you went into the tunnel. He was bleeding, like, profusely, and he staggered outside. I don't think he even knew where he was. I heard him scream. And then I heard people running in the streets."

She must have seen Michael's anger forming on his face: *And you didn't* warn *me?* "No, not the Rapture," she said. "The Bellows in the street. But they weren't Bellows anymore."

A realization slowly dawned inside him. He had been

running around in an *empty* street.

The hundreds of corpses that he'd had to high-step an hour ago were *gone*. How? He didn't understand.

So add that to the fugging list. Move.

He began pushing the door shut, and a rippingly bright agony flowed up his arm again. He cried out, snapping his hand back.

"Oh man," Holly said pityingly. For the first time, she looked at him without fury on her face. "That needs a bandage." She began climbing up the side of the Hummer toward the roof. By now, the jack-o'-lantern balloon, tethered atop the Hummer, had deflated, its hot-air fabric messily collapsed into its passenger basket.

"What are you doing?" Michael said.

"There's a first aid kit in the balloon."

"It's empty," he said.

"What? How do you know?"

Trust me, he thought.

Holly hopped back down. "Well, we're going to wrap it with *something*. You're losing too much . . ." But she trailed off.

Holly was staring at his bloody sleeve, her forehead kneading in concentration.

"Blood. Red," she breathed. "You've got red all over you."

"Yeah," he said confusedly. "I hear that's what happens when you get shot in the hand."

But Holly did not respond to his comment. A strange half smile twitched on her lips. She grabbed his flashlight from his good hand and turned away, casting the beam onto the road that had been so recently clotted with not-yet-resurrected Shrieks. "Look," she said, her half smile now full, her palm pressed to her forehead as if in disbelief. "Look at the road."

What? Nothing there besides snow.

"The blood—the Bellows' dried blood!"

The street was crisscrossed with mangled patterns of dark color: the blood spilled from the Bellows that Cady Gibson had bitten to convert them into carriers of his mutation. Michael stared, understanding not at all why this mattered.

"It's *black*," Holly said. "Your blood is different: it's red. The same color as Jopek's when he got shot. The same as anyone normal's blood."

"It only looks black because it's dried," Michael began, but he stopped. Hank's blood had dripped onto Patrick from the ceiling in the bank . . . *and that blood had been black, too.*

"Michael," said Holly, and the wind howled, and she rose her voice against it to tell him, "I don't think you're infected!"

"But you said that Cady had to have been infected by a scratch. You said the virus was mutating—"

"As it turns out, Holly was wrong! The virus is mutating, but—I guess not the basic stuff. Scratches still don't cause an infection. Although how *did* Cady get sick? And where the hell did all the monsters go?" she said as if to herself.

"Shit," Michael said. "No no, shit shit."

"How is being uninfected bad news?!"

Because it shows how freaking wrong I always am, Holly. Because I was fooled. "It's not. I just was so stupid, I should've figured it out somehow—"

"GOD!" Holly shouted.

Michael flinched.

"Michael, do you know what your problem is? You think the whole world *is* 'your problem.' You think that you can *fix* everything."

And, flinching again, for a different reason, Michael said, "So—what? 'Michael, don't try to help people. Don't try to save your mom. Don't try to save Patrick.'"

"You should try," spat Holly. "But what the *hell* is the point of feeling so sorry for yourself? You didn't take Patrick; *they* did!"

"But I didn't stop them."

Holly shook her head. "So, congratulations. You're not God." She raised her palms, as if in exasperation. "Look, you said you left your mom? Even if she *had* gone with you on Halloween, how long until she would've wanted to go back for Ron? Even if the world hadn't ended and your mom did talk to the police, how do you know that she wouldn't let him come home later anyway, and everything would have gone back to the way it was? I know you said your mom's 'good,' Michael. But God, people are a *lot* of things. Her life doesn't suck because you 'didn't save her.' Michael, her life is like that because she's *weak*."

His heart twisted. What she was saying sounded true . . . but it sounded true like The Game sounded true: it would just be him trying to make himself feel better. Holly went toward the passenger door, Michael to the driver's seat, getting ready to drive back to Coalmount.

Wait. Wait.

How long until she would have made you go back? Holly had said.

The idea set off something else inside him.

Go back . . .

Cady Gibson, though unbitten, had died in the mine.

There are some viruses that actually make infected animals migrate to the place on Earth where the virus originated, Holly had said on their "date" in the Capitol.

The mine. Oh my God, the mine.

The reason Cady Gibson had returned from the dead without a bite mark from a Bellow—the reason he had changed into a Shriek before any of the others—was that Cady had received the virus in some different way. The little boy who wandered into a mountaintop mine had stumbled upon something dreadful in the dark, and so he had become the first human on Earth to be given the disease.

Then how did it spread?

Maybe Cady bit someone else *before he died,* Michael thought. Maybe a miner; perhaps the very miner that had been tied to the altar in the Rapture's church; Coalmount's "First." And with that first poisoned bite, a diluted form of the disease had passed from its first son out into the world.

Maybe.

But with horror threading up his spine, Michael knew something for sure: the disease hadn't originated in Iran, or some terrorists' lab. . . . *And those were not the places the Bellows had been marching toward.*

"I know where the Shrieks went," Michael breathed.

"What? Where?" Holly shut the passenger door behind her.

How had Cady gotten the terrible virus? *What* had given it to him in that mine? *I don't know.*

But Michael remembered looking into Cady's eyes and seeing something ancient peering back at him, like a beast blinking from inside a human skull. And Michael was afraid.

"They went home," he said.

CHAPTER THIRTY-SIX

COALMOUNT

MOUNTAINTOP QUARRY

MINE #1337

!!! DANGER CAUTION DANGER !!!

BLASTING AREA—NO TRESPASSING—*NO SMOKING!!!*

(SAFETY, ITS OUR #1 RESOURCE!)

Spray-painted below:

TELL IT TO CADY (BEAUTIFULL BOY), U CORPRAT BASTERDS!

Michael drove over that rusted sign and parked the Hummer on the top of the world.

How much time had passed? He didn't know.

Sightless windows of skyscrapers had flashed past. The silvery trails of the Rapture's tire tracks and the Shriek's footprints in the headlight-lit snow. And then the on-ramp to the abandoned highway, which climbed out of the city, taking him back into the dark fortress of the West Virginia mountains.

'Cause nothing changes, Michael. The past doesn't really die; it just comes back to life, his mind had hissed as he drove into the black hills. *You're looking for Patrick in the mountains, like when you woke up in the woods and you couldn't find him. But you can't just pull him out of the trees this time. He fell off the end of the world.*

It's not a game, but it's still over.

Patrick. Patrick.

"Do we have, like, weapons?" Michael had thought to ask only as the city vanished from their sideview mirrors.

"What about the pistol?" Holly had replied, paling. "The one you took from Jopek?" He tried not to mentally add "you retard?" to the end of her sentence.

"I dropped it . . . back at the bank. . . ." Michael said.

The snow streaked through the headlights; following the trails of the Rapture and the Shrieks, Michael turned off the highway, onto a rutted, country road. And Holly, still angry and disappointed, looked at him for the absolute minimum amount of time.

"I've got pepper spray," she finally said. "My dad gave it to me the day I got my license." After a minute, almost to herself: "I remember thinking, 'Daddy, seriously: quit being so overprotective.'"

Gravel popped beneath the tires. The newly rough way was barely wide enough for the Hummer: bare branches of trees scratched the windows. Michael heard Holly jolt several times. As if to simply occupy herself, she tugged at the belly pocket of her hoodie until the seams popped; she found electrical tape in the glove compartment, then wrapped the cloth as a filthy bandage around Michael's blood-crusted hand. It made the nerves in his wound screech, but he didn't let himself cry out. She needed that distraction, and what other help did he have left to give her?

As they reached Main Street in Coalmount, Michael saw something glimmer in the headlights off to the right. His heart nearly imploded when he realized it was a Pop-Tart wrapper.

Patrick, Patrick. Sounding in Michael's head like a bell. *Patrick Dale Faris, Patrick Dale Faris—*

Sounding in his head like a prayer.

Please, he thought, feeling sick with weakness, *please help me, God, Universe, whatever. If You're there, if Anybody is there, please!*

But what did he expect? What the hell did he *expect*? The night was quiet, except for his car. And there was nothing in the sky but the cold witch-fire of the stars.

Holly sat there, inches away, finishing his bandage, but Michael had never felt so alone.

Nor so hopeless. Coalmount, an average coal town he'd explored by sled, now reminded him of a place obliterated by a hurricane. Great hectic gashes were torn into the storefronts; lampposts were ripped from their concrete; old burnt-out cars had been turned pathetically onto their sides. Past the Food'N'Such grocery store (*tomato soup*, he thought, his chest clutching), Michael saw that the big, yellow school bus that once had blockaded the street was now in two pieces, the metal shredded down the center by some massive force. On the cramped Charleston streets and winding mountain roads, the sheer number of the Shrieks' footprints had been disguised by the Rapture's own tire tracks. But now, traveling through these wide-open ruins and taking the one and only road out of Coalmount, Michael began to truly understand what it was he was steering toward in this ghost's world. Not just the Rapture.

Every Bellow—*every one of the Bellows that had lain in every Charleston street*—had risen again as Shrieks and led this lunatics' stampede, drawn by some dark instinctive signal of the blood. *Every. Effing. One.* He tried to picture Them, but their sheer number somehow made it impossible.

A random memory occurred: lying in a whispering field of timothy grass when he was a boy, asking Mom how many miles were in outer space.

Not miles, she whispered. She had smiled for him. *It just goes and goes and goes,* she said.

The idea of infinity—both simple and unimaginable—had horrified him, somehow.

What'm I going to do? What?

But that was when the Hummer made a dramatic turn, and uphill, perhaps a mile away, the mountain road ended with what *should* have been a gentle mountain peak.

But of course, the peak wasn't there.

The gentle, heartbeat-measurement-like mountain range was killed dead, the summit ripped away. In place of the apex, there was instead only a severe line of decapitation.

COALMOUNT MOUNTAINTOP QUARRY

"We're here," Holly whispered.

Michael gulped, turning off the headlights, slowing to ten miles an hour.

Even with the headlamps off, there was light enough to steer by: an eerie glow shot straight up from the earth ahead. *Like high school football-field lights.* It made him think of Ron, and there was one frightening, bitter moment when Michael nearly burst into laughter at the thought that Ron had once been his ultimate idea of evil.

The electric light radiated from the "decapitation" line, which marked the end of both the road and the mountain's ascent.

"It's the quarry pit for the mine," Michael whispered. Which was supposed to, what, sound insightful?

What's happening in there? What are they doing to Patrick?

As the Hummer inched up the mountain, the light filled the cab, sickly blue-white. So effing *bright.* What if Rapture lookouts were watching? *At least the windshield's bulletproof,* Michael told himself when his foot twitched on the brake.

I think.

Gravel ground underneath them. The pit was so wide as they approached—a quarter mile at least—and the Shriek prints spread across the whole span of it. All the way to the ledge. They're all in that pit, Michael. And they're going to come over it now, *now,* like poison boiling over the edge of a pot, because you were too slow, you're not *good,* and Patrick is dead—

"Please what?" said Holly.

"Huh?" Michael replied, startled.

"You said please." She sounded scared.

Michael's teeth snapped together, *click.* "Nothing," he said.

Finally, he stopped the Hummer a few feet from the rim of the quarry: close enough that, if he sat up from his seat, he could look over the edge and see what was in the pit. He had an urge to delay the moment, to think of something to say to Holly.

But Holly's seat squeaked. She was already leaning forward.

"What the ass are they doing down there?" she whispered, bewildered.

The Rapture, all still alive, were gathered in the crater in the earth. The walking-dead worshippers, the dozen of them, stood at the far end of the excavated hollow. The great oval crater—maybe a hundred feet deep and set on all sides with steeply cut rock faces (they staggered down, like stairs outside a temple)—was illuminated by enormous fluorescent light poles and dotted with mining equipment: cranes, conveyor belts, load trucks, silos, miniature mountains of coal. It was all fossilized by the snow.

But the Rapture weren't looking at *any* of that.

They were gazing unmovingly in the other direction, into the blank face of rock wall before them.

"Do you see him?" Michael said.

Holly scanned the crowd, then shook her head. "I don't see Rulon either," she said softly. "Is it just me, or does it seem like the rest of them are *waiting*?"

Looking again, closer, at the wall, into which all the Shriek footprints funneled. The wall, with a squat, square, black hole at the base of it.

The entrance to the mine.

"The Shrieks went into the mine," he said. *And what was there to say hi to 'em?* Cady's eyes, ancient and unfathomable, flashed again in Michael's head. "And Rulon must have taken Patrick in after them," he finished.

Michael looked to Holly. This was a different game than they had known they would have to play here.

But despite her fear, she would not blink.

"Then I guess that's where we're going," she said.

God, Michael thought. It was the spontaneous *goodness* that made it hard for him to find his voice. Whatever the anger and confusion that had passed between them before, this was just *her*: good, despite the world.

"I don't have a plan, Holly. We have to get into the mine, but I don't know how. Maybe I'll just . . . ram through the Rapture with the car." He tried to convince himself that that was not the world's stupidest suicide.

She reluctantly said, "Isn't there gas in some mines, though? I mean, couldn't the car accidentally make us, y'know . . . ?" She made a "blow-up" motion with her hands.

"Maybe."

She's going to say: *that plan doesn't make sense.*

She's going to say: *your stupid ideas aren't good enough.*

She said: "For those taking notes, that would have actually been an *okay* time to lie." Holly half laughed weakly. Still hurt. Maybe still furious. But: a peace offering.

Michael made a small smile.

Wished he could actually deserve the offer.

But what was the point in delaying? He began to lift his foot from the brake, then paused. "If I don't make it . . . tell Patrick I'm . . ."

You're what? What are you, Michael?

"Tell him 'I ya-ya.'"

Holly wrinkled her forehead: *You what, now?* "Nothing," Michael replied, shaking his head, yanking the shift into DRIVE with his good hand. "When Bub was little-little, he couldn't say 'Love you.' I just wanted him to feel good about himself. You know? To make him feel normal. So I said it— *ya-ya*—like him. I guess I thought . . .

"I thought I could make him feel 'good' enough that he really would become normal." He looked to her. "Holly, I'm sorry. I did that a whole freaking lot."

Something strange—like a revelation—crossed Holly's face.

But that was when they heard the knock, behind them, on the rear door of the Hummer.

Everything inside Michael jolted.

He spun in his seat, to look back through the sliding panel between the front and rear compartments of the Hummer. But it was Holly who got the first look. Before he could even see a single thing, Holly slid the panel closed.

Michael said, "What are y—"

"Listen to me." And when she spoke, it was with beautiful, semi-crazed determination on her face. "If *I* don't make it, will you tell Michael that I hate that he lied."

She was coming closer to him, so the skin of their noses nearly touched, so close that, if he hadn't been so shocked, he could have felt her breath—

"But the reason he lied? That's the real him. And that, I honestly have a big ol' crush on."

Michael felt something in his chest seem to open up an inch.

And it happened.

There.

In the freezing Hummer, with the neon light flooding the cabin vivid and full: the distance between them evaporated.

Holly put her hands on his space-suited chest, and then her lips were on top of his.

It did not feel like a cut-scene in a game; he didn't feel like they were kissing in front of a bursting sunset, or a victory field.

He closed his eyes, and he felt: her lips.

Warm. Dry, but wondrously soft.

And his heart was hammering like that of a panicked animal who has finally been cornered, but when he opened his eyes, Holly's lashes had parted, and her green eyes looked at him, directly into and *at* him in the full-blast exposure of the light.

Holly's lips twitched against his. *Smiling. She's smiling.* Crazily, he thought: *Which means I'm good at this?* Gently, she broke away, and before he could say anything, she placed her warm, smooth cheek to his. *"Michael-Michael-Michael."* A whisper in his ear. *"I'll trust you, if you'll trust me."*

Michael blinked as she pulled back. *Trust you for . . . ?*

Holly placed her hand dead center on the car horn, and pushed.

Hooonk! it blatted through the quiet. *HONK-HONK! HONK-HONK-HOOOOOOOOONK!!!* so air-slappingly loud that it might as well have added a cartoony *Ah-ROOOO-ga!*

"Holly what are you doing?!"

Awareness was rippling across the Rapture crowd in the quarry: heads turning, searching for the source of the sound, looking at the sky, *looking at the Hummer.*

Their surprise was blown.

And Michael realized what Holly was doing only when he saw her hand reaching for his door handle beside him.

The door that he'd been leaning on tilted away.

He tipped backward, gasping. He grabbed out but grabbed nothing, and flew out of the car, landing on his hip in soaked, trampled snow.

"I lost Hank," Holly shouted over the horn, *which she was still honking.* "I am *emphatically* not losing you guys, too!"

Michael lunged, but Holly transferred to the driver's seat and pulled the door out of his reach.

"Now," she said, and offered him a heartbreakingly shaky smile, "let's see that skinny ass *move.*"

"ARE YOU INSA—"

The door slammed shut, the motor revved; the tires spun, ripped snow, caught hold. Holly ignited the roof-mounted spotlights and flickered them like strobes. Michael didn't even get to stand: he was still stumbling up, screamingly shocked, when the Hummer grabbed air over the edge of the canyon and missiled down the access road, straight toward the Rapture below.

What are you doing? Michael thought. *Stop her stop her go go go,* as he scrambled over the ledge, trailing Holly down the access road, impossibly far behind.

The Hummer was flashing and honking and be-bopping back and forth. It skied, scattering snow as it leveled out on the "ground floor" of the pit, clipping the rear bumper of a SOUTHERN WV COAL/GAS dump truck. The deflated hot-air balloon, which had been knocking madly atop the roof, finally snapped free of its retraints and pirouetted heavily to the ground.

Did Holly think she could just drive into the crowd and scatter them? *Oh crap, Holly you are wrong*: already on a hair trigger, the Rapture crowd burst apart when she got within fifty feet, yeah, most of the men and women spreading like startled quail.

But some of the believers made their stand.

Their machine guns rising, rising . . .

"NO!"

Thunder crashed across the crater.

Michael'd been right. The windshield *was* bulletproof.

The thing was, the tires were not.

The front two tires detonated with flat airbursts: the car wrenched violently left, fishtailed, and Michael was still on the access road, still a hundred feet back when the Hummer finally flapped to a stop and a tall man with a dust-caked mouth and a red coat scrambled to the driver's door, his gun clumsily spitting bullets with every step he took.

As Red Coat wrenched opened the driver's door, Holly screamed, "Don't shoot, he made me, he made me!" Red Coat yanked her out of the cab by her hair. "He's here!" Holly shouted. "HE'S RIGHT THERE IN THE BACKSEAT!"

Michael skidded to a stop in the snow, stunned, confused.

He thought wildly, as he once had before: *Holly, you're a crappy liar.* But then he understood her plan, and his head filled with light.

Red Coat seemed to sense Holly's lie.

But Hammy didn't. Hammy was already opening the back

Hummer door when Red Coat cried: *"Stop that. Right now! Belinda, it's a trick!"*

Even from this distance, Michael understood the emotion that flew across the face of the woman who had questioned Rulon's prophecies in the First Bank of Charleston. The rear Hummer doors creaked on their hinges, revealing what was within, and Hammy was not filled with terror.

Nor surprise.

Just . . . heartbreak.

Devastation that all hope had led to this. Michael knew, more than ever before, how freaking much that this was not a game. In games, you don't pity the enemy.

An earsplitting cry came out from the dark of the Hummer. Far overhead, one of the field lights burst apart, showering sparks and glass.

Captain Horace Jopek, mutated and risen, launched out of the back of his Hummer.

The sightless, bone-clawed captain collided into Hammy, ripping into her throat before she had even struck the ground. Red dimes of blood flew.

Jopek's vocal cords issued a second shriek, and with it, pandemonium burst. Most of the remaining Rapture near the Hummer fled in all directions; those who had already run tripled their speed as Hammy's pleas gurgled and faded. Two or three of the Rapture stood rooted and mesmerized, not knowing what to do when the camouflaged Shriek looked up from Hammy with their friend's blood and skull fragments on its teeth, and began to chase after them, too. . . .

Through the chaos: *"Michael, go!"*

Michael's gazed snapped upward. Having escaped from Red Coat, Holly stood on the roof of the Hummer, waving frantically.

She thrust her arm toward the entrance of the mine. The

now-unguarded entrance to the mine.

"*GOOOOO!*" she shouted.

"*I'll trust you, if you trust me.*"

Gratitude and emotion flooded Michael. He did not feel his blood. Clearly, certainly, with no lie between it and himself: Michael felt his *heart*.

CHAPTER THIRTY-SEVEN

He dashed, with the Rapture's screams resounding from the four walls of the world.

Thank you. Oh man, oh God, thank you so, so much.

Weaving through the fleeing members of the Rapture (who did not care to stop him), darting between mountains of coal and ancient machinery, his breath whistling into him, out from him, and he felt every flowing inch.

And then—nearly unbelievably—Michael realized he was going to make it.

He passed under thick wooden beams of the mine entrance; the air, already bitter, seemed to die off ten degrees; the carpet of snow changed to gritty coal. Michael ran. With tears of thank-you in his eyes, he ran into the homeplace of the virus that ended the world . . . and Whatever had created it.

Don't scream for Bub. Don't let Rulon know you're here.

Though his face was drippy with sweat, and his pulse slammed inside his eardrums, just twenty feet into the mine Michael made himself slow. His crunchy footsteps were way too loud. The sounds of the world had faded back with eerie speed: the havoc back in the quarry had a from-the-other-side-of-the-tunnel quality, no realer than a movie playing in a different room.

And Michael had no weapons. *Except, maybe, surprise.*

Yeah. Yes. Slow down, not too much, but be quiet—do it.

Rulon isn't slowing down, his mind hissed.

Shit. Damn it.

Michael jogged.

The mine around him looked like pictures he'd seen in school: the roof rough and chokingly low (he could almost reach up and touch it); the walls a rippling black that were squared with wooden beams. But the pictures couldn't tell how the nightmare of the mine *felt.* They couldn't describe the cold, so sharp it was nearly like breathing glass. They couldn't describe the smell, like the back of a basement, with a cloying stink of . . . was that gas? Could that poison you?

It feels like being swallowed, Michael thought. *And Bub went through this.*

Oh, Bub, I'm sorry. Ya-ya, I ya-ya.

Water, somewhere in the dark throat ahead: a delicate *drip,* trailed by a ghostly chuckling echo. Michael tasted fine metallic fear on the back of his mouth. Images pushed into his mind. Bone-hands blossoming from the loose soil at his feet. Faces rising white and thin from the dark. Cady Gibson spidering toward him on the ceiling . . .

Michael glanced back at the entrance. Only a hundred feet into the mine, now. How had he not gone farther?

Michael swallowed and went on.

Ahead, the shaft of the mine curved sharply, almost a right angle. To continue would be to lose sight of the entrance. Michael spied around the corner. The light reached another twenty steps. After that: inner casket.

Doesn't matter, Michael jabbered at himself, beginning to move again now, slowly, keeping one hand to the wall, trying not to picture Cady Gibson floating from the outer rim of the darkness ahead.

It won't just be Cady, though, Mikey. Look at the footprints in the coal dust. All those footprints. The evidence of the unimaginable size of the migration. *Like the mind-frying, infinite black of space.*

Michael's hand passed over one of the wooden beams. He saw that it and all the others were cracked, ragged with splinters. They'd been sideswiped by deadly force. Oh Jeezus, what was he walking toward?

Keep going. You're scared, that's true, but. Maybe the Shrieks aren't going to come back out. Maybe they just came home, and they're going to stay here. Maybe—

He had turned the corner, and was approaching the very last ledge of the outside world's light, when he heard the dead people shrieking.

Michael's head snapped reflexively back, a jagged outcropping punching into the back of his scalp so hard that it made his eyes water.

But it wasn't the pain that made Michael's head swim, or that blanked his brain, or short-circuited all sense of himself in reality. It was the *sound.*

He had heard dead people bellow and shriek. He'd heard thousands at once, on Government Plaza. But nothing had ever sounded like this. Nothing on Earth.

Place your ear on train tracks at midnight; listen to the nearing thunder; let a ten-thousand-ton roaring black freight train highball to you and take off your head.

This was much worse.

Michael's hands clamped over his ears, but there was no denying this. The coal ground under his feet rumbled like thimbles in an earthquake. Particles shivered from the ceiling. Wind sped from the secret chambers and passages of the earth, flying through his hair and freezing him through his clothes.

It was primeval; it was first power; it was whatever unholy sound comes from ten thousand or more dead throats as they begin a game.

Michael's skull seemed to shake with harmonic vibration.

That's not wind. It's air pressure: they're coming.

And for one second, one shivering terror-blank second, Michael thought: *Leave! Go back! Bub's not down here. And if he is, it's too late.* Sounded true. Sounded smart and grown-up.

Leave now, and you can still get out with Holly before those monsters get here. Leave now, and maybe you can go back and get the cure. Maybe you can still save Mom! Doesn't that sound good, Michael?

Leave, and you can save yoursel—

"NOOOOO!" Michael shouted, and he ran toward the dark.

As if in response, the shriek cut off.

The ground still vibrated, and that wall of air pressure still barreled toward him.

But Michael heard a different, single, high scream flying through the darkness, now not far away. Footsteps, pattering toward him. His chest leapt. *Oh my God. Oh my God, is that . . . ?*

Echoing somewhere: *"Child, come here! Meet your fate, boy! Come back to me now! Oh, I can make it so much worse if you don't!"*

Rulon's chasing him.

And Michael stood there, hypnotized, a sunburst of amazement flooding him as Patrick sprinted out of the darkness.

How? How is he—?

Patrick looked like a kid escaping the boogeyman: his lips were strung back by strain and terror, his elbows scissoring, his breath coming in frightened little hiccups.

His face registered astonishment as he saw Michael, but for only a second before horror overtook it again. He slammed full speed into Michael, not hugging him, bouncing back and stuttering:

"Help help help me help me please HELPHELP—" A hand-shaped bruise covered almost half of his face. *"Can you, will you, help, PLEASE PLEASE!"*

"Bub, it's okay!"

"He's comin'!" Patrick gasped. "The cheater's comin'! The deer, the deer knocked 'im down, *then I was brave, but the bad man's comin'!"*

Deer? What?!

Patrick shook his head, pleading. His coat was shredded away at his elbow, blood leaked out from a knife-slit wound. Patrick looked very pale. His tiny hands suddenly grabbed at the belly of Michael's space suit, his eyes bulging and white.

"Let's go, please!" he cried. *"He's so bad! MICHAEL, NOTHING IS PRETEND ANYMORE!"*

Michael still did not understand how Patrick had been saved from the "Freaking" pit inside himself. But there was no time to consider it. He pulled Patrick's quivering body against him, planning to retreat out of the mine shaft and up into the light of the world.

The mega-shriek blasted once more, this time much closer, the rancid air pressure surging.

And over Bub's shoulder, Rulon's yellow grin materialized in the mine shaft, like the world's final, possessed jack-o'-lantern, come back from Halloween.

The priest's face was the twisted rag of a man who cannot wake from a nightmare. Hell-winds caught the folds of his tattered robes and hauled them in all directions. One of his eye sockets was a cratered soup: the eyeball had been pierced and popped, like the Old Testament justice, so Rulon wept both tears and ooze.

He bore the hunter's knife in his right hand.

"Michael Faris?" said Rulon. As if confused. Stopping for one second.

"R-r-reach—" Patrick was stuttering. He unzipped his jacket pocket, pulled out his orange plastic gun. "R-reach fer the s—"

Rulon snapped out of it. "If you know what will please your soul, boy," he growled to Michael, *"give me the sacrifice, give him to me!"*

Michael pulled his brother closer.

The sounds of the Shrieks, building like drums of doom.

"Sacrifice yourself, asshole!" Michael bellowed.

The priest's face went savage with rage. His knife sang upward. Rulon lunged toward them.

Michael had no time to plan: as Rulon attacked, Michael shoved Patrick away and out of Rulon's path, then leapt in the opposite direction like a boy dodging the train in the very last moment in a game of chicken. Rulon screamed fury as Michael evaded him. Out of the corner of his eye, Michael saw the priest try to rein back the momentum of his lunge, but perhaps there comes a time when momentum is fate: Rulon's knife stabbed down, yes, but not on Michael or Patrick:

His blade came down, with his full force and hatred behind it, into the fractured wood of a support beam.

The support snapped like a wishbone.

The ceiling rumbled.

Rulon looked up, blinked.

The ceiling came down in front of Michael with a guttural roar. Air displaced. Michael threw up his hands, shouting, certain his life was over.

But a second later he looked up, still uncrushed. Only part

of the ceiling had fallen in. How much, though, he didn't know: the air was a swirling, nostril-burning haze.

"Bub?"

He heard Patrick hack. *Over there, left, left!* Michael crawled, feeling out like a blind man.

His hand found Patrick's delicate chest, which was heaving and hacking viciously.

"Got you, Bub, here I am." He looked down at Patrick, and he realized he *could* see now: light, low and weak, was illuminating Patrick. Which meant, oh thank God, that the way to the exit had not been blocked by the cave-in. In fact, all he had to do was go around that corner a few steps away, and he would be able to take them out of the mine shaft the same way he had come.

"H-here, M-Michael!" Patrick coughed.

Run. Now. That's all. Just run around that corner and out of the mine, and this is over.

"I know. I've got you, Bub."

"N-no, I mean," Patrick racked, shaking his head, *"They're* here*! THEM!"*

Goose chills screamed up Michael's back.

With a sensation familiar from a hundred childhood nightmares—his vision being sucked, against every wish, toward some grim, waiting horror—Michael looked into the descending heart of the mine.

Past the mound of coal Rulon had brought down, something had come out of the depths.

Michael thought, *It's the Shrieks!* but he immediately knew that wasn't right. The Things invading the outer rim of light were eyeless, yes, and they hung upon the walls and ceiling like pale death-spiders. But they were not Shrieks, not any more than they were still Bellows.

Michael and Patrick were in the mine with something new, something ancient, and God help them.

Cady Gibson, clattering on the ceiling, led them, smiling its damned, everlasting smile.

Cady, who had entered this mine as a nine-year-old kid, still bore a ruined memory of the face, almost hurtfully beautiful, of the child it had been.

Cady Gibson, endgame mutation, was more bone than boy. The flesh of its arms was stripped entirely. Its fingers were a fan of fine, bleached blades. In its floating ribs, gray lung-sacks flapped. Raw tendon—taut and red—spiraled over the bones like the strings of a marionette brought to jigging life by some demoniacally grinning puppet master. Cady Gibson, the Terror, crawled across the black sky toward Michael and his brother, pealing forth cry after cry: a little boy leading its own hellish children outside to play.

"Michael, he's the bad boy!" Patrick screamed.

Michael stood up, his knees threatening to betray him. And in that infinite, black instant, Michael caught a glimpse of Something just past Cady—another creature, clittering along the ceiling of the mine shaft—that he knew would haunt the corridors of his dreams forever.

It was a Hell-dream, a beast of shock-white flesh. It had golden-rimmed eyes with slits for pupils. It had a red and lolling tongue that dangled and clocked from its mouth like a long, burst vein. With a shattering clarity, Michael understood: Cady and all the Shrieks had returned to this mine so They could *get this creature.* They had come to retrieve the Thing that had birthed the virus and ended the Earth, the Thing that had infected Cady in the first place.

Oh God, that's their MOTHER!

GOOOOOOOOOOOOOOOOOO!

Patrick burst into tears, and Michael lifted him into his arms and turned in the quaking mine shaft. He dashed around the corner, seeing the lighted rectangle of the entrance a billion miles up ahead. The fractured support beams were snapping now in the force of the stampede: Michael wove through a collapsing storm of earth and stone. The creatures howled in rage as the caving ceiling slowed their flight, but this was still like trying to outrun the wind. And Michael held on to Patrick as tightly as he had ever held anything, as tight as his own heart.

"Michael?" Patrick sobbed into his ear.

Answer him. You might not get to again. "Yeah?" Michael breathed.

Patrick said: "I love you."

The end of the mine, twenty feet away, ten, six, three—

The dead at their back, their shrieks deafening, air pressure flying like poisonous waves—

And then—Michael never understood how—he ran out of the mine.

Did it matter? No. Nowhere to run: he looked back into the mine and saw the Shrieks bursting through the fallen ceiling, and even if he got into the Hummer right this moment, it was too late—the field lights dazzled Michael's eyes—his ears were ringing—

"Holly!" Patrick gasped.

Something was coming, straight across the quarry field, almost *bouncing* on the ground. Something big. *Balloon!* Not quite inflated, the jack-o'-lantern aircraft, piloted by Holly, its basket half dragging across the snowy ground toward them. Michael's heart burst in amazement.

"Patrick! Michael!" Holly called. *"Come on!"*

Wind gusted, throwing snow from the peaks of the coal

mounds, snapping the inflating pumpkin face to the left, parallel with the rock wall containing the entrance to the mine. Michael sprinted to catch up. Holly released the burner for a moment to reach out for them, but Michael shouted, *"No no, keep filling the balloon!"* and he desperately tossed Patrick into the basket. He placed his good hand on the wicker rim and there came another gust of wind, and the jerk of the balloon nearly pulled his arm out of its socket. He screamed, but held on, the lip of the basket now as high as his chest. He leapt with all his strength, pulling himself up, over the wicker brim.

He tumbled in.

"Up up, go go go!"

"Absolutely," Holly breathed shakily. She yanked down the overhead handle harder, enlarging the blue burner flame.

And slowly their balloon began to lift toward the sky.

They ascended, fifteen feet, twenty. *Holy crap. We . . . I . . .*

We made it. The thought shimmered in his mind, nearly too huge and beautiful to grasp. *We* made it!

Michael looked over the edge of the basket. Fifty feet up now. The new creatures were vomiting out from the mouth of the mine, small in the fluorescent field lights.

Cady Gibson emerged, stopped, gazed up with those ancient eyes.

The monster couldn't grab them. Not now. *Not when we're flying—*

But suddenly Michael's hope threatened to flicker out.

No. What happens when we have to land?

And that was when he turned and saw Patrick holding his orange gun in his hands.

"Bad bad guys," Patrick hissed viciously. His eyes glittered with vengeance. It was not just fury at someone who wasn't playing The Game right: it was something beyond childhood, it was

full hatred, grown-up's hatred, and utterly without innocence.

Patrick hooked one arm over the edge of the basket so that he could look to the ground, aiming the bright plastic gun down to the lead creature, as if to shoot Cady Gibson with a make-believe projectile from "the weapon" the Game Master had given him.

Michael thought, *That's just a toy, Patrick. Just a toy.*

But then a secret understanding, both horrible and wonder-struck, fit into place inside Michael's heart, like clockwork.

It's not *a toy!*

Michael grabbed Patrick's wrist, steering Bub's weapon upward half an inch at the last moment. He did not even know why; it was simply as if something were directing his hand as much as he guided his brother's.

Patrick's finger tensed, and he roared with the biggest voice Michael had ever heard him use:

"REACH FER THE SKYYYYYYY!"

And Patrick pulled the trigger of his flare gun.

A cry of light; a sparkler scream.

A fiery red contrail blazed forth from the barrel. The flare gun launched its glittering charge across the West Virginia night, a fizzing, dazzling, screeching light, like the racing sparks of a fuse strung across the world. Yes, like the fuse of some unimaginable bomb.

The flare struck Cady Gibson.

There was a sudden floating fire-rose on the dead boy's chest, like a hideous fake, where a heart would be.

That was when the mountain blew up.

"OH SHI—" Patrick screamed as the first flame pyred out of the mine.

Michael grabbed at Bub and Holly, and threw them both down to the floor of the basket as it happened. He had been wrong about the "toy" gun, but Holly had been right about the gas: it *was* there, packed within all the subterranean nooks and catacombs of the mine, like patient, invisible dynamite. And as the flare ignited it, there was a tide of fire that even the monsters could not outrun.

Roaring yellow-red light filled the world, making Michael blind and deaf. In the storm of heat, he found Patrick and Holly and hugged them to him, to let them know that he was there. And they hugged him back, to let him know that they were, too.

AFTER THE END . . .

After their balloon had hurled and pitched in the sky like a
bouy in a hurricane; after the earth-tearing chain of explosions stopped; after the light and heat began to fade; after
Michael and Holly sat up, stunned silent but asking *Did we
just . . . save the . . . ?*

After Patrick gaped at the flare gun in his hand like a kid
blinking at the fist that has finally fought back against the bully,
but also somehow accidentally killed him . . .

After Patrick burst into tears that Michael and Holly could
do nothing to stop . . .

After the wind carried them into the night, and the flame-
filled quarry began to look no larger than embers. After Patrick
finally, simply exhausted himself and fell into an uneasy sleep.
After Michael and Holly rigged the burner-handle down with
a rope from the canvas bag labeled CAPTAIN H. C. JOPEK, which
Holly had grabbed from the back of the Hummer (the bag had
safety flares, tourniquets, a blanket, radio, "space food," bat-
teries, and a *Playboy* magazine, which Holly rolled her eyes at
and flung out of the basket). After they asked each other, *Did
we just end this? I mean, is that possible—if all the Shrieks*

came home, did we just kill them all? Holly said she didn't know, that she really doubted it. But Michael saw the hope in her eyes. He recognized it, from what he almost felt in his own heart.

Maybe all the Shrieks *did die, though,* Holly said. *I mean, since Cady was the thing that changed them into* Shrieks, *right? So maybe the only Things left are . . . like, Bellows that are scattered and by themselves.*

She added: *'Cause it* couldn't *have been all of them, right? Right?*

After the moon rose and the storm calmed and they drifted through a star-shot sky, wondering at the world that was slipping by in the smooth—silent?—darkness far below their feet:

Holly told Michael they should sleep in shifts. Michael tried to say he couldn't sleep, and for a while he couldn't; it was too quiet up here. So he turned on the army radio Holly had brought, and the white noise at least relaxed him. And he did sleep. And, same as always, dreamed of Mom.

It was Christmas morning, and thick, white flakes were falling past his window in a lightly moaning wind. He could smell pine, and the cookies (lemon) Mom had left for Rudolph. As he leapt from bed, he was aware of the cold on his ankles at the ends of his too-short pajamas. Mom stood at the bottom of the stairs. Her hair was drawn down in front of her face, and Michael had a terrible feeling that if she looked up, she wasn't going to have any eyes.

On the bottom stair, between her feet, lay a gift topped by a looping red bow. Inside the box, a sheet of paper, with a single word. And when Michael looked up with a question on his lips, Mom had disappeared. He was scared, lost-in-a-department-store scared. He came to realize that the howling outside was not a wind, but people at the windows. Gray-faced people. He shouted, but Mom wouldn't answer. Finally, he looked at the paper.

The word on it read:

Pocket

Snow.

He could feel snow.

Michael lay in the cold, then sniffed. He opened his eyes, looking around, brushing the flakes off his nose with the back of his hand. He wasn't totally surprised to feel tears there, too.

Purple light, over the rim of the basket. Snow falling gently. He could see the pink underbellies of clouds that told him it was almost sunrise—though the clouds were a lot closer than usual. He watched one that looked like a lowercase *t* drift past. He started to sit up, but noticed Holly's head lying against his shoulder, her eyes closed, her breath steady. *Sleepin' on the job, lady,* he thought, grinning. He hesitated a second, then thought, *Well, it's okay 'cause she kissed me first,* and he leaned in and kissed her, quick and light, on the edge of her lips. Man. Seriously: so *soft.* Holly shifted in her sleep, the side of her mouth tugging into a little half smile.

Michael thought: *pocket.*

Pocket? What's in my pocket?

Patrick was sitting across from him, looking at the wicker floor, his back against the opposite wall, one knee drawn to his chest. In his hands, he held the vial that Holly had stuffed into Michael's pocket in the First Bank of Charleston.

The ropes creaked overhead. They drifted. Patrick looked up at Michael, then back down at the wicker floor, his lips twitching and pursing. He seemed to be gathering something to say in his head. After perhaps ten minutes, he said softly, "There's no more Game Master, is there? Everyone can cheat now, huh?"

Michael watched him, unsure how to respond. He lifted Holly's head from his shoulder, positioning it gently against a corner. He scooted toward Bub, and the question within Michael was: What lie should he try to assemble for Patrick? But he realized he did not know. Right then, sitting across from his little brother in the waking sky, Patrick seemed a kind of mystery to him. *How did you save yourself, Bub?* Michael thought wonderingly. *How did you fall into yourself and come out? I tried so hard to save you; I did my best. But I didn't control this.*

"Do you think the Bellows cheated where Mommy is, too?" Patrick asked.

Michael felt his pulse, his breath, searching his stillness: the old automatic habit, waiting for some secret aspect of himself to present him with the Truth about the future of his Game. . . . But nothing came this time, of course. That was all over.

What if Mom did *make it to Richmond, and she's still okay?* some small part of him thought. *Is that possible?*

After the pain and terror of all his own false predictions, Michael tried to push down the idea. Jopek had said the Safe Zone in Richmond was overrun.

But Jopek had lied about a lot of things. I don't "know" for sure that things are good . . . but maybe that doesn't necessarily mean that they're bad. I don't know, but I'm going to keep going, anyway. And maybe that was hope.

"I . . . I dunno, Bub," Michael said honestly.

Patrick nodded, his lips pulling into his mouth. He didn't blink, but a moment later, the half-light in the sky lit the trails down his cheeks. He clenched the vial tighter in his small hands. How had the vial survived all Michael's falls since the bank? I mean, *How?* For some reason, Michael thought of what Patrick had said. *The deer. The deer knocked 'im down.* Bobbie could have been right, Michael supposed. There could be something watching over them. *But if there is*, he thought, *I don't think I could understand it in a billion years.*

"*If I give this to other Good Guys,*" Patrick whispered, "*it'll really make everything all better?*"

Michael found himself smiling. "I think it will." He searched himself, and he found, with a relief like warm wind, that he wasn't lying. Or, he didn't think he was.

"I m-m-miss Mommy," Patrick said. "She's a good . . ." Patrick blinked, frankly confused. He struggled to find the word. "She's *good*," he finally decided.

Yes, she was good, Bub. Is. Maybe is, Michael thought. *Holly was right: Mom's weak. But not just weak. Yeah, Bub. She's also good.*

Patrick stood up, placing his hands on the edge of the basket, and looked out. Holly shifted again and cough-snorted in her sleep. It was kind of ridiculously cute.

Patrick whispered, "*Girlfriend, now?*"

Michael blushed a little. Nodded.

"Wow," Patrick said, pretending to be amazed. "I have a *girlfriend.*"

"Bub, jeesh!"

Patrick shrugged with one shoulder. Laughed a little. *I think he's going to be okay. I can't believe it, but I think he really is.* The Game was fake . . . but this was real. *He really got past* The End.

The first pale, fragile yellow of dawn was touching the mountains and the valleys. A water tower loomed through the fog, drifting before being vanished. Silos, delicate roads, a toy-size tractor in the white. Look at the world. Wonder: What is this place? It seemed like a new earth, scarless, their sphere to shape. And even if Michael had learned enough to know the lie in that, he couldn't help but find it beautiful.

And he wasn't scared. *Liar,* his mind whispered. Well . . . okay. Okay, he *was* scared, but just then he had a feeling he'd never quite had before: like the fear didn't encompass him. Like he was other things, too.

"Michael?" whispered Patrick.

"Yeah?"

"Low-five."

Michael tried to slap his hand. Patrick pulled away. "Too slow," Patrick said.

Michael laughed. "Yeah, I get that a lo—"

But he stopped when they both heard the sound. A hissy sort of sound, and his first thought was that the hot-air burner was running low on gas.

But the sound had shaken Holly awake: it was that loud. And when it happened again, she didn't look up toward the burner. Her eyes slid down to the canvas bag. To the long, rectangular shape inside it. Shaped almost like an old phone.

Holly whispered, *"What the?"*

Patrick said, "Did that just—?"

The man on the radio, cutting off the white noise that had sent Michael off to sleep, said: *"—broadcast zone—"*

Michael, Holly, Patrick: gawping.

It was Patrick who lunged for the handheld walkie-talkie. He pounced down so hard, it was almost funny: the balloon basket swung a few feet underneath them.

"—zone, please respond—" said the radio. The voice coming through the waffle-fencing on the speaker sounded crinkly, far-off, a tin-can sound.

Patrick pushed down the red SEND button on the side of the walkie, with some effort. *"Y'hello, baby?!"* he shouted into it.

"Patrick!" Holly called, her voice shaky with tension. Patrick smiled up at her and, despite the suspense of the silence that followed, he looked pleased at making her laugh.

"Bub, here, let me." Michael took the walkie from Patrick's hands. *Oh my God. Holy freaking crap. Is that a* person? *Is it really?*

No. No, you don't know. It might just be a recording. Don't, Michael: don't get your hopes up.

But: why not? some other part of him said, his hands shaking. *Seriously: why* not?

And he was bringing the walkie up to his mouth—there was a brief burst of static and feedback—when a man, on the crackling speaker, sounding shocked, replied, *"Hello?"*

Michael's finger eased up from the worn, red rectangle SEND button.

The moment hung in the air between them all. The sun peaked over behind a mountain; Michael squinted, feeling dazed. The voice of a stranger, snatched from the air and sounding from this thing in his palm . . . it was like magic.

"Repeat: Is anyone there? Come in."

Holly put her arm around Michael's shoulder and squeezed a couple times.

"Repeat: Sir, are you there?" said the man on the radio. "Over."

Michael, gulping, stared at the walkie. . . .

And pushed down SEND.

"Y-yeah." His voice felt fragile, like glass. "Here. Uh, over."

He had barely let up the button when the walkie exploded, "Son of a *GUN*!"

Michael pictured a young guy falling back in his chair, hands flying to his headphones with the amazement of a man who has just heard a miracle. "Whelp, you—*wow*!" said Radio Man, as Holly laughed in wonder. "Hell-*oh*! Hey! Pal! It is *good* to hear a voice out there in radio land! How the hell are *you*?"

Still nervous, Michael smiled a little. "Compared to what?"

He heard Radio Man guffaw: "Do I hear that? I sure do!" Muttering in the background of the other end of the line. Michael pictured other people gathered around Radio Man's machine. He . . . he imagined soldiers.

"Ah, sir," the walkie-talkie said: a more official, man-in-charge tone. "How many are in your party, sir? Over."

"Three," Michael replied. It felt dizzying, the truth. "You?" Grinning hugely, Holly mouthed to him: *over.* "O-over," Michael said into the walkie-talkie.

There was a pause across the airwaves. And then Radio Man said, "More," with his smiling voice—his *beaming* voice, actually. "*More* than three.

"Three out there in radio land," he said disbelievingly. "Oh, boy. Thank G . . ." For some reason, he sounded nearly like he was going to cry.

"Hey, pal, your signal's going out; let's get your location info before we lose each other, okay?" said Radio Man after a moment. "I've just got to ask: Who *are* you?"

Who are you?

Michael closed his eyes.

And while he rode the wind that carried them into his unpredictable dawn, he pushed down the SEND button, and answered.

AUTHOR'S NOTE

The End Games is a work of fiction that contains some nonfiction elements. For example, Charleston and virus mutations really do exist, but for the story's sake, I've taken creative liberties with both. Other aspects of the book are invented whole cloth, including: Southern West Virginia Coal and Natural Gas, Coalmount, Atipax, and of course the existence of Bellows.

ACKNOWLEDGMENTS

Here is a truth about a novel (and perhaps especially a debut): The author's name is emblazoned on the jacket, but the story within is a kind of topographic map of his past and his heart—and neither of those things can formed in isolation.

I'm grateful to many, many people for their guidance and companionship in creating my particular map. Here are their names, with a few special explanations at the end.

Bridgeport: Scott Faris, Brendan Gibat, Heidi Griffith, Charles and Joanna Kovalan, Amy Lohmann, Alice Rowe, and Jeff Toquinto.

Family: Everyone, but especially my grandparents (Bobbie and Jack Crouse, Tom and Louise Martin), my wonderful second family (Rick, Abbie, Will, and Billie Layne, and Bill and Jeanne McNamara), my siblings (Matt, Molly, and Patrick), and my uncle Jimmy, who inspired my love of fear in the first place.

Film school: Ted Ferris, Jordan Kerner, Laura Hart McKinney, Bill Mai, Joseph Mills, Tom O'Keefe, Laura Hauser O'Keefe (who is also a talented designer/illustrator who helped me with my website), Dale Pollock, Ron Stacker Thompson, and Andrew Young. Most of all here, though, I owe a profound thanks to

Dona Cooper, whose generosity of spirit and wisdom shaped my understanding and love of storytelling.

At HarperCollins: Alessandra Balzer, Molly O'Neill, Viana Siniscalchi, and Jon Smith.

Misc. people who have been nice/inspiring to me: Pilar Alessandra, Leo Babauta, Brene Brown, Brook Bishop, Jack Canfield, Father Harry Cramer, Paula Friedland, Seth Godin, Michael Hyatt, Harry Knowles, Robert McKee, Ammi-Joan Paquette, Carson Reeves, Anthony Robbins, Craig Skistimas, and Gary Vee.

New Leaf Literary & Media: Danielle Barthell, Kathleen Ortiz, Pouya Shahbazian, and Suzie Townsend.

Winston-Salem: Tom and Sarah Jane Bost, Tanya Gunter, Caleb and Emily Masters, Ed and Pat Mayfield, Michelle Reed and the Bagel Station Crew, and Jamie Rogers Southern.

Writer friends/supporters: Bryan Bliss, S.A. Bodeen, Joshua Ferris, Ridley Pearson, Stephanie Perkins, Carrie Ryan, R.L. Stine, and Nova Ren Suma.

YouTubers who inspired and/or supported me: Ed Bassmaster, Elmify, LiveLavaLive, BertieBertG, Link Neal of RhettAndLink, and the VlogBrothers.

And, especially:

My editor, Donna Bray, who I think is literally ingenious. Donna's insights, patience, and unbelievable *care* made me transcend everything I'd allowed myself to hope *The End Games* could be. Thank you so much, Donna.

My mom and dad, Kim and Mike Martin, whose steadfast support of my writing gave me the strength to fight monsters in my stories (and my self).

My little brother, Patrick Martin. The "Michael and Patrick" in this novel are not *us*, but being the older brother of an awesome kid who loved zombies as much as I did made *The End Games* possible. You rule, Bub.

My agent and best advocate, Joanna Volpe, who is a voice of calm in times of writer-y confusion, and who understood *The End Games* from the beginning and did so much to make this dream become true.

Sara Zarr, whose kindness and friendship changed my life, and whose mentorship led me toward the endgame of this novel. Here is another truth: Without SZ, there would simply be no novel.

And finally, more than anyone else, I want to thank my wife, Sarah Louise Martin, whose "Sarahpo" artwork delights me and whose love fills my life with light and hope. There can be no overstating this: Having Sarah in my life is a miracle, and I love her with my whole heart.